COVEN BOUND

WINGS OF REBELLION BOOK 3

BREE MOORE

PREQUEL NOVELLA

BOOK ONE

BOOK TWO

BOOK THREE

BONUS NOVELLA

BONUS NOVELLA

BECCA + AVAAN

IAN + KAMRI

BOOK FOUR

CHAPTER ONE

MANDI

DEEP, SLOW BREATHS.

Visualize. Keep thoughts positive.

The coven was meeting tonight in the astral realm, and Mandi was determined to make it. No one would have to take notes for her. She'd figure out how to separate her spirit from its mortal cage and fly through time and space to the purple tree with a starlit canopy and blue algae growing on its trunk. A place where the witches could discuss their private coven matters with confidence that no one, and no thing, would be listening in. The others talked about astral projection like others talked about breathing or walking. If that was the case, Mandi was the infant who hadn't figured it out yet. A late bloomer, as Violet would say.

Blobs of color floated in Mandi's vision, and she couldn't help but feel resignation instead of excitement. That was how it started. Her usual sea of darkness, lit by strange, wavering clouds of color. Sometimes she saw faces, a random blip of an image, but she'd been blind too long for her subconscious to keep populating her dreams.

The colors faded. That was how it always ended. She'd enter a deeper sleep state, now. Her mind grew heavy and sleep crawled in, despite her fighting it. No astral projection. No flying over cities, no creating new worlds, no meeting spirit guides or coven sisters. No Sight. No one was sure why, but as a blind witch, Mandi seemed barred from the limbo realm. Why should one need working eyes to See the different planes?

The unmistakable sound of glass breaking shattered the nothingness. Shouting echoed as if from the inside of a tunnel, and a werewolf howled. Not Zeke.

Footsteps. They came fast, the thudding, rustling, muted steps of several people running over grass. Panting.

"...Merry meet and Merry part and Merry meet again. You may all step forward and say a few words, as moved upon. I only ask that you respect the dead and each other in the utmost." Violet's voice drifted through the air. The words she would speak at a funeral. Fletcher's funeral? Someone coughed.

Feet pounded and a sound like wings unfurling caught the air.

Gasps and cries. A bellow came from the direction of the woods. Fire crackled nearby, but instead of heat it let off a strange, whispering energy.

Violet. What had happened to Violet? Were her other friends there?

"They're dead!" a voice cried. It sounded like Honey. Honey was there. Mandi tried to speak, but her voice didn't work. She reached out to touch someone, anyone, but despite the nearby voices her fingers grasped nothing. It was like she was there, but a ghost, only to observe with her limited senses.

It sounded like an action film, the battle scene, a cacophony of sound with no way to ground herself in what was happening.

A dragon's bellow split the sky. Mandi crouched, terror pounding in her heart.

Hot air puffed into Mandi's face. She woke, gasping and gagging, Zeke's wolfish face right up against her own. Ugh. Werewolf breath. A heavy, comforting weight pressed into her side, and she reached her hands out, meeting thick fur. Her body relaxed as the dream bled away. She shoved Zeke's head away, redirecting his dog breath.

"Just a dream," she muttered. The terror took a long time to leave her heart. She must have been thinking of the funeral for Fletcher happening later that day. She still felt tired, indicating she hadn't had enough sleep for it to be morning. She lay in bed, agitated that it was still early enough she couldn't wake anyone up.

Unless...Violet could still be working. She had insisted on finishing her retrograde spells and excused herself from the astral meeting, though Mandi suspected her desire to be alone had to do with Fletcher's suicide.

Mandi ignored the prodding sadness in her chest and flipped the covers off, wriggling away from Zeke's sleeping form to avoid waking him.

It was chilly in the room away from Zeke's warmth. Mandi reached for her shawl on the hook by the door and wrapped it around her shoulders. The click of the doorknob turning caused the wolf to stir. The blankets rustled, and he jumped off the bed with a thud.

Mandi sighed. "Go back to bed. I'm just going to see Violet."

He didn't say anything. He couldn't speak in his wolf form. Instead, he leaned firmly into Mandi's side with a quiet chuff, insisting he come along. She wrapped her fingers into his fur;

his back was up to her waist. His presence helped her steel her nerves. *I'm telling her about a dream, is all.* A dream where the funeral was interrupted by an attack and Violet had died. Mandi dug her fingers deeper into Zeke's fur, adjusting her grip with sweaty fingers, and padded down the hall.

An indiscernible murmur came from the common room. Some of the residents were early risers or night owls. What time *was* it? Mandi listened, but it didn't sound as if they spoke of anything important, and Violet wasn't with them.

Zeke stopped. Mandi had forgotten to count steps, and they stood outside Violet's door. She knocked softly, then pushed it open.

"Oh. Hello, Mandi." Still awake, or had Violet gotten up early to finish her spells? Her voice sounded strained. Perhaps just tired.

"How are the spells coming?" Mandi kept her tone hopeful and curious, trying to lighten the mood before she started talking about death and dreams. Zeke panted, and she heard him lay down on the floor nearby.

"Something is blocking me. I feel opposing efforts trying to prevent me from forming these protective spells correctly. There's a snag somewhere if I could just find it…" Violet rustled through papers, and jars clinked as she moved things around. The air smelled strongly of the sage she'd been burning to clear the energies of the room.

"Have you tried recharging your ingredients?" Mandi walked forward, stopping when her hand brushed the worktable. Her fingers roamed over the gathered stones, lightly touching each one. The other residents wondered how she did any "witch work," being blind. It was hard to explain, but each stone's energy resonated in Mandi with a different tone. Like a tuning fork. She could sense some of the more powerful symbols used in spells, as well. Herbs she'd learned by smell and touch, mainly, but they, too, had a subtle language she could sometimes hear or a signature to feel. For everything else, there was puff paint.

Mandi's mouth stretched into a smile as she felt the raised marks on the page next to the spell casting. It was Violet's idea. The witch's version of braille. Mandi didn't like braille; it had never caught on for her. But meaning flowed from the smooth surface of the puff paint, taking on the unique curves and lines of the symbols essential for spell casting, and Mandi understood each one.

Luckily, spellwork cast with puff paint worked as well as ink. Her coven made their own, and each batch was blessed and put into special plastic, pen-like tubes. The paint had to flow in a steady, unbroken stream. If the paint didn't connect in any spot, the symbol was broken and wouldn't do its job. In Violet's miniature pentagram drawn on the spellboard, there was one line that faltered under Mandi's fingertip.

Mandi found a puff-paint pen on the counter and gave it a squeeze to let out any air. A steady squirt bridged the troubled spot and a deep sense of rightness settled in Mandi's gut.

"What did you do?" Violet demanded. Mandi assumed she would have been watching, but she must have been occupied somewhere else.

"Just straightened the paint. It feels better now." Mandi rubbed her fingers along the length of the pen.

"It does, but it didn't fix everything. Whatever I'm sensing…it's like an attack, Mandi," Violet said.

Mandi breathed in sharply. It was too close to her dream. "Wouldn't your wards prevent an attack?"

"If it were coming from outside, yes." Violet's tone was hard-edged, her anger grating on Mandi's ears.

The pen dropped from Mandi's hand and rolled across the table. "It's coming from inside? Who would do that?" Surely not any of her coven sisters. But a rogue...that was a possibility. She swallowed. "You need more help. We need more help. Another more advanced witch would..."

"We're at the maximum number of witches allowed in a camp already. You know that." The sharp edge of Violet's voice cut into Mandi.

Mandi curled her fingers in on themselves. "I only meant..." She trailed off. She knew the rules. They weren't allowed to even come close to the forbidden number thirteen. Thirteen witches could form a full coven, with exponentially greater powers. "I could help."

"You? You're barely a witch." The sharp rethort came like a slap. Zeke growled from his corner, his claws scratching on the floor as he stood. He wouldn't hold for any insults brought against Mandi.

Mandi's lip quivered, and her hands formed tighter fists, arms quaking, but she didn't unleash the hurt and anger on Violet. Violet was exhausted and stressed. She didn't know what she was saying. Mandi held her hand up toward Zeke. He quieted, but didn't lay down again.

Violet sighed, and her clothes rustled. Her hand cupped Mandi's cheek. "I didn't mean for it to come out like that. Forgive my harsh words. I've been meaning to talk with you about this for a while now. I always hoped you grow into your abilities and take over after me. We've all been expecting it. Only, you haven't done that. You're a strong woman with a brilliant mind for witchcraft, but I'm afraid your powers may be inaccessible after all. To lead a Naturalization camp, you must prove you can handle even the strongest witch that may come through here."

"Are you saying...that I can't do it?" Mandi's heart plummeted. She'd studied and trained her whole life to be the kind of witch that could take over after Violet retired. At least at the camp Mandi would continue to do magic. What little magic she could. Mandi bit her lip.

"What I mean is, you'll need help. Magical help. A werewolf is strong, but there are protections strength can't provide. It's too big a job for one witch. Even I have James." Violet sighed. "This really isn't the time for this conversation. I only wanted you to know so you didn't feel so much pressure to take part in the coven meetings. I'm sure the council will consider a dual-witch partnership. Perhaps one of your coven sisters? Think on it."

"I've had a vision," Mandi blurted. "Like a prophecy, or something."

The base of a jar slapped the wooden table, as if set down with a little too much force. "You don't have to prove anything to me. And this spell has to be finished before Mars rises."

"You're always telling us to pay attention to our dreams."

"Yes, as a way to practice for astral travel. We all have dreams. Hundreds in a night sometimes. They usually mean little."

Desperation climbed inside of Mandi. Her throat choked up. She had to tell someone. "This one was scarier. More real than I've ever dreamt. You were in it."

Violet sighed again, a bone-weary sound that made Mandi's heart fall. "I don't have time for nightmares. I'm living one. I have to meet with Fletcher's parents in a few hours. Right now, the only thing I care about is finding the words to tell them their son is dead." Her searing words made Mandi's chest constrict. "Go back to bed, Mandi."

Panic rose in Mandi's throat, and tears came hot to the corners of her eyes. "You died, Violet. You and James. And Drake, and there was fighting..." She trailed off. She did sound like a frightened little girl woken up from a nightmare. Maybe that was all it had been. Her fingers trembled as they twisted together in front of her.

Violet's skirts rustled, and her herbal scent swirled in Mandi's senses. Violet sighed again, and a heavy hand settled on Mandi's shoulder. She rubbed her thumb in soothing circles, though it didn't erase the fear from the dream.

"We cannot let our lives be ruled by the whims of an unknown future, or even particularly vivid dreams." She went silent, and her hand fell away. "I have done much I regret in my time here. It will catch up to me eventually. It's already begun, with IPC after me, looking for any reason to take me down and ruin this camp. With Fletcher." A small sob broke from her, and Mandi's own lungs squeezed tightly, pushing air out in a rush and struggling to draw again. Grief tightened its hold. Mandi's head floated. She needed to sit down, or she might pass out.

Zeke nudged his cold, wet nose into her hand, grounding her. The urge to swoon stopped, and air expanded her lungs. Her heart still throbbed, but she remained upright.

Violet sniffed. "Get some more sleep. All will be well." Her skirts moved again, and Mandi sensed the distance between them growing. Mandi wondered if she should press harder with the urgency she felt, but as she was about to speak again, Zeke's nose pushed into her hand insistently.

"I know, I know." Mandi ran her hand across his head until it rested in the usual place between his shoulders. They left the apothecary together and made their way through the quiet cabin halls.

Back in her room, Mandi flopped onto the bed, curling up and using her shawl like a blanket. A rather ineffective one. Zeke's head brushed the back of her calves as he gripped the real blankets in his teeth and yanked them over her. Mandi smiled as he settled against her back. As long as he was in her room, Zeke remained in wolf form. Nothing stopped the gossip chain, but the others had only their imaginations to supply any lies being passed around.

She dug her fingertips into Zeke's fur and sighed. She'd gotten used to the coarse feel and the steady way his sides expanded against her when he breathed. Mandi's body felt tired, but her mind churned with worry. She wouldn't fall asleep that way. She sat up, scooting out of the bed. Zeke chuffed quietly, questioning.

"Don't worry. I'm staying in my room." Mandi felt her way to the shelves holding various spell components. Simple things. Most everything was in the shared apothecary where Violet worked, and the younger witches weren't allowed to keep the more potent items in their possession. Mandi had her crystals, which were barely considered magic by government standards. After all, they only saw pretty rocks. Mandi knew different.

She ran her fingers along the shelf, the different vibrations and tones from the rocks singing out to her, as individual as human voices. Labradorite, quartz, lapis, opal...Crystals decorated every surface in her room, and a giant amethyst stood sentinel in one corner. Its presence promoted positive emotion and guarded against negative influences, a birthday present from Violet and James. Mandi touched the tip of it and moved on to her dresser, where an ever-evolving collection of stones made up interconnected patterns.

Regardless of whether Violet took her seriously, or even considered her proper witch material, Mandi was going to be prepared. Crystals could guard, make one almost invisible to enemies. They could induce courage or cunning, inspire and protect. Mandi shuffled the stones on the wooden dresser, erasing the patterns she'd previously created. She picked them up one at a time and placed or discarded them, keeping her dream and Violet at the forefront of her mind, building a spell with her stones.

Spell-casting with crystals was not a taught form of magic. Other spells utilized the properties of crystals to enhance and support the magic, but few people knew that a spell could be cast entirely of stone. Mandi knew. She'd gotten to know the stones, and she knew at a touch when she'd chosen the right or wrong crystal for a purpose.

Violet needed mental support in the face of the attacks she felt from an unknown source.

Mandi frowned, fingers passing over stones until she reached hematite. It buzzed beneath her fingers, not angry, but fierce. Mandi rolled it over in her hand, considering.

What had Violet meant about the things she'd done catching up with her? A lot of paranormals disagreed with Naturalization, and by all appearances, as a camp moderator, Violet was a supporter. She might have enemies among the rebellious factions out there. And Violet's original coven had been destroyed, some members killed, others gone missing. Everyone had lost people during the first years after the Reveal. Was Violet still on some headhunter's list from long ago?

Mandi could only speculate. Violet shielded her from the harsh realities of the past, and James didn't talk about everything in his class; just enough to scare the residents into behaving and working towards Naturalization. For witches, that meant receiving a government assignment. You used your powers and knowledge to benefit their agenda, and you got to live in society. If you refused, the fate was prison or worse. Most witches signed on as parole officers that monitored other Naturalized paranormals. Some witches like Violet managed the camps. There was a camp in about half of the states, and more popped up every year.

She placed the Hematite in the center of a growing circle of stones. A pulsing warmth drew her to a small Dragon's Eye. Described to her as a dark rock with hypnotizing bands of shifting red, it was a good choice against psychic attacks. Combined with obsidian...Mandi put both rocks in her palm and a reaction like a spark igniting filled her chest. She breathed a spell over the two rocks, strengthening the fire they created, and set them at the center of her circle. She focused on the love and care she had for Violet and imagined it winding through the stones, circling them, giving power to the spell. She sat back, sensing the motions of the energy as the stones spoke and interacted with each other.

Mandi was tired, but not ready for sleep. Her brain wouldn't turn off. The old question of why she stayed at Camp Silver Lake despite having numerous opportunities to leave and find a steady job elsewhere, rattled in her mind.

She told people she was after Violet's job. Until tonight, she had meant it. But if Violet didn't think Mandi had it in her...Mandi gripped the edge of the dresser. Her heart constricted, and she swallowed the sensation, straightening up with a resolve to go to bed.

One of the troubles with being blind was that she had no visual cue to fall asleep. She had interrupted her sleep cycle to talk to Violet, and now her body rebelled, thinking it was morning. Mandi crawled under the blankets, shoving Zeke over, and buried her face in her pillow. It sent warm, stagnant air back into her face, and the sound of her breathing grew louder.

A nudge on her shoulder from Zeke woke her sometime later. Mandi rolled over, rubbing at her face, waiting for the heaviness of sleep to lift from her mind and limbs. She kept her face pointed to the ceiling, seeing nothing, as usual.

"Morning, Zeke," she said after a final yawn. The energetic hum in the room was louder than usual, and it took her a moment to remember her work of the previous night. The crystal spell did its work from her desk, sending off waves of psychic armor for Violet's protection. The amethyst in the corner had activated as well, and Mandi frowned until she realized it was working on *her*. A stuck sensation lingered in her chest after the conversation with Violet about Mandi's future at the camp, though it seemed to be loosening with the work of the amethyst. Mandi thanked the stone in her mind and pulled the bedcovers off.

Zeke yipped his good morning, sounding muffled. Something dropped into Mandi's lap, a ribbed material. She recognized the feel of one of her shirts. He nosed a soft skirt into her hands as well.

"You're color blind. I don't know that I trust your choices." The long-standing joke never lost amusement for her.

The tell-tale click of the door and Zeke's immediate bark from outside the door let her know that he'd given her the essential privacy. She got dressed and made her bed by feel, then combed through her kinky curls with her fingers. Today she wrangled them into a poof on top of her head and grabbed a grey woven headband from the dresser. There was a little bead woven into it, the shape telling her which color it was. Her coven sister Honey had made them for her. Earrings go next, a conservative dangling pair. She avoided the bright feathery ones she preferred, knowing she was dressing for a funeral.

Finally, she ran her hands along the desk surface until she found her wooden box. Opening the lid, her special collection of rare and powerful crystals and gems sang at her. More like a vibration beneath her fingertips, like a stringed instrument being played. These were the stones she'd taken greatest care to collect, unblemished and pure.

Her hand hovered over one, drawn by the sense of order that clicked in her mind. Labradorite helped soothe irrational fears. Were her fears irrational, though? Or would the funeral be impacted by some form of chaos as predicted in her dream? Even if it wasn't as desperate as her dream indicated, it could be nice to have a stone that leveled her thinking. She rolled it in her hand, feeling it out, and her knuckles brushed another stone in the box. The second stone hummed, and the labradorite grew cold in her hand. She released it, seeking the humming stone. When she found it, the crackling of fire came to mind. Not the draining, energy-fire from her dream, but the comfortable sort she liked to curl up in front of with a blanket and a mug of hot tea. Fire agate.

That one inspired action, and the clarity of direction to do what needed to be done. It could repel energetic attacks as well. None of the stones would give her super strength or be much help in a fight. They were small tools but used well they could turn the tide of a conversation or situation, she knew that by experience. Perhaps her preparation would be enough that Violet and the others could see that she was capable of protecting herself, and that some day she could protect the entire camp.

Mandi slipped the fire agate into her pocket. The next four stones came in quick succession, each one building on the last. Jet stone, for healing grief. Celestite, a soothing stone with a gentle vibration. Smoky quartz to hide her from those with ill intentions. And clear quartz, which would act as an amplifier for the other stones.

The crystals rattled together in her pocket, all five of them placed on her right side. She didn't feel like separating them would be wise.

Hushed voices whispered outside her door. Mandi picked up the word "funeral." She pulled on her socks and boots. Last but not least, she reached for the cane leaning against the wall beneath her lightswitch. She ran her hands along its length until she reached the subtle button switch and the seam partway down the handle. In a moment's notice, she could extend the cane into a staff for physical protection. She had trained with it to have something besides her magic for self-defense. She felt better with its heavy weight in her hand and hopeful that she wouldn't have cause to use it.

The conversation stopped when she opened the door. She stepped out into thick, tense air.

"Hey, Mandi!" Beckett said. Mandi smiled at the cheer in his voice, but her hand gripped the top of her cane extra hard at its falseness. She cocked her head, smile widening into more of a grimace.

Zeke cleared his throat, and the beads in his dreads clicked together. "Beckett was updating me on the funeral arrangements. I mean, it's more of a memorial service, since there's not...there's no..."

No body. Mandi's throat constricted with sadness, and she coughed to clear it before speaking again. "I'm sad to hear that, but not surprised. Everything else all right?" Mandi asked, holding her head cocked, giving the men a chance to come clean about whatever they'd been whispering. There wasn't anything secret they couldn't tell her—they were *choosing* not to tell her for reasons of their own.

The silence killed her. She knew looks and body language she couldn't interpret were being exchanged. She reached into her left pocket to grip the Celestite for comfort. It was working, but barely. Mandi let her curiosity take over, suppressing the last of the slight irritation still trickling through her mind.

"Hey guys, don't leave me hanging." She kept her tone light.

"Sorry, Mandi." Guilt laced Beckett's tone. He was pretty good about not leaving her out of things, maybe because he knew what it felt like. Not many three-legged werewolves in the world.

Beckett cleared his throat and continued, "We're trying to keep this on the down-low, but my patrol from last night showed increased rogue activity."

The fire agate in her pocket pulsed like a shock against her leg. Mandi covered her pocket with her hand, feeling the low thrum of the activated crystal. She got the sense the crystal warned her of something coming. Mandi licked her lips. In conjunction with her dream, it did not bode well.

"We think they might try something during the service," Zeke added.

"Zeke, that's what I heard last night in my dream. I know Violet didn't think much of it, but...it was like a prophecy." An auditory prophecy. She'd never heard of such a thing, but why not? A shudder passed through her.

"I'll talk to James. He can set up some extra warding where we're having the service. Be ready to step in, he might ask the rest of the coven for help if Violet is still out of it," Zeke said.

Mandi froze. "What's wrong with Violet?"

"Violet had a breakdown this morning after Fletcher's parents left. She received a phone call from a contact in D.C. and went off her rocker. James had to sedate her. Mildly. More like, put her to sleep because she never went to bed last night, and she was exhausted." Zeke's rambling made Mandi think there was more than he was saying. Why not tell her? She was one of Violet's coven sisters.

Mandi spun away from Zeke and headed down the hall at a reckless pace, cane tapping staccato before her. No matter what Violet thought of Mandi's abilities as a witch, Mandi was still her coven sister. She had to help.

CHAPTER TWO

MANDI

"MANDI, STOP! SHE'S NOT seeing anyone." Zeke yelled. He jogged after her, catching up after a few strides. He put his hand on her elbow from behind.

Mandi jerked her arm away. "I need to see her. I need to make sure she's all right."

"She's sleeping," Zeke repeated. "James will be furious if you disturb her. He didn't put her under very deep, just enough for her natural sleep cycle to take over. She'll be awake for the service in an hour. We'll get you some breakfast, and I'm sure she'll be down by then."

"She needs me, Zeke." Mandi slowed her stride, halting in the hallway. She felt someone brush past on her other side, a whiff of sea air wafting into her nostrils. Ian, possibly. The siren always smelled like the ocean.

"And you need your strength for today." The tone of his voice was firm and unbending. Mandi didn't like it, but she would concede for now. In her mind, she was determined to check on Violet as soon as she finished breakfast. She wove her arm through Zeke's again. The smells and sounds of breakfast greeted her, growing as they entered the hall.

"Zeke!" Luis, a packmate, called out. Mandi smiled at the familiar hubbub in the kitchen.

Zeke's voice rumbled in Mandi's ear. "I'm going to get his report. I'll bring you something, okay?"

"Zeke, Mandi!" Honey's gentle voice floated through the air. "Don't worry, I've got her. You do what you have to do." A cool hand cupped the top of Mandi's and seemed to reach into her soul. She smiled. Her dearest coven sister had the power of empathy and the ability to pierce any clouded feelings and bring comfort or clarity.

"I'll see you later, Mandi," Zeke said. Mandi waved, trying to look in his direction and give him a reassuring smile. He was doing so well at appearing strong for everyone else, but she sensed that he held back the real flood of feelings.

"He's a dreamboat, Mandi. The way he looks at you...Snatch him up before I do," Honey said, leading Mandi to an empty seat. "How are you feeling?"

"Tired already." Mandi set her cane beside her, leaning it against the table.

"I've drawn up some shielding for myself. You ought to do the same. It's going to be a trying day for us all. Wait here, I'll get us some bowls." Honey's warmth disappeared, and Mandi put her chin in her hand, leaning into the table and closing her eyes for a moment. She enjoyed the relaxation of letting her muscles go.

After a moment, she sensed others sliding into the empty spaces across from her and breathed in the familiar scents of herbs and ink. The rest of her sisters had arrived. Dana, Meg, and Anita, the other witches of the coven besides Lilith, who was certainly filling in for Violet where needed.

Honey returned, greeting everyone. Dishes clinked in the air behind Mandi, and Honey guided her hand to the spoon. Mandi dug into the oatmeal. She focused on the hint of cinnamon in her food while listening to the chatter of her sisters.

"I hope you slept well, Mandi. It was a mess this morning," Anita said. "Curses everywhere. We've been cleansing the front hall for most of the morning."

"You could have woken me. I would have helped," Mandi said. Did they all think her incompetent? She put her spoon down. "What happened, exactly?"

"She went on a rampage. I saw the end of it," Dana said. "I don't think she got much sleep last night."

"She said she felt like she was under attack when I saw her," Mandi stirred her oatmeal. It was already getting cold.

"You talked to her last night?" Honey asked. She sounded crestfallen. "Then the spell to open your Sight didn't work?"

Mandi shook her head sadly. "I drank the tea exactly ten minutes before bed, I double checked the stone circle we made. It was the same as always. Kicked out before I even got in. Thanks for trying. You have the best ideas, Honey." Her friends had tried dozens of spells and varying totems, blessed and spelled and prepared with auspicious timing in conjunction with planetary movements, but none of them had helped Mandi project.

Honey sighed. "Couldn't you sleep?"

Mandi described her encounter with Violet, and her sisters listened intently. "I can't shake the feeling the dream was a prophecy, that it really might happen," Mandi finished.

"How is your relationship with Violet lately?" Anita asked around a mouthful of breakfast. She paused and spoke again, her words more distinct. "I mean, dreams are more about the person dreaming than anything real."

"I think what Anita is trying to say," Dana said, "Is that it *could* be prophetic. But more symbolic. Or it could be an expression of your own inner turmoil."

"She brushed it off. Like I was a child having a nightmare." Mandi swallowed. Tears pricked her eyes when she thought about what Violet had said. *Barely a witch.* Perhaps it was more about her relationship with Violet than she thought. She took a deep breath. "She's been busy with the retrograde protection spells and doesn't want my help. Why did she insist on doing it alone?"

"She is under a lot of pressure. Maybe Dana's right. You're feeling distant from her, even angry. The dragon and all the fighting could represent your growing anger and resentment. You're afraid your relationship with Violet is coming to an end. I mean, it makes sense. She's like a mother to you." Honey threaded her arm through Mandi's, and Mandi grabbed her cane before standing. What she said made a lot of sense. Mandi should have grabbed the labradorite to calm her unreasonable fears after all.

"I guess I hoped by now she might see me as more of an equal, and less like a student," Mandi said at last as they moved together towards the door. Everyone muttered a quiet agreement.

The back door to the cabin opened. Airborne water prickled on Mandi's skin. The mist chilled her, and she wished she'd brought her shawl. Shoes rustled through the grass. Another stone activated in Mandi's pocket—no, two of them. Jet and smoky quartz. Her neck tingled, and her ears strained for any sound of running feet, of panting, of a dragon's roar...She shook her head and released the impression of her dream, focusing instead on the low murmur of voices drifting across the field.

The respectful whispering didn't reveal who was present. Tone was difficult to discern from a whisper.

"Is Violet here?" Mandi asked in a hushed voice.

"No," Dana and Honey answered together. A thick lump formed in Mandi's throat. Should they go look for her? Did she need help dressing? James was probably already with her. Mandi opened her mouth to suggest they go make sure, when a collective sigh rippled through the group, the tension breaking. Footsteps drew up to Mandi's left, slow and even.

"There she is," Honey said.

"She looks terrible," Anita whispered. Several people hushed her.

"Sisters, thank you for being here." Violet touched Mandi's arm in passing. Had Violet finished the protective wards in time? Mandi tried to feel for them, but the tumultuous grief energy bouncing across the gathered circle of mourners scrambled her senses.

Without any preamble, Violet chanted the death rites. James' baritone voice joined with hers, rising and falling in the muted air.

"By the Air that is Her Breath
By the Fire of Her bright Spirit
By the Waters of Her Womb
By the Earth that is Her Body
May the circle be open, but unbroken
May the peace of the Goddess be ever in your heart
Merry meet and Merry part and Merry meet again."

Mandi's heart pounded. The words from her dream. But she didn't hear any panting or running. She rubbed her sweaty palms on her skirt, brushing against the stones in her pockets.

"You may all step forward and say a few words, as moved upon. I ask that you respect the dead and each other in the utmost." Violet went silent. No one spoke. Someone coughed. Mandi fidgeted with the stones in her pockets, rolling them around and around, her agitation growing.

A roaring sound split the circle, like a helicopter or an airplane passing too close overhead. But Violet's wards were too good for that, so it couldn't be...

Several screams split the air, and a whoosh of air struck Mandi's face. Fire crackled, the air zinging with an electric-like energy. Screams erupted. Two hands pulled back on Mandi's arms.

"Something's happening, Mandi. We need to leave, now." Honey, voice strained and quivering, tugged on Mandi's arms again.

"What's happening? What is it?" Her voice sounded panicked and foreign to her ears. Her dream. It was real. And if it was real, then the fire crackling in front of her with no heat meant...

She sensed the presence of another person stepping in front of them.

"Violet and James are dead. Get inside, now." Zeke, voice gruff. There was brokenness there, too. "You have her, Honey?"

"I do. Come on, Mandi."

Violet and James are dead. Mandi staggered, using her cane to support herself. Fire agate throbbed in her pocket. The sounds of fighting carried across the field. Violet and James prostrate on the ground, burning in a fire without heat. Whoever killed them could be back there on the field. Why was she running away?

Mandi pulled out of Honey's arms. Despair and anger surged in her, the Fire Agate igniting a strong desire for action, for retribution. She turned away from the cabin and faced the field. From the sound of things, a full battle had broken out.

Honey tried to drag her back. "No! Mandi, you can't. It's too much. There are rogue wolves and vampires, and Drake is somewhere out there Mandi, I can *feel* him." She broke off, a sob in her voice.

Mandi pressed a button on her cane, holding it out before her as the end shot out, turning the cane into a staff. She spun it in her hand. She couldn't do much with the crystals in her pockets except draw strength from them. Residents weren't allowed to enact spells they could fight with, but at least Mandi wasn't entirely helpless with the staff in her hands.

A roar reverberated, and the ground shook with the stride of a large animal. The roar from her dream. Bear-shifter? Mandi gripped her staff and crouched to center her weight.

A massive paw smashed into her chest, and she flew backward, losing her cane and crashing hard into the ground. The chaos of battle around her amplified, then quieted, as if someone fiddled with some universal volume dial. Her head rang, and her ribs throbbed with each breath.

No. This wasn't how it was supposed to go. Mandi propped herself on her elbows, head swimming, trying to get a read on where the bear would charge next. The thudding on the ground warned her, and she screamed, bracing for impact, helpless without her cane.

"Zeke!" His name flung from her lips without thought. The bear-shifter rolled her with ease, her body flipping over rocks and grass, burning her skin as she skidded to a stop feet away. She was a pile of useless bones and sinew. It wouldn't take much to break her apart.

And then Zeke was there standing over her, the warmth from his furred body and the strength of his rage surrounding her as he snarled at her opponent. Zeke. Her fingers brushed the fur on his side, pressing in to feel his muscles quivering, preparing for the attack. His back legs kicked at her, scratching her, but the meaning was clear enough: run.

Mandi couldn't run, but she could crawl. She scooted out from beneath him and army crawled, limbs and ribs screaming at the effort.

A bellow rent the sky, rattling the ground with its ferocity—the rogue dragon-shifter, the one she had seen in her vision. Mandi tucked her head under her arms, measly protection against the flame-breath she was certain would come any moment.

"Powers that be, listen to me. Cease at once." A clear voice rang out from somewhere in the back, louder than humanly possible. Mandi recognized the voice of Lilith. All sound and vibration stopped. Her own limbs were immobilized, frozen in the desperate throes of escape. Lilith's command quivered in Mandi's veins, a power she couldn't counteract. Footsteps drew nearer to where Mandi laid prostrate on the ground in a mid-army crawl position.

"This is no way to treat your brothers and sisters." Her voice slid over Mandi like water, cooling the heat of her panic, and the adrenaline racing through her limbs subsided. She was suddenly tired. Part of her brain said she should still be afraid, she still needed to run, but it was growing quieter and quieter. "We should work together in this time of distress. I will release you, and you will separate into your own groups without lifting another violent hand towards one another while I meet with the pack leaders. You may send one individual in for medical supplies."

Her voice turned away from Mandi, opening in a chant. "Powers that be, listen to me. Release at once." A whoosh of air, accompanied with a loud swishing sound, passed through the field. Thuds echoed around her as those caught in mid-leap fell to the grass. Such simple words, but Mandi knew it was more than just saying them that caused the power to activate. She rolled over, wincing as her wounds screamed, and when no impending attack from the bear shifter ended her, she allowed air to fill her lungs and release, breathing through the pain. Someone bumped against Mandi's side, and she flinched.

"It's me," Zeke spoke hoarsely. He'd shifted into human form. She sensed that he sat up, leaning over her. His hand braced her head, stroking over her hair.

It felt nice. His warmth, his touch, his...What was she thinking? She was delusional. She gripped his arm, halting the path of his hand and clinging to him. A whimper. Had that come from her?

"I'm sorry, Mandi." His voice cracked. "You look...does it hurt?"

Mandi's resolve not to cry crumbled. How bad did she look? "Yes," she managed to say. She sniffed, and his scent filled her nostrils, a mix of sweat and almonds layered beneath the dominant dog-like smell.

"Lay still. I'll go in and get supplies." He stood. Mandi wanted him to come back, to stay with her.

Lilith's voice broke over the field again. "Zeke and Drake, come with me to the cabin. All others tend to the wounded and have patience. I hope we can come to an arrangement that will please everyone."

Mandi squeezed her eyes shut. This couldn't be happening. Rogues had attacked the camp. They must have killed Violet and James. How could Lilith sound so calm?

Zeke's hand pushed down on her shoulder. "I will be back." Then he was gone.

Mandi clung to Zeke's promise as her body shivered uncontrollably. Her breathing increased, coming in rapid gasps. Surely someone would notice her. Surely she wouldn't be left alone to die.

CHAPTER THREE

MANDI

HONEY SUCKED AIR THROUGH her teeth and the crystals clacked in her palm.

Mandi laughed. "Lighten up, Honey. It's not surgery."

"You should be having surgery. Be glad you can't see this. Shouldn't we be adding spells to this? I thought crystals were just for amplification," Honey said. The cool surface of a jasper stone whispered over the skin on Mandi's knee. Heat instantly blossomed there, increasing circulation to the wound.

Mandi sighed, relishing the warmth and relaxation that flowed through her.

Honey laughed. "I'll gladly rub rocks all over your body if it will get you well," she teased.

Mandi laughed, then winced and put an arm to her ribs. "Ah, that hurts." She sucked air in through her teeth. "Crystals do so much more than support spells. They can *be* the spells."

The crystals clinked again. Mandi closed her eyelids. She could sense the stones in Honey's hand. Mandi had picked them out. Three stones left. Only one was needed to finish the healing cycle that Mandi orchestrated through Honey. She hurt too much to place the crystals herself, so Honey had offered.

One of the stones flared, and Mandi flinched. "Not that one."

"I barely touched the rose quartz. It's a healing stone, isn't it?"

"All of the crystals in your hand are. That's why we chose them. But we need the master healer to tie this all together. Clear quartz," Mandi insisted.

"They're both quartz," Honey muttered, but she was good natured and picked up the clear quartz. It thrummed, and Mandi's pulse quickened.

"Can you feel that?" she asked. "The rightness of it?"

"It seems a little warmer?" Honey's voice lilted up at the end, like a question. She put the stone on Mandi's chest. *Click.* Mandi's body responded immediately, vibrating with a forceful energy that meant that they'd done it right. The right stones, in the right order, their magic flowing through her body and speeding up the healing of the wounds inflicted by the bear shifter some days ago.

Mandi shoved those thoughts away hard. It still hurt. It would hurt for a long while. She knew from experience that grief never fully went away, it just dulled a bit and became bearable. A memory of pain, rather than the fresh emotional wound she faced now.

Violet and James were dead, as her dream had predicted. If she'd been a stronger witch, maybe Violet would have heeded the prophetic nature of her dream and been prepared to face whoever had taken her life.

If Mandi had been a stronger witch, she wouldn't be laying wounded in this bed, and the rogues wouldn't be making themselves at home upstairs, welcomed back as residents as if nothing had ever happened to make them leave. They were dissenters, disrespectful of authority, and looking to turn every little thing into a fight, but Lilith seemed to have them in hand. For now. What did the future of the camp look like filled with

A rap came at the door, and Honey answered it.

"Honey!" Lilith's clear, cheerful voice carried into the room. "How is she?"

"More alert than last time you visited," Honey replied.

Mandi didn't remember the last time Lilith visited. The witch probably wanted to talk to Mandi about the camp, which meant talking about James and Violet. Emotions roiled beneath the surface. Violet was supposed to retire, leaving Mandi in charge of the camp with Zeke. But she hadn't retired. She'd been killed. And Mandi had never gotten a chance to prove that Violet was wrong; that she could, in fact, manage the camp despite her limited abilities.

Honey's soft hand touched Mandi's where it rested on the bed. "Do you feel up to talking, Mandi? Lilith needs to discuss something important with you."

"I'm tired," Mandi replied. She didn't have to pretend to look exhausted. Anyone who saw her still gasped at the appearance of her bandaged leg and ribs, except Honey and Zeke, who took turns at her side and were used to it by now.

"It's rather important, or I wouldn't have disturbed your healing," Lilith insisted.

Mandi shifted her shoulders, relaxing the tension building there, and focused on the thrumming of the crystals where they rested on her body, noting the signature of each. They would all need to be charged after this.

"Are you hungry? I could get you something to eat," Honey said. "I'm sure you're sick of me by now. Talking to Lilith will be a nice respite."

"I'd never tire of you, Honey," Mandi said with a smile. "I guess some food would be good."

Mandi heard the door close. Lilith's presence lingered, a sort of vibration that Mandi would recognize even if Lilith's perfume weren't so distinctive.

"That's quite the arrangement you have there. It's creating quite a powerful energy." Lilith's weight bounced the bed as she sat down. Mandi hardly felt it with the stones working their power.

"Crystals are as powerful as anything if you know how to use them."

"You have a gift." Silence passed between them. Lilith cleared her throat. "That is, in fact, what I came to speak with you about."

"My crystals?" Mandi asked.

"Not exactly," Lilith paused, as if considering her choice of words. "What did Violet tell you was the reason you cannot travel in the astral realm? The reason your spells often need shoring up, despite years of study and a precision of execution the rest of us envy?"

Mandi waved at the words, wishing the motion would take away the pain they brought with them. She swallowed the block of hurt that rose in her throat. "She, uh, always said it was the fever. The one that took my vision. She said it crippled my abilities somehow, that I might never...that I should be grateful because it made me less of a threat to those who wanted to harm me."

Lilith tsked. "I suspected as much. People say the most ridiculous things when they're envious."

Mandi's brow furrowed. "Envious? Violet didn't envy me."

"Listen." Lilith moved up on the bed and took Mandi's hand in her own cool, soft ones. "I know this is difficult to hear so close to the tragedy. But our coven needs a leader, and I think it ought to be you."

Mandi gasped. Her hand pulled away from Lilith's grasp. "How could you think such a thing at a time like this? Violet was murdered less than a week ago. We still haven't found the culprit. And I'm the last person who should be leading the coven. I can't even walk!"

"My dear, that's hardly the measure of a witch or warlock's ability to lead a coven. You have unimaginable power, untapped, hiding in the depths of your soul. Violet was frightened, understandably. Too frightened to help you release it. Oh, of course she pretended. She tried things to placate you, gave you books, allowed your friends to help you. But she led you on a wild goose chase, knowing full well what was needed to give you access to the astral realm and your abilities."

Mandi tried to let the idea sink in, but the words wouldn't penetrate her pounding heart, the heart that had learned from and adored her mentor. Could Violet have withheld her knowledge all these years? Tears pricked the corner's of Mandi's eyes and she used her thumb to rub them away.

The vibration of the stones laid across her body diminished. Their charge had nearly run out, their healing power spent. The pain lay in wait, a low throbbing that should remain bearable for a few hours.

"I believe," Lilith began, her floral scent wafting over Mandi as she leaned in. "That you could be among the most powerful of witches, if given the right opportunities."

"Why not one of my sisters? They are stronger. More able. Why me?" Mandi gestured with frustration. The whiplash of negative energy sucked the stones dry, and they stopped thrumming. Mandi dropped her hand down on the blankets and turned her head toward the wall.

"Because you, my dear, understand what it is to struggle. What do your friends know of that? They have it easy in comparison. They are kind girls, but they pity you. Coddle you. Keep things from you. Have you noticed?"

She *had* noticed. Especially lately. Even before the battle at Fletcher's funeral. They claimed they could handle it, that they didn't want to bother her, but could it be something else? Could they actually believe that she would weigh them down? That she held them back? That they needed to treat her like a child?

She turned her face back to Lilith.

"I can see what they have closed their eyes to. You have untapped potential that will someday rival us all."

Mandi's breath caught in her throat. "You think so?"

"I wouldn't say it if I didn't mean it." Lilith's tone held a sincerity that Mandi couldn't deny. "The way I see it, you just need a nudge…but it will take more power than we currently have. I've sent for some help. A few friends who owe me favors. They will get here before the next full moon."

Mandi squeezed her eyelids shut, trying to visualize it, to imagine a world where she had the power to do anything, where the others looked to her for guidance, rather than looking to see how they could best keep her safe.

Mandi nodded once, firmly. "I'll do it. I'll lead the coven."

She could hear Lilith's smile. "Wonderful news. I'll continue as liaison between the various camp factions. I think that would be best, especially while you regain your strength. Don't you think that would be best?"

Mandi hesitated. "Lilith? I'm not entirely sure how to lead a coven. I've never done this before."

"You're a natural leader, Mandi. But if you have any questions, I'd be glad to give what guidance I can."

"Why aren't you going to lead the coven? You'll still be part of it, won't you?"

"Of course I will. I'm not going anywhere. But running the camp and leading a coven are more than one person can handle. You saw how Violet got in the days preceding the...incident at Fletcher's funeral. She ran herself ragged. She was in no fit state to protect herself, or anyone else for that matter. I'm not going to make the same mistake. No, I don't desire to be the most recognized witch in the room. I'm happy to pass some of that off to you." Lilith patted Mandi's shoulder and chuckled. Then her tone changed.

"If I'm to be fully honest, I'm also concerned for our future. Tom reported the recent deaths to the International Paranormal Council and requested back up in the form of a Supernatural Task Force Squad. He disappeared immediately after, obviously knowing that his actions would have repercussions for the camp as a whole and not wanting to be held responsible for any more deaths."

"Deaths?" Mandi gasped. "Would it really come to that?"

Lilith's tone lowered. "I'm afraid so. The response from the government was clear. They will use any force necessary to subdue and capture the residents here for relocation. We cannot allow this to happen. We must be willing to act first, even if those actions seem extreme or strange. Will you help me to convince them and be a voice of reason in these trying times?"

"Of course," Mandi said. "And your friends, when they come, will they help me expand my abilities?"

"They will indeed. And who knows? You may eventually receive your heart's desire. A full coven can do many incredible things together. The lame may walk. The blind may see."

Mandi's hands drifted to touch her eyelids. A smile worked its way onto her face.

"I'm so glad we made time for this chat. I see us doing great and powerful things together, Mandi. History-making things. Now, I have to go attend to my duties. Would you like to tell your friends about your new role, or should I?"

"I'll tell them," Mandi said in a daze.

Lilith patted her shoulder one last time, then left the room.

Mandi collected the stones Honey had placed on her in a pile on the bed as she processed what had just happened.

She'd been made the leader of the coven. Without fanfare, without ceremony. Was there usually a ceremony? Violet hadn't been one for throwing parties or participating in silly rituals. She held a brief initiation for each witch that came to Camp Silver Lake, so they felt welcomed and a part of something even if it wasn't a proper coven, and even though they would be expected to serve the government the rest of their lives.

A knock interrupted Mandi's thoughts, and by the heavy way the hand fell on the door, she knew it was Zeke.

"Come in," she said, surprise lacing her voice.

The door creaked open.

"I brought you a sandwich. Honey asked if I could deliver it to you. She said she needed to fill the herb stores and went out with Meg and Dana. She'll be back later." Zeke laid a plate beside her.

"Thank you." Mandi's smile came out more of a grimace. Herb gathering was one thing she couldn't do well. Leaves were hard to differentiate by touch, and plants didn't speak to her the way they spoke to Meg.

"I passed Lilith on my way. What did she want?" Zeke's words muffled at the end as he bit into a sandwich of his own, or so Mandi assumed. A chair creaked as he settled into it.

Mandi took a bite of her sandwich, chewed, and swallowed before answering. "She offered me the priestess position in the coven." She shrugged nonchalantly.

Zeke's plate clattered on the dresser, disturbing the stones there. That made Mandi wince. She'd have to organize them later.

"Mandi, that's huge! I thought she'd take it on for sure, at least for a few years. Do you feel up to it right now?"

"There isn't much to it. Just lead, guide, protect." She smiled at that last one. With her new position at the head of the coven, her sisters wouldn't be able to leave her out of things. They'd have to tell her what was going on, and she would no longer miss out. Lilith had assured her she'd take care of the astral projection issue when her friends arrived. It was almost enough to make her forget the horrifying events that had occurred earlier in the week.

The door to her room burst open.

"Kamri!" Zeke said with alarm.

"The vamps and the rogue werewolves are at it again. I need your help." Kamri was breathless, and a whine edged her voice. It must have gotten pretty desperate.

"Let's go. Sorry, Mandi. I have to handle this."

The door shut behind the two of them, and Mandi was alone once more. She ate her lunch in silence. There were plenty of exciting things to come, if they could keep the camp from tearing itself apart before then.

CHAPTER FOUR

ZEKE

ONE MONTH LATER.

"Come on, we're going to be late!" Kamri hissed, racing for the front door of the cabin.

"You're certain it's coming this time?" Zeke beat her to the door and opened it, earning an eye roll for his chivalry. The past two weeks the truck hadn't showed, claiming engine failures and a new driver who "got lost." The stores at the cabin grew lower and lower, most of the fresh food gone. No one had any answers that satisfied Zeke.

"They said a driver was on the way for certain. On the road, headed this way," Kamri said, breathless. She and Zeke shed their outer clothes on the porch, stripping off jeans and t-shirts and leaving biker shorts and, in Kamri's case, a sports bra. She worked on shoving her clothes into a tiny pack so she could change before they reached the food truck.

Kamri's red-and-black-dyed hair fell across her back as she stood and stretched. She was built thicker, like a weightlifter. Zeke tried to sense the passion that he was supposed to feel between them as intended bondmates, but though he felt respect and admiration, no mystical soul-mate sensation came through for him.

You shifting, or not? Kamri spoke through the pack mind channel. Zeke shook out of his thoughts and pressed into that space inside that felt wild and other, a pulsing hot mass beneath his heart. He breathed in, and the change raced through his limbs. It was harder outside of the full moon. Zeke caught up to Kamri easily, paws spraying gravel and then dirt as they veered off into the trees. Kamri's grey and white coat stood out in the brightness of the forest; she was more of a timber wolf, made to blend in with a grey mountain background.

His sense of smell magnified a thousand times. He picked up squirrels, birds, pine, dirt. Everything filtered through that singular, master sense. There weren't any deer or other large prey in the woods. They'd all been hunted or frightened off by the paranormal's presence at the camp. Rejected by humans and animals alike. Sometimes Zeke wondered if paranormals had come from another world and somehow landed on Earth, like the extraterrestrials of so many science fiction stories.

Zeke darted around a tree. The truck should have been visible through the trees by now, but the road ahead appeared empty at the usual check-in point.

The two wolves dropped their packs and shifted out of sight of the road. They slipped on their clothes and a pair of minimalist sandals, the kind that rolled up small and tight. At least they didn't look like barefoot hobos. Kamri straightened her ponytail, then strode out to the road.

"Another new driver?" Zeke asked.

Kamri shook her head. "They didn't say anything about that." She ran her fingers through her hair, cursing the empty road.

Zeke frowned. Something seemed wrong. He sniffed the air. His nose wasn't as strong in his human form, but he could sense more than a typical human. Nothing alerted him, and the tension eased from his neck. He rolled his shoulders, then picked up a rock and bounced it in his hand. "We'll have to wait and see if they show."

"Great." Kamri rolled her eyes. She maintained her cool, aloof attitude, and Zeke couldn't tell if she felt any worry at all. He'd always been terrible at reading her.

A bird flew overhead, a predator-type Zeke couldn't identify from the distance, but the shadow of its wings on the road sent a flashback through his mind. *A raven-shifter flying overhead. The crackle of energy filling the air and silver fire striking down Violet and James together, their bodies burning.* He rubbed a hand over his eyes, shaking off the memory. It had been weeks, but it felt like yesterday, the terrible smell that filled the air for days afterward, the confusion of the rogues going from attacking to taking over the cabin. People he'd known for years leaving, abandoning the progress they'd made on their Naturalization records. And the constant flow of questions - how had James and Violet's personal wards failed? How had Harper gotten access to dark magic? *If* she was the one who had killed them. Maybe she was the reason Dr. Hartford and Tyson Miller had disappeared when it happened. Had they been killed too?

"Since we have a few minutes to catch up. How's Mandi?" The gleam in Kamri's eyes told Zeke she'd been waiting to talk to him about this.

Grateful for the distraction from his morbid thoughts, Zeke shrugged and sat down on the side of the road, picking up little rocks and throwing them. Kamri joined him. "The same, you know. Just friends. What about you and Ian?"

"Oh, we're not a thing." Kamri waved him off, leaning back and looking at the sky.

Zeke snorted. "You're totally a thing. You can't deny it to me, I'm your intended mate. We're supposed to be able to read each other's minds, remember?" Zeke laughed, but Kamri only gave a half-hearted chuckle. It was a sensitive subject. Zeke had always heard there was a connection, an urge, associated with being someone's bondmate, but he had never felt it with Kamri. She told him two years ago that it was the same for her.

Kamri stared off in the distance, a wisp of red hair blowing past her cheek on the breeze. She pulled her knees up and hugged them. "With Ian, it's just that he doesn't see me that way, you know?" Kamri glanced down, scuffing a sandaled foot in the gravel at the edge of the road. "How could we possibly be a good fit for each other? He's so..."

"Dainty?"

She elbowed him. "I was going to say quiet, you moron. And sensible."

Zeke grabbed a handful of gravel and let it slide from his palm to the ground. "Ian will surprise you. My mom always said the bond is never wrong." Of course, she hadn't been referring to this unnatural pairing between species. What would she think of his feelings for Mandi?

Kamri shot him an odd look. "Your mom is lupin?"

Zeke dropped the second handful of gravel and dusted off his hands. The road stood empty in front of them. Mentioning his mom and wondering what she would think if she were there dug at his heart. He thought he had numbed himself to the constricting pain, the fear that he'd never see her or the rest of his family again. Apparently, he'd been wrong.

Kamri stuck out her bottom lip, face pensive. "For me it was my dad. He abused it, though."

Kamri was a runaway. She'd tried to make it on the streets as part of an alley pack. Zeke didn't know what had happened to her there, but she was actually relieved when Violet had picked her up. A bit scrawny at first, but she'd worked hard for her position as co-alpha, and a few months at Camp Silver Lake had made her into another creature entirely. Zeke admired Kamri for a lot of reasons. He just wasn't in love with her.

He checked the road again. "They should be here by now." He turned to stare at Kamri's downturned face until she met his gaze. "We should tell them. The pack. About us. That we don't want to be...that we *aren't* bondmates."

Kamri flipped a piece of hair over her shoulder. She chewed her lip, then nodded. "They deserve to know. If we have to leave the camp, our pack has to trust us. They're going to wonder why we let two humans run around with us, slowing us down. Because be honest, if we bug out you aren't leaving Mandi."

"She's not my bondmate though." As much as he wanted her to be, it was *supposed* to be Kamri. Being with Mandi would be against tradition and every law of nature that ruled the werewolf packs.

It was Kamri's turn to snort. "I didn't say she was. But you wouldn't leave her. Like I wouldn't leave Ian."

Zeke sat up straight. "The moment we announce they'll see it as a direct opening to challenge me to win a position at your side."

Kamri stood, brushing off her pants. "I'm not going for any of those buffoons, and they know it." She paused, then gazed at him with her blue-violet eyes. "We're not backing out of it just because some rogue idiots think they'd make a better pack leader than you or me. If we get challenged, we'll defeat them, and then see where we stand with the rest of the pack. I'm willing to wager that most of them stand behind us, no matter who we're in a relationship with."

Zeke nodded. The breeze changed direction, and he finally caught it. The wrong scent. The scent that shouldn't have been there. A growl rumbled low in his throat.

"Trouble?" Kamri asked.

Zeke caught sight of fur erupting around the collar of her shirt as she started to shift. "Hold on," he cupped his hands around his mouth and called out. "Gavin, I know you're there."

The bushes across the street rustled, and two wolves emerged, a large grey and a smaller, sandy brown. Zeke gritted his teeth. Gavin had roped the kid into this? Whatever this was.

The two wolves trotted across the street, then shifted, revealing a grown man and an acne-faced teenager. The man, Gavin, crossed his muscled arms and gave Zeke a cocky grin.

"Fancy seeing you here, chief."

"That's alpha to you," Zeke said, working hard to keep his tone level. "We had food truck duty today. Was the roster too confusing for you? Who's covering the north side?"

Gavin chuckled. "Confused? Naw. We felt our talents would be better put to use doing something more meaningful for the pack."

Kamri's lip curled in a snarl. "Thought that being the ones to bring the food in would put you in high graces with the pack, did you? You're both idiots."

"Are we, now? We're not the ones who have to inform the pack that the truck didn't show. For the third week in a row. Food stores are running low. What are the alphas going to do?" Gavin sneered, and Keith mimicked his stance and expression. The stupid pup.

Zeke straightened, but kept his arms relaxed. His alpha authority could shut down an attack from betas like Gavin and Keith, as long as they didn't issue an alpha challenge call, but he preferred not to provoke an attack if it could be avoided.

"How do we know you haven't run them off, sabotaged the camp?" Zeke asked, his tone hard.

"This camp is done for. Just look around, *alpha*. Ever since those so-called leaders died the camp as you know it has fallen apart. Following the old rules isn't going to work anymore. Someone new is in charge. If you can't see that, maybe it's time for a new alpha," Gavin said.

Kamri threw off her shirt and shifted so fast she was a blur to Zeke's human eyes. Her claws hit the gravel, sending it scattering. Her hind legs kicked off the loose shorts she'd donned in human form, and she postured at Gavin and Keith, lip curled to show her fangs. Then, she barked. It cracked through the air like a whip, the full force of her alpha authority behind it, and Gavin and Keith flinched. Keith whimpered.

Zeke closed his eyes and breathed in. Kamri had a much shorter fuse than he did. He felt anger at blatant shows of dissension and division like the ones Gavin and Keith were showing now, but getting angry didn't have to mean losing control. He couldn't directly contradict Kamri in front of the two betas, however. The alphas had to remain united or lose their influence over the pack.

"Let's head back to the cabin and talk about this there. You guys will have to answer for skipping your surveillance assignment, and Lilith should know about the truck." Zeke held up his hands in a peaceable gesture, and to his surprise, the two guys only glanced at each other before shifting. Zeke stripped off his loose clothes and bundled them again, grabbing Kamri's as well, before he shifted.

Back to the cabin. Now. Wait in your rooms until I send for you. If either of you even think of ignoring my instructions again, there'll be hell to pay.

Yes, alpha. Both wolves replied, seeming properly cowed. Zeke kept his senses trained on them. He'd have to watch for those two in the future. Either one could end up challenging him for the alpha position.

I'm going to run ahead and tell Lilith about the truck, see if she'll place a call about it. Kamri's voice came into Zeke's mind with a distinct tone of worry. She bounded ahead.

It'll be fine, Kamri. We'll figure this out, Zeke offered what comfort he could through their pack connection, but it sounded false even to him. Running out of food was a serious problem. Maybe he could take some of the pack to the nearest town and buy some food. He had a Naturalization license, after all, and could legally be off camp grounds. He'd have to get permission from Lilith.

The lodge stood quiet as they came upon it, and for a moment Zeke could believe that nothing was different. Just another day at Camp Silver Lake. He stood, taking it in for a moment, while Gavin and Keith shifted and entered the lodge, supposedly following his order to shut themselves in their rooms. He'd address their insubordination as soon as he heard what Lilith had to say about getting food for the residents.

He shifted and got dressed on the porch, then opened the door. Shouts filled the lodge. Zeke followed the sound, taking the stairs two at a time and striding to the apothecary where a small crowd gathered in the hall.

"What's going on?" Zeke asked Ian, who stood towards the back of the crowd.

"Kamri's pretty upset."

"With Lilith?" Zeke knew Kamri didn't like the witch, but she hadn't blown up like this before.

Ian nodded. "You better get in there before it gets bloody."

Zeke pushed through the crowd, shoving onlookers aside. Most of them were rogues, he noted, and they looked more excited than worried. Almost like they wanted a fight to break out. Well, he'd put a hard stop to that.

Lilith sat back in a chair with a calm expression.

"This is an abuse of power, and you know it! We need food, Lilith!" Kamri yelled, eyes bulging, the veins in her forehead standing out. Fur spiked up along her arms and face and her fangs elongated, only to be forced back into human form as she fought the change.

Zeke stepped between the two women, holding out his arm toward Kamri as if the gesture alone would calm her. "What's going on, Kamri?"

"Lilith won't do anything. She won't make the call, and she won't let anyone else leave to get food. She says 'it will sort itself out'. If you ask me, she did this on purpose," Kamri snarled, and her chest heaved.

"I don't know what you're talking about, dear. I'm just as invested in the residents here as you are, more, perhaps. But you and I have different priorities." The witch clasped a mug of tea, blowing on it and sipping the brown liquid.

"Lilith, food is a priority," Zeke said, his tone quiet, but laced with anger. It rose in response to Kamri's, as he could feel it through their mental connection, and pack loyalty caused him to want to shift and protect. He couldn't do that right now. Attacking Lilith wouldn't solve anything. He counted to ten and breathed in, then out. He gritted his teeth. "Do you know something we don't?"

Lilith's self-satisfied smile dug its way under Zeke's skin. He hated that she kept information from them. Violet and James had at least tried to include him and Mandi, to train them on the ins and outs of managing the camp. Everyone knew that Mandi and Zeke were slated to take over once James and Violet decided to retire, but in the chaos and confusion after the rogues had attacked the camp, Lilith had assumed the role of mediator. A role that was taking on an increasing amount of authority.

Lilith waved her hand. "I see no reason to get into a panic. We have enough shelf-stable items to last for a few days more, at least." She tipped her mug again.

Kamri growled.

Zeke raised a hand, preventing her from responding. "I can't speak for everyone, but my pack can't go without meat. We lose energy, we get cranky. You don't want to see what cramped quarters looks like with a bunch of hangry werewolves." He trembled, suppressing the fiery sensation that shot through his veins. The wolf wanted to be fed. Hunger was always the worst after a transformation. Kamri would be dealing with the same need for fuel. Hangry barely began to describe it. Zeke focused on relaxing the tension in his jaw and shoulders, breathing through the fire.

"Do not overreact. The universe will provide, as it does." She spoke in a dreamy, far-off voice, and Zeke snorted. Every wolf knew you had to provide for yourself. The "universe" might send a deer across your path, but it also sent the hunter, the frost, and the sharp rock that injured your paw. The universe couldn't be trusted any more than Lilith.

Lilith suddenly thrust her mug away, splashing the table beside her with tea, and stood. "They're here! This is wonderful. What was I just saying?" She grinned, as if she had solved everything with those words. She pushed through the gathered onlookers in the hall.

Zeke exchanged a look with Kamri. "Who's they?" she asked.

"Hopefully the food truck. Maybe she sensed something?" Zeke headed for the door.

"If it's not, I'm going for her throat first. Witch on the menu tonight."

Zeke forced a smile. "Maybe you should go eat something?"

Kamri shook her head, crossing her arms over her chest and shifting her weight to one leg. He saw her swallow hard.

"No one wants to deal with your hangry self. Go on. A command from your pack leader." Zeke's mouth twitched with the edge of a smile. His commands held no authority for Kamri. It was a bit of a joke between them. In the tension of that moment, however, the joke was lost.

Kamri turned towards the lodge door and the kitchen. "Are you coming with?"

Zeke shook his head. "Not until I see the truck unloaded. Make me something." Then he made his way down the stairs and out the still-open front door.

He stopped dead on the porch, blinking with disbelief. No white truck backed up to the receiving area. Instead, a bright red Ford sat on the drive with a tarp bulging in the back. Drake climbed out of the drivers' side first, smirking at Zeke as he slammed the truck's door and started removing the straps holding the tarp down. From the passenger side, the truck's other occupants emerged.

Seven. How had seven women crammed into the cab of a truck? They started squealing and shouting when they saw Lilith in the drive, embracing as if they were family.

Why had Lilith said this would make everything all right? More mouths to feed? More strangers to fill their ranks? They *needed* that food. Zeke crossed his arms over his chest, pursing his lips in a thin line. He'd keep his thoughts to himself as long as Lilith could explain her reasoning.

Drake threw off the last rope and yanked on the tarp covering the contents of the truck.

Crates and bags of food crammed together in the truck bed. Drake hopped up and started unloading, handing parcels off to rogues and residents alike who passed Zeke standing frozen on the porch.

Lilith walked up, breathless with excitement. "Zeke, meet my sisters. You can thank them for the food. They heard of our plight and answered at once. Isn't it marvelous?" Her eyes flashed as a self-satisfied smile spread across her face. Zeke watched the seven women work with the residents to unpack the food. Lilith had played her hand well.

Zeke cleared his throat. "You could have told us."

"And ruin the surprise?" She chuckled, touching Zeke's arm. He moved it out of her reach.

Currently, there were six witches at Camp Silver Lake. Seven new witches would make a full thirteen-member coven for the first time in the camp's existence.

A full coven gathering anywhere, especially on government grounds, was illegal.

There was only one thing Lilith could be planning to do with the majority sway over a full-strength coven and a pack of rogue paranormals at her disposal: she was going to initiate a revolt against the United States government.

CHAPTER FIVE

TYSON

THE TV PRATTLED ON in the background of the dimly lit apartment. It was well after noon, but the lump on the bed still hadn't moved. Light filtered through closed blinds, and dust motes swirled in the air. With a huff, the polar bear rolled, his white mass making the bed creak.

Tyson felt like a blimp hovering on the edge of a cliff as he shifted his bulk again and heaved a sigh. Too uncomfortable to lay still, and too depressed to move.

A short grunt came from across the room, and a split second later, Tyson got a face full of cotton. Becca snorted. Tyson huffed and rolled further, his claws raking the carpet as he landed on all fours beside the bed, wavering with drowsiness. His massive jaws opened in a yawn, and his rear bumped the lamp on the bedside table.

"So much for our deposit," a man said from the far corner of the room. Becca's leech on a leash. Tyson bared his teeth at him.

"Our deal was no talking and you get to live." Becca's voice floated over from a chair in Tyson's corner of the room. She must have thrown the pillow. Her lip curled up in a near-snarl as she glared at Avaan. The charmer stroked his short black beard and stared at her like she was the last woman on earth.

"Could you become human again? You're going to break more than Felix's patience can handle," Becca snapped. She fingered the cord around her neck, the wooden flute an obvious lump beneath her shirt. Tyson was still hazy on the details, but from what she'd explained to him she was the last of the Lamia, an ancient race of snake people that the Thueban used to wage war on other tribes in the Middle East. That simple wooden flute could be used to override her free will and control the snake that rested just beneath the surface.

Sleep deprivation wasn't helping things. They slept in shifts to keep their eyes on Avaan, otherwise, he could steal the flute and use it against Becca again.

Tyson groaned, letting his bones melt and his massive, white-furred body deflate, reverting once again to his frail human state. The sense of bigness, of power, fled, and he was left with the full weight of a crushing sense of failure.

He was their payment to the bartender, Felix, for allowing them to stay in this room above his bar. His dreamwalker abilities were supposed to heal the man's wife. June. She was bedridden, sick with some sort of Cancer in advanced stages, but no amount of radiation or extreme therapy had healed her. Felix had hinted that they'd tried some magical things recommended by a witch, but the results hadn't been what they hoped. June was still sick, and Tyson had no idea how to cure her. He'd spent hours at her bedside, prodding his mind to give him the answer. He'd felt so confident when he offered, but now he was little more than a fleshy lump taking up space that the barkeeper could rent out to pay the debts caused by his wife's sickness.

Becca had been like a coach for Tyson. She had aggravated him into shifting, not just into a polar bear, but a mountain goat and a raven as well. She kept trying to get him into the more spiritual stuff, like astral projection, but it was like Tyson was blocked.

Ever since Harper and Quinn were hijacked by Lilith, the demon disguised as a mortal witch. They had obeyed her every command, even to the point of pursuing and attempting to kill their friends. One moment Tyson was kissing Harper in a corner, the next he was running for his life from the same woman.

"You're thinking about her again." Becca stood and crossed the room, picking up the pillow she'd thrown and tossing it back on the bed.

"And if I am?" Tyson stood up from his crouch on the floor wearing only boxer shorts. He could maintain loose-fitting clothing when he shifted, which was unusual for shape-shifters and weres. Even pants and shirts didn't shred, they became part of the form.

Becca shrugged. "Just...if you want to talk about it..."

"Put some clothes on, please. It's disgraceful. We all share this room." Avaan crossed his legs over on the opposite side, straightening his chair. He wasn't allowed to leave the chair except to sleep, use the bathroom, and go with Becca to get groceries.

Tyson stared flatly at Becca, ignoring Avaan. "I don't want to talk about it. Not until we pay our debt to Felix and get out of here."

Becca jutted her thumb over her shoulder. "I signed you up for an online course in astral projection. Take a look." She climbed into the bed.

Tyson grabbed a t-shirt that didn't smell too bad off the back of another chair and pulled it over his head. Still yawning, he pulled the chair back from the desk and sat down at the laptop Becca indicated. On the screen, surrounded in a swirling, computer-generated blue and purple cloud with misty sparkles, were the words *The Astral Travel Guidebook: How to have your first out of Body Experiance.*

"It's not even spelled right. How can I trust the wellbeing of my spiritual self to someone that can't spell?" Tyson gestured at the screen. He was tempted to click away and browse the internet for more mind-numbing entertainment, but Becca's mumble caught him with his cursor hovering over a new tab.

"Get over yourself. This guy is a guru in the astral arts. There's a section on healing from the astral realm. Or maybe someone you contact through there will know how to heal June. Just learn *something*." The last part came out smashed between her face and the pillow. A moment later, she was snoring softly.

Reluctantly, Tyson clicked the "start the course" button and waited for the screen to load. The bar's internet was not the fastest. He tapped out a rhythm on the tabletop, rocking his chair back on two legs.

"She's right." Avaan's voice nearly sent Tyson toppling.

"Geez, man, you scared me." He righted his chair, keeping all four legs firmly on the ground this time.

He shrugged one shoulder. "She's right. You must hone your abilities. I practiced many hours with my great-great grandfather's flute before I was ready to test it on a live Lamia. When I saw Rebecca's sleek coils emerge at the call of my flute-song, I knew all of my practice had paid off."

"You know you're talking about my cousin, right? It's really insulting. She'd kill you if she heard you call her Rebecca." Tyson grimaced at Avaan, then turned back to his screen. A man spoke in Video #1, crystals wrapped in the three prongs of his beard.

Tyson snorted, chin in his hands. "This man is a total quack."

"Be careful insulting those that know more than you," Avaan warned. He had a book in hand now, but Tyson didn't think he was actually reading. "If you knew more than he did, we wouldn't be on the verge of being evicted."

"Felix said he'd give us more time. Given the circumstances," Tyson muttered, hands flexing around the seat of the chair beneath him.

"How much time does his wife have?" Avaan managed to sound genuinely concerned.

Tyson ignored Avaan. A roiling pit of guilt and fear ground like boulders in his gut, and he squirmed in his chair. Instead, he tried to focus on Crystal Guy. He was talking about the wonders of astral projection. Twenty-four planes, or dimensions of existence, and something about the "Eternal Source" all things stemmed from.

"The things you find in the astral realm may seem frightening at first, but remember, you cannot be killed there. Only thrust back to your body. The biggest danger is in getting lost and being unable to find your way back to the Physical plane, or losing yourself in a spiritual or mental sense, and basically going mad. You must take these three steps to avoid getting lost."

Tyson slid open the table drawer and found a paper pad and pen. He jotted the items down.

One, Stay with Your Spirit Guide. He got a spirit guide? Awesome.

Two, Take Care of Physical Needs for Food, Water, and Rest. Apparently, his body wouldn't actually sleep while in the astral realm. Too much projecting could cause serious sleep deprivation. Noted.

Three, Slow and Steady Wins the Race.

Basically, he shouldn't try to explore the entire astral realm in one night. The planes went up in vibration as well as down. Further down, the beings became more conniving and horrifying, all the way down to the Big Bad himself, who was something like Christianity's Satan. Further up, everything from the lower planes was mirrored in kind, until the Eternal Source, a colorless sea lit with blue flame and the Creator of all things. Except, it wasn't God as Tyson had been taught, and apparently love had very little to do with the way this Almighty created. Tyson frowned. The religious aspect was a bit heavy for him. He'd always believed in a higher power, call it God, the Universe, Fate, whatever. But he'd always held to the thought that love was at the Source. According to this guy, Jaco Korin, all of that was wrong. But then, Tyson could find out for himself, of course. He just had to split his spirit from his body. Easy peasy.

Jaco continued in Video #3, *All About Spirits*. "Can you talk to the dead? Yes, you can. If you can find them and interest them in your mortal self. Depending on how long the spirit has been in the astral realm and the quality of their spirit, as well as what plane you find them on, you may notice their memory has deteriorated. If they're on a plane you're unable to reach, you'll simply need to find the right guide, or gain experience and strength to find them yourself."

Like a video game. Level up, you can talk to the right people, obtain the right items, accomplish the quest. Tyson sat back, rubbing his chin. He could find out what really happened to Reya. He'd have to be careful not to get distracted from the real purpose of finding Harper. He could apologize to Reya, at least. But for what? For being a scared kid pressured by adults? It wouldn't absolve him of the guilt he felt. Not for her, and not for Fletcher.

Tyson slapped the table and let out a loud, exasperated sound. He tapped the spacebar to get Jaco to shut up about low vibe spirits and high vibe spirits. Tyson leaned into his hands and rubbed his eyes. He'd done everything wrong. Everything in his life. He never should have confirmed Reya's abilities to those people who came to his house. He never should have gone into paranormal psychology or gotten a job at the camp. He could have lived a quiet, normal life serving food at fast-food restaurants, or whatever pathetic losers did those days.

Now, Tyson. Is that any way to talk to yourself? His mother's voice floated through his mind, making him laugh a bit as he ground his palms into his dampened eyes. She always said stuff like that, giving him pep talks when school got hard, when other kids teased him, when he would get down on himself. He blinked to clear his vision, and sniffed, then looked up at the computer again. He glanced at Avaan, who seemed absorbed in his book.

He scrolled through the sections in the course until he found a video titled, "Your First Projection." He could probably jump to it and go back to the information stuff. He might as well see if he could even do it before he wasted any more time. Tyson opened the video. Soothing, ethereal music played behind Jaco's voice, which had taken on a dream-like tone.

"Make yourself comfortable, laying down if possible."

Tyson leaned back as far as he could in his chair without tipping it, resting his neck on the top.

"Take a few deep, slow breaths, and tell yourself it's okay to succeed or fail. Either way, you tried today, and you can try again tomorrow."

Tyson muttered the words, trying to play along. Becca would be proud.

Jaco continued, "Notice your breathing. Deepen each breath, make it longer, slower. Control your breathing. There should be nothing in your mind except the sound and feeling of your breath.

"You will begin to feel strange. Everyone feels this stage differently. You might feel like you're floating, or your limbs are tingling. Your entire body might go numb. You may start to panic. This sensation is normal. Tell yourself that. Tell yourself right now, and go on controlling your breath. In, out. Deep breathing."

Tyson sank down. His limbs did feel a bit lighter, or something. Were his feet buzzing because it was working, or because they were simply falling asleep? He didn't dare shake them and disturb the process, but they felt like Jell-o. Definitely asleep.

"A heavy blanket, or perhaps a wave, will roll across your body. Allow this to happen, but keep your mind clear. Your cells will start vibrating in a moment."

Tingling spread across his body. *I'm going to be paralyzed. I'm going to die. I can't breathe.*

Tyson sat upright, gasping and heart pounding as he struck pause on the keyboard and slapped the laptop lid down. That was enough for today. He gripped the table, but it wasn't grounding enough. He needed to feel the earth beneath his feet. He stood and found his jeans from the day before, getting his toes caught in a hole in the knee and nearly falling over. He used the bed to stay upright and got both legs in their proper holes. He jabbed a finger in Avaan's face.

"If you move from that chair, I don't care what Becca says; I'll rip your face off." He bared his teeth, and Avaan nodded as if unfazed, but the hand holding his book quivered. The desire to commit violence shuddered through Tyson, shocking him.

He turned swiftly and half walked, half ran down the stairs and through the bar downstairs, then burst through the doors and onto the rain-soaked street.

Drops landed on his face and head, wet and cold and just enough to shock Tyson back into a better frame of mind. He breathed in and out, the smell of gasoline mixing with the rain and burning the back of his throat in a sort of pleasant way. He was still on the earth, still in his body, still alive. He breathed in again, counting to ten, then let it all out, clearing panic from his veins.

People passed Tyson, walking the streets with their auras flickering in and out of Tyson's vision like broken Christmas lights. He blinked, wishing he could get rid of the extra colors for even a moment. He'd gotten used to Avaan's and Becca's auras; he almost didn't notice them anymore. *Becca.* Panic sparked in Tyson's chest. How could he be so stupid? He bolted back into the bar, dodging an alarmed patron with a violet drink in his hand. It sloshed on the man's shirt and he exclaimed.

"Sorry!" Tyson shouted over his shoulder, thrusting his way through the door to the upstairs apartment.

Tyson surged through the doorway to find Becca holding Avaan in a headlock between her legs, wrestling the flute from his grip. Avaan escaped her hold and dove for the flute. Without thinking, Tyson shifted into his polar bear form and roared.

Avaan fell back against the far wall, holding his hands up defensively. "Sorry, sorry, it's not what it looks like," he stuttered.

"You were stealing the flute," Becca held up the wooden instrument and jabbed a finger in Avaan's face. "If I suspected you intended to do anything else, I would let Tyson kill you."

A continuous growl rumbled low in Tyson's throat. He snapped his jaw, just to hear Avaan scream. He yelped. Good enough. Avaan bent backward away from Tyson, sliding along the edge of the bed. Tyson turned his head, watching Avaan scramble back to his place.

Tyson turned his attention back to Becca, shifting from bear to human, reluctant to give up the feeling of power, but wanting his voice back. Anger still throbbed through his veins. Anger and guilt, which pushed up into his throat. If he'd been a few moments later...

"Why did you leave?" Becca demanded, face twisted in anger.

"I needed a bit of fresh air." Tyson crossed his arm over his chest. He resisted hunching his shoulders, forcing himself to face Becca. "That course you signed me up for nearly killed me."

Becca rolled her eyes. "Astral projection can't kill you. I've done my own research. You just panicked. And look what nearly happened! You can't take off like that. At least take him with you next time. You can't leave him alone with me. That's the whole point of this opposite sleep arrangement." Becca retied the flute cord and slipped it back under her shirt.

"You're the one who's afraid to do something about him." Tyson sucked in a breath, steadying himself.

"Oh, like let you kill him? Is that what you want? I think Harper's been a bad influence on you," Becca shot back.

Tyson blinked. Had it come to that? The anger bled out of him, leaving him feeling empty and tired. Charmer or not, Avaan didn't deserve to die. Tyson ran his fingers through his hair. He met Becca's gaze. "I don't want to kill him. And I'm sorry I left."

"Good." She acted as if that was the end of it, laying down to go back to sleep.

"Becca, you can't keep up this way. *We* can't." Tyson kept his voice soft.

She pulled the covers up to her ears, rolling to face the opposite wall. "What do you want me to do? I can't see a way out. If you find one, let me know."

Tyson watched her until her breathing changed, becoming deep and low. He remembered better times. Times at family reunions when they'd run wild together—playing at being shifters, watching paranormal documentaries and thrillers, wishing they had the same powers. Now they did, and both of them just wished they could get rid of them.

Tyson had always assumed paranormals wanted to become human. It was how he'd approached every case. But meeting Harper, and living his own new reality made him realize that maybe people were happiest being the way they started out. In his case, he just wanted to go back to being human. It'd been simpler to be ignorant.

He had all the signs of classic paranormal depression. Except, it didn't need to be labeled 'paranormal' at all. Depression was depression, human or not. His psychology texts paraded before his eyes with suggestions for treatment. He knew all the answers, but those books hadn't helped Fletcher. They hadn't helped Harper. Hell, he wondered if he'd helped anyone do anything other than disillusion themselves.

Tyson put his head in his hands and pressed his palms into his eyes. Getting out of this situation seemed hopeless. Finding Harper and Quinn, impossible. Even if they did find them, how could they break through whatever hold Lilith had on them?

Avaan left, mumbling something about food. He came back a moment later with three plates and left two of them beside Tyson, who sat staring blankly from his seat at the desk.

"Thanks," he said a moment later. Avaan grunted in acknowledgement.

Eventually, Tyson heard Avaan snoring from the other bed. The alarm clocks on the bed stand read after 11 p.m. Tyson glanced at Becca's sleeping form. She had a freaking curse on her, but she wasn't giving up. Tyson couldn't either. His friends needed his help.

He glanced towards the computer. It was the last thing he wanted to do, but it was the only thing he had. Besides, it was something to keep him awake while Becca slept. He could go back over the section he skipped and just absorb information; he didn't have to attempt projecting again, at least not right away. The screen flickered to life, and he turned the volume down so he wouldn't wake anyone up. He unpaused the video.

"Let's go, Jaco," he muttered.

CHAPTER SIX

ZEKE

ZEKE CAME UP FROM the water, gasping for air. He slicked the water back from his face and blew out, holding onto the side of the basement pool. Without proper maintenance, the water smelled a bit funky. He wouldn't have gotten in except he *needed* to burn off some nervous energy triggered by the swarm of witches that had descended on Camp Silver Lake.

He had to let his thoughts settle without leaving the lodge, and the pool was rarely used anymore. The water reflected silvery light from the few narrow windows, making wavering lines on the ceiling. He should get out. But perhaps he'd do a few more laps first...

Voices echoed down the hall. Zeke froze, listening as they drew closer. He recognized Drake, and the other voice belonged to one of the werewolves that followed the dragon shifter around like a pup follows its mother. Zeke had seen pack-like behaviors among other rogues in the camp. Was it possible Drake had some sort of alpha authority, even outside his species? That didn't bode well.

"Man, those witches stink," the werewolf, Vance, complained. Zeke wrinkled his nose. Vance didn't have much room to talk. He smelled like he'd been rolling in something dead.

"It'll be worth it when they finish the spells to lock this place in," Drake growled. "We need a more defensible position."

"But why?" Vance whined. "Why not attack now?"

"The witch has a plan. I don't normally hold for trusting her kind, but she's good for her word, Vance. She's giving us a critical role in this rebellion, one that will take us to the capitol."

Zeke let out a shuddering breath. Water dripped from his hair into the pool. Drake had confirmed what Zeke suspected Lilith would do with a full coven at her disposal: they were going to take on the U.S. government. A rebellion.

Zeke shifted his arms, preparing to get out of the pool, when the voices drew closer. He hesitated, not wanting to miss what they said or draw their attention to his presence.

"What about those who aren't in agreement, Drake? I don't see that alpha and some of his friends letting this sort of thing happen. They keep asking about Naturalization. Whiny babies can't appreciate what's been handed to them." Vance snorted.

"Oh, we'll take care of them," Drake lowered his voice, and Zeke barely heard it over the lapping of the water. "Lilith's tasked me with that, she has. Said she's relying on me to find out who we can trust. Let's just say things could get bloody." He laughed, and Vance wheezed along with him.

Zeke thrust himself out of the pool, making the water slosh and sending a large splash over the side. He grabbed a towel and rubbed at his face furiously. Who cared if they heard? He wrapped the towel around his waist and stalked from the room, glancing down the hall. It stood empty at both ends.

He clenched and released his hands, then looked toward Mandi's room. He had to talk to her. About the witches, about what he'd just heard, about all of it. He strode down the hall and raised a hand to knock, but froze. He was still in swim trunks and a towel.

"Dude, she can't see you. What's your problem?" He muttered, letting out a long, slow breath. The thought made him feel both guilty and relieved at the same time.

"Zeke?" Mandi called from inside. Damnit, she'd heard him talking to himself. Again. He pushed the door open and slid into the room. He flicked on the light. It didn't matter to Mandi if she sat in the dark, but Zeke preferred to see her face.

Zeke cleared his throat, the reason he'd come sitting heavy in his chest. "Hey, how are you feeling?"

Mandi was propped up in bed, dressed, with her hair done. She looked perfect. "You smell like the pool."

"Yeah. I needed a swim."

She waved a magazine in her hand. "Honey and Meg came by. They outlined everything in puffy paint so I can 'read' it. They regret that James Bordin's behind isn't as luxurious a view this way, but…"

Zeke laughed. "They did that? Wow." He sat on the edge of her bed.

"I know, right? The best." She handed the magazine over. It was one of those trashy celebrity magazines, the kind they sold in supermarket checkout lines. "Lose seven pounds in three days" kind of headlines. Zeke snorted at the cover bedazzled with different shades of puff paint.

"Impressive sight, I'm sure." She offered.

"Yeah, that. More like color vomit. Seems effective, though." He handed it back to her. His mouth dried up. He wanted to sit and listen to her careless banter for the rest of the day, not discuss the tension in the cabin or what Lilith was planning to do with a full coven of witches.

"They did an herbal magazine, too. I could have written it. And more correctly." Her head bowed. Her hands fidget in her lap. "Bedrest is super fun, let me tell you."

She was still recovering from some pretty severe injuries dealt by that bear-shifter. The one sitting in the common room upstairs. He'd received a week in solitary confinement, released when he promised to "be good." Zeke wanted to rip his throat out, dig into his intestines, tear his fingers off one by one...

Mandi snapped her fingers in front of his face. "Oy, you got quiet there. You getting caught up in a revenge dream again?"

Zeke wiped the drool off his face. Damn wolf. A shudder passed through him, and his mind slowly came back to the present. Back to being human, or nearly enough. "Sorry. Your ribs still pretty sore?"

"I walked around the room today." It was a deliberate dodge. She wanted to be back in action so badly, but wounds inflicted by a bear, much less a paranormal one, took a long time to heal.

"And how long did you sleep afterward?" Zeke grinned, despite the fact that she couldn't see it. He swore she could hear it.

She picked up a pillow and threw it. Zeke ducked, letting the pillow sail over.

"Blast your reflexes. It would be really satisfying to hear it hit you one of these days."

Zeke retrieved the pillow, handing it back to her. "I'll sit still this time."

"Really?"

A laugh escaped his throat. "No. But I thought the offer might make you feel better."

She smiled. "You always know how to make me feel better."

"I wish that was the only reason I'd come to see you." Zeke's smile faltered. He fidgeted with the black stone on a cord around his neck. What had Mandi said it was? Black something. It started with a 't' sound. He could never remember.

"Oh? What's going on?" She straightened, suddenly very interested. Her eyes gazed almost directly into his, one of the rare moments when he felt like she could see him with that cloudy, white stare. Her eyes were pretty, like limestone, or the foam of the sea. "Zeke? You're staring."

"How can you always tell?"

She smirked. "Don't change the subject. What were you going to tell me?"

Zeke flexed his fingers, staring down at them. Where to start? "Did you know Lilith was planning to bring in more witches? A coven's worth?"

"They've come?" Mandi's face lit up. "She told me she'd sent for some friends, someone to help us...Zeke, do you know what this means?" She shrieked and threw her arms around him from the side, burying her face in his bare shoulder.

She sounded...happy.

"Mandi?" Zeke asked hesitantly.

She peeled herself off of him. "I'm sorry, it's just that, I never thought this day would come. Violet would never entertain the thought, of course, even temporarily. But so far, everything I've read mentions that you need a lot of power to restore physical functioning like sight. So, a full coven might have enough..." Mandi bit her lip.

Zeke blinked, feeling dazed by her unexpected reaction. "We're supposed to be continuing James' and Violet's legacy here, not encouraging dissent and...and chaos."

Mandi cocked her head to the side. "Be honest. Did you plan to take their place and spend the rest of your life checking paranormals in, helping them get Naturalized, and hoping you never attend their funerals?" Her brow creased, and Zeke resisted the urge to smooth away the wrinkles with his thumb. He held his hands tightly in his lap.

"I hoped it would change, given time. I never thought I'd be part of it changing," he finally said.

Mandi turned her head to the side. "Before Fletcher, I was complacent too. What happened to him..." Her voice broke. She breathed deeply and tilted her face up toward Zeke. "That shouldn't happen to anyone. I don't think I can be part of it anymore."

Zeke rubbed his thighs and blew air through his lips. "So, you'll join the coven."

"There's nothing for us in Naturalization, in following these broken laws. The world is on the cusp of changing. Can you feel it? I want to be part of it."

He stared at her, palms growing hot as he continued to rub them against his jeans. What could he say to that? The only thing he felt changing was their relationship. He wasn't sure where they stood or how they would make it through what came next, especially if Mandi stayed at the camp and his pack voted to go somewhere else.

Mandi fidgeted with a frayed edge of her blanket. "You don't have to decide right now, and I'm exhausted. Could you find my toothbrush, please?"

Zeke couldn't find the words to tell her that he did, in fact, have to decide right then. And if Mandi couldn't be convinced to leave, that meant he would stay. Until she agreed to leave or said she didn't want him. They could talk about it more in the morning. He stood up and brought her toothbrush and a cup of water. He turned the light off, and Mandi settled back onto her pillows, sighing.

"Are you coming to bed?" Mandi spoke so casually one would think they *were* lovers.

Zeke smiled sadly, leaning his head against the room's door frame. "I have a meeting with the pack tonight."

"Oh. Goodnight, then." Was that disappointment in her tone?

Zeke sighed. "Goodnight, Mandi." He shut the door tight and strode down the hall to where he'd left his street clothes, feeling mushy inside. He needed to harden himself. Gavin was bound to give him grief tonight. The meeting would end in bloodshed unless Zeke could focus their attention on the importance of getting the pack out of the camp.

Kamri waited for him on the front porch of the cabin, pushing herself in the wooden swing. "It's about time. I think I've seen everyone else leave."

Zeke just nodded and sat next to her. The bench creaked. A rush of wind traveled through the forest in front of them, cracking limbs, bending trees. He shuddered, feeling the new witches' presence in the cabin like a blight on an otherwise perfect fruit.

"Kamri..."

"I know. We have to leave." Her voice choked.

Zeke looked at her, noting the furrow of her brow and the hardness of her gaze. "You're worried about the witches too."

"If Lilith wants to try to bring down Goliath, good for her. But I don't think she's going about it in the right way, and I'm not willing to offer up my pack to her insanity. She does not have my loyalty. I'd rather risk life out on the run."

Zeke didn't respond.

Kamri frowned. "You aren't coming with us."

"Mandi won't leave the coven," he said quietly. When he looked at Kamri, he saw a flash of pain there. "I'm sorry, Kamri. If I could feel any differently..."

"This whole alpha-bond thing is bogus, isn't it?" She laughed. "It's not that you've broken my heart or anything. I just always pictured us leading the pack together. Now it feels like starting over. I'll have to fend off wanna be alpha suitors while I reestablish the pack by myself."

"I don't want to do this to you, to the pack. But Mandi..."

"What about you? Lone wolves walk a dangerous path. You need a pack to keep you sane, that's a fact. Mandi can't be your pack." Kamri rocked the swing with a hard push of her feet off the porch.

Zeke stopped the motion of the swing, putting his feet down and abruptly standing. He gazed into Mandi's eyes. They would make a powerful couple. They respected each other. They trusted each other. Love would come with time, like it often did in an arranged marriage. Zeke's grandparents had an arranged marriage. They drove each other crazy, but it was the kind delivered with so much love anyone in the room could feel it. They could both be gone if he ever managed to get back.

But first, he had to convince the pack to leave without him.

Kamri stood, ignoring the hand he offered, and stripped down. Zeke tossed his clothes on the porch and transformed, his bones shaking and grinding. The sounds around him sharpened, the fireflies' lights dimmed, and his sense of scent erupted with a thousand messages. Time to meet the pack.

Zeke raised his snout and howled. Kamri's higher tone joined his, arching through the star-riddled sky. A chorus of howls responded in the distance. Kamri shot him a glance, challenge in her amber eyes, and shot off the porch, bolting for the woods.

Zeke followed, relishing the race through the cool, end-of-summer air. His human stress bled away for an instant, burned off by the adrenaline pumping through his canine veins.

A quick run through the woods was followed by a careful descent down a cliffside. Zeke tried not to look over the edge to avoid the memory of finding Fletcher's broken body at the bottom. Not this particular cliff, but the flashback threatened to overwhelm him regardless. A shudder passed through him as he wound down the rocky path behind Kamri, nearing the caves where their pack met for the fire circle.

Zeke sniffed at the air, taking in familiar scents. No rogues. Good. The eleven wolves that had originally resided at Camp Silver Lake were piled around the entrance to the cave, the crackling fire in the pit at their center the only indicator that they weren't regular wolves. That, and the intelligence that gleamed from their green, gold, and amber eyes, unlike anything that could be mistaken for a wild wolf.

All eyes turned toward the pack leaders as they trotted into the circle. Zeke and Kamri took their places at the opening to the cave on the raised ledge jutting out slightly higher than where the rest of the pack rested.

Zeke met the eyes of each wolf. There was Beckett, his three legs sprawled out sideways where he lay on the stone. Gavin stood at the farthest edge of the pack, near the cliff ledge. Keith was there beside him, refusing to meet Zeke's eyes. A red-brown she-wolf called Mavis paced nearby.

Zeke shook himself away from watching them and turned his attention to the rest of the pack.

I'm not going to dance around with pretty words and false promises, Kamri began, projecting her thoughts to the pack. Zeke couldn't stop the snort that escaped him. Trust Kamri to bulldoze her way through this. *We can't stay here.*

Everyone looked up, some with alarm, some with tails wagging in excitement.

Where will we go? It was Lana, a dainty grey wolf sitting towards the front of the pack, orange firelight glinting off her fur. Wolves around her shifted positions restlessly.

I have connections in Canada, Sarah piped up. Her tail wagged. *We could travel as a pack, at night. I'm sure we'd make it. There's plenty of woodland between here and there.*

We don't look like your typical wolf pack. We'd draw the attention of some scientist or campers and get reported, Zeke pointed out.

Smaller groups wouldn't get noticed as easily, Kamri said. *We stay close enough to communicate, but not close enough to be associated.*

We shouldn't leave now. Gavin interrupted Zeke's reply. *The camp is finally ours - truly ours. Lilith will do something about the faithless government. She talks of retaliation, of paying them back for everything they've done to us. This could be the rebellion we've been waiting for.*

Zeke's entire body went rigid. *I do not trust Lilith,* he said at last.

The larger the pack, the stronger we are. We should join with the rogues and stay and fight for our rights, Gavin insisted, his tone taking on a frustrated edge. Mavis stopped her pacing and stood next to him, ears flicking back.

Zeke scraped his paw against the stone and whined low.

That's one way to end up with a lot of dead werewolves. Kamri kept her tone level. *But we will not exercise our alpha rights to force anyone to come with us. You are free to choose your pack.*

Pack? Gavin's laughter echoed in their minds. *Are we still pretending to be a true pack? A true pack has leaders who will mate and bring success to the pack through their combined bloodlines. Not leaders who are "just friends" who mate outside of our species.*

Zeke's lip curled.

Beside him, Kamri snarled. *Watch your words, wolf. Whatever your accusations, we are still the alphas.*

Then you admit what he says is true? Mavis asked, bobbing her head. *We all see Zeke with that blind witch. And you with your fishy friend.*

Kamri snarled and stepped slightly forward. *Zeke and I are not bonded with each other. We will not force the bond.*

Yeah, well, it's time for new alphas, I think. Gavin edged forward. He glanced around at the others gathered around the fire, and then raised his snout into the air and howled. Mavis joined him. The challenge call.

Zeke shuddered with the force of it passing through him. The power of the alpha flickered, then severed inside of him. Until he won the challenge, he wouldn't have access to the power to command the pack.

The other wolves moved to the entrance of the cave, opening the ledge up for the pending fight. A log in the fire snapped, sending sparks flying into the air. Zeke noticed Keith slinking off in the darkness, but he couldn't worry about that at the moment.

Gavin and Mavis paced on the far side of the ledge.

The challenge call is a serious

Why are you doing this, Gavin? Zeke asked. *We won't stop you or any wolf from staying here, if that's what you want. Let those who want to leave go in peace.*

And lose half of our strength to your cowardice? An alpha is supposed to protect the interests of the pack. You want us to leave here and become vagabonds, but any fool can see that we need to stand together and fight the giant that's been keeping us down so long. Your path will see us scattered, recaptured, and put down like wild dogs. Gavin bared his teeth.

Kamri's ears flattened and she barked at him. *Staying here opens us to being used by a witch who is headed in a dangerous direction. How can that be better?*

We're done talking. Mavis cut in. She barked and lunged forward, Gavin at her side. They targeted Zeke first, snapping towards his neck, his underbelly.

Zeke grabbed the scruff of Gavin's neck and flipped him. Gavin kicked up at Zeke's stomach, scraping him. Zeke snarled and went for Gavin's throat. He didn't have time to be human about this. All of his wolf intuition said to kill the challenger, and to do it as quickly as possible. A sharp pain flared on his rump, and he jerked back in spite of himself. Mavis had bitten him, but a yelp from the she-wolf told him Kamri had her well in hand.

In the moment of his distraction, Zeke had lost his chance at Gavin's throat. The challenger was up on all fours and rushing Zeke before he could make another attack. Zeke pushed forward, angling down. He thrust the other wolf up and back, knocking Gavin off of his feet. Gavin lay still. Zeke didn't waste this chance. He rushed the weakened wolf. His jaws snapped down towards the wolf's exposed neck.

Gavin came snarling to life, paws scattering loose rock on the cliff ledge. He caught hold of Zeke's throat briefly, but Zeke shook free and ripped at Gavin's ear.

Mavis broke from Kamri and joined Gavin, harrying Zeke back. Zeke glimpsed the cliff edge behind him, too close for comfort. Kamri came up behind the two challengers, jumping on Gavin's back and biting at his spine, but the wolf thrust her off. He was focused on Zeke, on getting him over the side of the cliff. Zeke thrust off from the ground, leaping over the two wolves. He ran back towards the caves, putting the fire between himself and the cliff edge. Kamri tried to follow, but Mavis bit her tail and dragged her back. Gavin pounced, pummeling Kamri with his hind legs, biting at her face.

The watching wolves howled. Zeke couldn't leave Kamri to succumb to their attacks. He gathered his strength and darted forward. Mavis blocked him, her dark face spattered with Kamri's blood. Her jaws clamped around Zeke's foreleg. He snarled and bit at her face, at her neck, anywhere he could reach. Kamri's whines filled the air. Gavin rammed into her, sending her body into a nearby rock. She slumped to the ground and didn't get up.

Zeke ripped his leg out of Mavis' jaws, ignoring the searing pain. She might have bitten down to the bone. Blood dripped and spread in dark spots on the stone beneath him. He fought desperately against the two challenging wolves, more and more aware of how effectively they drove him back, and the energy that drained rapidly from his body. His strength flagged.

Gavin's bulk slammed into his side and his claws raked down Zeke's body. Zeke's head hit the ground, ringing from the impact. He lay there, stunned, waiting for the bite that would take his life, but Gavin stood over him, Mavis looking on. He leaned in close, a satisfied grin spreading across his muzzle.

Zeke closed his eyes. He didn't have much strength left, bleeding from several wounds, and his head swam from the strike he'd taken. Mavis and Gavin still seemed at full strength, standing tall.

I'm not a heretic. Wolf law states a challenge may end with death or with desertion. I'd give you the choice, except I know that you'd prefer death over abandoning this lot. So, instead, I'm giving you your life. Take the gift and leave. It won't be offered again. If you try to stay and fight, or if you ever return, you'll end up like your mate. Gavin sneered the last word, clearly meaning it as an insult.

Zeke raised his head. He looked over the remaining wolves in the pack, their faces illuminated by the fire as they waited to see who their leaders would be. With Kamri gone, even if Zeke won, he'd be expected to choose another female to lead the pack with. He knew, as he had known for some time now, that it would never be another wolf that he wanted.

You'd better do right by this pack, Gavin, Zeke growled. Gavin stepped off, letting Zeke struggle to his feet. No one came forward to help, and as Zeke painstakingly walked away, still trailing blood, mournful howls erupted behind him, clashing with the celebratory howls from Gavin and Mavis.

Shadows emerged from the cave and the path ahead. The hulking forms of the rogue werewolves, with Keith at their head. Gavin barked, welcoming them. Zeke closed his eyes. That had been Gavin's plan all along: challenge the alphas, get control of the pack, and merge with the rogues.

Make sure he leaves. Escort him to the nearest border, Gavin gave the order. Zeke sensed the alpha authority in his words, a power that shuddered through him without touching him.

He was a lone wolf, now. No pack, no protection, no home, and no authority.

Two rogues nipped at his heels. Zeke growled and snapped back, but increased his speed to a trot, barely above a walk. He had to survive this. Had to find a way to get a message to Mandi, to convince her to leave with him before it was too late.

CHAPTER SEVEN

MANDI

MANDI WOKE SWEAT-DRENCHED FROM a nightmare, Zeke's name on her lips. Her hands fumbled across the bed for him, but she didn't feel his thick, warm fur hide or hear the reassurance of his breath. He was gone. Had he come after the fire circle? Mandi put a hand to her head. It ached fiercely, pulsing and throbbing. Her mouth felt dry, her lips chapped. She felt for the cup of water always within reach on her dresser, but her clumsy fingers knocked it over. Water ran across the surface, spattering on the wood chair.

Mandi's hands splashed in it uselessly as she tried to get a grip on her emotions. She breathed in through her nose, then steadily out through her mouth and cleared her mind. The water dripped. He hadn't come in, but then, he didn't always. Her dream had been about...about wolves. Coincidentally enough. Wolves fighting. But it didn't mean anything. People could have dozens, sometimes hundreds of dreams in a night and none of them would be prophecy.

But she'd had one before that had turned out to be real.

Mandi gulped air and went for the door. She grabbed her cane and pulled the door open, walking straight into someone standing outside.

"Oof! Mandi!" Dana's familiar voice cried out. "What are you doing up?" She untangled herself from Mandi, holding her at arm's length.

"I-I had a bad dream. I woke and noticed Zeke missing. I had to see, to know—" she stammered.

"There was an alpha challenge put out at the meeting last night. And Kamri...Kamri was killed."

Mandi gasped, putting a hand to her mouth. Her hand trembled on her cane. "No! I can't believe it...is Zeke hurt? Where is he?" Her chest felt as if it were being squeezed in a vice. She wanted to run, to find Zeke, to be reassured that he was all right.

"He's walking. Injured, but walking. He was banished from the pack."

Banished was better than dead. For a moment, Mandi's heart went out to Ian. He had feelings for Kamri, perhaps beyond the friendship they shared. Mandi would find him and make sure he was all right, but for now she had to find out more about Zeke.

"Who are the new alphas?" Mandi asked.

"I'm not sure. No one has seen the pack today." Dana's voice sounded shaky. "Beckett seemed so scared. He was hurt, too, like he'd been fighting. He gave me Zeke's message and took off without saying anything else."

Mandi took her staff in both hands, its solidity grounding her. First Fletcher, then Violet and James, and now Kamri...her entire world was shifting out from beneath her feet. Would she even recognize it when everything settled?

"So, Zeke..." Mandi trailed off, hardly daring to ask. She wasn't sure she could take any more bad news, and hearing that Zeke had left and would never return would gut her.

Dana put a hand on her arm. "Zeke wants you to meet him at the border. He said he was on the west side, by the split boulder. You can't walk there with your injuries, so I'm taking you." Dana's jacket rustled, and Mandi realized she was dressed and ready to go. "I have your jacket here."

Mandi held up her arm, holding her cane in the opposite hand. "The border is miles out. How are we going to get there?"

"Portal," Dana said the word so quietly, Mandi's sharp ears nearly missed it. The sleeve of her jacket pulled up over her outstretched arm, and then Mandi switched, letting Dana help her other arm into the jacket.

"But...how? We always had to do so much paperwork before," Mandi said. "And it's the middle of the night."

"Near dawn, actually. I figured, if Lilith isn't filing paperwork, how's anyone to know? It'll be a quick one. No big deal." Dana sounded so casual. She was remarkably good at portals, Mandi knew that. If anyone could open and close one without alerting the others, it would be Dana. Still, the idea of sneaking around didn't sit well with Mandi.

"Where do you want to do it?" Mandi asked.

"The pool room. The water will mask the energy signal of the portal."

The two women walked swiftly down the hall.

"Wait here," Dana said, just outside the room. Mandi waited in silence, listening to the water lap in the distance. It didn't sound like anyone was swimming, but then, the sirens could be eerily stealthy. They didn't splash when they swam.

"It's empty," Dana's whispered voice came back. She touched Mandi's elbow, then took her arm and led her into the room. It smelled of chlorine, and the air felt warm and damp. Mandi let Dana position her somewhere safe, presumably away from the edge and out of sight of the doors. Dana took a breath, and a moment later the bright, warm, slightly sucking energy of a portal opened before Mandi. It tugged at her skin, at her hair, inviting her in.

"Go, quickly. Oh, and take this with you." She shoved a plastic bag into Mandi's hand.

Mandi gripped the thin handles of the bag. It crinkled in her hands. "What's in here?"

"Supplies. He requested a few things. Just give it to him. I'll open the portal in ten minutes to bring you back."

"Could you bring Zeke, too?" Mandi asked.

Dana hesitated. "If he wants to come through, he'll be able to," she said at last.

Mandi breathed in through her nose, held out her cane, and stepped forward. The portal's energy washed through her, magic pricking against her arms and face, and then the late afternoon air of the forest swirled around her, smelling of pine. A bird chirped. Another answered.

A twig cracked.

"Zeke?" Mandi called out. "Is that you?"

"Yes," his smooth voice replied. A single-word reply didn't give Mandi much to go off of. She listened to his breathing. It hitched slightly when he moved, and she remembered that Dana said he was injured. How badly?

"It scared me when you didn't come in last night."

"I'm sorry. I didn't have much choice." His voice was laced with fatigue. Mandi wanted to run into his arms, touch his face, touch every inch of him to make certain he was all right.

The intimacy of her thoughts made her cheeks heat. She held the plastic bag out to him instead of acting on them. "Dana said you asked for some stuff. What's in here?"

"Bandages and antiseptic, I hope." He stepped forward, fingers brushing hers as he took the bag. "I could kiss that woman. She packed jerky."

Mandi crossed her arms, trying to ignore the kiss comment. "Bandages, Zeke?"

"Gavin didn't exactly ask politely." More rummaging. "Did she pack the WereCalm? Ah, yes she did." A plastic bag rustled. It was close to the full moon. Mandi knew Zeke would be in trouble if he was caught out in the open when he went wolf. No matter how much self-control he had, the moon overrode everything. WereCalm was a stimulant drug that wouldn't stop a transformation, but it would make the wolf sleep. Zeke hated taking it. Made him sick to his stomach, and he slept most of the day on it. Fortunately, he only needed one dose, and he would only take it if he couldn't confine himself somewhere. The fact that Dana had packed it meant that Zeke wasn't planning to stick around.

By the sound of things, Zeke had sat down on the ground. Mandi reached out her cane until she tapped Zeke's side, then plunked herself down next to him. Zeke ripped a package open and let out a moan. Mandi's mind spun as she tried to wrap it around the implications of the werewolf pack hierarchy being rearranged.

"Why not do this back at the lodge?" She asked.

"Can't," Zeke said around a mouthful. He was eating something. Jerky? "Gavin banished me. With his alpha status he could command any of the pack to chase me off or kill me on sight. Probably has already. Beckett managed to talk to me, but he sounded like he was fighting something. Orders, I imagine. Always was a bull-headed wolf." Zeke's chewing grew loud in the silence.

"So…you're not coming back?" Mandi's hands shook.

The chewing stopped. Zeke cleared his throat. His thigh pressed against Mandi's leg, and his hand found hers.

"Mandi, the pack is done with me. Whether they like it or not. Kamri is dead. Or seemed to be when I left last night. I haven't heard from her. I can't stay here. And I don't want you to stay here, either." His fingers rubbed across hers.

"What?" The touching was distracting. She tried to withdraw her fingers, but Zeke held on tight.

"I don't like what Lilith is planning. A rebellion means war, Mandi. People die in war. The most she can hope to accomplish is getting this camp shut down and its residents taken to a new camp, or worse."

Mandi struggled to find the words. "I can't, Zeke. This is my chance. Lilith can help me strengthen my powers. I'll be able to do all that Violet claimed I never would. A coven could give me everything I've wanted." Her voice faltered at the end. The coven wouldn't give her Zeke. In fact, it could drive him from her forever. The thought tore at her heart, and her throat constricted.

"You don't need a coven. Not like a wolf needs a pack." His voice broke, and Mandi heard the pain of being forced away from his wolves. Who else did he have, without his pack? Without her?

"Two people is hardly a pack, especially when one of them is human. What do you need me for?" Mandi didn't mean to snap, but he wasn't seeing clearly. Not if he was asking her to leave this, the one opportunity she had to gain both her astral and physical sight.

"I'm not sure need is the right word." Zeke's breathing hitched. He leaned closer, and his hand moved from clasping her fingers to holding her waist. He must be a mere inch from her face, the way she could feel his breath on her skin. One of her hands reached up, trembling, to touch him. Her fingers traveled up to his temple. There was a dried substance on his skin. Dirt? Or blood?

She smelled only the earthy scent of the forest around them, and beneath that a slight, sweet almond scent that she recognized as purely Zeke. She wanted to snuggle her head into his chest and let his warmth envelope her, but this new kind of touching was too new, too unsettling. They had come close to kissing dozens of times but never had acted on it, with Zeke needing to keep up appearances with Kamri and the pack. Now wasn't the time to start. She had to *think*, dangit.

"Mandi," Zeke said.

Mandi shushed him. "Give me a moment." She dropped her forehead to his shoulder, resting there, letting her thoughts swim through her mind until they lined up. She put a hand in her pocket, feeling the stones there. Only two today, amazonite and clear quartz. Communication and growth.

Mandi pulled the stones from her pocket, rolling them in her hand, then raised her head.

"What do these tell you?"

Zeke snorted. "You're the stone reader, not me."

"Just feel them out. They'll speak if you listen." Mandi pushed the rocks toward him.

Zeke sighed and picked them up from her hand. "I feel dumber than rocks when you ask me to do something witchy."

"Crystals aren't witchy. I mean, they are. But it doesn't take magic to receive from them. It's just energy. Try. Please?"

"Fine. I'm thinking...This blueish one...I don't like it," Zeke said, a note of exasperation in his voice.

Mandi cocked her head. "Why not?"

"Because when I look at it, I think, 'how can I ask her to leave the opportunity she has here?' and I know I shouldn't. I shouldn't tell you I want you to come with me, to be my pack, that I want you to know that…" He stopped.

Mandi bit her lip. She waited, letting the stones work. Even from Zeke's hand she could feel them heating up, humming, doing their work, bringing the words out.

"Okay, I get it. I won't ask. You don't want to come; I won't force you." He sounded angry. The stones dropped back into Mandi's lap and Zeke stood up, pacing away.

Mandi thrust the stones into her pocket, sensing the dissonance between their energy and Zeke's frustration. She scrambled to her feet, grabbing her cane, and moved towards the sound of Zeke's footsteps.

"Don't leave yet. Not like this," she cried.

"I'm not leaving. Just needed a break from those rocks. I swear they get into my mind." His voice sounded close enough that Mandi could believe him.

She relaxed, putting her hands on top of her cane and standing still. "This has nothing to do with you and everything to do with me. I'm not ready to give up. And I think there's something you still need to do."

"What's that?"

"You've never mentioned them, but I know you have a family. You came from somewhere. Do they know what happened to you?" The words surprised even Mandi. She felt the influence of Quartz thrumming through her. Clarity. Communication. Even hidden things became clear with Quartz.

"I can't." Zeke sounded small and frightened. Trapped.

"Lilith hasn't taken action to pursue any resident that has left this past month. There's a task force coming, and she's locking down the camp tonight. I don't see her reporting you to anyone. They'll be safe, Zeke." Mandi's throat clenched. She didn't want him to go without her either, but if he couldn't stay here, she wanted him to be happy.

"She might not be in charge here forever. And if she's ousted, whoever takes over would have full access to every step I take. It's all recorded."

The microchip. Mandi reached up to the tiny lump beyond the base of her neck on her back. The tracking device was slightly larger than a grain of rice. She swallowed. "What are you going to do?"

Zeke let out a long breath. "I was hoping you could help me remove it."

"Me?" Mandi's voice went up in pitch. "Zeke, I'm *blind*. I can't cut you!"

He snorted. "Sure you can. I've seen you chop vegetables, cut steak. You're more than capable."

"You're not vegetables!" Her voice squeaked at the end. Mandi breathed, trying to calm the pounding of her heart. "I left my surgical tools at home, wouldn't you know." Her hands still trembled. How could Zeke even think of asking her such a thing!

"Mandi, I have a knife. It's the only way I can go back. If they found my family...it's not an option." His voice held more care and hurt than she'd ever heard.

"What if I hurt you? Or you get an infection? Zeke, what if they *catch* you?" Her breath caught. What they did to Naturalized paranormals gone rogue was still something rumors were made of. Some claimed they were given the choice between serving in the government as military or as agents operating against their own kind—or lethal injection. Mandi realized she didn't know what Zeke would choose, and her skin broke out in a cool sweat at the thought.

Zeke's arm slid around her, drawing her into his chest. "Stop jumping to the worst conclusions. I'll be careful." His breathing shuddered.

Mandi basked in the embrace for a moment longer, then sighed, pushing away. "You'll have to kneel down for me to reach."

Zeke immediately complied, settling onto the forest floor in front of her. A rustling of fabric told her he had pulled his shirt off, and she hesitantly touched his shoulder. She swallowed hard, trying not to think about the warmth that blossomed inside at the feel of his skin beneath her fingertips. Zeke took her hand in his, placing the handle of a knife carefully in her grip, squeezing before letting go.

"Where is it?" She asked.

Zeke moved her hand to a place just over his shoulder blade. "Near here," he murmured. He released her.

Mandi felt for the tell-tale bump and found it. "This is it, right? You don't have any oddly shaped moles?"

Zeke gave a chuckle, making his shoulders move. "No moles to worry about, Mandi. Just make the cut and press it out."

"How deep do I have to go?" Mandi adjusted her grip on the knife.

"Deeper than you think. Just press the knife in, make a slice with the part near the tip. Pretend it's a steak." Zeke laughed at his own morbid joke, and then the forest fell silent. The air was still, except for tree leaves rustling. It was like the world had taken a breath with Mandi. She let out the air she'd been holding in, felt again for the place the tracker was lodged and ran her fingers tentatively along the flat side of the knife to make sure it was in place and her fingers were out of the way. She pressed in. Zeke stiffened and gasped. Mandi sunk the knife in a bit farther and heard the air suck in between Zeke's teeth. Her heart cried out for him, but she couldn't stop now. Something warm dripped over her fingers. She gritted her teeth and finished the cut.

"I need you to take this." Her own voice sounded disembodied. She passed the knife over Zeke's shoulder, and he took it from her. She found the wound she'd made, bleeding freely now. Mandi's grip kept slipping on the blood, and a sob rose in her throat. She tried to swallow it, but desperation and fear let it escape.

Zeke's hand found hers again. "Take a breath. It'll be alright, but you need to focus and get this done."

"I don't have bandages or anything," Mandi cried.

"They're in the backpack. I asked Dana for some, remember? I need you to get this out now." He kept hold of her, the light pressure calming her. Mandi bit her lip and breathed in, then pushed the skin together as hard as she could. The hard form of the tracker gave way, and Zeke's fingers explored the spot, then he turned, and Mandi could hear him searching the forest floor.

"It's out! You did it. It's out." He laughed in a strange, short burst, and then Mandi heard the sound of rocks clashing together and the slightest crunching sound as he destroyed the tracker.

A bubble of emotion popped in Mandi's chest. She sucked in a long breath, stepping back from Zeke, the blood drying on her hands making them sticky. Zeke walked up to her, feet crunching on the pine needle-riddled ground. His hands engulfed hers, and he kissed her forehead.

"Thank you."

"You're still bleeding," Mandi pointed out.

He bent down and grabbed the backpack, holding it between them as he rustled around inside. "There's a pretty big bandaid in here. That should do for now."

"How will we know if I cut too deep?" Mandi's voice hitched, but she kept it steady despite the trembling of her heart. Adrenaline still throbbed in her veins, keeping her on edge.

"If I soak through the bandaid too fast. I'll figure something out. But I think it's slowing already. You did really good. You'll have to clean your hands well, though. Sorry about that."

Mandi went to touch her skirts, then stopped just before her bloody hands touched them. She dropped her arms awkwardly by her sides, careful not to contact her clothes. Silence stretched between them.

Mandi cleared her throat. "Where are you headed? I'll look you up when...when I'm done here."

Zeke cleared his throat. "Chicago. Look under the name Costas."

Costas. His real surname. Mandi's heart clung to the name, knowing what it cost him to give it to her. "I'll find a way. I promise."

He drew close again. He breathed into her hair, his hands on her arms. "Are you sure you won't regret this?"

"Yes," Mandi replied, even though she didn't feel it.

His head lowered, and the softest brush of his lips graced her cheek. Mandi's senses tingled to life, fire racing from her face down her neck and spreading through the rest of her body.

A thrumming sound pulsed in discord with her rapid heartbeat. Dana's portal had reactivated. Zeke stepped back, and Mandi nearly told him not to go, but she swallowed the words. They would only hurt. The whirring energy field sucked at her slightly, drawing her towards it.

"Take care," Zeke said.

Mandi nodded. She turned in the direction of the portal and walked through swiftly. No last glances for her, just his words, rolling around in her mind, full of meaning she couldn't begin to digest in her emotional state. *Take care.*

The portal touched Mandi's skin like cool water. For the briefest of moments, she lost all orientation. Then she came through on the other side and quietness surrounded her.

"Did you speak to him?" Dana's voice came out of the darkness. Then a gasp. "What happened to your hands?"

Mandi flexed her fingers. The blood stiffened them as it dried. "He's leaving. The pack threw him out. We..." She swallowed. "We destroyed his tracker."

"Oh, Mandi, I'm sorry." Dana pulled her into an embrace. "I know how much he means to you."

Mandi breathed in Dana's herbal scent, strong on the lavender. She let it calm her, though it didn't seem to reach into the farthest places of her soul, the parts that already ached even though what had happened hadn't sunk in yet.

I made the right choice. Mandi thought to herself.

A door opened down the hall. "Ladies, it is as I said. I have reports from beyond borders. Our enemies move. Tell everyone it is time to circle up and ward the camp. They'll be on us within the hour." Lilith's voice rang full of purpose, determination, and not an ounce of fear.

"Is that even enough time for the warding?" Mandi asked.

"It will have to be. I've gotten a message to the elder sisters. Dana, find Meg and Honey and have everyone meet in the lower pentagram chamber."

Dana ran off to do as Lilith asked. Mandi made her way to the basement. She wanted to go to her room and curl up in her bed, but she steeled herself against that urge. She only stopped at the bathroom to scrub her hands as hard as she could, getting all the blood out from under her fingernails and letting her emotions wash down the drain with the soapy water.

She made her way to the opposite end of the lodge, using feel and the chatter of the other witches to lead her to the apothecary. Mandi took up her place in the pentagram circle with her coven sisters, old and new. She sensed the extra bodies, catching their scents mixing in the air. Sweet herbal smells, something spicy, an undercurrent of body odor. Witches weren't known for their use of deodorant. It wasn't a bad smell, but markedly present.

When would Lilith speak with the sisters as she promised, to help Mandi travel into the astral realm? They had only been here a few days, and Mandi barely knew their names. There had been no mention of aiding Mandi's abilities, but then, everyone had been busy preparing for the warding of the camp.

The conversation in the room reached a peak, and then quieted suddenly at the sound of hands clapping.

Lilith's voice floated over the gathered circle of witches. "Welcome, Sisters. Much has occurred, as of late. Most notably, the arrival of several friends who will help us usher in a new age for Camp Silver Lake. May our influence extend beyond the borders of this camp and encourage others to reclaim their freedom.

"The most pressing matter," she continued, "is that of our protection. Reinstating the wards. The previous leaders kept the resident witches, aside from themselves, out of much of the spellcasting. I have chosen to include you all, for the obvious fact that with a proper coven together at last, we will channel a vast power that will be able to shield us against the sort of magical attacks I suspect the camp will come under in the coming days and weeks. We are ready for the warding, and not a moment too soon. Meg?"

Clinking and shuffling sounds echoed around the room. Murmurs of thanks drew closer to where Mandi stood.

"Here." Something pressed into Mandi's palm. The twisted wires and smooth surface told her it was one of Meg's wrapped crystal wands. Mandi could sense the quartz and its ability to channel and emphasize her powers. It flooded her body with much-needed energy and relief. She was exhausted after her conversation with Zeke, but the coven would need all of them to prevent the government-sanctioned massacre that was coming.

Serena's voice took up a reedy chanting in an old tongue, dipping high and low in a sing-song way. Mandi tried to match her tone and failed; it was simply too high. She took a lower part. The wires wrapped around the crystal wand pressed into her palms as she held it before her.

The chanting stopped abruptly. A clatter of stones sounded from the center of the pentagram, as someone brought forward the anchor stones that had been etched with sigils and blessed for this purpose. Black tourmaline, obsidian, black kyanite. The witches in the circle stomped their feet and raised their hands to the air, pointing their crystal wands at the stones. They had to be reminded of their purpose: hold the ground. Protect. Repel.

Energy trickled from Mandi's body. She wavered, but held strong, reaching out to find Honey's arm waiting for her to take it. She smiled through her brow-furrowing concentration. The circle took up another chant, this time in English. A spell for breaking enchantments. A spell against curses. A spell to prevent stalkers and reporters.

Incense burned in Mandi's nose: cinnamon, as well as another scent. Dragon's blood? A potentially unstable scent to burn. It could increase the power of their spells on many levels, but it could also make them volatile and hard to maintain. It was invigorating, however, which was something she was grateful for in her state.

There was a tap on Mandi's chin. She opened her mouth, and her tongue tingled with the smoky, dark flavor of black ceremonial salt.

Time stretched and bent around the circle. It could have been twenty minutes or three hours; Mandi lost all sense of it as she clapped and chanted and waved until her arms grew heavy and her voice grew hoarse. Finally, Lilith performed a double clap and all chanting stopped on cue. Anticipation thickened the air, the lodge and the land outside listening.

"We must take up our corners. Three at each point, one in the center. Mandi," At Lilith's mention of her name, Mandi turned her face up, holding steady. "You will be our centerpoint."

Me? Centerpoint required a particular kind of strength and ability. Ability that Mandi was certain she fell short on. There was no way she could...

I will guide you. Can you hear me? Lilith's voice echoed in her mind, like an echo in a cave. Mandi swallowed her fear and nodded. She didn't know Lilith could mind-speak. What other abilities did Lilith have that she'd never shared with the coven? A thrill rose inside of Mandi. She could teach them so much. No more learning only herbs and tiny enchantments.

A tap on her shoulder made Mandi straighten, and she held out her hand. Three small stones landed in her palm, placed there by one of the others. Smooth malachite and moonstone, and squarish aquamarine. Mandi clasped them to her chest near her heart.

Transport on three. One...

Mandi's skin prickled. Transport meant she had to move her body through time and space in an instant, no portal needed. It could be done for short distances only. Mandi had only transported a few feet before, but she needed to go farther this time and make it to the center of the larger circle outside. The transportation aspect of the spell connected the inner pentagram of the lodge with the outer pentagram of the grounds, guarding both from magical infiltration such as spying and unauthorized portals.

Two...three.

Concentrating on that perfect center point, Mandi clapped her hands together, the stones and wand between them. A tinkling sound, like broken glass, cascaded around her. Her body buzzed, and Mandi smiled, knowing her transport had been successful moments before she popped back into existence.

Fresh air sucked into her nostrils as she breathed in. She turned 360 degrees, tapping her foot around her to make sure she was in the right spot. A slight vibration shook the ground to Mandi's left, so she adjusted. Everything lined up, shooting into the sky above, arcing through Mandi to her coven sisters on the perimeter. She wouldn't be able to see them even if her eyes worked, the outside pentagram was so large.

You know the words?

Mandi answered by invoking the chant. She spat down towards her feet, the salt lingering in her spit the activation for binding the spell to the salt that her sisters had sprinkled around the perimeter.

Repeat after me. Lilith intoned a list of latin words. Mandi quickly repeated them, recognizing words of shielding, concealing, and repelling. As soon as the words were spoken, there was a loud CRACK and instantly Mandi's hearing muffled. Had something gone wrong? Had she pronounced all the words correctly?

Plant the wand. Everything is well.

Mandi steadied her breathing and bent, pushing the crystal wand in the ground, tip pointing up. She set the rocks down, feeling their vibrations for the correct order and placement, fine-tuning to their vibrations. She stood and brought her hands out from her sides, palms exposed to the air. Gradually, she drew them up over her head, fighting a weight that threatened to hold them down. She gritted her teeth and clapped her hands and the suffocating sensation broke. She sighed with relief.

Keep your hands up!

Mandi straightened them again, embarrassed that in her relief that the spell was working, they had relaxed.

Prick your finger on the crystal.

Mandi licked her lips. They were dry and cracked beneath her tongue. Blood magic was not something Mandi had ever evoked before. She didn't recall Violet mentioning this in her description of the warding, but then, Violet had been known for withholding information she didn't think Mandi was ready for.

But Lilith's earlier question echoed in her mind. *Do you trust me?* Mandi had let Zeke go to receive this opportunity. She wouldn't fail now.

Mandi rested her fingertip on the crystal's fine point and pressed down. She gasped at the brief, sharp pain, then brought her finger up. It pulsed, as if her heart recognized the miniscule loss of life force. She held her finger out, uncertain what to do next.

A drop at each point. Feel it out and trust your intuition.

Mandi's breath quivered as she turned. There was the slightest click in her gut, and something inside told her that she was at the west point. She rotated until she faced North, knowing she needed to go in order. North, South, East, West. She squeezed her finger at each one, praying a full drop fell, unable to see for sure. When she finished, the ground heated beneath her feet and a rippling sensation waved out from the center point towards the perimeter. Mandi applied counterpressure to her finger, stemming the blood.

You've done well, Lilith said. *Already you blossom into your abilities. The sisters will gather tonight and begin the further awakening of your powers.*

A thrill ran down Mandi's spine, and she shivered. Mandi turned to leave the center point, to go to the cabin and tell Zeke the incredible news she'd just heard. But her footsteps faltered before she took the first one. He wasn't there. Her breath caught, and the satisfaction that had come from successfully placing the wards drained from her body.

She hugged her arms across her chest and limped back toward the cabin, avoiding the thought of how empty her room would feel without him there and trying to convince herself she'd made the right choice.

CHAPTER EIGHT

TYSON

BLEARILY, TYSON RUBBED HIS eyes. It was just after 5 a.m., and he'd finished the final video in the course. He'd skipped over the guided astral projection sessions, not willing to face the terrifying reality of separating from his body again.

The bed was empty. Becca was gone. Avaan's chair was vacant, too. A note scrawled on the hotel pad next to Tyson's computer said they'd gone out for groceries and to expect them back by six.

"At this hour?" Tyson muttered, rubbing the stubble on his chin. Then again, a corner store must be open somewhere, and they had to be careful about showing up at the local grocery store too often. Glancing at the clock again, Tyson decided he had time to shower. And then he'd visit June. He had to try *something* to help the bartender's wife.

Tyson scrubbed up and shaved, emerging from the shower and feeling like a new person. His inner spirit buzzed with energy, as Jaco would say. Water was filled with negative ions, which helped "charge up" empaths like Tyson, or something to that effect. He certainly felt charged up. For the first time in ages, he felt like he could do something productive. He left a note for Becca, in case she returned while he was gone, then jogged down the stairs to the bar. It was empty except for the barkeep, still closing up after a late night.

Tyson walked to the right of the counter where a black, unassuming door led to the part of the building that Felix shared with his wife. As Tyson reached for the door handle, a heavy hand landed on his shoulder. Tyson turned to face Felix. The low light of the bar glinted off the man's round glasses, emphasizing the serious expression on his face.

"Are you for real this time?" Felix asked, crossing his arms.

"I've never done this before," Tyson reminded the man. They'd confessed soon after arriving that Tyson was new to his abilities, but he had had a feeling in his gut that he could help June. Felix had given them a month, which was up any day, and they'd asked for more time. Five more days. They had five days for Tyson to awaken some ancient ability he only thought he had, and he'd been too caught up in self-pity after a half-dozen failed attempts to try again.

Felix turned back to the cleaning he'd been doing, bending down to reach under the cabinet.

"Are you sure there isn't something else I should know about her condition? There isn't a chance it's been magically induced?" Tyson asked.

Felix set a spray bottle down on the counter. He sighed, his shoulders coming down slightly, and gazed off at nothing in particular. "We wanted children. We met a witch, don't ask us how. She did some stuff. Herbs, spells, the like. But none of it ever worked." His eyes darted to Tyson, then away again.

"But you have children. I've seen the pictures in the hall. Adopted?" Tyson asked.

"Not exactly," Felix said, rubbing a spot on the counter half-heartedly. Tyson was pretty certain the man had already cleaned it a few times. "They were hatched."

"*Hatched?*" Tyson blinked. Was the couple part reptile somehow?

Felix muttered under his breath, then breathed in deeply. "I'm not interested in your judgement. My wife was wasting away, she was so desperate for children. We stole the eggs from a harpy's nest on good information that if we imprinted them with our will for children, they would hatch into what we desired. There were four eggs. Three of them hatched into beautiful babies, each two years apart. The fourth never hatched, must have been a dud. We kept it, just in case."

"So, you have three kids that you hatched," Tyson tried to keep a level tone, "from harpy's eggs, and an unhatched egg that never became what you imprinted it with. I'm assuming you imprinted it with the desire for another child?"

Felix fixed Tyson with a weary expression.

"harpy's eggs weren't covered in my paranormal psych classes," Tyson admitted.

Felix sighed. "Of course they weren't. Look, I'm not saying the witch or the harpy egg caused June's condition. I don't think they did, which is why I didn't mention it before. And it's obviously personal. But now you know, maybe you can do something with that."

Felix turned away without another word, waving his hand behind him as if he didn't care. Tyson watched with guilt clenching his heart. He took a shuddering breath in and pushed the door open before he could back out. The hall beyond was lit only with the soft light spilling from an open door at the far end. June's room. Looked like she might be awake.

Tyson knocked on the open door, noting that the woman's head turned to face him.

"Come in, Tyson." She was awake and coherent. He hadn't expected that. It seemed like a good sign. Most of the time he'd come to see her, she'd been asleep.

Tyson entered and took up a chair next to the bed, clasping his hands and leaning on his knees. He glanced over at the woman. With her wig in place, she hardly looked sick today. They had a hospice nurse to keep June comfortable until the end, but that was all mortal remedies had promised them.

"Come to work your magic on me?" June gave him a wry smile.

Tyson coughed, glancing around the room nervously.

"Holly isn't here. I sent her home late last night. And you know I won't spill your secret." She straightened her head, eyes looking toward the ceiling.

"I know. You and your husband have been more than tolerant in that regard. Thanks for...for your patience." Tyson shifted, straightening in the chair and rubbing his sweaty palms on his pants. The confidence and energy he'd gained from his shower seemed to be draining away the longer he sat here. What had he planned to do, anyway? Taking a single online course did not make him a dreamwalker.

June's aura flickered, almost as if in response to his doubt. He shook his head, clearing his thoughts of negativity. There was barely enough light around the woman to constitute an aura, based on Tyson's limited experience. It had dark, diseased-looking patches, huge holes of missing light, as if her soul had cavities. What light he could see was faint and a fevered yellow color.

"It's okay...if you can't." June licked her lips, eyes closed. "Felix wouldn't understand, but I would. And I mean it." Her green eyes opened, looking straight at Tyson. "This is the last time I want you to try. And then…you and your friends should leave. I need time to prepare him for my departure, and it'll be easier if you're not here."

Tyson nodded, heart pounding. He'd never held the life of another person in his hands this way before. Well, he had back at the camp, but he'd never understood it the way he did now.

"Okay," he replied. He looked at the woman, thinking about what Felix had said about the harpy eggs. Should he ask her about them? He didn't want to upset her.

Tyson looked down at the *ulu* knife in his lap. He picked it up and studied the carvings on its curved handle, an image standing out to him. He'd seen it dozens of times before, but never like this. A diamond with a dot in the middle. It seemed duller than the others, as if something was smudged on it. Tyson frowned and blew on the symbol, rubbing it with the hem of his t-shirt. The symbol burned red. He yelped and nearly dropped the knife, then looked at June. She appeared to have fallen asleep, despite his noise. Her chest rose and fell peacefully.

That symbol blazed back at him, red and orange. Tyson raised his finger in the air, not entirely sure what he was doing, only knowing that he had to do this. He breathed in, filling himself with the intention to heal, to make whole, then traced the diamond symbol in the air. Light erupted from his fingertip, and his breath caught. The completed mark hovered before him.

"Go on, then," Tyson murmured. He held up both palms and pushed toward the mark, sending it drifting toward June. The *ulu* knife grew uncomfortably warm in his lap, and Tyson picked it up, noticing all the symbols were glowing with an almost blinding orange light. The orange was becoming a white-hot yellow. Surprisingly enough, it didn't burn him. He turned back to June, holding the knife. The diamond symbol hovered in the air inches above her torso, waiting for him to do something else, but he didn't know what.

Tyson stood. He touched the closest corner of the diamond, and it tilted toward him, the dot at the center spreading and swirling, opening to give him a view into June's abdomen. It wasn't sinew or blood or organs he saw, but a writhing mass of fat, putrid worms. The worms surged forward, coming for his face. He reeled back, breath coming in quick gasps as he scrambled back across the floor. The knife thrummed in his hand. Tyson shot a look at it, then raised it desperately. The worms squealed and parted to either side of him, cascading to the floor.

It was working! The magic had exposed the source of June's illness. His victory was short-lived, as he realized he had to find a way to keep the worms from escaping and possibly infecting someone else. Unless...unless he was *supposed* to remove them. Tyson grimaced and pushed himself off the floor. He walked to June's body, prone on the bed. Was she still breathing? Yes, there, a slight rise and fall. He averted his eyes back to the mass in her stomach. Was she in pain? Her breathing held even, her face smooth and peaceful. The knife pulsed twice in his hand, and he felt it tug his hand toward her stomach.

He gulped. The meaning was clear as day in his mind, but he hesitated. Could he really cut into this woman? Would she survive it?

Tyson lowered the knife. He felt the first cut in his own stomach, a clear, burning slice that carved through his belly with ease. June moaned, her head rolling to the side. The worms writhed towards Tyson's arms, prevented from climbing by the light exuding from the knife.

Tyson was no surgeon. His eyes blurred with tears as he cut away the tuberous bodies of the worms. They fell away, what remained of their bodies shriveling inside June's body until Tyson saw the root, a single body the worms had grown from almost like a fungus. He saw through the hole in the diamond that it had tendrils gripping every organ in June's body. If he didn't release it, and June died, the parasite would likely find another host.

Felix.

He closed his eyes and his lips moved, but no words came out. Was he praying? He didn't know. His hand reached inside June's body and tugged up the enormous wriggling monstrosity, stretching it as far as he could. June's body seized, arching up toward him. Her eyes flew open and with a singular motion, Tyson swung the knife across the worm's body. It broke off with a horrifying squelch. Tyson stumbled back, breathing hard. He looked at the knife, at his hands. No blood. June's stomach was whole, the covers untouched. He'd somehow gone through them.

June lay still. Tyson approached her, resting two fingers against her neck. Her pulse was faint, but there. The diamond symbol hovering above her crept through the air until it hung in front of a picture on the wall beside the bed. The image depicted a much younger Felix and June standing together in wedding clothes.

The symbol pulsed three times, flashing brightly enough to leave an impression in Tyson's vision. He walked toward the picture, tucking the *ulu* knife into his back pocket. He ran his hand along the picture frame. He glanced at June. She made no indication that she saw him. Feeling guilty for prying into things, but certain that the *ulu* knife wouldn't lead him astray,

Tyson pulled on the frame. It swung open on a hinge, revealing a vault beneath.

"I don't know the code," Tyson breathed. As he did, six numbers on the keypad lit up in quick succession. 4-6-3-1-2-9. He punched them in, holding his breath. The vault door beeped softly, and he opened it. Inside, an egg sat in a velvet nest. It was bigger than a softball. Tyson took it out. The black surface gleamed in the dim golden light of the room.

The diamond symbol passed over it and Tyson looked through. Resting inside was a round object he didn't recognize.

"What am I supposed to do?" Tyson asked, as if the diamond symbol were sentient and could respond to him. It merely hovered, a fiery drawing in the air, trying to tell him something, but he didn't know what. It flashed once, then it went out, as if suddenly doused.

"Ah," June breathed. Her hand drifted from her side, reaching out toward Tyson and the egg. "The last egg. Felix told you?" She drew a long breath in again, this time the motion seemed easier for her.

Tyson nodded. He held the egg away from himself. "I think it's the source of your illness."

June stared at the egg, then finally nodded. "I think you're right. Perhaps it was already imprinted when we got it."

"Can a harpy egg be re-imprinted?" Tyson asked, gazing at the surface of the egg. He still wasn't sure what "imprinting" entailed, but he was intrigued. An egg that received the will of its owner and turned out the desired item or idea? Now that was powerful magic.

"I don't know," June said, shaking her head. She swallowed, and her body shuddered. "Water."

Tyson tucked the egg into the crook of his arm and managed to pick up the glass on the little table beside her bed.

A gasp came from behind, and then Felix rushed past Tyson, bending over his wife in her bed, running his hands down her face.

"Are you...did he?"

June smiled. "He did. And he found the source."

Felix looked from the egg up to Tyson's face. His face contorted, and Tyson braced for a lecture about opening the safe, a demand to put the egg back.

"Destroy it," Felix said firmly. "Get it out of here. I don't want to see it again, and it won't do anyone else any good."

Tyson hesitated a moment before replying. He stared at the egg, drawn to it somehow. He didn't need another problem to figure out, but something about the egg pulled at him. When would he ever get another opportunity? Something that could create anything was too powerful a tool to throw away. He'd have to be careful, of course, or he'd repeat what happened to June and Felix. "I-I want to try re-imprinting it. See if I can lift the darkness off it and make it a tool for good."

"Harpy eggs are tricky things," Felix warned. "But if you want it, it's yours. Just don't hold onto it if you start feeling off, like you're sick. You've seen what happened to June. We never should have kept it as long as we did."

"I'll keep that in mind," Tyson said.

"Keep what in mind?" Becca spoke from the doorway. Tyson turned and grinned. Becca and Avaan looked amazed, a look that turned to confusion when they noticed the egg he was holding.

Before he could say anything, Felix came up behind him clearing his throat. "I'm indebted to you, dreamwalker. I started to think you couldn't do it, but you've proved me wrong and I'm grateful. You and your friends may stay in our flat as long as you like."

Becca coughed. "Unfortunately, that's sooner than we hoped. We'll have to move on. Tonight."

"Tonight? What are you talking about?" Tyson asked.

Becca rocked on her heels, glancing at Avaan. "There's been a...development. We don't want to impose on your hospitality or put you at risk for anything." Becca jerked her head oddly, and it took Tyson a moment to realize she was indicating that they needed to leave.

"Er, okay. Felix, I guess we're leaving tonight."

Felix's brow creased, but he nodded. "I wish you well on your journey. I don't expect we'll see you again, and in that case, thank you." He glanced at his wife. "I can't ever thank you enough."

Tyson took in the scene for a moment, June and Felix, gazing at each other with deep affection that warmed him to his core. He left them that way, following Becca and Avaan down the hall and through the black door and into the bar. They entered another, identical door on the far end of the bar and made their way up the staircase to their room. As soon as the lock clicked behind them, Becca flung the backpack off her back. It sat limp, and Tyson realized it was empty. No food.

He set the egg on the bed, afraid he might drop it otherwise. He pulled the *ulu* knife from his pocket. "You didn't make it to the store?" He asked, looking between the two of them.

Becca collapsed on the bed, putting her head in her hands.

Avaan sat down in his chair, crossing one leg over the other. "I could have gotten in without setting it off, but she wouldn't let me."

"You don't know that!" Becca glared at him. She glanced at Tyson. "They've set up these new scanners. They detect whether there are any paranormal anomalies in your blood, and if it beeps, they demand your Naturalization I.D. If you don't have one, they take you in. They had an S.T.F. agent standing ready."

Tyson's eyes widened. "I heard rumors about the scanners. I didn't think they were that close to being utilized. I guess the technology finally caught up."

"And enough Stiff volunteers to station at most public places, or near enough. It's bad." Becca sighed, looking at the floor. "We saw someone get tagged, Tyson. I don't know what she was; a witch, I'm assuming. She wasn't Naturalized, and the Stiff swooped in on her in *moments.* I felt so bad for her when she tried to run..." Becca trailed off.

Tyson looked at the snake charmer. "So, what about what he said? I mean, he's human, right? Couldn't he get in without setting off the alarm?"

"I could, but she—"

Becca cut him off. "It's too risky. If it goes off and you get taken in, what choice do I have but to turn myself in too? Or did you forget that we're 'bonded'?"

"They never said it would be like this," Avaan muttered. "Lamia are supposed to like being bonded. It's better for you."

"Says the oppressor." Becca's temper was rising, and bond or not, she was about to lose her grip. Scales were spreading out from beneath the collar of her shirt, climbing up her neck.

"Uh, Becca?" Tyson gestured towards it.

"What?" She whirled on him, pupils dilating, irises changing into slits.

Tyson held himself steady, so she didn't see him flinch away from her. "Try some deep breaths, maybe?"

She finally got what he was trying to say, and her hand flew to her neck. Her face contorted with focus, and gradually, the scales drew back, her skin slowly returning to normal.

"Thanks," she said, not looking at him.

"Sure." Tyson shrugged like it wasn't a big deal that his cousin could turn into a serpent.

Becca stood, slapping her thighs, and headed to the closet. She tossed the jackets that hung there onto the bed, then disappeared into the bathroom.

"What are you doing?" Tyson asked.

"We have to go. If we cross the Mexican border, we'll be safe there. At least until they catch up to the U.S. with their security measures. I'll bet we have ten years."

"I've always wanted to see Mexico," Avaan said, as if they were planning a vacation destination and not discussing running for their lives. He stood and moved as if to help Becca pack, but froze when both Becca and Tyson glared at him. He sat down, muttering dark, curse-sounding words in Arabic.

"What about the harpy egg?" Tyson stared at the black oblong orb gleaming against the tan blankets.

Becca's gaze slid over the egg and then she shuddered. "Maybe give it back to the harpy? I wouldn't want it."

"Maybe I *should* destroy it," Tyson said. The others stayed silent, leaving the decision up to him. The surface gleamed. He touched it, and a zing traveled up his arm, making him shudder. Maybe he was being stupid, but he couldn't let it go now. He needed every resource he could get to help him find Harper and bring her back to herself.

Tyson slid the *ulu* knife back into its sealskin wrapping and placed it in an outer pocket of his backpack. He grabbed a shirt and wrapped it around the egg. He didn't know how delicate harpy eggs were, but he didn't want to risk it breaking all over his stuff. He zipped it up and pulled the straps over his shoulder.

Avaan stood suddenly. "We shouldn't leave now."

"You're crazy!" Becca shouted.

"Didn't you just say you always wanted to visit Mexico?" Tyson asked the snake charmer.

"Yes. But I have a bad feeling about leaving *now*. Timing is everything. *Jida* used to tell me, from the time I was this high," he gestured at his knee, "that I should always listen to the bad feelings in my heart. They would keep me safe. Now I'm having one, and this woman says to ignore it!" He gestured at Becca's back. She was at the door, hand on the knob and ready to leave.

She flipped her blonde ponytail over her shoulder and faced Avaan. "Listen, I've gotten comfortable here too, but if we can't eat, we can't stay. We'll find another way to track down our friends and break this curse on me. Meanwhile, we should go somewhere we can blend in better."

Tyson shrugged at Avaan. Normally, he'd be all for listening to your gut, but he had to admit that trusting the instincts of a foreign snake charmer intent on mind-controlling someone Tyson thought of like a sister wasn't going to happen.

"I will sit here. I will not move. You can't leave without me." Avaan gripped the edge of his seat as if they would try to lift him off and carry him.

"Tyson." Becca gestured towards the stubborn man. "A little help convincing him, please?"

Tyson stared at her. What did she...? Oh, right. Polar bear. He ripped off the backpack and let the pure power of the king of the arctic surge through him.

Avaan yelped and leaped from his chair as if it had burned him. "All right, all right, all right! I'll come. But whatever happens, I told you so."

Tyson merged back to human form and put the backpack back on. He felt winded, like he'd just run five miles with that half-transformation and coming back again. They passed through the bar. Felix was nowhere to be seen. Dust motes swirled through the air in the empty bar, and Tyson wondered if Felix would even open tonight. The bell above the door chimed as they left.

The auras Tyson saw walking down the street were stronger than ever. The colors almost entirely blocked out the peoples' features. Becca's was a pulsing green, not sure what that meant but it didn't seem good; Avaan's was red, glowing brilliantly. Healthy. Tyson seemed to automatically have a sense of that sort of thing, like he'd been able to tell that June's aura was very, very ill. He tried to file the impressions away in his mind to ponder later. Most people he saw had one main color with blotches of other colors, some brighter than others. Some auras were sick, spotted in a similar way to June's, or fractured with strange bits of light.

Becca started jogging down the street toward a bus stopped at the closest bench and sign. She jerked Avaan through the doors and waved frantically to Tyson, saying something to the driver over her shoulder. Tyson jumped onto the bus and they squeezed their way to an empty strap they could hold. It was standing room only. Tyson's eyes bugged out of his head at the bombardment of color around him, floating egg-shaped bubbles of color pressing in on every side.

Anxiety hit his chest like a pallet of bricks. His knees gave out, sending him to the floor on his hands where he gasped for air. His chest was constricted, everything being squeezed out of him. Becca dropped next to him, her hand on his back. His skin buzzed where she touched, like ants were swarming him. Tyson shook her off and coughed.

Words sounded like angry hornets in his ears. What was going on? Tyson had to get in control. He'd been so clear when he was with June, but now the magic was consuming him. He climbed to his feet, breathing in through his nose, out through his mouth in forceful gasps. The nausea slowly quelled until the bus turned a wide, fast corner. Tyson couldn't hold it in. His stomach clenched and he ran for the front of the bus.

"I have to puke!" he shouted. People fell into strangers' laps in their rush to get out of his way. The driver screeched the bus to a halt at a red light and threw open her door. Tyson rushed down the steps, stomach heaving. His vomit spattered the pavement and his shoes.

"Watch out!" The shout was faint, and Tyson's brain picked up the sound too late to get his legs to move him out of the motorcyclist's path.

The impact knocked him clean out of his body.

Tyson looked down at his...spirit self? He was floating. And his body sprawled on the ground. The driver of the bus ran towards it, pointing and mouthing words that Tyson couldn't hear. Blood pooled across the pavement beneath his body's head, dark and red. Was he dead?

"Welcome to the astral realm, dreamwalker." A guttural voice emerged from the air beside him. "It's about damn time."

CHAPTER NINE

ZEKE

ZEKE LIMPED THROUGH THE forest on his injured paw. He'd bandaged the foot in human form. It probably needed stitches, but he couldn't go to a hospital now. Fortunately, with his paranormal blood, it would heal in a few days with lingering soreness. He was miles out from the camp border and headed northeast. He'd told Mandi to look him up in Chicago, but could he really go back there? There were other options. He could hide out in a city on the coast. A change of view could be nice.

He turned west, sniffing, and immediately sneezed from a tickle in his snout. He rubbed at his nose with his paw, huffing to remove the irritant. He moved a few pawsteps in the direction of the Oregon coast. His gut clenched, and the desire to growl moved into his throat. Not there.

He turned, using his body like a compass. South. He could head to California. Lots of werewolves out there, apparently. His Naturalization license could be flagged if anyone saw it, considering he'd be out of his state's boundaries and the laws wouldn't have had time to change yet to allow Naturalized citizens beyond their state borders. But if he was going to risk getting caught out of state, there were places he'd rather go.

He turned east, back in the direction of the camp, trying not to think of Mandi. He didn't succeed. There was a gaping hole in his heart and mind that she'd filled. Being in wolf form muffled it, but the feelings were still discernible. He'd left her in danger. She could be killed, or worse, converted to a brand of witchcraft that would warp and change her. He'd fought going back every step he'd taken, but perhaps he should reconsider it?

The thought of Camp Silver Lake gave him the same horrid, sinking feeling that continuing toward the coast did. With great reluctance, Zeke turned his body slightly toward the north. Toward his hometown. Toward Chicago.

He sniffed the wind as if he could smell the oily vinegar and peppers on an italian beef sandwich and the fishy, foggy scent of the lake. He felt the city in his bones, the bite of winter, the strange city community that was somehow distant but close. He'd grown up in a tiny flat in Greektown, just off Lake Michigan, with all fourteen of his family members. Fifteen including Zeke, but he hadn't been home since his capture six years prior.

A thrill surged through him at the thought of going back, terror and excitement all at once. If the family pack accepted him back, he'd have a safe place to ride out the full moon, and he wouldn't have to use the WereCalm pills tucked in the pouch next to his Naturalization I.D.

He pushed thoughts of the small blue pills away and considered his next step. He needed a Ryde or a bus; Chicago wasn't a place he could easily reach on foot, especially with his injured leg. But first, he needed a phone. He had to make sure his family was still where he remembered them being...and that they wanted him back.

It was late when he reached the edge of the forest at the outskirts of a small city. He sniffed at the rocks and tree trunks, looking for the special sign that werewolves used to mark a clothing pod hidden nearby. He caught a whiff and dug beneath a rock, finding a backpack. He rummaged through, finding a slinky tee and leggings. Bad draw. He couldn't walk through the city in those clothes. At least not without gathering the very worst kind of attention. He re-buried the backpack for a future female werewolf to find and went searching for another cache. The next one was good. He transformed. It took an agonizing four minutes to shift from canine to human. The moon was nearly full. He had to make it back to his family before he was stuck as a wolf for 24 hours.

The shorts from the cache were too baggy, and he had to constantly hitch them up. The t-shirt was a size too large as well, but he appreciated the ballcap. It added to the outfit and made it into a sort of disguise. He put it on backward and slung the backpack over his shoulder. It was werewolf code to leave clothes where others could find them. Zeke had buried his own clothes near the clearing Mandi had left him in. It was too close to the camp to really be of use to anyone, but maybe they'd come in handy for someone in the future.

The backpack contained five dollars in ones and quarters, another perk. If he could get to a bank ATM, he could use his Naturalization ID to take money out of his account, money he'd earned working at the camp since his Naturalization. It would create an electronic trail if anyone reported him missing, but it was something he'd have to risk. He couldn't not eat for the days it would take him to get to Chicago.

Zeke straightened the backpack on the shoulder and hitched the shorts again, deciding the first thing he needed to buy was a belt. He kept his head down and tried to emit vibes that said, "You ignore me, I'll ignore you." Having been an alpha came in handy there. Confidence rolled off of Zeke in waves, and he caught the glance of a werewolf or two on the street. He could tell by the way they sniffed the air, sifting through the pheromones and the energy he exuded, that they sensed an authority about him and scampered away, shoulders hunched, or simply acknowledged him with a nod. There were only a handful, compared to Chicago. Chicago crawled with werewolves. Quite possibly the biggest network in the United States.

If he was In Chicago, the swagger he was putting out would be dangerous. It would draw the attention of the gang packs, and they either wanted to beat it out of you or start a pack war. And you better pray the mafia didn't get involved.

Zeke spotted a pay phone near a bus stop, its metal box tucked back under the eaves of a thrift store. Zeke casually ambled over to it, taking care not to look as urgent as he felt. His blood rushed and pumped in his ears. His heart rate was elevated, even for a werewolf. He needed to get it under control so he didn't trigger the change.

Zeke's hand landed on the phone handle, and he picked it up, then hesitated, quarter in hand. He nearly hung the phone up, but his gut got the better of him and he dropped the quarter in and dialed before he could change his mind. The phone rang.

Had he remembered the number right? It rang again.

And again.

On the fourth ring, Zeke shuffled his feet and sighed. Then the receiver clicked.

"Hello? Fat Cat Tats, what do you want done?" A gruff voice said on the other line.

Fat Cat Tats? *What happened to the butcher shop?* "Yeah, uh, can you tell me where Antoine's Butchery moved to?"

"No, I can't. They didn't leave a forwarding address." The man guffawed and hung up the phone. Zeke set the receiver down and leaned against the wall, heart clenching. They had moved the butchery. That meant they'd moved homes, since they used to live above the meat shop. Good cover for a werewolf family and all the meat they consumed. Zeke sent up a quick prayer that the butchery was still in business and hadn't folded under some hardship that had come from Zeke's disappearance.

Across the street, Zeke saw a sign for a public library. He could look up the butchery on a computer, maybe find someone to take him across state lines. Illegally.

He jogged across the street. His hand closed around the library door handle and pulled it open. He stepped through. The black stone on his chest heated up. He looked down at it, surprised it wasn't glowing or something. Mandi hadn't told him what it would do when she'd given it to him months ago. Just that it had "protective" properties. Zeke glanced around, not seeing any threats. He touched the stone absently. He was drawing attention to himself. He hurried through the doorway and about five feet away from the entrance, the stone cooled down.

Zeke looked back. The door seemed perfectly ordinary, the terminals that detected unchecked-out books stood sentinel, like any other library he'd visited. Except, in this run-down, small-town library, the terminals appeared brand-new and out of place. Could new tech have been developed that detected paranormals in public places? Suddenly, Zeke was much more grateful for Mandi's sentimental gift. He glanced around, subtly watching for a security guard to detect his presence, but no alarms sounded, and no one approached him.

Zeke spun on his heels and headed in a random direction through some shelves to get the librarians' eyes off of him. He browsed through some books, then ducked out at the end of the row and headed for the computers clustered in the middle of the room like a digital island. He found an unclaimed one and popped on the headphones while the computer loaded up.

Zeke sat as far from the librarians' line of sight as possible and dimmed the screen. There was no chance they could see what he was doing, which was good because he was about to use their search engine for illegal activity. He needed paranormal transportation. Secret and fast. But first, he needed an address.

A finger tapped his shoulder, and he jumped, turning to face a smiling librarian. She smelled strongly of mint and a synthetic floral lotion that burned his nostrils. He breathed out and forced a smile on his face.

"Hey," he said. "Er, is something wrong?" His heart pounded in his chest. He kept his hands locked to his sides, trying not to fidget.

The librarian pointed to the computer screen. "You're going to need a password for that. Do you have a library card?"

"Uh, no. I, uh," Zeke laughed nervously, trying to cover up his nerves with embarrassment. He rubbed the back of his neck. "I just moved here."

"Well then, that's just fine!" She cocked her head and smacked her lips together. "Come by the desk before you go and I'll get you the paperwork for a card. Meanwhile, just type any valid email address for a username and this is today's password." She jotted several capital letters on a sticky note and handed it to Zeke, who took it, smiling gratefully.

"Thanks,"

"My pleasure." Zeke watched her walk away, and once he was sure she didn't seem suspicious of him, he logged in and typed "Antoine's Butchery Chicago" into the computer's search engine. He got "Antoine's Prime Cuts" and clicked on it, not seeing the familiar family logo anywhere. But this had to be it. He scrolled around a bit, but the website was a dead-end. Unless his father had changed his name to "Shaun" and had gotten plastic surgery. He headed back to the search page and scrolled down to the next name. "Sweet Butchery." He clicked on it and immediately went to the "About Us" page. There they were. His father, grandfather, and oldest two brothers stood with their arms around each other, smiling. Well, except Phil, who had a straight expression that somehow suited the serious younger boy Zeke remembered him being. He must have been about nine when Zeke left. He shook himself out of the reverie and scrolled, finding the address of the new shop.

A stack of sticky notes rested on the desk beside Zeke, and he pilfered a pencil stub from the empty computer cubicle on his left, jotting down the address in a messy scrawl. He clicked into a map next, visualizing where the new butchery was. They moved from an older section of downtown to a newer one. Where would his dad have gotten the capital for that? It gave Zeke a queasy feeling. A bold business move, to be sure: more people to cater to, but dad hated debt, and Zeke had a feeling they hadn't purchased the new shop outright. The name was weird too—why get rid of the identity that had been respected in the community for decades and exchange it for a name like that? It didn't sound like something his father or grandfather would approve.

He clicked to the homepage of the website and his heart skipped a beat. There on the front screen was the reason why everything felt wrong. A man in a rich suit and a pleased, wolfish grin stood shaking Zeke's father's hand, standing in front of the new shop, which had an uncut ribbon across the doors.

Bruce. Leader of the Chicago mafia, and head of the biggest werewolf pack in the U.S., if not the world.

Something had gone horribly wrong. Zeke's father would never sign up with the mafia. When Zeke had tried to do it, his father had forbidden him from running around with "riff raff and criminals." It hadn't stopped Zeke, and he regretted not listening sooner. Now his father was in debt up to his neck. Was it Zeke's fault, somehow? Had his not being there to help keep the butchery running made his father get desperate and choose to sellout, rather than close up shop?

Someone sat next to Zeke. They glanced his way a bit nervously, and Zeke sniffed the air. His senses were somewhat muted as a human, but still more advanced than most. The metallic tang of blood wafted off the twitchy teen vamp. How did he get in there without setting off the alarm? He didn't have any obvious protection like Zeke's stone, but he must have had something. The teen glanced at him again, licking his lips, and Zeke let a growl rumble low in his throat.

The vampire froze, realizing Zeke was onto him, possibly understanding what he was as well, and he grabbed his stuff and moved one booth over. Zeke kept a wary eye on him. A vamp could drop a werewolf easily, and their venom was paralyzing. But what had he planned on doing? Sucking Zeke dry in the library?

After watching the vamp for a moment to make sure he wasn't going to try anything, Zeke brought his mind back to the next problem he needed to solve—transportation. His fingers hovered over the keyboard.

How did one search for local illegal businesses? He'd heard there was a paranormal dark web of sorts, but he didn't know how to access it. Even if he did, the library probably had firewalls against accessing it.

He typed "paranormal transport" and got nothing but laws for paranormals using public transit and articles about the recent changes going into effect at the start of the new year. The new laws would have allowed Zeke across state lines legally with his Naturalization I.D. Too bad they weren't in effect now.

Zeke's neck prickled with the sense of being watched, and he popped his head above the privacy partition to glance at the librarians. They were both focused on their computers. One got up and pushed a cartful of books toward the opposite end of the library. Neither gave a hint that they suspected Zeke of anything. He scanned the rest of the room. Zeke's eyes landed on the vampire just as he glanced away again.

"You got a problem?" Zeke hissed.

He shook his head hurriedly, clearly not wanting to get mixed up with a werewolf. Smart kid. He kicked at his backpack, as if trying to shove it under the desk. Or draw Zeke's attention to it. It was a plain black backpack, except for a symbol stitched in dark, almost imperceptible thread. A car with a flat arrow over the top. Zeke had seen that symbol before on a handful of cars next to their license plates, almost blending in with the car color and barely noticeable.

Zeke scooted his chair closer to the vamp. He leaned away but kept clicking on his computer.

"What is that?" Zeke whispered, pointing at the bag.

The vamp stayed stubbornly silent, setting his jaw and staring forward. Punishing Zeke for his threatening attitude earlier, maybe.

"Come on. I know you're bummed I'm not your next snack, but maybe you can help a guy out? I need to get somewhere."

The vamp's expression melted a little. He shifted uncomfortably, glancing around.

"I'm Z. What's your name?" Zeke didn't offer his hand. You didn't offer a hand to a vamp.

"Larson."

"Larson, thanks for your help." It was unlikely that was his real name, just like Z wasn't Zeke's, but there was an understanding between them now.

"There's a P.A.P. nearby," Larson said.

"P.A.P.?" Zeke asked, keeping his voice down. Their whispered conversation was drawing attention. Zeke needed to wrap it up.

"Paranormal Access Point. You need to get somewhere, they'll get you there. It's down on 53rd, at the Carco gas station. You want to talk to Greg and Steven." Larson's fingers typed furiously.

"They okay with my type?" Zeke asked.

"They don't care what your type is, so long as you can pay. And tell them I sent you." The kid rubbed his nose and brushed his shoulder against the side of his face, looking at Zeke briefly, then back at the screen.

Zeke hated the thought of what a couple of vampires would want as payment, but as his only option, he would have to give it a shot. "Thanks again, man. I'm lucky I found you. Never thought I'd say that about a vamp."

"Damn right," the kid muttered.

Zeke shrugged it off and did a quick internet search for the gas station he mentioned, taking down directions, then closed down the computer and stood up.

Paper with directions and addresses in hand, Zeke left the library, noticing the uncomfortably warm sensation returned when he passed through the library security terminals, and vanished again once he was back outside.

The Paranormal Access Point was nowhere to be seen when he arrived at the Carco. Zeke noticed gas pump number six had the car symbol on it, the same symbol from Larson's backpack. It was scratched into the paint on the side of the pump, barely visible among the other scratched-on graffiti. Zeke stood in front of the pump and scanned the button, then noticed the "call attendant" button. He pressed it, hoping he'd understood the message correctly, watching the front doors of the gas station. If the attendant came out, he might need a good explanation for why a pedestrian was standing in front of a gas station pump asking for help.

The glass doors stayed shut. A black car emerged from behind the gas station and pulled slowly around the entire parking lot, as if circling Zeke to get a good view. Zeke watched the car, turning as it went around again, then it pulled smoothly into stall number six. The window rolled down, and an Asian man with a smooth face leaned out, his arm resting on the windowsill.

"You need a ride, pal?"

Zeke shifted the nearly empty backpack on his shoulder. "Yeah. Larson told me about your service."

The man grunted. "Greg. This here's Steven." A man with an identical face waved from the passenger side, grinning widely. The men looked exactly alike. Like twins. Their smell wasn't vampire, like Zeke assumed it would be, though it seemed similar.

"Where're you headed?" Greg asked, squinting at Zeke.

"Chicago."

They both whistled. "That's a long drive. We charge by the mile. You fill us up, buy our food, we'll have you there no cop-stops, guaranteed." Greg's smiling brother, Steven, smiled even wider and rubbed his hands together.

Zeke slapped the top of the car. "You got a deal."

From a slim pouch he kept on an elastic belt beneath his clothes, Zeke pulled out his debit card. He only hesitated a moment before sticking the card in the slot on the pump to fill up the car. His family might need every penny they could get. He'd be as scrupulous as possible, and once he got there, he would work to help the family get out of debt.

The pump stopped, and Zeke put the nozzle away, then went to open the passenger seat. It was locked.

Greg rapped his knuckles on the side of the car. "Two cases of beer and the spiciest chips they got. And nuts. Lots of nuts. Get yourself something, too, and a few bottles of water. We'll need something to piss in, no stops."

"No stops?" Zeke echoed.

Steven cackled from the passenger side. "Just to eat and sh—"

Zeke held up a hand. "I get the idea."

He ran into the gas station and paid for the required goods. The attendant barely reacted to his Naturalization ID, just glanced at it without looking close at any details. Zeke dashed back to the car and Greg popped the trunk, letting Zeke throw his stuff in.

Steven held up a calculator. "1,964 miles. You pay half up front, half on arrival." He had an electric card processor in hand.

Zeke hesitated. "Isn't that traceable? The reader?"

"It's hacked to prevent info getting into the wrong hands," Greg explained.

Zeke gave Steven the card, watching the screen carefully to make sure he wasn't getting screwed. $2 per mile. The amount made him wince, but it had to be done if he was going to get home in time. Running, even with his enhanced form, would take a week. He'd get there in less than two days with these guys.

Zeke climbed into the back seat. His long legs had nowhere to go, so he angled himself sideways and leaned his hand on the windows.

"Rules of the road: No puking in the car. Holler if you need to step out, don't try to do it out the window. Human forms only. No magic, it interferes with the custom shields we have built into this baby." Greg tapped the dashboard with his hand, starting the car up with the other. It rumbled to life, and Zeke felt a tingle wash over him. The stone around his neck didn't react.

"Client chooses the music," Steven said, as if it was a huge perk.

Zeke waved his hand. "Pick something you like." He didn't listen to music often enough to really care.

He did get sick of the screaming rock "music" Steven gleefully selected after a few hours. He requested they turn on something calmer, and they went from gut-churning shrieking to classical instrumental. The difference jarred him, and a headache formed behind his eyes. Zeke cushioned his head on his arm, exhausted from a day of running through the forest. The smooshed sandwich and sticks of jerky he'd eaten sat in his stomach like rocks. The bread, combined with the stale stench of the car, made Zeke's stomach want to heave. He rolled down the window and stuck his head out, deliberately keeping his tongue in his mouth. It took a conscious effort to not stick it out.

"He's like a puppy, Greg, look at that." Either they assumed Zeke couldn't hear them, or they didn't care. Zeke ignored them.

The fresh air was worth a bit of ridicule. The sensation in his stomach subsided, and Zeke reluctantly rolled the window back up, then tried to get some more sleep.

When he woke up next, they were pulling up to one of those greasy cheap food joints. He stretched, yawning, and the beads in his dreads rattled as he shook the sleep out of his limbs.

"We getting out?" he asked between yawns.

Greg opened his door in answer.

"Yep!" Steven chirped, already outside. He slammed his door, rattling the car. Greg held his open as if waiting for Zeke to get out.

"The wards activate when this door shuts. You'll be stuck inside 'til we get back. That what you want?" Greg growled. He must have been tired from driving so long. They'd been on the road six or seven hours, and Steven hadn't taken the wheel yet.

Zeke hurriedly got out of the car, taking a moment to get his legs under him. The wolf yawned inside his chest, stretching and wakening, sending a burning urge through his veins. Be wolf, it said. Run. Hunt. Howl.

Zeke glanced at the moon. It was partially hidden behind clouds, but he could see it was nearly full. Two or three days at most. He kept it marked on a calendar at the camp, but he didn't have that with him. The pills in his pocket gave him some reassurance. If he shifted outside of a safehouse, he'd go mad. But it wouldn't get to that point. He'd take the pill if he thought he was in any danger of going full-moon wolf.

"We've got time," Greg said. "No fret, moon-face." He laughed at his joke. They seemed to have a pretty good idea of what Zeke was, but he didn't know anything about them, except that they weren't vampires.

The three men entered the restaurant together, and Greg and Steven placed their orders, indicating that Zeke was paying. He loaded his order up with as many burgers as he could get away with. About six, he'd found, before cashiers looked at him too funny. Six half pounders, skip the extras, add chicken nuggets for good measure. His stomach might hate him after two days of preservative-laden fast-food, but he had to eat something.

Greg and Steven ate like perfect gentlemen. Zeke watched them, mouth agape, as they tucked napkins in over their shirts and knifed and forked their burgers and fries. He became acutely aware of his own sloppy eating. He'd downed three burgers while they sipped their sodas and stabbed little pieces of burger and fry one by one.

Zeke finished a good twenty minutes before they did. He itched to go on a run, but he didn't want to get left behind. He wouldn't put it past these guys, even if they were neat freaks. Instead, he sat in the booth, looking anywhere but at the drivers, trying not to be rude and trying not to lose his mind. Finally, he gave up and excused himself to the bathroom.

A familiar feeling followed him. The persistent, sticky feeling of being watched. It clung to Zeke while he did his business, then soaped up his hands. When he got to the hand dryer, the sound ramped up his anxiety. The dryer was slow. His hands were still wet when he abandoned it, opening the door. He jogged down the orange-tiled hall and froze at the end, staring at the booth he'd left the two men in. It was empty.

He exploded out of the restaurant doors, throwing them open too wide, too fast with his extra strength. The hinges protested and the door swung back fast, almost catching Zeke. The car. The car was gone. He ran around the building to check, eyes squinting in the darkness. He sniffed the air. The moon pulled at him from the sky. It was difficult to resist the urge to change, especially in his panic.

The air gave him nothing. Not a whiff of their scent, but something else was on the air. Something strange, like a spice Zeke had never smelled before, barely perceptible beneath the overwhelming scents of grease and meat.

A car wound around the corner of the restaurant, coming the wrong way up the drive thru. It was late enough that no one was there. Zeke sighed with relief. It was them, the Japanese brothers. He waved his arms, but they didn't stop, instead turning and coasting back the way they'd come, parking at the farthest corner of the parking lot. Grumbling, Zeke broke into a jog. Whatever they were up to, it wasn't worth nearly five grand. He would give them a piece of his mind, he'd...

They stepped out of the car, and Zeke watched their bodies become molten.

In the dim light at the end of the parking lot, their skin marbleized. Human shades mixed with a deep royal blue that gleamed in the moonlight. Guttural growls and garbled howls broke the night air as tusks erupted from the upper jaws and horns emerged from their heads, straight and thick. They stretched and bulked out, muscles rippling. They looked like something out of Japanese legend, something about the squarish shapes of their faces...

Their pants clung by threads; their shirts hung like rags. The shorter of the two—possibly Steven, if Zeke remembered correctly through his rising panic—pounded his chest and roared at the sky, then advanced on Zeke. The ride service was some kind of front, then. Either that, or these two just really didn't like Zeke.

This was how it would end, then. Two sets of red, bloodthirsty demon eyes set on consuming Zeke, or his soul, however it worked. He cursed that teenage vampire from the library as he ran the hell away, stripping off his outer layer as he went. The change was effortless. So close to the full moon, it was quick and hot and pain free to merge from human to wolf.

Zeke bounded across the pavement with a lopsided gait, his wounds from the alpha fight still healing. He veered into the vacant field behind the restaurant, taking the fight away from the city lights, away from people that could get hurt. It was just him and those beasts.

Heavy footfalls came up fast behind Zeke. The monsters were huge, but they could run. *Damn.* Zeke glanced behind to gauge distance; the monsters were literally on his tail. One of them reached forward with a snarl and ripped a few hairs out of Zeke's streaming tail.

Zeke launched himself at the nearest monster, jaws clamping down hard on its arm. It roared and flung its arm about, tossing Zeke into the air. His teeth released, spitting and gagging on the bitter taste of the monster's blood. He twisted in the air and landed on all fours, skidding across the dry grass. Dirt and rocks sprayed around him. Zeke snarled as the monsters approached again.

One of the monsters chanted foreign words that Zeke didn't understand, and its forehead glowed with a symbol of an eyeball in the middle of sun rays. The air filled with a hot energy, and lightning crackled out of the sky and struck the ground near Zeke. He yelped and jumped out of reach, landing in the middle of a dirt road. Ultra-strength was one thing; he had no defenses against weather magic.

A truck engine revved. Zeke blinked in the brilliant glare, not sure if it was another lightning bolt or the truck's headlights flaring.

The truck veered off into the field and tires spat dirt as they spun to a stop. People piled out of the back in tactile suits. Zeke bolted down the road, not waiting for them to organize themselves and come after him. Whatever kind of team this was, whether Stiffs or some joy-riding weirdos, Zeke didn't want any part of it.

"Surround the Oni. Jack, aim for the third eye. Go, go, go!" a male voice shouted. The humans ran toward the bellowing demons. Zeke couldn't help but stop and turn around, going against every instinct he had. What the hell were they doing facing those monsters themselves?

The demons lunged for the nearest person. Crouching, the guy fired a crossbow-looking weapon. It missed. The person rolled between the demon's feet, then shouted, making the beast turn around. He was lunch, for sure. Except there was a twang and the demon when silent, standing still as a statue.

"He's going down, watch it folks." Sure enough, the demon fell with an earth-shaking thud. Its fellow bellowed his displeasure and got on all fours, charging madly at the remaining crew. They scattered, several taking shots, one getting it in the shoulder. It only grew madder, thrashing around and breaking off the shaft of the weapon. The truck lights illuminated the fight, which grew more frantic on the humans' end. One guy got too close, and the demon's hand swiped him into the air. His scream ended when he hit the ground, and Zeke flinched. Time for him to go. He didn't need to witness the massacre. As it was, they had gotten themselves into the mess, and Zeke didn't owe them anything. More than likely they'd give him the same treatment as the demons.

As Zeke slunk away into the darkness, a triumphant shout broke the air. He turned to see the team high-fiving one of their guys. The second demon, once Greg or Steven, lay in an awkward prone position, not stirring.

Their victory was short lived. They checked on their friend, who groaned and moved, so it seemed he was alive, if a bit broken. Curiosity made Zeke want to stay and find out what they planned to do with the beasts that had tried to kill him, and who they were, since they didn't bear the official insignia of the Supernatural Task Force. Some sort of vigilante cowboys, maybe. Bull riders looking for a thrill. But Zeke couldn't afford to get caught. He forced himself away for a second time, taking off at a trot.

Out of the darkness, Zeke caught a click and a whistling sound, like a rope swinging fast through the air. A weighted net sent his nose skidding into the ground. He lay panting for a second before leaping to his feet and digging at the edge of the net. He strained. It budged maybe an inch. The weights were heavy.

Someone approached from the left and Zeke snarled.

"Easy, there. You're not in as much trouble as you think." A flashlight shone in Zeke's face, then away. "Are you a shifter? Nod and pick up your paw if you are."

Zeke gritted his teeth and laid his ears flat, growling again. Being a shifter had never served him well in his life. If he had the chance, he'd play dumb animal as long as he could.

"Hey Jack, I think we're mistaken. This one's wild."

Another guy jogged up and glanced at Zeke. "No way. I'm never wrong."

"You are this time." The one guy smirked at Jack, who glared back.

Jack addressed Zeke. "You're being an idiot. We're on your side, dope." He waved his crossbow. "Do you see any S.T.F. logos? Those demons are unconscious, they'll wake up any second, and we have to get you out of here before the S.T.F. *does* come. I guarantee someone called in the noise those Oni made."

Zeke gave the guy a second glance. He was right about the Stiffs, and Jack didn't exactly seem the redneck, cowboy type Zeke had first pegged him and his guys for, even if he did have the accent.

Zeke nodded his head and lifted his paw, and Jack fist-pumped the air.

"Told you." He slapped his companion on the back.

The other guy huffed, then looked at Zeke. "I'm going to take the net off, but you're coming with us, all right? Give us a chance to explain who we are and what we do, then you can decide if you want to be part of it."

Zeke didn't see another choice. He was surrounded at that point, as two of their friends came up. One grinned ferally at him, and he shuddered. Her scent had the cloying musk of a big cat shifter. Jack and his buddy were definitely human, but this girl and her friend definitely weren't. What was going on here?

The guy lifted one side of the rope net, grunting as he did. Zeke slipped under, glancing over his shoulder at the dark, open field behind him, contemplating making a break for it.

"I know it's a full moon, but can you shift? We've got some clothes in the trunk." Jack threw his weapon in the back of the truck and grabbed some clothes, tossing them at Zeke. "Everyone turn, give the guy some privacy."

Zeke shifted, the transition much harder going from wolf to human. It took him some time, grunting and pushing through the pain and the resistance. Damn moon. He grabbed the basketball shorts and t-shirt and threw them on. Once dressed, he straightened.

"New recruit?" Zeke asked, trying not to sound out of breath after shifting. He walked up behind Jack, who spun, grinning at him and holding out his hand.

"Yeah, man. Welcome to the rebellion."

CHAPTER TEN

MANDI

THE DAY FOLLOWING THE warding was filled with bated breaths as the camp waited to see if the witches' protections would hold or fail. Fortunately, they held, and no government task force raided the camp. Werewolf surveillance reported movement on the borders, but no magical activity. They were safe. For now.

And the best part was that Lilith had informed Mandi that in the late afternoon, after she addressed the residents of the camp about their uncertain future, the coven would begin the work of opening Mandi up to her full powers, starting with astral travel. It would require a magical splint, and Lilith herself had offered to be the one to perform it.

Now, Lilith stood at the center of the lodge kitchen, speaking to the group of paranormals who remained at Camp Silver Lake.

"We are starting anew," Lilith announced. "You've seen for yourselves what pathetic help the government has offered to allow you to integrate into a fearful society. I've made contact with those from other Naturalization camps who are tired of oppression. They have agreed to join us. In a few days, a plan will be put into motion across the country to bring the balance of power into our favor."

Shouts of agreement and a scattering of applause filled the room. Mandi clapped along, heart pounding with excitement and uncertainty both. What would a world look like without the restrictions—and structure—the camps had provided?

Mandi heard a subtle click. A clamor rose around her.

"Who turned off the lights?" someone yelled.

"The power went out," another answered.

Mandi didn't recognize the voices; she was still learning the tones that went along with the rogues.

"Be calm," Lilith instructed. "I assumed such would happen. The government has withdrawn their aid. We've made it clear we no longer answer to them. It is time we made our own way."

"Where will we get our blood?" That one was Heath. His tone had a sharp, angry edge to it that bit into Mandi's ears. How low were the vampires' supplies? A chill went through Mandi. Had Lilith truly thought this all the way through? The vampires wouldn't last long on the tiny forest animals within the camp boundaries, and larger prey avoided the area. Out of necessity, the vampires would turn on those within the lodge before long.

"All will be supplied. Trust me," Lilith's voice soothed. Stones in her pocket hummed. The black tourmaline vibrated, sensing a spell at work.

The room fell eerily silent.

"What happened?" Mandi whispered, leaning in toward Honey.

"She's...put them all to sleep." Honey sounded stunned. "All of the residents, except for the coven."

"What?" Mandi's heart skipped a beat.

Lilith cleared her throat. "A necessary precaution. And temporary, I assure you. They will not perish under this spell."

"It is a kindness." Serena's high-pitched voice floated through the air. "They will not thirst or hunger."

Mandi wondered what sort of spell could allow for that. Certainly nothing Violet had taught them.

"Then you haven't solved the blood supply issue?" Meg asked. "And the food?"

"We are leaving soon. I saw no point arranging something for this location when we wouldn't remain here long," Lilith explained.

"Leaving? Where?" Mandi asked. After all the effort they had put into defenses, Lilith wanted to leave?

"We cannot change the world from here." Lilith chuckled. "No, we are expected in Washington. And if we are to make it in time and at our full strength, Mandi's splinting must happen. You all read the pages I marked in the *Elysium Arcanum*, I presume?"

Honey had read them aloud to Mandi so she knew what to expect during the splinting that evening. It was a complicated spell, and if it failed, Mandi could be blocked from the astral realm for the rest of her life. But then, so could Lilith. The spell held risks for both of them, and it humbled Mandi to realize what Lilith was willing to do to ensure that Mandi reached her full potential.

Mandi lay carefully on the floor in the apothecary. The coven had gathered there to perform the splinting spell.

Shuffling surrounded Mandi in the darkness that made up her world. Her breathing hitched and she flexed her fingers. Someone knelt by her head, skirts swishing as they folded against the ground.

"Are you sure you want to do this?" Honey's voice floated into her ear, a bare whisper that the others wouldn't have heard.

Mandi let a small smile spread across her lips at the concern Honey showed her. "I've wanted this for years, Honey. I know what I'm doing."

"None of us have tried magic like this before." Mandi could almost hear the wrinkle in Honey's brow.

"You'll do great." Mandi reached her hand up, feeling for Honey's soft fingers and grasping them in her own.

"It's time to light the candles." Lilith's voice filled the room with an edge of authority. Honey dropped Mandi's hand and stood to take her place.

Mandi's whole body felt cold with Honey's absence. Her hand reached into her pocket for the stones she had placed there.

"Mandi," Lilith said firmly. "There cannot be any disturbances in the energy field within the circle during the splinting. There's something on your person that could cause a disastrous outcome."

"My...my stones?" She'd chosen stones of amplification, to strengthen the bonds of magic about to be performed. She had felt such comfort in them, and yet Lilith claimed they were dangerous? Mandi had never chosen wrong, but then, she'd never considered that no stones would be needed.

"Yes, the stones are protecting you, and they will fight this sort of magic that is aimed at your innermost self. You must let them go." Her voice softened, growing more persuasive.

Mandi withdrew the stones, rubbing them in her palm, feeling a resistance from them. They didn't want to leave her. Skirts swished again and someone, possibly Honey again, bent down and removed the stones with a smooth motion. Her smell was wrong. All bitter herbs and a sickly-sweet rose, no gentleness. Not Honey, then. One of the others, one of Lilith's coven sisters.

Mandi drew in a shaky breath to fill the void left behind as the stones withdrew from her auric circle. She steeled herself for what was to come.

"Several of those in this circle are novices to the type of magic we are about to perform. I must ask that no matter what you see, hear, or feel, you remain loyal to the circle and our sister within it. You will not step back, you will not go to her, you will not drop your candle or let it go out. Control your breathing, do not gasp or cry out or let your emotions get the better of you. I have seen you all and fully expect that you can handle this. Consider it a test for what is to come, a sign of what we can accomplish together." Mandi imagined Lilith's gaze resting on each member of the circle, lingering on the sisters Mandi had grown into her magic with. Their hands might tremble, but she knew their loyalty would not falter. Thinking of them made her throat constrict. What they were doing for her, to provide her with this ability to project, was priceless. She would owe them everything.

"Now then, we will begin. Serena, take up the North. We need a stronger presence there."

Honey was at the northpoint, holding the circle together. Mandi felt a chill at the last-minute switch. She desperately licked her lips, wetting them, but the moisture evaporated instantaneously.

"Honey, your presence is more fluid, it serves the southwest," Lilith directed.

Mandi flexed her hands. Her neck ached with tension, and she breathed out through her nose, attempting to relax her body. Lilith crossed into the circle and laid down beside Mandi, their hands almost touching.

"In this ceremony, part of my essence will be transferred inside of you, to brace you up. Serena will lead. She has done this before." Calmness radiated from her presence beside Mandi. Like a tangible blanket being pulled across her body. Mandi accepted the soothing, calming the pacing tiger of emotion in her chest. *It will be fine.* And for some reason, a sensation rose like fur brushing past her face, and she thought of Zeke. What was he doing now?

Best not to think of Zeke. Mandi breathed in, then out, and cleared her mind.

Serena's alto voice rose in a chant. Mandi didn't know the words, and they weren't in English. They chilled her. Her arms and legs melded with the floor. Pinpricks of pain indicated each of the points as they were called in reverse order. Her sides, her feet, and the top of her head. They drew together to her navel and hot wax oozed onto her skin. Ropes twined swiftly around Mandi's wrists, and she felt the rope lengthen away and tighten, as if they'd been tied down to something on the ground. She didn't move, did not scream, no matter how frightened she felt. She would not be the one to interrupt this spell. She would be strong enough.

Beside her, Lilith let out a long, slow breath, like a moan without sound, the slightest hitch in her breathing telling Mandi that something painful, or perhaps unanticipated, had happened to the witch. All was silent.

Serena whispered in the foreign tongue and the word slid down Mandi's back like the cool, slithering body of a snake. She shivered without intending to, then froze as a sensation like a knife point pricked the spot between her eyes, pinning her third eye chakra between earth and sky. The clear, bright pain slid to one side, then to the other, and the word Serena spoke this time was in English.

"Open." The witch breathed in deeply and the knife point vanished, replaced with fingers prying the skin apart across Mandi's scalp. Or at least, that's what it felt like.

Mandi couldn't withhold the scream. Blood dripped into her eyes. The knife pricked her heart, and she knew in that moment that she was going to die, she was surely going to be sacrificed to some dark magic that Lilith worked. Lilith had lied.

Blinding white light filled Mandi's vision. Light that crystallized and flared, then faded into blackness, but the blackness was dotted with tiny lights. Things that Mandi had only heard described. Could it be...stars? Her eyes filled with them.

"We're not through yet, Mandi." Lilith stood beside her in a white robe that draped loosely over her lithe frame, open to her navel. Mandi glanced down and realized she was dressed similarly.

"How can I see you?" She reveled in the sight of the other woman, her pale, silvery hair, her milky skin, contrasted with Mandi's own dark skin tone, which nearly blended in with the night sky that surrounded them on every side.

"This is the beginning. We have made it to the astral realm. You must still receive my essence to maintain this ability of your own volition."

"What will happen next?" Mandi's voice sounded thin and reedy in her own ears.

"We now rely on Selena to complete the splinting of your soul. I am strong enough to see through the veils between worlds, but only just. She is approaching us with the wands." Lilith's voice had a far-off, ethereal tone. Her eyes contained a glassy sheen.

"Wands?" Mandi asked. But Lilith's reply was cut off by the pain that pierced Mandi's left side, just beneath her rib cage. Her vision darkened again, and a scream erupted from her throat, echoing into the void. Something pointed and stiff worked its way into her body, sliding past bone and sinew to rest just below her pulsing heart.

"Awake!" a voice that was many voices bellowed, and a great rushing wind carried her, slamming her with unnatural force back into her body.

Mandi gasped and tried to sit up. Her hands strained at their bonds; her side split with pain.

"With these wands of crystal, bone, and wood, spirits bond," Serena's soothing alto voice intoned, and all the hands of the circle clapped as one. A whooshing sensation flooded the circle. Sweat pricked Mandi's brow. She was in darkness once more, trapped in a mortal body and having no sense of her physical surroundings other than what sound, smell, and touch provided. The stone beneath her felt damp and sticky. Her side ached with each throb of her heart. She wanted to touch the area, to make certain she was okay, that her life force wasn't bleeding out, but her hands wouldn't obey her thoughts.

Her head swam. Thoughts became difficult to form. If the growing wetness beneath her was any indicator, she was losing blood, and fast. Why didn't they see? Why didn't they stop and help her? No Sight was worth this.

"Please," Mandi gasped out, straining against her bonds in the direction she remembered Honey standing. "Help me."

The slightest gasping sob sounded, stifled in a hand or sleeve, but loud enough for Mandi to hear. Honey had heard her. The others had also. But none of them would step forward to save her. After all, she had wanted this.

Mandi turned her face to the sky, prepared to die. What a fool she had been. What would Violet say if she were here now? Mandi flexed her hands, feeling the silk bindings on her wrists rub against her skin.

Serena started a chant, at first a low hum, and the other voices rose to join her. The floor vibrated beneath Mandi. Her head rattled, her limbs resisted at first, the strength draining from them. A whisper trickled into her ear, something unintelligible and inhuman. It entered like a warm draft of air, surrounding her brain, travelling to her brain stem. Mandi shivered as it oozed down her spine. It made its way to the foreign object lodged in her chest.

The wisp drew itself into the wand and the crystal hummed, burning with a bright light that Mandi could somehow see, not with her eyes, but with her mind. It glowed a sickly yellow, and then the light dimmed and vanished.

Strength surged back into her limbs. Breath regained its rhythm in her lungs. Mandi sucked in the precious life-giving substance. Was it over?

"Join me." A hand grabbed hers, but somehow didn't grab it, and she was pulled up and out. Out of her body, out of the room. A palm pressed over both of her eyes, then lifted, and it was as if scales fell away from her eyes, cracking and falling to the ground. She could see. The body of a young black woman, naked and prostrate on the stone floor, wrists bound, a pool of blood beneath. And beside her, a pale and fair woman, more mature in body and face but still beautiful, blonde hair spread out around her like a halo, hands clasped over her bare chest. Lilith.

"Are we dead?" Mandi asked, turning to face the person who had pulled her from her body.

Lilith smiled. "No, dear. We sleep. Our wounds are closed, though it does not look like it. Our sisters light candles for us, to remind us of the way back." She gestured, and Mandi did indeed see the coven members leaving their place in the circle one by one to place the candles around them until seven candles outlined Mandi's and Lilith's bodies.

Mandi tore her eyes away from her body. She noticed the horizon lightening, a pale pink and orange light washing away the night sky that had surrounded them. Her feet, she realized, rested on nothing. The pain in her side was now a dull ache, and she could think through the pain. She moved her hand to rub at the area, but she couldn't feel anything. Her physical body didn't exist in this plane.

"Don't go too far," Lilith warned.

Mandi meant to say she didn't mean to go anywhere, but the horizon drew her. She only had to think of herself as there, and her spirit sped through time and space to reach the destination she desired. Below, waves lapped on a smooth shore with stark, black sand. She'd heard the waves, she'd felt the sand beneath her feet, her physical body knew these things, but her mind had never had an image for them before. Now it did, and it drank them in. The treeline. The brush. The way the water reflected the sunset. Surely, it couldn't be a scene from reality, and yet she remembered learning something about volcanic sands in the islands. This must be like those. It was beautiful, and yet void of life. What else was out there?

An eagerness consumed her. She gazed at the horizon, knowing that more lay beyond, and yet hearing Lilith's words not to go far. Would she find her way back if she did? She glanced over her shoulder, laughter bubbling through her that a simple gesture like her head turning could give her the information she sought.

No more relying on sound and other physical sensations. She could *see.*

Mandi felt a tugging beneath her breastbone. A pinpoint of flickering candlelight came into view. Another, then another, until seven shone in a circle. Mandi resisted the tugging. She recognized she was being called back into her body, but that body was damaged. She would no longer be able to see the vivid colors, and light...the light she would miss most of all. The tugging turned into an insistent pulling, dragging her across the distance from the sunrise on the lava-sand beach back to those seven points of light. She let it carry her, neither helping nor resisting.

With a slight sucking sound and sensation, she fell back into her body, her vision once again closing into the pitch dark of her physical blindness. Her breath moved in and out of her body, growing stronger as she came more into herself. Soft hands grasped at the knots on her wrists, scrambling to untie the bonds that held her. Little gasping sobs came from someone above her.

Mandi reached up a hand as it was freed and touched the face of the person who knelt beside her. They clasped the hand, pressing it into their cheek damp with tears.

"Oh, Mandi, it was more terrible than I..." Honey broke off into sobs.

"Honey, I could see. For a moment. I saw...everything." Mandi's other hand slid down her side, feeling bandages wrapped around her torso.

"You lost so much blood, I...I thought you were dead." Honey hiccupped.

"How do you feel?" Dana pressed.

Mandi's brow furrowed. No weakness weighed her limbs, no fatigue. She felt better than she had since the rebels had attacked the camp upon Violet's and James' deaths.

"I feel...excellent." She turned her exploration inward, trying to determine if she could sense the object she'd felt placed into her body. There it was, humming away, a toothpick-sized crystal wand with a yellow aura she felt more than saw. "It's so small."

Honey leaned in. Mandi knew it was her from the sweet scent that wafted into her nose. Her voice dropped to a faint whisper. "Mandi, this is blood magic."

"I know. But if it's given me my Sight..." She trailed off. Violet had made them promise not to participate in blood magic if they could help it. Each time they did, they bound their physical and spiritual beings more tightly to the lower realms and the entities within them. *"It is possible for a witch to become so tangled in bonds that she loses herself."*

Mandi swallowed. Surely a spell like this would enhance her powers, now that she could travel to the astral plane with real vision like any other witch. She wasn't the weak link anymore.

Mandi turned her hand into Honey's and gripped, pushing off with her other hand. Honey helped her stand, and Dana held her elbow to steady her. Clothing was pushed at Mandi. A plush robe. She threaded her arms into the soft, thick fabric, surprised that the wound in her side didn't hurt at all.

"You have all done very well. The bond is complete, the splinting accomplished. Mandi will now be able to join us at our astral meetings. Our coven will be stronger for it." Lilith's voice beamed with pride. Her hand landed on Mandi's shoulder. "You must, however, be aware that the bond between us will be permanently damaged if you go beyond the boundary of the magic tying us together. I do not yet know what the radius is, but at first it will not be large."

"Mandi," Honey said, her voice containing a subtle urgent energy that made Mandi's heart rate pick up pace. "Can we talk to you for a moment in private?"

"Privacy simply isn't possible with the proximity we must keep. For Mandi's safety, and mine," Lilith emphasized.

"Could you step just outside the door to the room, Lilith? I want our sisters to feel confident speaking with me." Mandi quaked at asking, but held her head high. She was priestess of the coven. One of her roles was acting as confidant to the sisters within the coven. Surely Lilith would understand.

"I will be just outside. Tell me if you feel sharp pain at any point, and we will find another way for you to have your private conversation."

Relief flooded Mandi. "Thank you, Lilith." She braced for any of the new witches to object to being excluded from the conversation, but they filed out of the room quietly.

Lilith cleared her throat. She hadn't gone, then. "Should you choose to utilize divination, I have a lovely blend that you can use in your tea. The Amethyst Moon blend. I'll fetch it for you. I keep it at the back, there are some rather rare herbs in it."

There was a rustling as herbs were scooped into a bag, and then the bag was passed into Mandi's hands. She held the fragrant tea blend, the sweet floral notes wafting into her nostrils. She took a deep breath in and instantly felt calmer.

The pressure of Mandi's hands vanished. Footsteps crossed the room, a door opened, then shut tight. Lilith had left them alone.

"Is Anita here?" Mandi asked. She hated that she had to ask. Having had sight ripped from her again when she re-entered her body was a crushing feeling, but the slight throbbing of the crystal in her left side reminded her that it was possible. She could do it again.

"I am," Anita said, but her voice seemed blunt, as if she didn't truly want to be there. "I don't understand why we can't tell the others. What's so secretive, Honey? Having doubts?"

"Well, yes," Honey admitted. "We did this splinting spell for you, Mandi, but..." Mandi heard her shiver in the slight tremor of her voice. "Being part of it, I felt something dark settle on the room. It didn't wish us ill, but rather, it was reveling in the fact that we had called it to us."

"I felt it too!" Dana exclaimed.

"I'm certain I heard a name mentioned, as if we'd summoned a being into our midst," Meg said, her voice laced with anxiety.

Mandi wished she had her stones so she could pass one to her friend. Meg needed black tourmaline, and Mandi herself wished she held a blue lace agate to help ease the tension in the conversation.

"Most of these powerful spells call on an entity from an alternate dimension to power them. Violet didn't like using them, and look where it got her," Anita said.

"That's not fair," Honey insisted. "Violet had clear principles. We trusted her. Can you say the same about Lilith?"

"We need a coven to be at its strongest for whatever is coming. Lilith said that it is time to fight for our rights, and I think I agree with her," Dana said.

Mandi listened to the back and forth, puzzling over the swirl of thoughts in her mind. It wasn't until silence filled the space between them that she realized they were looking at her, waiting for her response.

"Lilith has a very different perspective than Violet on many things, that's true," Mandi said, choosing her words carefully. "But she's also advancing our education and abilities far faster than Violet ever would."

"Rushing isn't always a good thing. We still don't fully understand what this splinting of your Sight has done. You're still blind?" Meg asked, her voice a little hesitant.

Mandi tried not to snap back. "Yes, I'm still blind. But I was able to see in the astral realm during the spell. I've never been able to do that before. And Lilith says that with time and practice, the splint can be removed, and I'll be able to travel astrally without her help. This is temporary."

"It's just that we're nervous," Honey interjected. "And we've been taught to value our intuition. Perhaps it's time to put our fears to rest and do some divination to determine if this is the right path for us. For all of us."

Mandi reluctantly nodded. "That's fair enough."

Cups clinked. One of the other girls retrieved a tea set from Violet's cupboards. It was odd to think of them as Violet's still when she was no longer there.

"I've got the burner," Megan called. "Dana, will you fill a pitcher?"

"This kettle is filthy. Who used it last?" Honey said, a note of disgust in her voice.

Mandi smiled at the banter among her friends. "Probably James." They laughed together, remembering the warlock's forgetful tendencies with fondness. Water rushed from a tap across the room.

The portable stove hissed slightly when the iron tea kettle was placed on it. Mandi recognized the sound from dozens of tea readings just like this one. They didn't always read the tea leaves.

Sometimes they used tea bags. The future was confusing enough without reading it every morning.

"What's in Lilith's blend?" Mandi asked, passing the tea blend to the person next to her. Meg, she thought, by the sweet and acrid smell of sage and cigarettes.

"By all appearances," Meg began. "Rose hips, black tea, orange peel, blue cornflowers, and hibiscus. I'm not sure what herbs are in here, I don't recognize some of the leaves."

"Weird combination," Anita said.

"What's our question? It's gotta be clear," Dana piped up.

The water started to simmer. Could her friends hear it? Or was it just her practiced hearing that could tell the different stages of water boiling?

"Are we all asking the same question? There's no need for that. We can make it personal," Honey reminded them.

"It feels right that it should be the same. And we'll compare all the leaves' symbols. Wherever we go, we hope it's together, don't we?" Mandi asked. Silence. The water's boiling increased.

The burner clicked as it was turned off. Packaging rustled and the leaves made a gentle fizzing sound as they touched the water.

"As you drink, consider this," Meg piped up. Her voice held the heavy, familiar tone of prophecy. It was a distinction Mandi had learned to listen for. She sat up straighter, turning her head towards the sound of Meg's voice. "Should the coven stay together in the new order Lilith has created? Are we meant to go our separate ways? What will following Lilith mean for each of us?"

"That's not just one question," Dana fretted. "How can we get a clear answer?"

"Cream, Mandi?" Honey asked. "Think of the question most important to you, Dana."

"Let me try it with just the honey, please," Mandi said. What would Lilith's special tea blend taste like? She waited for the light touch on her arm that indicated her cup was ready. When the fingers rested against her skin, she reached her hands slowly forward. Someone, possibly Honey, guided her hands toward the cup. Mandi grasped the handle and saucer. Heat radiated out from the tea. She brought it towards her lips and blew gently.

Silence passed through the group. They would normally chatter about recent events, relationships among the residents, spells they were struggling or succeeding with, but tonight they shared silence.

Mandi sipped. She had already decided to stay with Lilith, to learn astral projection and eventually gain her real physical sight, as Lilith had promised. After the bonding spell, feeling the strength and power of a full coven surge through her, Mandi was confident Lilith could do it. Perhaps Violet had said it wasn't possible within the realms of white magic because they didn't have a full coven. She'd never explained it in a way that made sense to Mandi.

Cups clinked as they were turned upside down on their saucers. Mandi drained her cup and did the same, turning it three times one way and twice the other, completing the motions for the divination. She turned it right side up swiftly.

"Pass to the left," Meg said.

No one passed their cup to Mandi, of course. She held hers, waiting to hear about the readings.

"I see an anchor," Honey announced. "This is Dana's cup," she added for Mandi's sake.

"Right side up?" Mandi asked.

Honey coughed. "No. There's also an arrow. It points to the cup handle. And Meg, I need your input here."

"It's a door," Meg said with confidence.

Mandi wished she could see. But she had studied the symbols and knew what they meant. She could still be part of the conversation. "Open or closed?"

"Ambiguous," Honey said. Meg murmured in agreement.

Mandi ticked off the symbols on her fingers. "Arrow, anchor, door. Focus on family. Instability. Opportunity to be had, or lost. What was the question you focused on, Dana?"

"Should I stay with the coven?" Dana's voice sounded small. "You all know I don't have a real family. What does it mean, then?"

"The coven could be your family. Easily," Honey said. Always quick to comfort. Mandi smiled halfway.

"But the upside-down anchor...instability?"

"Things don't feel very solid right now, do they?" Meg asked. "Let's look at the other cups. Our intention was to read them all and decide together, so that's what we're going to do."

A moment of silence, and then Dana spoke, her voice in a tremble. "I've got Meg's. There's a door again. Same as mine. And...a monkey? What does monkey mean?"

"Ape is the symbol in our book," Honey said. "It means a hidden enemy."

"There's a fire underneath it. She's going to set her enemy on fire?" Dana sounded perplexed.

"Fire at the bottom of the cup warns against haste. There's danger in moving hastily," Mandi muttered, fingering the bottom of her chin. Her hand tired of holding the cup and saucer in her lap. She rested her arm across her leg and leaned forward.

"Okay, so, opportunity, danger in haste, and an enemy," Meg rattled off. "Next is Honey's. The door is there again. Obviously, that's a symbol we need to pay attention to. I think we're all facing an opportunity that could be lost but isn't yet. Here we also have a pitchfork."

"I know that one!" Dana exclaimed. Mandi imagined her bouncing with excitement in her seated position on the floor. "It's stirring up trouble deliberately."

"Yes," Meg said. "And it's combined with a rat here. The rat is someone to not be trusted. So that could be the same person as the ape or someone different." Her tone changed inflection, a note that most people would have missed. Mandi wondered who Meg didn't trust. Was it one of them? Was it Mandi herself?

A long pause filled the room.

"Is it Lilith?" Dana blurted.

Tension rose immediately, clenching at Mandi's chest. Of course it wasn't Lilith. Lilith wanted to help them. She wanted to give them new spells, expand their magic and potential as a coven. She had opportunities for them...Mandi's thoughts snagged on that. She envisioned a door opening and closing. Opportunity to be had or lost.

"There are often many facets to these meanings. We need to dig deeper, like Violet always told us." Honey's voice sounded constricted, as if she held something back. "I'll gather the cups, now." Her hand bumped Mandi's arm, and Mandi handed her cup over. It rattled on the saucer, and Honey's breath hitched.

"What is it?" Mandi demanded.

"Nothing." Honey replied, voice trembling.

Meg leaned across Mandi. "I've never seen that one before. What were you thinking about while drinking?"

Mandi felt the weight of their gazes. She swallowed. She hadn't told them what Lilith had promised her. They had all heard Violet say regenerating human sight wasn't possible. They deserved to know if they were going to make a decision about staying, that much Mandi knew. She'd been wrong to withhold it from them.

Her fists relaxed. She hadn't even realized she'd been holding her hands so tightly. "Lilith's sisters are old and powerful. We all felt that when they arrived. Joining with them as a full coven is an opportunity that few have in these modern times, when bloodlines are watered down, and the old witches remain in hiding." Mandi took a shaky breath in and slowly let it out. "None of you have asked why this decision is so easy for me to make, why I already know that I want to stay with Lilith. Not only did she promise to splint my magic so I could project into the astral realm, but she has the key to restoring my vision. My real, physical sight. I couldn't say no to that."

"That's why you didn't go with Zeke," Dana said, snapping her fingers. "We wondered. We figured you'd had a lover's row, but we didn't want to pry."

Mandi's face flushed. "You know we weren't lovers."

"All but," Meg said. "Don't think we didn't see it, Mandi. You two were inseparable."

"As friends only," Mandi insisted. Inside, she squirmed. Her coven sisters hadn't said much about Zeke since he'd left, and Mandi had been grateful for the excuse to try to forget him. After all, he was long gone by now. Headed for his family, hopefully, to make things right there. And she might never be near him again.

"Sure, sure." Honey's voice held a smile that Mandi could hear. "Still, it surprised us all when you said he'd left. I never thought he'd leave your side."

Mandi snorted, shaking her head. "What's in the cup that has you all gasping?"

"I didn't see it yet. Can I?" Dana asked. The cup clinked against the rings she wore on nearly all her fingers. Mandi had felt them before. "Oh, it looks like a bat?"

"Yes, a bat," Honey said solemnly.

"An animal bat? A bat can mean lots of things," Mandi said in a rush. Her mind reeled. What had Violet said when she read the book to Mandi?

"The bat is a symbol of sickness and trouble when it is found by itself. It means hope has failed to bring healing, happiness, or success, and sorrow is left in its wake. In true tassiographic fashion, it can mean both death and rebirth. Usually symbolic, of course, but I'm always wary when I see a bat in my cup. The only times it has happened, I've experienced the greatest sorrows of my life." Violet's voice repeated in Mandi's mind.

"When combined with the pistol," Honey sounded as if she were reading from a book, "the bat can indicate the physical death of the person who possesses the leaves being read, or the death of someone within their immediate circle."

Mandi licked her lips. "You saw a pistol?"

Honey cleared her throat. "I saw two."

CHAPTER ELEVEN

Tyson

"I'm dead." Tyson stared numbly at the body on the ground, disbelieving that a moment ago, he had occupied that body.

"That's up to you, actually. Your body needs you to tell it that you want to live." The voice came from his left, a man's body with a fox head.

If Tyson hadn't been in an alternate plane, he would have thoroughly soiled his pants.

"Who *are* you?" Tyson asked. He stared at a blonde woman who had knelt at his side, cautiously touching his neck, checking for a pulse. Her hands shook, and tears streaked her face when she looked up, shouting for someone. Becca. It was Becca.

The fox-man folded his arms. "Your spirit guide. Call me Tod."

An ambulance wove through traffic. *No, no, no.* Not an ambulance. Anywhere but the hospital.

Tyson wasn't paying attention. Dark-haired Avaan tugged on Becca's arm, glancing anxiously at the gathering crowd, and she stood with him, watching emergency personnel climb off the ambulance. Avaan pulled her into the crowd, away from the questions and watching eyes. She resisted, but she couldn't stay. Not if they wanted to avoid scrutiny. As much as Tyson hated to see it, he was grateful Avaan still had his head on his shoulders. Even if the snake charmer had strong ulterior motives.

Tyson watched them load his body onto a stretcher. He couldn't go to the hospital. They were worse than airports, drawing blood, testing it for paranormalcy. They'd have those scanners Becca mentioned for sure.

A hand landed on Tyson's shoulder, and he startled. The fox-man's honey-colored eyes glittered. "Get back to your body. Keep it alive. I'll come to get you tonight, and we can talk more."

Tyson looked away from the scene, wondering if he should follow his body or stay in the astral realm, now that he'd made it here, and look around. He felt a tug and glanced down, realizing with shock that a golden thread twisted from his chest.

"Where does that go?" He asked.

The fox-head scrutinized him. "You shouldn't concern yourself with it right now. It's not near as important as getting back into your body so it knows you want it to keep your heart pumping, your lungs breathing. What can I say to convince you?"

Tyson drifted forward. Could it be a key to finding Harper? Feelings had grown between them in the time they had known each other. Was it possible they'd formed a bond strong enough it could lead him to her?

"Are soulmates a thing here?"

"That bird woman isn't your soulmate," Todd snapped. He took Tyson by the shoulders and steered him in the direction of the ambulance. "And even if she were, every second you stay here you send your body further into shock. If it dies, you're trapped here. Think about your body and you'll be there in an instant. Get going." He shoved Tyson, and Tyson stumbled forward, but he didn't think about his body. He thought about Harper, and to his amazement, it worked.

Todd's face vanished in a blink, and Tyson found himself stumbling through a dark corridor of smoke-like mist. It was fog, except black. Having no sense of smell or touch made it disorienting to walk through. The golden light on his chest still shot into the distance.

Where was he? The further he walked, the thicker the fog grew. The path he was on narrowed, then branched off. Tyson eyed one of the off-shooting pathways, then turned, walking briskly down it. A cage popped up so fast he nearly ran into it. A gnarled hand reached for him, brushing the front of his shirt. Tyson fell back, drifting back the path as fast as he could go. A horrible cackling followed him, and a frightened sensation tightened in his head like a vice.

Harper. If the line in his chest led to her, then was she in one of these cages? Tyson floated faster, zipping past the off-shooting paths until the golden thread whipped to the left.

The cage loomed, so quiet Tyson thought it was empty until the being inside parted its ink-dark wings and lifted her head.

"Harper," Tyson fell to his knees. He reached through the bars toward her. She made no move toward him, and her face held no recognition. Tyson swallowed. "I'm going to get you out of here. I promise." He glanced around for evidence of an opening, a lock, anything.

A popping sound echoed behind him. A growl penetrated the still air.

Tyson's head whipped around, then relaxed when he saw Tod. "Help me, will you? This thing has to have an opening."

"You are an idiot. Coming here without a guide. I should let the Essences consume you, but you're needed. You need to get back in your body. Now." Tod's arm shot out and grabbed the collar of Tyson's shirt. He launched into the air, dragging Tyson with him.

"No, you don't understand!" Tyson kicked his incorporeal legs. Terror filled him as the space between himself and the ground increased. A shriek erupted from Harper's cage. Tyson fought harder, and then his insides wavered. He blinked and they were back in the daylight, shooting down the middle of the street toward an ambulance with flashing lights. Harper was gone.

Todd went into a dive and thrust Tyson into the vehicle, right through the closed doors. Tyson fell into his body and immediately woke, coughing and gasping. His head throbbed. One of the guys in the bright greenish-yellow jackets shushed him, holding him down to the cot as he tightened the straps across his shoulders. Tyson's hearing returned in a sudden flood, all sirens and shouts in a language he didn't understand. No, he recognized English words, he just didn't understand their medical jargon.

"I thought for sure this one was a goner," the man beside him shouted.

"Seems like a fighter," the woman across from him responded, and she smiled reassuringly at Tyson, the last thing he saw before he passed out from the pain.

The sounds of the hospital filtered through Tyson's groggy consciousness like he was coming up from underwater. A nurse in grey scrubs with straight brown hair stood next to the monitors, clicking away on a computer. He reached a hand up and felt a hard plastic face mask with tubes winding out of it attached to his face.

The nurse turned, her straight brown hair swinging forward over her shoulder. "It's good to see you awake. How does your head feel?"

Tyson felt at the lumpy bandage. His skull throbbed underneath, but otherwise didn't hurt much. "It's good." His voice sounded tinny and strange inside the plastic mask. He pointed at it. "Can I take this off?"

"In a minute. Let me get your vitals and see what the doctor thinks. You took a pretty hard hit. You're lucky nothing else is broken." The nurse glanced towards the door as if she expected someone to come through at any moment. She put the stethoscope earpieces in her ears and leaned in, reaching under Tyson's hospital gown and placing the device against his chest. He gasped at the feel of the cold metal on his skin.

"What happened?"

The nurse removed the stethoscope and turned back to the computer to type something in. "Witnesses say you ran off the bus and were sick in the road, and a motorcyclist swerved around the stopped bus and hit you. It's a miracle you made it, you lost a lot of blood and your concussion was pretty severe."

"And...how long have I been unconscious?"

"A little less than 24 hours."

Tyson rubbed his mouth with his non-bandaged hand and breathed out, then in again, focusing on the familiar action to keep calm. His head swam and throbbed, a faint edge of pain piercing through the cloud of medication. The nurse seemed perfectly calm, not like someone who had discovered her patient had paranormal blood. But then, perhaps she was used to it by now; maybe it happened every day. Tyson cleared his throat. "Did they find anything unusual?"

The nurse tilted her head, her expression shifting to confusion.

"I mean with my head," Tyson rushed to cover for his awkward phrasing. The last thing he wanted to do was *cause* suspicion if there wasn't any already.

The nurse sat on the bed with her hands folded over her stethoscope. "The doctor will tell you all about it, but what I can say is that everything will be fine. You're in good hands."

Tyson relaxed slightly. He still couldn't be positive, but if she hadn't mentioned anything, and there didn't seem to be any extra precautions in the room to hold a magic-user, they likely didn't know.

Tyson clasped his hands together. "Have I had any visitors? When can I leave?"

"No visitors yet. Is there someone you'd like to call?"

"Not right now." Tyson nodded to the nurse, noticing her name badge for the first time. "Thank you, Sonja."

"You're welcome." She stood, putting the stethoscope away and going back to the computer. "The doctor will be in to do some tests, make sure your brain function is normal. You'll get to see some x-rays, probably. We'll need to do more. Your brain injury was traumatic enough you'll be here for another four days minimum, but it all depends on what the doctor thinks. It could be a couple weeks if he thinks you need inpatient observation and testing."

The blood pressure cuff on Tyson's arm beeped.

Sonja replaced the empty bag on the IV stand. "If you start to feel any pain, even a headache, let me know. I'll get the doctor to come in and check you out."

She walked swiftly from the room, the swish of her grey scrubs fading, then disappearing as she closed the door. Tyson didn't dare sit up on his own quite yet, but he pressed the button on the bed to elevate himself. The lines on the monitors remained steady, and he felt fine.

The nurse, Sonja, gave no indication that she suspected anything. Tyson held his free hand in front of his face, staring at it as if he could see through the skin into the cells in his blood and see the changed DNA. Would it show up when they took his blood to the lab? What if he started healing faster than expected? He'd somehow made it through the scanners, assuming they were installed at this hospital. Maybe dreamwalkers didn't have magic in their DNA.

The door opened, and Tyson stiffened. The curtain drew back to reveal a woman with dark skin and hair wearing jungle-themed scrubs.

"Welcome back to the land of the living!" The nurse had a peppy voice that didn't match her wide-eyed, intense expression. Something about the tilt of her head and the tone of her voice made Tyson realize that she knew.

She knew he was paranormal.

Tyson bolted upright and threw up his hands, like he was about to shoot magic fireballs or something.

The nurse's eyes got wider. She stuck a hand on her hip. "And what do you think you're going to do? You've got loads of magical mutations in your blood and seven genetic markers for paranormalcy. There's Stiffs at every door. You going to take on the whole hospital?"

Tyson slowly lowered his hands, then licked his dry lips and shifted his seat on the bed. "Are you going to report me?"

"Nah," the nurse said, waving a dismissive hand. She stepped closer. Tyson blinked rapidly. Either the lights had flickered, or her eyes had changed color. Weren't they brown before? They'd become a vivid green. Her eyes were definitely green. They shimmered oddly in the fluorescent lights. "That's not my job. My job is to get you out of here without anyone else finding out."

Tyson stared at her. The revelation that she was somehow, miraculously, on his side, that she was *not* going to report him, stunned him more than a hospital-wide alarm would have.

"How—why—*how* did I get through the sensors?"

The nurse smiled. "I'm Jackie." She stuck her hand out toward Tyson, and he shook it cautiously. "I keep them malfunctioning with a few different tricks. They go off with a number of patients who mysteriously never test for paranormalcy. As long as I can disprove the blood test, like I did with you, all the humans just think the tech is buggy."

Tyson swallowed, gripping the blankets. "So, uh, no one else knows?"

Jackie shook her head, then cocked it to the side. "Well, that's not entirely true is it?" she muttered to herself. She straightened and looked ahead, past Tyson. As Tyson watched, the woman's skin lightened to a summery tan, her hair lengthened and straightened, then bled to red. Her stature stretched, thinning and becoming taller.

A completely different person sat at the edge of Tyson's bed.

"I'm Melanie." The woman held out her hand. Tyson stared at it, then back at the freckled face framed with red hair. "I'm a chimera. A human chimera. I have a twin form. I can change my physical appearance into a nearly opposite human form. It's very scientific, actually. Two sets of genes exist in one body. We're the same mind, just different forms."

"I'm not scared, just amazed," Tyson replied. "I mean, I can change into a polar bear, but what you just did is incredible! They didn't mention your kind of paranormal in my classes."

"A scholar, eh? What degree?"

"Paranormal Psychology," Tyson said.

"So, wait, did you know you were a magic user when you went to school?" Melanie asked.

Tyson smacked the blankets on his legs and smoothed them. "You know, I didn't? I actually worked for a Naturalization camp for a few years. Yeah. Didn't find out until after I left."

Melanie laughed. "Fascinating! I want to hear your whole story, but it'll have to be later. I need to check on a few other patients. None as interesting as you." Melanie put her hand up to her mouth as if telling a secret. "I'm not supposed to be in here. Jackie isn't either. But there's one more thing you need to know: I'm a member of the Transcendental Redemption Society. We're one of several rebel factions working to free paranormals from the unrighteous dominion of the United States government. If you'll work with me, we can get you out of here."

Tyson breathed in deep. The TRS had found him again, after all. "I joined, actually. Hal recruited me. You know him? Big Black guy, eye tattoos literally all over his body."

Melanie smiled. Her nose scrunched a little, making the freckles move. "No, I don't know him. There's a lot of interesting people in various locations. Maybe you can introduce us. Anyway, I'm guessing that beneath that bandage you're probably healed. You're not acting like most brain trauma patients we see. Do you mind if I take a look?"

Tyson leaned his head towards her. "Go ahead."

Melanie unwrapped the bandages, clicking softly with her tongue. "That's what I thought. It's worse, really. You're completely healed. All the staples and stitches are gone. Well, the staples are here," She held out her hand. "They were stuck to the bandage. The stitches are already absorbed. Your hair is even growing back some."

Tyson felt the fine hairs poking up through his scalp. Definitely longer hairs than a freshly shaved scalp should have. "What do we do about that?"

Melanie stood and logged into the computer near the monitors. "I can hold them off by saying I changed your dressings. The biggest problem will be when the doctor wants to check it out later today or tomorrow. If they find you've healed, we'll have a problem because then they'll know that I've tampered with the results of your blood sample. Well, that Jackie tampered. So we'll have to get you out before then. If I get implicated in too many more escapes, they'll get me. It's nearly time for me to move on from here." Melanie shut off the screen and turned back to Tyson, morphing into Jackie as she went. It took about a full minute, and her eyes lingered green for a while before muddying back to brown. Tyson blinked again, feeling twitchy from watching the transformation.

"See that pager button on your bed frame?" Jackie said. She had a slightly southern accent, a bit deeper than Melanie. Richer.

Tyson found it and pointed. "This green one with the phone?"

"That's the one. I've managed to have it wired so it calls me directly. If you have any trouble, or if anyone comes in here and starts questioning you, push that button and I'll get you out of it if I can. I won't endanger my own life unduly, or that of any of the other patients here. I also cannot act too rashly, or I risk exposing T.R.S. We've operated for a long time without getting put on the S.T.F. radar, and we'd like to keep it that way."

"Got it," he said, nodding firmly.

"Good. Let me rewrap your head, then, and I'll contact my team and see what we can do about getting you out of here."

Jackie applied new antibiotic cream and gauze, for authenticity, she said.

Jackie wrapped it all in a tight, turban-like fashion. Tyson patted at the bandage. It felt so strange to wear it when he knew that his wound was mostly healed.

"Jackie?"

She turned away from her clean up, smiling at me. "Hm?"

"Do you think that accident could affect my abilities in any way?"

She looked thoughtful. "An injury to the brain could definitely affect them. It could enhance them or make it more difficult to use them. If you experiment, be careful not to let anyone catch you."

"Okay. One more thing: was anything brought in with me? A blue backpack, by chance?"

Jackie snapped her fingers. "Yes. I sensed some strong energy coming from it, so I hid it. I'll bring it by when I check on you during Melanie's shift tomorrow morning. Do you need anything else?"

"I'm a bit hungry."

Jackie nodded. "Of course. I'll call for some food for you." She wished Tyson a good night and left.

Tyson watched the curtain until it stopped moving. How did it all work with Melanie and Jackie? Were they both employed at the hospital? Did she work two shifts? What happened if they got scheduled at the same time? She must have excessive stamina or something. Did she have to get two degrees in nursing, too? His curiosity was running away with him. It wasn't really important right then. Finding a way to contact Becca, to let her know he was alive...He remembered the expression on her face when she had seen his body after the accident.

He checked the clock on the wall. It read just after 6 p.m. The door opened again a few minutes later. It was a nurse he didn't know, bringing a tray of food. They exchanged niceties, she took his vitals and inputted the information into the computer, scanning her badge.

Tyson felt her eyes on him as he dug into the meal like a starving man. He hadn't eaten anything in over 24 hours, and he was definitely hungry. After a few minutes, she seemed satisfied he wouldn't choke, and she left the room.

After eating, fatigue slammed into Tyson. He laid the bed flat and just before he lost consciousness, he felt a familiar catch in his brain, like a fishhook had landed in the folds of his mind. He followed it, letting it drag him up, up, up and out of his body. His body slumped to the bed, his steady breathing the only way he could tell he was still alive. He whooped, pumping his astral-fist into the air and swooping around the room, then swooping through the walls. He didn't want to fly into any other rooms, for fear of seeing some surgical gore or a naked person and the like, so he flew through the outer wall of the hospital, hovering twenty feet above the street.

There was exhilaration but not like he expected. No wind existed in the astral realm, so he didn't feel it rushing past his face, and gravity seemed to be a personally fabricated thing. As he glanced around, he noticed others walking around more solid-looking, so he assumed they were on his side of things, not people walking around on the physical plane. He tried to remember what the guy said in the videos back at the bar, but he had fallen asleep during some of the lessons, so he didn't remember that part.

"Welcome to the Higher Astral Plane," a familiar guttural voice blurted behind him, preceded by a literal "popping" noise.

Tyson whirled around to see Todd, his fox-head grinning unnaturally wide.

Tyson's anger flared. "What did you think you were doing? I was trying to save Harper, and you whooshed in and forced me back into my body. What gives?"

"You are naive yet to the ways of the planes," Todd said, baring his teeth. "Your rampant traveling took you to the Lower Mental Plane, where the human mind breaks down without extensive training on how to withstand the mind-scrambling winds."

"I didn't feel any wind," Tyson insisted. "Just lots of smoke. Or fog, or whatever. Look, my friend is trapped down there, and I can't just leave her, especially knowing it's affecting her mind."

The fox folded his arms. "I'll agree to help free her if you agree to listen to what I say to you. Here, I have the knowledge you need to not get your soul fragmented, your body possessed, your mind driven mad. Capice?"

Tyson set his jaw. "Got it. But be quick about it, maybe."

Todd clapped his hands and rubbed his palms together. "Excellent. Okay, lesson one: planes."

Tyson looked around, up at the sky, then back at Todd. "How many planes *are* there?"

"Nine. Well, nine that you need to concern yourself with learning about for now. There are sub-planes and other dimensions with their own versions of the nine original planes, but for now, there are nine."

Tyson worked to wrap his head around that, storing the information away for later. "Which plane are we on now?"

"The Higher Astral plane. It's just barely above the Physical plane, which should be the obvious one. Going down you have the Lower Astral Plane, the Lower Mental Plane, the First Abyss, and the Second Abyss. Going up you have the Higher

Mental Plane, the Formative Plane, and the Eternal Source." Todd moved his hands, switching them to demonstrate levels going up.

"So how does one get there? To the Eternal Source? Is it like coming here? Do I fall asleep on this plane, or something?" Tyson asked.

"Not all the planes are so simple to travel to. It's difficult to explain…" Todd snapped his human fingers. Which, now that Tyson had noticed them, seemed more feminine than masculine. Long, slender fingers with manicured nails. The body was more difficult to discern beneath the layers of clothes the fox-person wore—heavy military coat and pants, padded with other clothes beneath. Tyson thought of Todd as male because of the fox-person's guttural voice, but that could be misleading, he supposed. Thinking of it as a 'him' was simpler for Tyson. Todd cleared his throat, raising a bushy brow at Tyson. "If you've finished scrutinizing me."

"Oh, of course. Sorry." Tyson shook his head, his cheeks burning slightly. He glanced to his left, where someone walked straight up the side of a building and over instead of going around. "Who are all these people?"

"Focus. I'm explaining travel to the other planes. Unless you don't care to learn that?"

"No, no. Go ahead." Tyson put his hands on his hips, shifting his footing. He lifted his heels, rocking, still watching the people—beings—around him.

"You know that popular children's novel, Alice in Wonderland?"

"I only saw the movie. The cartoon." Tyson shrugged.

The fox-person tsked. "Shame. Look, it's like that. The winding paths of this place can take you anywhere, but if you don't have a specific intention, you could end up somewhere you don't want to be. Or somewhere incredible, but you won't know how you got there and getting back might not be so simple."

"So I think about where I want to go, and pick a path, and it will take me there?" Tyson asked, folding one arm over his chest and resting his chin on the other.

"In a manner of speaking. But the highest two levels are different. You can have every intention of going, but if your vibration isn't high enough to withstand the vast currents of energy flowing through them, you'll wind up walking in circles. Some well-meaning pursuers of 'enlightenment,'" Todd used air quotes, emphasizing the word, "have searched for the Eternal Source until their physical bodies have perished. Spirits aren't in the same danger, but they can be lost or lose their sanity. A specific invitation is required for a lower vibrational being to visit the higher-level planes."

"And the lower levels—"

"Aren't places you want to go," Todd said firmly. He made a slicing motion with his hand. "Your light, dreamwalker, shines brighter than many others. You'll need to be watchful, so you do not get possessed."

Tyson's thoughts turned to Harper, the glassy look in her eyes when she'd looked at him last, and the complete lack of recognition as Lilith commanded that she attack Tyson and their friends back at the village. "Is Harper...Is that what happened to her?"

Todd looked at him sharply. "I do not know what happened to your bird friend. It would be best if you keep your focus on the task at hand."

Tyson snorted. "What good is a guide who won't take me where I need to go?"

"I should have let the Essences get you on the Lower Mental Plane. Teach you a lesson. Unfortunately, they actually change your personality. And who *knows* what I'd be dealing with then. Each plane has its dangers, even the higher ones."

Tyson glanced around, gesturing widely. "Looks pretty benign to me."

"From the first level. A level at which your experiences are largely shaped by your own subconscious. You can interact with others here, even be invited into their subconscious experiences, but as long as you remain inside your own thought plane it's extremely unlikely that you'll be attacked or taken advantage of. You have to invite others inside in order for that to happen."

Tyson blinked. "You mean...like I invited you in? Did I invite you in?"

Todd sighed. "I'm your guide. I was assigned to you."

"Oh, and which realm do you come from?"

"Plane. Not realm. I've been to all of them. All except the Eternal Source and...well, the lowest one." His tail twitched. He seemed ashamed, shuffling his feet, not making eye contact.

"So, I've got a bum guide," Tyson said, tongue-in-cheek.

Todd's head snapped up. "You do not have a bum guide." His voice—If he really was a he—crept up in pitch until it sounded remarkably feminine. He coughed and continued. "Only true heroes need a guide to the darkest of underworlds or the highest of heavens. And you, sir, are not that. You're an amatuer dreamwalker who had to nearly *die* in order to achieve transcendence."

Tyson swallowed against his constricted throat. "But I achieved it, didn't I?"

"Congratulations. Real special." Todd slow-clapped, and Tyson wanted to wipe the smirk off the fox-man's face. He dropped his arms to his sides, holding them rigid and flexing his fingers as they tried to curl into fists.

"If I'm not here to find Harper or Hal, what am I here for?" Tyson said through gritted teeth. He worked his jaw, trying to release the tension of his pride taking a hit.

"You're here to learn. But you know what? I don't think you're ready." Todd stepped forward, hand pressing into Tyson's chest and shoving him. "A student must be humble. You're so full of it nothing I say seems to be getting through. And I'm…" He shoved again, forcing Tyson back. A pit opened up behind Tyson. Wasn't he in control of this level, or whatever? "Not going…" Another push. Tyson gazed back at Todd, who grinned a sharp-toothed grin and leaned in so close, his nose nearly touched Tyson's and the golden rims of his eyes burned. "To waste my time."

The tiniest nudge from his hand sent Tyson reeling backward. He wheeled his arms, trying not to fall, but despite the seemingly automatic floating he'd been doing before, gravity took hold of him again and pulled him down into the depths of the pit.

Tyson slammed back into his body with a gasp. The heart machine attached to him went nuts. It only took a few seconds before a nurse came racing through the door. Tyson's hand rubbed his chest. Being forced back into his body felt like getting hit by that motorcycle all over again. His head throbbed, and his breath came in short gasps. The nurse rubbed and patted his back, eyes going to the monitor.

"There, now. Bad dream?" She asked.

Tyson nodded, gulping, not trusting himself to speak clearly. He blinked, still seeing multi-colored spots and hearing that damned fox's laugh. He had blown it. And now he knew that Harper was in immediate danger. Those Essences the fox had talked about could be alternating Harper's personality while he sat uselessly in the hospital. But how could he fight against something intangible?

"It's coming down nicely," the nurse muttered, still looking at the monitor. "How are you feeling, sweetie? It's a bit early, but the cafeteria just opened, and I can get you some breakfast."

"Yeah," Tyson managed.

The nurse smiled. She scanned her badge into the computer and made some notes. "Looks like you're cleared to eat."

"I ate last night."

"Good. And kept it down, I see. That's what we want to hear. I'll be right back."

"Nurse?" Tyson called. His heart was galloping much more slowly now. His hand dropped into the blankets, fingers finding the plastic band on his wrist that grounded him and reminded him that he was in a hospital. Traveling to other realms should probably wait until he got out again. "Could I make a phone call?"

"Sure thing, sweetie."

Tyson collapsed back against his pillows. Todd had just wanted to freak him out. Shake up the newbie, force some respect for the next time they encountered each other. Tyson figured he could learn his way around the astral realm without a special guide. He had always learned better by experiencing things for himself. Was there any way to convince Todd of that? Tyson could explore, discover what the astral realm was all about, and find some clues that might lead him to Harper. Or at least Harper's body. She would still be possessed.

The nurse came back with a food tray, and she brought a phone from a table near the computer over to his bed.

"Don't you think about breaking out of here. The doctor still has to examine that head of yours, and there was something funny about your bloodwork. It seems to have gotten mixed up with another patient's. No worries, I'll work it out," the nurse said as Tyson picked up the phone. He froze. Could she know, somehow? The nurse laughed at the look on his face, and Tyson smiled weakly.

"Do people really do that?" He gave a faint laugh.

The nurse laughed loudly. "Sometimes," she said at last. "I'll leave you to it. Visiting hours start at ten."

She turned and left the room. Tyson held the phone between his ear and shoulder while it rang so he could use both hands to open the jello. Why was it always jello? At least it was red, not that nasty green stuff. He licked the foil wrapper. The phone clicked.

"Hello?" Tyson said. Static.

He'd tried the number for the room above the bar, assuming she'd go back. But what if Becca wasn't there? What if she'd left the state with Avaan, or been captured after his accident?

"Tyson?" Becca's voice came through after a moment. "Tyson! Oh my gosh. Are you okay?"

"A bit of a headache, that's all," Tyson said lightly.

"I can't get in to visit you. They've got those blasted scanners at every entrance. Avaan might be able to come in. We don't know yet how sensitive they are. Have they...have they figured you out yet?"

Tyson glanced toward the door the nurse had disappeared through. "Not yet. There's a nurse here who works for the rebellion. She's trying to get me out. Are you safe?" Despite the danger they were both in, it felt good to talk to someone he knew.

Someone mortal, who made sense in a way he was used to. He felt his blood pressure dropping, his heart rate slowing.

"That's good you're not alone in there. I figured the worst, you know? And we've been trying to think of a way to get you out. Let that nurse know that we're out here waiting and ready to help if we're needed."

"I don't want you to stick around the hospital. You'll draw suspicion."

"We're keeping on the move. Don't worry about us. Just...get better and get out." A worried note in Becca's voice came through the line.

Tyson grimaced. He hadn't meant to worry her. "I'll let you know as soon as there's an update."

"Okay. My number might change. I'll call you if it does. See you soon." Such a hopeful phrase. Tyson heard a click on Becca's end of the line. He held onto the phone for a long time after, letting the hopeful tone linger in his mind. Then, with a deep breath, he hung up and turned back to his food.

He picked up a pastry from his tray and frowned. There was a blue post-it note stuck to the bottom. He peeled it off.

Another nurse suspects something is up with your blood work results. She caught Melanie switching vials and questioned her. We think we got her off the trail, but just in case we've accelerated motions to get you out of here. Your condition should be stable enough. When we ask you if you want a sticker for being a good patient, say yes. The sticker we will give you is a hidden deactivator patch for the paranormal detection terminals at the entrance to the hospital. This is your signal to leave as soon as we exit the room. Your clothes are in the backpack on the couch to your left. Put them on under your gown and be ready.

- M - J

Could he get one of those stickers for Becca? Though, if this was happening as soon as they said, she probably didn't need one. He could meet her once he made it out. Tyson glanced at the couch near the left-hand wall. His backpack, filthy as ever, stood upright against the stiff cushions. He moved his breakfast tray and tossed off the covers, swinging his legs over the side of the bed. A sudden surge of nerves stopping him from sliding off. What if his legs crumpled and he fell? What if he was paralyzed? He pinched his thighs, wincing and rubbing at the small red spots left by his fingers. Okay, not paralyzed. He took a deep breath and let gravity pull him towards the floor.

His muscles felt like jello, but they propelled him forward normally enough. He unzipped the backpack. Neatly folded jeans and an unassuming blue polo were accompanied by stiff-looking boxer shorts and socks, all tucked in next to the tennis shoes he'd been wearing when he got hit. He tugged them out and found the harpy egg gleaming inside one shoe, and the *Ulu* knife rested in the bottom of the bag. He stared at it, unblinking. It seemed like a lifetime ago he'd first gotten cut by it and received a vision of Alaska from his ancestor's perspective. Could he use it to show him a vision of his own future, rather than the past?

Tyson put the clothes and shoes down in a pile on the couch and reached into the backpack, picking up the knife.

The door to the hospital room swung open.

"What are you doing out of bed?" The female voice rang out with a forceful tone. Tyson nearly dropped the knife as he shoved it into his backpack as hard as he could, somehow avoiding cutting himself. He swallowed and glanced back, finding Sonja with a packet in one hand and her other hand on her hip. She used her free hand to point at the bed.

"You shouldn't be up yet. You were hit pretty hard." She smiled, but it didn't reach her eyes.

"I just wanted to put on some normal clothes. The gown itches." He tugged at the shoulder of it and made a face, hoping he sounded convincing enough. He pointed at the package. "What's that?"

The plastic wrapper crinkled as Sonja moved slightly and glanced down at it. "Doctor wants you on blood thinners to avoid clots after that strike you had. Jump back up and I'll administer it. Then we can move on to the tests I mentioned. We'll have you taken care of in no time." She pulled over a small table on wheels, blocking Tyson's view of what she was doing with her body. He cautiously climbed onto the bed, not settling in too deeply in case Sonja turned on him. He noticed a syringe and a tiny glass bottle. The clear liquid went into the syringe, and Sonja turned back to him.

"You know, you really should have told us there was something different about your blood. Now things are going to get harder." Her tone hardened. She stepped toward him. "You can start by telling me who helped you get in without detection. Is it the same person who was going to help you escape?"

Tyson licked his lips and pushed himself further up the bed away from her, eyeing the needle in her hand. "I don't know what you're talking about."

Sonja laughed. "I've seen plenty like you in my day, Miller. Most honestly didn't know about the secret hiding in their blood, but others did. And some of them escaped. I want to know how. If you work with me, I can make your transition much easier than I've made it for others."

Tyson's thoughts spun. His eyes darted down and he slammed his hand down on the button and scrambled off the bed. His instincts took over, and the form he'd become most familiar with over the past few weeks flowed through him, changing the structure of his muscles, bones and sinew. His polar bear form was too big for the space between the bench and the bed, and his bulk shoved the bed back, throwing Sonja and her syringe backward. Somewhere, glass broke. Tyson grabbed the backpack in his jaws and stepped around the bed. Sonja lay between him and the door, which was blocked by another figure.

"Hold it right there." An armed security guard stood in the doorway, holding a walkie talkie up to his mouth. "We've got a 4-1-1. I repeat, a 4-1-1."

Tyson turned his massive head to look out the window. Second story. Could a polar bear manage the fall? Probably not. Nothing to help him climb down, either. He looked back at the officer, and Sonja propping herself up, eyeing the still-loaded syringe on the floor a few feet away.

The only way Tyson was getting out was through, and his window of opportunity was closing fast.

CHAPTER TWELVE

ZEKE

Japanese demons. That's what Greg and Steve were, at least according to Jake, who claimed to be some kind of expert on paranormal creatures.

"I'd have loved to harvest their horns. Don't worry, they grow back. Don't think it would go over so well when we tried to recruit them, though." Jake shot Zeke a lopsided grin. Zeke squirmed in his seat. Not much got to him, but poaching paranormal body parts wasn't a conversation he was going to have willingly. Even if the demons had tried to kill him.

"You're going to recruit them?" Zeke asked.

"Of course. They'll be under heavy guard at first, but if we can convince them, why the heck not? Can't discriminate when you're running a rebellion and the other guys have a bigger army. We only knocked them out because in their demon forms they're a bit unreasonable. You must have noticed that."

Zeke shifted in his seat and changed the subject. "What's this rebellion of yours called?"

"The Transcendental Redemption Society. T.R.S for short." Jake glanced from the road to Zeke and back. "Heard of it?"

Zeke sniffed, rubbing at his nose. Something in this car, some scent, made him twitchy. He'd never spelled the spicy, somehow bitter scent that wafted forward from the back of the cab. Laughter drifted up from the bed of the truck, filled with the two unconscious Oni trussed up like turkeys. "Can't say I have. But then, I've been in a camp up until a few days back."

Jake whistled. "Naturalization camp? Man, you're lucky we grabbed you."

"I didn't know what they were. My source implied they were vamps."

Jake barked a laugh. "Well, you're lucky we picked you up. Otherwise, your organs would've been spread across that parking lot."

"Listen, I don't know how to thank you, but I can't join your rebellion. I've got..." Zeke struggled to find the words. "Things to attend to. Loose ends. You know?"

"I know." Jake's tone implied that he did, in fact, know what Zeke was going through. He exuded confidence. And cheap body spray. Definitely human. "Most of us do. I'm sure we can find a place for you. Where is your business taking you?"

Zeke hesitated before responding. "Chicago."

"What part?"

"Westside," Zeke offered vaguely.

"Got a pack there? You know what, it's none of my business. But I've got a guy who was getting ready to leave to deliver this package. Super important. Tell you what: you go in his stead, we'll give you transportation, and we'll be in touch about your role with us. Just get that package to my buddy, right?"

Zeke shook his head, his dreads swinging against his jawline. "Why would you trust me with something like that? We met less than an hour ago."

"He's got a point, Jake." A man from the back put a hand on the shoulder of Zeke's seat, leaning forward. "That package is critical."

"I need Silver for something else. It's gotta get there somehow, and I don't see you volunteering, Slim." Jake said cryptically.

The other guy, Slim, sat back, muttering to himself. Zeke didn't try to decipher it.

"Well, I'd appreciate the ride. What's in this package?" He tried to keep the curiosity from seeping into his voice. He didn't want to seem nosy, but a man would be a fool to transport something potentially harmful.

"Better if you don't know," Jake said with finality. "You know, I've just got a sense for people. You're a trustworthy one, I know it."

"The amulet helps," Slim said. He seemed like he had a pretty big chip on his shoulder.

Zeke glanced sideways at Jake, who had a slight smirk on his face. Sure enough, something glowed dimly beneath the man's t-shirt, just visible in the gap in his leather jacket.

"What does it do?" Zeke asked. He'd seen magical objects before, a few, back at the camp. Sometimes residents had them confiscated when they arrived. Violet had kept them under magical lock and key and far out of the resident's sight.

Jake patted the glowing lump and shot a glance toward the back seat. "That's supposed to be kept a secret, Slim."

"Yeah, well, you don't hide it very well. Might as well stop giving people the illusion that you have some sort of superpower," Slim snapped.

Jake raised his eyebrows at Zeke. "Someone is jealous," he whispered loudly. Then he laughed, looking out the front window at the road illuminated in his headlights. He didn't answer Zeke's question about the amulet.

Zeke decided he didn't like the man very much. Too flippant to be a good leader. But his wolf senses didn't trigger any red flags, so he knew the man was likely telling the truth about who he was and what he was about, at least.

The truck turned off the main road and bumped along a narrow dirt trail. Zeke couldn't call it a road, not with the number of potholes that sent him bouncing off his seat. He was actually grateful for the seatbelt.

Jake stopped the truck abruptly and flicked off his seatbelt, pulling the keys from the ignition and flinging open his door. "You in any rush to get going…?" He trailed off, as if realizing he didn't know Zeke's name.

"Call me Z," Zeke said.

"Well, Z, we can get you set up in a bunk tonight, get some food in you." He swirled the keys around in his hand.

Zeke fumbled with the seat buckle. "No, no, I'd rather, you know, get going." That sensation in his navel was growing, the itch of the full-moon transformation. He still had about a day and a half of travel ahead. The sooner he left, the better.

"All right," Jake slapped the side of the truck. "We'll get you loaded up. Slim, you've got that package ready?"

"Yeah, yeah, one sec." Slim slammed his door as Zeke opened his. His feet hit the ground, and Jake was there in front of him, hands casually in his pocket.

"So, a buddy of mine is working an angle for us with the White City pack, you know them? They might give you some trouble at first."

Hell. Yes, Zeke knew the White City pack. They were the ones…Well, they were part of the reason he had been sent to

Camp Silver Lake in the first place. And now their leader held some deal over his father.

"You're not…" Jake thumbed his nose and laughed, glancing around. "One of them? Are you, by chance?"

"No." Zeke wasn't. He'd been in the middle of his initiation when it all blew up, though. It had been quite a few years. Would they remember him as the kid who messed up so badly back then? "I can handle myself well enough, don't worry about that."

Jake chuckled. "Oh, I'm not worried about you. You'll do just fine. Just don't let them recruit you before we do."

Zeke resisted rolling his eyes. He wasn't up for recruiting by anyone.

A rumble came from somewhere behind the house, and a small pair of headlights appeared from the darkness. An engine revved and the headlights bobbed up as the motorcycle surged forward.

Slim stopped in front of them, spewing dirt, and pulled off the helmet. "What do you think, eh?" He patted the blue paint job on the motorcycle.

Zeke whistled appreciatively. He didn't care if he was driving a beater, so long as it ran, but the motorcycle was pretty sweet. "How will I get this back to you?"

"Consider it a loan. You wreck it, you buy it, but otherwise, I expect to see you again at some point. You'll return it." Jake slapped Zeke's shoulder. "You sure we can't convince you to join us? I know you're eager to conduct whatever business you have in the Westside, but a night's rest after being hunted by Japanese demons would do you good."

"No, but thanks again." Zeke reached for the helmet, which Slim handed over somewhat reluctantly. He climbed off the bike, and Zeke noticed the cardboard package strapped to the back.

"Look, you're showing a lot of trust in a stranger. I just want you to know that I've got this. And I appreciate the ride more than you know."

"I know. Remember?" Jake tapped the amulet beneath his shirt and winked, then whipped out a piece of paper and a pen from an inner pocket of his leather jacket. He scrawled a name, a phone number, and some words Zeke couldn't make out, then folded it and passed it to Zeke.

"That's my friend and his place of residence. The phone number is for me. Call when you've completed your first mission for the T.R.S., my friend. We could use an intelligent man with your level of self-control on the team."

"I'll call," Zeke said, putting the paper in the pocket of the borrowed basketball shorts. He swung his leg over the seat of the bike, feeling exposed wearing flimsy shorts and a t-shirt on the motorbike. First stop might be to find proper clothing for riding. He fitted the helmet, squeezing it down over his thick dreads, then brought the motorbike to life with a rumble. He gave Jake and Slim a thumbs up. Jake returned it double as Zeke pulled away, leaving a cloud of dust in his wake.

He'd gotten insanely lucky. They could have forced him to stay, swear binding oaths, or even killed him just for knowing they existed. Instead, they'd handed him a motorcycle and a valuable package and sent him on his way. Nuts.

Zeke made good time. He practically flew to the border, reaching a small motel in Pine Bluffs, Wyoming at three a.m. He rented a room and let the transformation take him, curling up as a wolf on the bed. Let the cleaners try to figure out how the coarse dog-like hairs had gotten there in the morning.

He snagged five decent hours of sleep and then painstakingly shifted back into human form, took a shower to wake himself up, and grabbed a plate full of breakfast sausage and bacon from the continental breakfast station, inhaling piece after piece. He had two days, at most, before he'd be unable to shift into human form. He estimated he had another ten hours on the road, and he'd have to drive straight through to get there in time. But first... he found a small clothing store with jeans and a fake leather jacket in his size, plus tennis shoes and socks. Properly dressed, he filled up on gas and pulled out of the sleepy town, headed for the Windy City.

Zeke's mind turned to Mandi. It seemed like ages since he'd left her standing in that forest clearing. She hadn't wanted to come with him, and could he blame her? Not when regaining her sight was on the table. But he didn't like whatever Lilith was planning. As soon as he finished with his family, he'd head back. Return Jake's motorcycle and find a way to get to Mandi.

His nose itched. He rubbed the sensation away and fought back the urge to shift, gripping the handlebars of the bike more firmly. Scenery whipped past, a blur. He made another pit stop, just after noon, grabbing lunch and topping off the bike at the same time. Back on the road.

The horizon darkened from pale blue to a light yellow- orange, then purple. In the dusk, glittering towers rose from the earth, and Zeke took a deep breath in, catching a whiff of smoke and the rotten-egg smell of the river coated in fried foods and something chemically sweet.

Home sweet home.

Zeke flexed his hands on the bike grips and urged the bike forward with a bit of extra gas, burying himself in the heart of Chicago. He'd passed the area Antoine's Butchery—and his home—used to be. Going off what he remembered from the post-it in his wallet, the new place was called "Sweet Butchery." It was…distasteful, to say the least. It didn't sound like something Zeke's dad would take to, but if he was relying on the mafia's funding for the place, he'd likely been muscled into accepting the name. Dad had never cowed to anyone, and when Zeke had tried to join the mafia six years prior, he'd threatened to disown Zeke. Which told Zeke that if his family was under the mafia's thumb at last, things had to be bad. Real bad.

Zeke's motorbike pulled up to the curb, and he tore off his helmet, pulling his dreads away from his sweaty face. The warm breeze did little to cool him down after hours stuffed into the stifling helmet. He sat on the motorcycle, staring at the shop. An electric sign on the glass door read "Closed," and above it, yellow lights illuminated the dark lettering of the shop name, "Sweet Butchery." All modern block letters and no class. The shop opened at 7 a.m.

No point in spending the night in the gutter. Zeke patted the pocket containing his wallet, fatigue settling in over him as he stuck the helmet back on and pulled away from the sidewalk and merged with traffic. Paranormal-friendly hotels had pawprints in the windows. Which felt insanely discriminatory to Zeke, but what could he do about it? The "we're all human" argument didn't apply, and too many business owners and travelers didn't want a werewolf boarding with them, no matter how "house trained" they claimed to be.

Zeke hadn't asked for this. He'd been born a werewolf, and he'd die a werewolf, as would his family. But none of them had to deal with the kind of discrimination he'd been introduced to ever since his Naturalization. At least before, no one had known what he was. They judged him off his appearance, and his family. Respect for the Costas name had more than made up for the hooligan Zeke had been back in the day.

But now...now his I.D. had the truth stamped across it for all to see. The fake name he'd given the camp officials when he arrived, a picture of his human face, and next to it a shot of the golden-eyed wolf that hid in his DNA. The fewer people who saw it, the better. Just his presence, combined with the damning evidence on that card, could condemn his entire family to a camp just like the one he'd left.

He drove ten more minutes to find a dingy place with a paw-print sign tucked in a far corner of the window. He nearly missed it. He glanced at the place, then down at the motorbike. It was a pretty fancy thing to leave parked out in the open all night long. He'd better see if there were any vacancies first. Zeke peeled off his helmet, bringing it with him into the pinkish lighting of the motel lobby. Cigarette smoke and stale, donut-tainted air rushed him as the heavy glass door swung open at his push.

A man with magenta hair sat at the desk, typing rapidly on a computer so old, Zeke was surprised they hadn't sold it as an antique on the web to pay for repairs. And the place was in need of a good repair. Paint peeled from the walls, too faded and stained to determine the color it had once been. Perhaps the reason for the eye-bending pink light bulbs that adorned every fixture in the entryway. Zeke hoped the rooms were a more normal color; the pink made his eyes twitch.

The man at the desk pounded a few final keys and looked up, smiling and interlocking his fingers on his desk.

"And how may I help you?" His grin seemed a little too wide. Were his incisors pointed? Zeke sniffed the air. The man didn't smell like a vampire. He certainly didn't look like one, either. And there was a distinctly sulphuric smell to him. Demon?

Zeke raised an eyebrow and closed the distance to the desk. "Do you have a room? One night."

"No one ever stays here just one night," the man said, raising his own eyebrows to match Zeke's.

"Just the one," Zeke insisted.

"Whatever you say." The man grinned. His teeth were definitely more pointed than a normal human's would be. He clicked around on the computer. "We have two rooms open. Do you prefer a coffin or a dog bed?" He cackled, and Zeke rolled his eyes at the joke in poor taste. The man fell quiet. "I.D.," he said, more abruptly, and held out his pale hand.

Zeke passed the Naturalization license over to the man, who turned it over and over again, scanning every aspect of the card. He muttered to himself.

"You're far from home, pooch." The man glanced at Zeke.

Zeke let a growl rumble from the depths of his throat. "Is this place even to code? Seems like you're bending a lot of rules yourself."

The man held up both hands defensively. "If you get offended at every little thing, you're in for a world of hurt in this city. Everything checks out. Lucky for you, we care more about our bottom line than what the government thinks." He passed Zeke his Naturalization license and a printed paper detailing the cost of the room.

"What's this fifty dollar 'obscurance' fee?"

"The dog hair. And smell. Not to mention the time of the month it is. Your room comes with complementary industry-standard were-proof metal door and reinforced walls, with optional chain collar and bindings at additional cost. Not to mention, we won't tell anyone you were here." The man reached into a nearby drawer and drew out a heavy iron collar, nearly dropping it on his keyboard.

Zeke slammed the paper down, jabbing it with his finger. "I won't have any need for your chains. And this fee is robbery, straight up. I won't pay it." He bared his teeth, feeling the fangs as they grew, his jaw elongating...He restrained the transformation, panting with the effort.

The magenta spikes of hair on the man's head seemed to harden, taking on a glassy sheen. The corners of his eyes narrowed, becoming pointed, and his chin elongated. The tip of his tongue flickered out of his mouth, and it might have been the blasted lighting, but Zeke could have sworn that the man's skin turned ashen. The sulphur smell thickened in the air.

"If you'd like, I can call lower management. They're sure to answer all of your concerns to your satisfaction," the demon hissed.

The black tourmaline pendant on Zeke's chest heated up. It wouldn't do much if the being attacked him. It was more for subtle magic. Zeke held that diamond-eyed gaze and pulled out his transaction card. He laid it on the counter. *Lower management* wasn't something he wanted to get mixed up in. Not worth a fight that might risk his soul.

Magenta-hair cocked his head, swiped the card from the counter, and ran it through the machine on the desk. "Sign," he hissed again, indicating the paper.

Zeke read it three times to be sure he didn't miss anything about the sale of his eternal soul and, finding it satisfactory, signed. Magenta-hair passed him two cards back, one of which was a keycard.

"Down the hall and to your left. Six doors down." He smiled, more pleasantly that time, and Zeke noticed his features were shifting back to the more human ones he had first worn when Zeke entered the motel.

Zeke moved toward the hall, then hesitated, glancing back at the desk. "Do you have a place for motorbikes to be stored securely?"

"There's a cage out back. Twenty-five a night," the demon kept a simpering smile on his face. Zeke held back an eye roll and handed his card back to pay the fee.

Once the bike was settled, he made a beeline for his room. It was after 10 p.m., and his eyelids felt sore. He was also hungry, but nothing in the motel vending machine looked palatable, so he locked the door to his room, stripped off his clothes, and shifted with immense relief. Tail practically dragging, he jumped onto the bed and circled until the covers were properly rumpled and nest-like, then lay down, drifting to sleep amidst the memories of falling asleep beside a certain lovely witch he'd left miles behind.

Beyond the cheap vinyl blinds and thin cotton drapes covering the window, the near-perfect circle of the moon shone down on the city, and howls could faintly be heard amongst the usual late-night sounds on the streets. The wolves were out, and they were ravenous. Soon, Zeke wouldn't have any choice but to join them or drug himself into a stupor so deep he would sleep through the insatiable wolf hunger.

CHAPTER THIRTEEN

TYSON

MUSCLES BUNCHED BENEATH TYSON'S heavy fur coat. He stared down Sonja, who seemed to be calculating if she could get to the syringe before he mauled her. He *wasn't* going to maul her, but there was no way she could know that. He had to get out of there before S.T.F. backup swarmed the halls, and they had an uncanny response time.

He lunged, then skidded to a halt, seeing Melanie's familiar face at the door. She shook her head. Sonja screamed and twisted her torso, hand grasping the syringe. The dark-haired nurse sat up with the needle glinting from her fist, wild-eyed, hair astray, panting. Her expression changed to one of confusion.

"Sonja, that's hardly necessary at this point. You don't have enough sedative to take out a thousand-pound polar bear," Melanie said, tossing a strand of bright red curls over her shoulder. Tyson couldn't tell if she was bluffing or not. "Let me talk to him."

"S.T.F. is on the way, ma'am, you should stand by and let professionals handle this." The security guard thumbed his belt where a taser and a gun hung, both still holstered.

Melanie looked him up and down. "I happen to have more than a bit of experience de-escalating these types of situations. Would you rather face down a polar bear or a man?"

The security guard stammered for a moment, looking flustered. He eyed Tyson. "You really think you can get it to change back?"

It. That kind of attitude was the kind that gave paranormals so little reason to want to blend in with humans. Tyson felt anger course through his veins, brief, but so familiar. He'd always been on the other side of it, feeling it come from the residents at Camp Silver Lake, never understanding why they seemed so defensive when he tried to calm them down. He'd been wrong so often, and now there he was, being forced to live through some of what they dealt with.

He stamped the powerful feelings down, separating them from the bear instinct that coexisted in his body and made him want to flee from this place with its strange smells and noises. He focused his breathing, keeping his eyes on Melanie.

She held up her hands. "Tyson, I know you want to get out of here. You're afraid. You're hurt. But you have to listen to me. These people just want to get you some help."

Tyson couldn't help the snort that puffed out of his nostrils, along with a bearish grunt. He knew Melanie was putting on a show for the sake of the others, and she must have some plan, but the idea that the Naturalization camps helped anyone was laughable to him now. A shameful part of his past that he hoped he could somehow be redeemed from.

"It will go so much better for you, for everyone, if you return to human form."

A form moved in the corner of his eye. Sonja sprang forward, faster than Tyson could react.

Melanie jumped at the same time and crashed into Sonja. Both women fell to the ground, and Tyson scooted away as they rolled across the ground, fighting for control of the syringe. He couldn't get involved in helping Melanie without hurting both women, he was too large. And helping her could implicate her as a member of the rebellion. Melanie reached for the needle and Sonja jerked away. Melanie's momentum sent her arm straight into the needle point. She gasped and reared back. Sonja released the needle and scrambled away, panting and straightening her scrubs.

Tyson watched Melanie's eyes roll back into her head. She collapsed against the machine that had recorded Tyson's vitals, and everything went silent. And then her skin started flashing. Her hair grew and shrank, curly and straight. She was changing. Her form settled. Sonja shrieked. The guard reeled back from the door.

The chimera was frozen in-between forms. Half black woman, half white, a distorted face twisted between two bone structures. Her entire body was that way.

A crowd of footsteps pounded in the hall. Tyson didn't think twice. He shoved the bed out of the way and was to Melanie-Jackie in just a few steps. He growled in Sonja's direction, hoping she'd get the hint and stay back. With some creative maneuvering of his snout, he got Melanie-Jackie slung across his broad shoulders, then faced the man at the door.

He counted to three and charged. He didn't want to hurt the man, who fortunately saw sense and dropped the gun in his hand in favor of diving out of the way. The tactical force that arrived at the doorway in just that moment, on the other hand, wasn't so lucky. Tyson bowled into a group of five, knocking them aside like bowling pins. He tugged Melanie-Jackie back over his shoulder, glanced two ways, then took off down the less-obstructed hall. A locked door blocked the exit to the hospital wing. He reared up, feeling the woman slide off his back, then slammed his front paws against the doors. They buckled. He reared up again, slamming back down. They crunched, and one swung off its hinge, still slightly attached at the top.

Tyson turned and picked up Melanie-Jackie in his massive paws. He wasn't as fast on his hind legs, but he could carry her more safely. The crackle of a taser caught his attention. The Stiffs were rallying, and several had guns out, approaching with practiced form.

Tyson bolted. Running on two legs was not a natural phenomenon for this form. He needed another plan. He followed green exit signs, using a single powerful swipe of his arm to shove chairs and other furnishings he passed into the hall to slow the Stiffs coming up behind him. He kept his eyes darting back and forth, looking for stairs. An elevator would never hold him.

He passed more people now. They screamed and ran or dove out of the way as he passed.

Stiffs shouted behind. Did they have someone waiting for him at the front doors? Tyson rounded a corner into the hospital lobby and through his polar bear gaze he found a crowd lining the open hall, barricaded back by the tactical shields of several dozen Stiffs. Beyond them, the reinforced glass doors of the hospital exit gleamed. They were guarding the doors, all right.

Tyson froze. How could he get out of this? Harper would have done something insane like fly to the ceiling and break through one of the higher window panes, but Tyson could only do that if he dropped Melanie-Jackie, and he wasn't going to abandon her, not after she risked her job and even her life to help him escape. He shifted the unconscious woman in his arms, grateful for the tireless bear strength still coursing through him with the adrenaline and considered the visored faces of the S.T.F. team he faced.

They had tasers, yellow and black at the front of the belts at their waists, capable of taking down magical creatures with clout much more significant than a simple polar bear. And who knew what else they had up their sleeves? He couldn't charge straight through.

The backpack in his mouth buzzed. Like a giant cell phone vibrating with a call. The *ulu* knife. Tyson felt an answering tug in his gut. He closed his eyes, even as the apparent leader of the tactical force barked a command, and a front line of Stiffs advanced at a crouching crawl with shields raised and their free hand on their tasers.

Tyson tried to focus on the energy zinging through him, rather than what it would feel like to have the voltage of those guns course through his body. He searched inside and found an open space, almost cavity-like, filled with a sort of blueish-green light. He opened his eyes and released the light in the cavern.

Everything stopped. A whooshing sound, sort of like the gentle shush of ocean waves, filled the room along with the same teal light that filled his body and mind. Ribbons of brighter light danced across the floor, through the air. Tyson took a step forward, and the Stiffs remained frozen, unblinking, unmoving. Had he stopped time? It didn't matter. He wasn't sure how long this would last, but he could sense the reservoir in his body diminishing, so it couldn't last forever. And if it ran out, could it be replenished? He didn't want to find out now, not when he was just beginning to discover his abilities.

Tyson surged toward the door. It opened automatically when he approached, as if he were just another visitor at the hospital allowed to come and go as he pleased. The beginnings of a headache pulsed in the back of his skull. He held onto the magic behind him, his body quivering with effort as he stepped through another set of automatic doors and into the broad daylight, where nothing was frozen, and people took up their cell phones to dial S.T.F. lines. Some screamed and ran or hid. A polar bear carrying an unconscious woman was hardly a comforting sight.

A navy-blue armored vehicle stood parked out front, and a stocky woman jumped out. She was dressed in street clothes and a bullet-proof vest. She threw open the back doors of the van and gestured to Tyson.

"We've been waiting for you. Get in!" The woman yelled. Her ponytail swung as she glanced around the street. No one tried to stop her. No one even seemed to notice her.

Tyson hesitated. Could she be a Stiff in disguise trying to trick him into compliance? It didn't seem their way. Jackie-Melanie had said that someone would be waiting for him outside when she gave her signal, but she hadn't had a chance to do that.

The woman jogged over to him. "Is that MJ? Dammit. Cover blown. What happened to y'all in there?" She shot a look over her shoulder at the armored van. "Nevermind that. Just get in, for Pete's sake. Transform if you can. I'm sure a naked man isn't too much more for the public than a polar bear."

Tyson decided to trust her. She knew Jackie-Melanie. She had to be with the rebellion. Tyson held his polar bear form and walked with Jackie-Melanie to the back of the car. As soon as he stepped over the curb, he felt his connection to the magic bubble he'd created in the hospital lobby snap, and the magic rushed back into him. He staggered, leaning forward and managing to drop Jackie-Melanie on the floor of the van. He rolled to avoid crushing her with his bulk, eyes rolling into the back of his head.

He never hit the ground. Or so he thought.

The lump on his head when he woke up inside the van, laying on the floor in human form, told him he'd hit, and that he'd hit hard. It felt like a golf ball. His backpack leaned against his side, and the hospital gown covered him to his knees.

"I know it's not the smoothest ride down there, but I'd stay put if I were you." The woman from before spoke before Tyson could even lift his head and look around. "You're going to have some headache. Warn me next time you decide to pass out as a 1,000lb animal, m'kay?"

Tyson turned his head and noticed the woman held Jackie-Melanie's head on her lap. The woman was fully Melanie now, with her long red hair and paler, freckled face.

"Is she all right, then?"

"The sedative is wearing off." The woman eyed him. "You want to tell me what happened?"

"Give me your name, first. And tell me where we're headed." Harper would be proud he hadn't caved at the first question. He wasn't naturally suspicious. Never had been. But being parano rmal...It changed things.

She considered him, sucking her cheek in on one side and then sighing. She pulled out her ponytail and dragged her hand through her dirty blond hair, shaking it out, then tying it back up. "They call me Sandy. MJ said you're Tyson in her correspondence." It wasn't a question. "What are you? Polar bear shifter?"

"No." That was all he could think to say. Sandy accepted it, nodding as if in agreement with his lack of willingness to share information.

"We're all a bit afraid at first. Been burned a few too many times. But we're the good guys, Tyson. We're on your side, for once. You can trust those who are part of the T.R.S."

Tyson flexed his hands at his sides. He'd believed that he was one of the good guys, too. He'd convinced dozens of wary paranormals to trust him, to trust Tom. How many had ended up like Fletcher?

He forced himself to swallow the pain of regret that bottled up in his throat and cleared it, then turned his head back to face Sandy. "You never said where we were going."

"Headquarters. Well, one of them. If you want me to give you a full history of the T.R.S. on this drive, though, that ain't happening. I'll leave it to the tour guides." She tucked a strand of hair behind her ears and shifted, Melanie's head still on her lap.

The truck swerved and hit a bump. Sandy looked up. "Nearly there, now."

Tyson wanted to sit up, but the truck was still swaying, and he didn't want to risk being knocked over again. He remained on the floor feeling exposed and ridiculous. When the truck stopped, he slowly rolled onto his stomach and pushed with his arms to sit up on his knees.

Tyson stood up, legs feeling steady enough. The back doors on the truck flew open, and a woman climbed in and flung herself at Tyson. All Tyson could tell was that she wore a black hoodie. He held his hands out, startled by the assault of affection from an apparent stranger. When the woman backed off, rubbing her arms, Tyson saw the face under the hood.

"Becca?" he asked incredulously.

She slugged his arm. "Who else did you think it was? Do you know a lot of women that would greet you that way?" She snorted.

"It's good to see you. I didn't know how I'd find you after things at the hospital went so wrong." He glanced at the drive behind the open truck doors, but only a few men in plainclothes stood there, watching as Sandy draped MJ's arm around her neck. One of the men jumped up to help. "Where's Avaan?"

"Shadowing me, as always. Just staying out of the way." Becca gestured vaguely. "The T.R.S. approached me when they spotted me outside the hospital. I thought they were Stiffs and tried to run, but they calmed me down pretty quick with their rebellion spiel. Of course, Avaan doesn't want to be here. He's going on about 'returning to our homeland.'" She rolled her eyes and crossed her arms. When she glanced back over her shoulder, one of the men gestured for them to get out of the truck.

"Are you in, then? Are you joining?" Tyson asked.

She jumped down. "I don't know."

Tyson sat and slid from the truck bed, holding the hospital gown down.

Becca laughed. "I guess we should see about getting you a change of clothes."

"I don't know how girls wear dresses," Tyson complained.

"Our behinds aren't usually hanging out."

Tyson blushed, putting a hand behind him, feeling the slit in the gown, and Becca laughed again. "Here, I'll stand behind you." She positioned herself at his back, a solution only slightly better than letting a stranger glimpse his butt.

They were taken to a room with a few armchairs and couches, a sort of closed-off receiving area. Several doors led out of the room, and Tyson was asked his size, then handed a pile of clothes. A bathroom was revealed behind one of the numerous doors. The jeans were a bit short and tight, and the shirt too big, but miles better than the hospital gown. Fortunately, the tennis shoes fit him well enough. He came out to find Becca conversing quietly with Avaan. They stopped when they noticed Tyson standing there.

"I am glad you didn't get captured." Avaan smiled at Tyson, his teeth brilliant white. He seemed sincere.

"You too. Both of you." Tyson flopped down on an armchair near the couch they sat on and slapped the top of his thighs, rubbing his hands on the denim and trying to resist tugging on them to find a more comfortable position in the too-tight pants. "What happened after I was...taken?"

"We tried to follow, but when we saw the sensors at the hospital entrance we had to leave in a hurry." Becca's hands flexed in her lap. One of them reached up and scratched at a patch of skin on her cheek that Tyson noticed was flaking rather horribly. Becca seemed to realize what she was doing and stopped, clenching her fists again. "The transformation...my transformation...is accelerating. At least according to him." She motioned at Avaan with her head.

"My journals indicate that you are beyond the prime timing for the full bonding. If you continue to resist, you could go mad," he explained matter-of-factly.

"By full transformation, do you mean she'll be a snake lady full time, or...?" Tyson asked.

"No. Her skin will transform from human flesh to mature Lamia scales. She will no longer be able to hide among humans. The bonding I've performed up to this point was only a partial ceremony, rushed and under duress. The true ceremony takes several days and is much more...involved."

Tyson could only guess what such a ceremony entailed, and judging by Becca's fiery glare at Avaan, he didn't want to inquire.

Avaan cleared his throat and tore his eyes from Becca's back to Tyson. "Her choices are to go into hiding forever, or to accept her destiny."

"I'm not joining your harem. And I'm not going into hiding, either," Becca retorted.

"It's hardly a harem with one woman," Avaan sputtered.

Becca waved a hand. "Either way. I've been doing my research, digging on the ParaWeb. And there's another option."

Both Avaan and Tyson looked at her in surprise.

"There can be no other option. The journals make it quite clear..." Avaan began.

"No one writing your precious journals would want someone to free a Lamia intentionally," Becca snapped. She ran a hand through her hair, making it pouf up a bit on one side and giving her a harried look. "There's a group located in Texas that helps Lamia rehabilitate. And I'm going to see if they can help me."

Avaan crossed his arms. "It's a joke, surely. I won't go and sully the name and honor of my ancestors."

"You will go. Or you'll lose me to this madness you're so fond of going on about."

Tyson had never seen Becca so livid. Most guys would have played it cool, waited until she calmed down, but not Avaan. He straightened, his dark eyebrows coming together in a fierce expression.

"I've been congenial and respectful up until this point, Rebecca, but I don't have to cater to your whims. I would remind you that I hold the power to bond to you with or without your consent, though I'd much rather it be with."

Becca tapped the long, thin shape beneath her shirt on her chest. "Not without this, you won't."

"Don't think I can't take it back." His nostrils flared. It was the first evidence of a backbone Tyson had seen since meeting Avaan.

"Oh, so you're 'allowing' this rebellion to take place? Your ancestors must be so proud," Becca mocked. She could be scathing when she was in a bad mood.

Avaan opened his mouth in retort, and Tyson cut him off. "Hey, can you guys do this later? I've already got a headache,and you're making it worse."

The two fell into silence, Becca examining her nails, Avaan the wall.

Tyson coughed, then continued. "It sounds like you're not planning to stay, wherever you're going. What about me? Can I trust these people here?"

"I should hope that was obvious by now," a voice said from the doorway. Tyson hadn't even heard it open. A tall man stood there, dressed casually in a long-sleeve shirt and jeans. "One of our own risked her job, her freedom, even her life to bust you out of that hospital."

"Dak." Becca stood, straightening her hair behind her ears and tugging on her sleeves, as if to hide the green scales Tyson could see peeking out on the backs of her hands. They were on her neck, too. How much longer until they covered her?

"Becca," Dak acknowledged. He nodded to Avaan as well, then gazed back at Tyson.

"I'm not ungrateful. I know Jackie—er, Melanie?—took a huge risk. And she can't go back to the hospital now. I just don't know if here is where *I* need to be," Tyson finished lamely.

Dak spread his arms. "If you want freedom and equal rights for paranormals, you're in the right place, my friend. It's all we stand for, it's all we do. Government's too slow, so we're forging our own way. And I've heard you have some inside knowledge and talents that could help us get there."

"You have?" Tyson blinked, looking at Becca.

Becca gestured to Dak. "I told him a bit about you. What you did for June. You could be a huge asset here, Tyson."

"I'm not that good. I'm new, I—"

"What do you want, Tyson Miller?" Dak asked, moving forward into the room. "Maybe our agendas aren't so different as they seem."

"It's just..." Tyson stammered, then stopped himself and took a breath. "I'm looking for a friend of mine. This is exactly the sort of thing she would love to join, but for me, I'm new to this magic-user thing. I don't know where I fit or what I want. I just need to find her because..." He trailed off. It wasn't that he owed Harper anything. His life was destroyed almost from the moment she entered it. Sure, she had saved his life, but only after endangering it. And they might have kissed, but how much had that meant to her? He wanted to find out. Mostly, he felt a bit lost without her. "She's a friend." He said at last.

Dak nodded. "We've all got friends out there, Miller. Some more lost than others, if you catch my drift. But if you help us, we'll help you with whatever resources we have available to us. At the very least, you'll have a secure place to start your search from. Just give us a little bit of your time. We'll have our experienced projectors train you in the astral arts, strengthen your confidence and your abilities. If what your friends here say is true, you already met one of our own and agreed to join the Transcendental Redemption Society, so you're well on your way to becoming part of the next movement to rattle history for good. What do you say?"

Dak was right. Tyson had agreed to join with Hal. But it had been easy to say yes before they'd encountered Lilith and discovered what she was capable of. It wasn't just the government the T.R.S. had to look out for. And how could Tyson be sure they weren't working *for* Lilith? Just because Hal had seemed to fight against her didn't mean it hadn't been a front.

Harper would tell him he was being an idiot. Tyson could see the expression on her face now. The T.R.S. headquarters would be the safest place he could stay while he looked for her.

"Okay," Tyson finally said. His breath wooshed out of him in a sigh. He flexed his fingers. "I'll do it."

"Excellent. I'll need to introduce you to your team." Dak turned to Becca and Avaan. "I hear you two won't be staying, however. Is that a final decision?"

"Yes," Becca said firmly. "I'm afraid we won't be much help to you until we've worked out a few things between us." She glared at Avaan.

Tyson swallowed the words he wanted to speak, to ask her to stay. He had lost Harper; he didn't want to lose her too. He could feel the depression that had kept him in a polar bear half-hibernation state the past few weeks yawning in his chest. If she left, who would ground him? Who would give him pep talks?

Becca smiled knowingly at him. "You'll do great, Tyson. If there's one thing you're good at, it's making friends. And I have something that might help you." She turned to a backpack on the couch, rummaging through it. She pulled out a few random items—colorful rocks, a bundle of leaves, a container of salt, and several small amber bottles. She gestured at the spread, looking pleased with herself.

Tyson cocked his head. "What am I looking at?"

Becca rolled her eyes. "I bought it from a witch. She said the stones help with projecting, the sage clears the space of negative energy, and the essential oils help you access your inner strength."

"Er, thanks." Tyson gave her a wry smile. Becca grabbed the satchel and pulled it onto her shoulder, then gestured at Avaan.

"That's it, then. Time for us to go. You can expect us back if everything goes well," she said, looking from Tyson to Dak.

Dak pulled one hand from his pocket and held it out to her. Becca moved forward and shook it.

"Thanks for everything. Especially taking on this guy." She jutted her thumb at Tyson.

"He's going to be a great asset to our cause," Dak replied.

Avaan even shook the man's hand.

And then Becca turned back to Tyson. "Don't be stupid about this. About Harper. Nothing rash."

"Me? Rash? Do you even know me?" Tyson joked.

Becca embraced him. "I'll be in touch as soon as it's safe," she said over his shoulder. Her warmth pulled away from him, and she bounced from the room, stopping at the doorway for one last glance and a wave.

Tyson watched her leave until she turned a corner, and he couldn't see her anymore. Once she was gone, his stomach seemed to drop right out of his abdomen. He was truly alone, now.

CHAPTER FOURTEEN

MANDI

MANDI STOOD IN THE warm basement chamber holding hands with Meg and Dana. A low thrum came from her throat and reverberated with the hums of the others, filling the room until at last, the ritual that opened their meeting was completed.

In the midst of the dwindling notes. Lilith spoke, "There is one matter we must take care of before we activate the portal and leave here. When I said Dr. Thomas Hartford had fled, I was not being entirely truthful."

A gasp went up from Mandi's coven sisters. She heard Honey withhold a cry.

Beside her, Dana squeezed her hand and leaned in to whisper in her ear. "It's Dr. Hartford. Tom. He...he looks terrible, Mandi. All skin and bones."

A rattling cough echoed in the small room and a chair creaked at the center of the pentagram. Mandi's heart clenched. He was here. Dr. Hartford was in the room. What were they to do with him?

"It's as if he's aged years...No, decades. Hasn't shaved at all." Dana's voice trailed off, as if it was too horrible to continue.

Beneath the incense in the air, Mandi caught the hint of another smell, a putrid stench that belonged to something dead, rather than living.

No one else moved or spoke.

"What happened to him?" Mandi finally called out.

Lilith's voice took on a harsh tone. "He betrayed us. Or rather, tried to. From the moment Violet and James were killed, this man took action against the remaining residents here. He called in the Supernatural Task Force with orders to remove us. A camp without leaders, he reasoned, was a danger to the world. So, without consulting a single other being and without reason, Thomas Hartford sought the destruction of the people living here."

"No," Mandi gasped. Tom had always been one of the kindest, most understanding souls she knew. An advocate for justice.

"He wouldn't do such a thing," Honey cried.

"Do you deny that you called the S.T.F. squad, Thomas?" Lilith asked.

The man at the center of the circle coughed. "No," he wheezed.

"And do you deny that they had orders to permanently remove residents from this camp?"

"No," came the solitary word.

"But...why?" The words fell from Mandi's lips. She wanted to know. She *needed* to know how this man could betray her and all of those he'd lived among and counseled over the years.

"I would not see the camp fall..." Dr. Hartford rasped.

Lilith cut him off with a sharp word. "Enough! There is no excuse for what you've done. Isn't it clear? He had every intention of becoming a hero out of tragedy. Of sacrificing good people for the sake of his own reputation. I could not very well let him go his own way after that. A man with his knowledge could do much damage to our community here I've kept him locked up, but there's no sense in continuing imprisonment. I call on you, my coven sisters, to help mete out judgement upon this man. Is he worthy of release? Or perhaps his soul should vanish from the earth, right there in this room?"

Someone sobbed. Mandi thought it might be Honey.

"This isn't right," Mandi murmured. And suddenly, Lilith's presence was in front of her, excluding an icy cold sensation the same way any other human would let off heat.

"Who else is there to judge? Do we send the police for him? A human judge in a court of law? Would they not side with his reasoning, justify his cause, and release him? And what danger might it cause those who have sought refuge here?" Her words dripped with honey and venom, a hatred that Mandi hadn't heard from the woman before.

"Do we have any other evidence that he intended us harm? I've known him since he came here, and he's always been good and safe and given no indication of deceit." Mandi's throat choked up. Dana squeezed Mandi's hand several times. Mandi gulped past her fear and breathed in deeply, waiting for Lilith's reply.

"You speak wisely, Mandi. Of course, I wouldn't expect an intelligent woman like yourself to be a harsh or swift judge with a case like this. But the facts have been presented, and there are no other witnesses to call. What faculties can you rely on in the face of such a situation?" Lilith's voice slid through her ears.

"A truth spell," Anita piped up. "We could ask him anything, and he'd have to answer."

Lilith laughed, a chilling sound that rang through the room. "A truth spell is only as reliable as the asker, and tricky to manage. Have any of you young ones even cast one?"

Mandi knew they hadn't. Violet had been about to teach them, but truth spells were complex and rather advanced. She hadn't wanted to rush them.

Lilith continued. "I've subjected him to several rounds of questioning, of course, but I sense that you do not trust my word alone. And in the face of an accusation with such dire implications, I suppose I do not blame you. Ultimately, it is more important to me that we are united in our decisions. I can set aside my pride for this. I hope you will not mind if I ask one of those with more experience in our circle to cast the spell?"

Murmured assent went up, Mandi's voice among them. She hated to doubt Lilith after all the witch had done for her personally, but she wanted Honey and the others to trust as well. If this was the only way, then...

"Isabel?" Lilith questioned.

"Yes, Lilith." Isabel's heels clicked as she took several steps into the circle. The man let out a low, wheezing moan.

"Not...again..." He gasped.

Why wouldn't he allow a truth spell? Mandi had never seen one performed, but surely it wasn't bad.

Isabel whispered an incantation for fire and Mandi heard the slight whoosh as it lit. The gentle cascade of herbs and possibly dirt or salt being sprinkled entered her ears, and a musty, earthy smell trickled into her nose. A paper tore. Mandi imagined it being tossed into the fire, as was often the procedure in spells involving fire. It would have Dr. Hartford's name written on it.

Dr. Hartford let out a long, gut-wrenching yell.

"You're hurting him!" Honey cried. Mandi wanted to cry with her, but she bit her tongue. Surely, Lilith knew what she was doing. Surely, if there was another way, she would choose it.

The scream faded and the man was left panting. "Ask your questions, witch," he spat.

The gruff voice certainly didn't sound like it belonged to the kind man Mandi knew. But then, if Lilith had done this several times, was it possible she had broken his spirit and turned him against them? Or had he always felt that way, deep down, and Lilith's questioning had brought it to the surface at last?

"Did you place a phone call to the dispatch center on the eve of Violet's and James' deaths?" Isabel's melodic voice asked.

"I did."

"And why did you place the call?" Isabel continued.

The therapist remained silent.

Isabel coughed politely. "Note this, girls, even Truth spells have limitations. Yes or no questions are all he is compelled to answer. The spell urges him to speak and answer other questions, but the consequences of resistance are much less dire. And so, he may resist. I'll ask another and you'll see. Mr. Hartford, did you place the call in order to have residents at this camp removed forcefully?"

A pause. For a moment, Mandi thought he had successfully resisted again, but then a horrific, tormented yell ripped from his throat. Once, twice, three times he yelled, and the legs of the chair banged and scraped as if he thrashed about.

"He'll harm himself," Dana whispered. "See his veins bulge?"

Mandi didn't. She knew Dana knew she didn't, either. For once, she was glad she couldn't see to witness this man's attempts to withhold the truth.

"Yes!" He barked and then retched, as if the word had been forced from the depths of his body.

"Thank you. Girls, any other questions?" Isabel asked.

A fearful silence followed. Mandi cleared her throat. Her limbs trembled as she spoke. "Ask him if his intention was to protect others within the camp, or only those outside it."

"Yes or no questions are best," Lilith reminded her.

"Just the first part, then." Mandi hated feeling as if she'd gotten an answer wrong in class. She silently urged Dr. Hartford to answer the question as it was asked and not try to resist.

"Was your intention by calling the S.T.F. squad to protect others within the camp?" Isabel asked.

"Yes," Dr. Hartford spoke with a tone of relief. A question he wanted to answer, it seemed. "From the rogues."

"What do you mean?" Mandi asked, without thinking. The truth spell only held if the person who cast it asked the questions, she knew that. And it wasn't a yes or no question.

"They seek to destroy everything we've built here. Anyone who allows their influence must intend the same." Dr. Hartford's voice sounded strained, but his meaning was clear. He accused Lilith of betraying the camp and those in it, just as she accused him.

"Would you do anything, including sacrificing another resident, in order to maintain the status quo within the camp?" Lilith demanded. Isabel repeated the question.

Dr. Hartford grunted, and Mandi braced herself for another scream, but it never came. A breathy sigh of air drifted through the room, and the chair at the center of the circle creaked, and then silence.

"Is he...?" Anita squeaked.

A shuffling sound. "Yes," Isabel spoke. "His heart has stopped. The strain of resisting the spell was too much for him."

Why had he resisted? Mandi massaged her throat, trying to gulp past the lump there.

"Do his own actions not prove his guilt?" Lilith said, that sharp edge in her voice again. "It seems he would rather die than reveal his betrayal to you. I am sorry, girls. I know he helped—or seemed to help—many of you. But you must put his teachings behind you. The world we aim to create together will not include Naturalization, its restrictions or its bylaws. Paranormals hold the power, and it is we who deserve to have a place among, if not over, humans. Can you imagine a world where they must cater to our needs and desires, rather than us catering to their fears?"

Mandi's spine shivered. Her skin suddenly itched, and she wanted to scratch until the discomfort went away. She rubbed one arm and sucked in air, breathing through the overwhelming sensations. Dr. Hartford was dead. He'd been a good man. Perhaps misguided. After all, he'd been helping Fletcher alongside Tyson Miller, and they had failed to hear the blue jay shifter's cries for help. How many more would have to die before the right people heard?

"Lilith," Mandi said, her voice sounding as if it would get swallowed up in the tension that permeated the room. "How exactly do you intend to see that paranormal people get the freedoms they deserve? How is that possible without the world turning to chaos and bloodshed?"

Lilith's footsteps padded towards Mandi and away again as the witch walked around the circle. "Have you ever studied the great uprisings in history, Mandi? Do you recall the prices that were paid? It could be argued that true, lasting change cannot be made without the payment of lives. Think of it as a unique sort of blood magic. Enough blood spilt, enough intention put forth, even dull-witted and magic-less humans can cast spells and change entire societies. Of course, they've all had help from those like us, reading the charges in energy, helping it along…but you didn't think these things happened by accident, or even more naive, peacefully?"

As the witch spoke, Mandi heard the sound of a chair scraping on pavement. Someone was moving Dr. Hartford's body.

"You must prepare yourselves, my dears. Violet was a kind, even generous teacher, but she coddled you, kept you blind to the violence of magic. She did you no service neglecting the darker ways we witches influence others. It's influence or be influenced in this world. I intend to teach you true power, true influence. We will force the world to change, or we will destroy it and create a new world. This is our legacy." Her voice grew in volume and force, gaining an ephemeral tone that rang in Mandi's ears the same way it had when Violet used to share the visions she'd seen. Truth, from the Mother of the Earth, served through her servant Lilith.

Mandi found herself nodding. She didn't want to see the world destroyed, of course. She would do everything to encourage change in those who resisted it. They must see that bringing humans and paranormals level with each other was the right thing to do. She'd lived her life hiding her magic and who she was. When their coven succeeded under the guidance of Lilith to bring about this historic change to the world over, no one would ever have to hide or alter who they were again. No more deaths as needless as Fletcher's. No more camps, no more segregation, no more laws. Only equality. It made perfect sense.

Fingers snapped, and Mandi's concentration broke. She drew in a gasping breath.

"I can see some of you catching the vision," Lilith said, her voice infused with an infectious joy. Others chimed in with their assent. They all felt it. Mandi's heart lifted.

"What did you do with Dr. Hartford?" Honey's sweet, sad voice broke through the chatter.

"We couldn't leave him in the midst of our circle. He might have tainted the pentagram," Jasper said. Mandi had only heard her speak a few times, she tended to keep her thoughts to herself.

"Yes, but what did you do with him?" Honey's voice seemed like a hollow reflection of itself.

"His body will be disposed of in a manner befitting his betrayal of this camp," Lilith shouted hoarsely. She gasped, and her sob pierced Mandi's heart. "I'm sorry. He was a colleague. Someone I thought I could trust. I'm sure many of you feel the same way."

Mandi had never heard Lilith so distraught. She stepped out of her place to go to her, to comfort her, but someone beat her there.

"There, now, sister." One of the new witches. Serena, Mandi thought.

Mandi altered her course, going to put her arm around Honey. "It was a hard thing to hear that he wasn't who we thought he was. We have to let him go and move forward. I think Violet would have wanted this for us. Don't you want it for us?"

"Not if more people are going to die," Honey whispered.

"Please," Mandi said. "Please try to be strong through this. I know it's in you."

"I—" Honey's voice faltered. "I'll try."

Mandi squeezed her. "Thank you. I can't imagine trying to do this without you."

"Just don't let me lose myself." Honey gripped Mandi's hand in hers, her fingers cold and clammy.

"I won't." Mandi felt another set of arms around her and smelled Meg's herbal scent and heard Dana's quick breathing. They huddled for a moment, undisturbed.

"Come back together with us, ladies. We have work yet to do. I want to show you the scope of what I've been working on." Lilith clapped and Mandi and her friends separated, back to their places in the circle.

"Meet me in the next plane," Lilith said, her voice taking on a dreamy quality.

Mandi's heart raced. She would get to See again! She had practiced a little in her dreams, but Lilith had warned that she needed to go slowly. She lowered herself to the floor, using her arm as a pillow on the cool cement. She breathed in and let her mind drift. The crystal splint in her side began to vibrate as she drew near to subconsciousness, and a ping sounded in her mind.

She soared out of her body and into the air. She saw everyone else laying prone, their astral selves hovering above their bodies.

"I call upon north, upon south and east and west," Lilith intoned, gesturing to the four directions. I call for the High Priestesses and Priests of the Covens of Ragranoth to gather."

Ragranoth. Mandi had never heard the name, but it filled the room and made everything vibrate on a deep level that shook her chakras. In her mind's eye she saw them pause for a breathtaking moment, then reverse their spin. Lilith swept with her hand, gesturing around the circle, and a silvery strand appeared from each astral form to Lilith's fist. A line sank into Mandi's own chest, not something she could feel until Lilith pulled. Mandi's astral form moved forward. It didn't hurt, but the sensation was overwhelming, especially combined with the sight of her surroundings blurring. They were traveling somewhere.

A watery, pressurized sensation filled her head, and then her ears popped as they descended. When her surroundings settled, she saw twelve bodies standing in thick mist, their faces obscured.

"Gathering is risky," Lilith whispered. "We risk drawing unsavory attention. But you must understand the scope of what we undertake." There was a short gust of wind past Mandi's cheek, and a fourteenth figure appeared standing next to Lilith in the center of the circle.

"Elspeth," Lilith said, gesturing at the circle. "Meet my sisters."

"It is well." The figure, Elspeth, nodded.

Gust after gust came, until thirteen additional individuals stood amidst the circle of Mandi's coven sisters, which had gradually grown bigger to accommodate them. Now, it seemed they had all arrived.

"These are the High Priestesses and Priests of twelve other covens across the United States. Their exact designated degree on the map correlates with a critical point on this diagram, which is, of course, familiar to us all." Lilith's hands raised and spread apart. Streaming from them was a glowing orange pentagram with wavering lines, almost like flickering fire in the air. "Each one contains thirteen powerful and willing witches and warlocks, who will, when they receive the signal, take up their place and take part in a nation-wide ceremony to call forth our champion."

"What champion?" Mandi asked, her voice rising in the flat silence of the strange plane of existence. A shadow moved beyond their circle, as if drawn by her voice. Mandi shuddered. Was this one of the unsavory beings Lilith had warned her about?

"We are taking on the world bone country at a time. We're going to need a champion," one of the warlocks said, his voice tinged with disdain. Stupid question, foolish girl, his words seemed to indicate.

"Alone, as mortals, we are not powerful enough to enact worldwide acceptance of paranormals. With our champion, we will. I will not answer more questions here. Speaking the name of our champion in this place will certainly draw more attention than is needful." Lilith turned to the figures around her, and for a moment, the fog drifted apart, and Mandi could see Lilith's youthful, flawless face. Her skin was tinged purple-grey, her eyes glowed deep amber. Something about her seemed…changed. "Thank you for meeting my sisters. They are prepared to serve the Deep One, and now all is ready. Go now, make your preparations. The time is nearly at hand for us to act."

The thirteen others *bowed* to Lilith, and Mandi caught a murmur of agreement on the air as one by one the figures dissipated, leaving on a gust of wind just as they'd come. The last one lingered, still bowing near Lilith, reaching a trembling hand toward her.

"Has a vessel been chosen?" Her voice creaked with the ancient tones of a true crone, a witch who had lived many centuries.

"It is unwilling, but I am told she prefers them that way." Lilith's face was again obscured by fog. Mandi strained her eyes trying to see. Shadows gathered beyond their circle, growing clearer even than her own friends' faces.

"You've done well." The crone turned, pausing at a figure across the circle from Mandi. "This one does not have the heart for our task."

"I am aware. A plan is being made. It must be done…carefully. She is beloved."

The crone figure nodded slowly. "Do it quickly." And then she, too, disappeared.

Mandi could not discern who the crone had referenced. Was it one of her sisters? One of Lilith's? They might not be in the same order as the circle they stood in back on the Earth plane. But she could recognize, hovering in the air above the coven member, the faint shadows of a bat and a pistol, and her heart seized.

"We must go." With a harsh swipe of her hand through the air, Lilith gathered the silver ties that bound them to her, and they were once again taken through time and space, back to the first plane.

Mandi stumbled on landing, despite being within her astral form. There was no solid ground beneath her feet, and yet some catch within her body had made her stumble through the air just as if she had tripped.

"They are powerful allies, Lilith," said a deep alto. Hecuba. Mandi drank in the woman's scarred face, determined to memorize it for reference when her sight dimmed again, and she could no longer see.

"But will it be enough?" a bird-like voice asked. It belonged to Beatrice, a woman as slight and trembling as a sparrow in a cat's mouth. Her astral form twitched and fidgeted.

"It will be enough to cast the largest circle that has ever been cast the world over. We are gathered, and yet there are still preparations to be made. Our own pentagram sits dark, awaiting our power to charge it for a portal that will take us to Washington. There we will procure our vessel and call forth our champion."

"Lilith, who is our champion?" Dana asked, her voice sweet and clear. Her eyes were wide. Mandi glanced at her other friends across the circle. Anita observed her fingernails, as if afraid of Lilith's reaction to Dana's innocent questioning. Meg stood with hands clasped, quietly observing. And Honey...Honey's narrow face seemed hollowed out, pale and grey with fear. Mandi wanted to rush to her friend, to make her a cup of tea and tell her it would be all right, but she didn't dare move while Lilith turned slowly, staring them all down. Her flesh had returned to normal, her eyes a vivid blue as they always were. Had Mandi imagined the changes she'd seen before?

"This name is a name of power, and you'd do well not to forget that. Our champion is none other than the Deep One herself: Ragranoth."

Mandi's body reacted viscerally to the name as it was spoken. She'd heard it before, when Lilith had called the priests and priestesses forth to meet them in the astral realm, but she recalled another time. A time sitting beside Violet, being told in a whispered tone surrounded by totems of protection, the names of the great demons that dwelled in the lower astral realms.

"I tell them to you once. You will remember them, without need to study, for studying even their names can attract darkness to your soul." Violet's voice of warning rang in Mandi's ears. *"Sogerith, Vaken, Zal'gadol, Ragranoth..."*

"But...that being is a *demon*. Aren't they...evil?" Mandi asked.

Lilith faced her, the smile on her face unpleasantly stretched, as if it strained her to maintain it. "Demon is such a crass term. More accurate to think of them as 'lower vibrational beings,' and before you ask whether we couldn't recruit a being from a higher dimension, they have refused to hear our petitions." Lilith's brow furrowed, darkening her eyes into a hooded glower. Her expression lightened almost immediately after, however, a shift that left Mandi's mind reeling. "But never mind that. We will have all the power we need once we purify a body for her."

"Let us return. I'm eager to begin," Jasper said with a rush. Her cheeks were flushed, perhaps excited at the prospect of working with such a powerful alternate-dimension being. But Mandi's heart clenched at the thought, years of Violet's warnings about dealing with demons swirling in her mind.

Jasper disappeared. Dana gave Mandi a wave and a slight smile before disappearing herself. Mandi blinked. She'd hardly looked at her friend's face this time. She was already taking this sight for granted.

In a moment, she was alone with Lilith. "Do not dally. We are waiting for you." Lilith, too, vanished.

Mandi stood taking in the room, the pentagram chamber in the basement of the cabin of Camp Silver Lake, she noted the large black vault in the corner, a wooden table, and in the center of the room, the large star-shape etched into the cement floor. Reluctantly, she moved to her body and laid down, letting darkness fold back over her as she reconnected with her physical self.

Blind again. The stark difference was enough to make her chest and head ache with the desire to cry, but she stifled the feelings and sat up slowly, the crystal twinging in her side, and then the sensation left.

"What is the plan once we are in D.C.?" Dana's voice inquired.

"We need to obtain the vessel, the body in which Ragranoth will dwell. I'm counting on Mandi for this. You'll play a pivotal part in obtaining an audience with this person. After all, how can she refuse you? A disabled person of color come to petition on behalf of the most disadvantaged population in the country," Lilith said, then chuckled deeply.

A politician, then. "This person...she knows that I'm a witch?"

"No. She believes you to be part of a human-based organization that supports paranormal rights. A gift will be opened in her presence, one that will render her unconscious. Then we will open a portal and bring her to us."

Mandi's eyebrows raised. "This seems risky for the coven. Capturing a high-profile politician in broad daylight with an unauthorized portal? I understand what you intend with this champion, but is it really in the best interest of the coven?"

Silence followed her words. Mandi kept her chin up. She was priestess of the coven. Lilith herself had given her charge over their care and keeping. It was her right to question this ambition that Lilith now drew them into.

"It's obvious you care for the safety of our coven sisters, Mandi. I admire that. But this has gone beyond our simple coven. What we do now is in the best interest of all our brothers and sisters in magic, for witches and warlocks the world over. Do not limit your scope of influence. You have an opportunity to be a key part in. Don't you trust me?"

Her side throbbed, right near the tiny crystal wand that splinted her magic. She had trusted Lilith with her life, then. Could she trust Lilith with her future, and the future of the coven, as a whole?

"I do. I trust you," Mandi said.

"Ready," Hecuba announced. Mandi heard the crackle of energy that indicated an active portal.

"Wait, we aren't going to pack?" Meg asked.

"No. All we need we can obtain at our destination. The time is now," Lilith said.

Mandi's heart sank. Her stones. They sang to her from her room, now next to Lilith's, crying for her from their velvet-lined boxes. She took in a shuddering breath and steeled herself. She would return for them when this was over. And there would be crystal shops near the nation's capital. She could replace some of her favorites, at least. For now, all she had was a single rose quartz. She touched it for comfort, glad she'd picked it up that morning.

Lilith's hand touched Mandi's arm, making her jump. "Go on, dear. I'll come through with you, and the others will follow."

Mandi breathed in and moved in the direction of the portal. She felt its energy tingle across her skin, not hot or cold, pulling at her slightly. She stepped through, feeling the magic pass through her cells, changing them, rearranging them.

She stood on the other side; the sound of a distant crowd muffled by walls around her. Was she in a room?

"This way, Mandi," Lilith's voice called from a short distance ahead. Mandi walked until she felt a brick wall. It was slightly damp, indicating she was outdoors. She ran her fingers along the wall, avoiding objects at her feet, walking around a large metal object that seemed like it could be a dumpster. She was in an alley of sorts. When she emerged from the entrance onto the main sidewalk, the crowd grew much louder. People surged past her, bumping her on all sides.

"Mandi!" Dana's familiar voice cried out. Mandi turned toward it, waving an arm, hoping she faced the right direction.

Dana breathlessly came up, accompanied by another person. "I've got Meg and Honey with me."

"What's happening? Where are we?" Mandi asked, clasping hands with her friend.

"I'm not sure. D.C. for sure, at a parade, I think."

"A parade?"

"I don't know. Not exactly. A crowd of people is gathered. They're looking at…" Dana gasped.

"I want to see," Mandi muttered. She reached out and grabbed one of the hands of her friends that touched her arm. "Catch me," she said, only giving the person a moment before she split from her body, her astral form hovering above the crowd. She looked down and saw Honey and Meg trying to adjust their grip on Mandi's unconscious body and keep her from falling into the street.

"Have you guessed yet?" Lilith's voice floated out of seemingly nowhere. Mandi glanced around, noticing Lilith hovering a slight distance away.

"Guessed what?"

"Who our vessel will be?" Lilith's arm straightened, pointing to the podium ahead.

Following Lilith's arm with her eyes, Mandi's gaze landed on a woman with dark, carefully coiffed hair and an immaculate blue suit. She stepped down from the podium, headed towards a waiting car in a cleared pocket in the crowd. Suited men and women with wires in their ears surrounded her, holding people back as she climbed into a shiny black car. The woman's face turned, and she waved at the crowd of onlookers, who cheered and waved signs and flags.

Mandi's entire being went rigid as it struck her who this woman must be. She'd never seen that face before, but there was no mistaking why the people would be gathered, why the news crew cameras followed the armored car, reporters jabbering about the event that had just taken place.

It was the president. Lilith was going to let a demon possess the President of the United States.

CHAPTER FIFTEEN
ZEKE

ZEKE'S BONES GROANED AT the effort it took him to transform into his human form. A full hour later, he stood in the bathroom, freshly showered and shaved, wishing he'd thought to have his clothes cleaned the night before. It wasn't how he wanted to present himself to his family after five years missing. He wanted to make a good impression.

He adjusted the black tourmaline on the cord around his neck, untwisting it so it laid flat again. Tonight would be the full moon, and he'd either be safely at home, protected by the physical and magical precautions his parents always had in place when the family pack transformed or back here, locked in his room alone. It all depended on if they disowned him or not.

If they did disown him, he wouldn't blame them.

Zeke's motorcycle took him through downtown Chicago to the west side. He parked in front of a building that smelled of blood and his childhood. Sweet Butchery. He removed his helmet, eyeing the package strapped to the back, and after a moment, decided to bring it with him. He tucked it under his arm and entered the building, bell ringing on the door as it swung open.

White linoleum, stainless steel case filled with various cuts of meat. Zeke didn't recognize the man working the counter at first. He was most likely a relative, but which one?

The man froze in his wiping down of the register when he saw Zeke.

"You!" He exclaimed. He glanced over his shoulder. No one else was by the slicers and tables behind him, they were all in the back. He looked back to Zeke. "Ezekiel?"

The squint in the man's eyes gave Zeke his first clue. "Cyril!" Good ol' Uncle Cyril, his father's youngest brother.

"Man, I never thought I'd see you alive again. Come here," Cyril gestured with his beefy arms, moving around the edge of the counter and coming to clap Zeke on the shoulders. He gazed into Zeke's eyes so long and hard, Zeke caught himself shifting his stance. No. Channel the alpha energy. He had to maintain the upper hand, not become a pup again.

Cyril laughed. "So you went and found yourself a pack. Not hard to guess, given that color in your eyes. But still, one has to wonder why your own pack wasn't good enough. You settle down?"

"Nah. They tried to pair me with the alpha female, but she was in love with a siren." *And I am in love with a witch.* Zeke kept that part to himself. It wouldn't go over well. "It was a necessity, not so much a choice."

Cyril chuckled. "We figured you got yourself into some kind of trouble. Your pa looked for you, you know. Months. Years. After the butchery nearly closed down, he had to quit. Where'd you end up, son?"

Zeke avoided Cyril's curious gaze and watched as a young woman entered with a cart full of various packages. She hauled them onto the tables, unwrapping some, carrying an armload of others to the case at the front of the store. She stopped, barely catching the top packages as they tried to cascade from her arms.

"Girls, you remember your oldest brother," Cyril said, grinning and spreading his arms. "He's back!"

"Agetha?" Zeke hadn't been able to keep his triplet sisters apart when he'd lived with them. Another girl burst through the back doors, dark hair put up in a hairnet and looking identical to the girl carrying the meat. Another face appeared behind hers, then they both fled into the back room. The one that remained, her arms full of meat, unloaded hastily into the case, eyes darting to Zeke with unsuppressed terror.

Zeke forced his face to soften, careful not to bare his teeth. "There now, pup. No need to be afraid. Do you know where pa is?"

She shook her head, glancing to Cyril, then wiped her hands on her apron and ran from the room.

Cyril clicked his tongue. "They're skittish these days. Seeing you, it's like a ghost. We assumed you were dead. Why didn't you call?"

"I need to talk to my father, Cyril. Is he here?" Zeke moved to go behind the counter, but Cyril blocked him, crossing his arms over his bulky chest.

"He's not in the back. He's in a meeting. You'd best wait here until he's done." Cyril gestured with his head.

Zeke saw the door, now. He'd assumed it was a fire exit. He walked over, ignoring Cyril's sputtering, and pushed on the handle.

Modern classical music wafted over him, along with a thousand good smells. Chandelier light cascaded down, lights twinkling amidst soaring architecture. Zeke gaped. It was the type of place he'd never be able to afford an appetizer, much less a plate.

The tables were empty this time of the morning, all except for one. Five men sat at a table, three in suits, two in the white aprons of the butcher trade. Zeke's eyes narrowed at the man with the perfectly gelled hair sitting between the other two suits.

Their voices drifted over to him.

"An extension is going to cost you, Antonio, you know that. Why not pay now? I know your shop is doing well enough." The man in the center pointed at the paperwork in front of him on the table.

"Well enough, if it weren't for the skimming you're doing," Antonio, Zeke's father, growled, holding his arms folded over his chest. "We barely make enough after your fees to support our family."

The man chuckled. "If you'd let some of the whelps work for me, you wouldn't have so many mouths to feed."

"We don't sell our own." The man next to Zeke's father spoke up. Zeke couldn't believe it was Robert; his oldest younger brother had grown taller than their father in the past few years, from shrimp to giant.

"You sure there ain't inbreeding going on? There's more of you every time I look." One of the other suited men sneered at Zeke's father, and Zeke's fists clenched. Hairs grew on the side of Robert's face, and his mouth and nose began to elongate. Antonio placed a hand on Robert's arm. It was a dangerous day to test tempers, this close to the full moon.

Zeke breathed hard, then walked up to the table.

"What does he owe?" he asked quietly. All of the men glanced, then stared at him.

Bruno's grin widened, looking from Antonio to Zeke and back again. "This is one of your pups, isn't it? The eldest, returned at last. Well, then, this could change things significantly." He looked Zeke up and down.

Antonio blinked slowly, turning to face Bruno without reacting to Zeke's appearance. "Our agreement stands. We will make next month's payment as usual. Thank you for your time." He pressed his hands on the table and stood, moving more stiffly than Zeke ever remembered. His hair was streaked with grey, too, and his face relaxed into an exhausted expression.

"Dad, I have money. I could—" Zeke grabbed his father's arm. Antonio looked at him, almost sadly, then used his other hand to remove Zeke's fingers in a single swift motion. He still had plenty of strength, it appeared.

"You weren't here to get into it, so stay out of it." Antonio grabbed a cane from beside his chair and walked steadily toward the door to the butchery. Robert glared at Zeke, a mixture of shock and anger, and followed their father out.

When Zeke glanced back at Bruno, the man was putting on his suit coat, his men gathering up the papers and putting them into a briefcase. Bruno noticed Zeke still standing there and motioned with two fingers.

"Come with me to my car. I'd like to speak with you."

Zeke hesitated. He'd gotten caught up in mob business before. Adolescent mob business, but all the same, it had landed him in a Naturalization camp. But meeting privately with Bruno would give him a chance to offer the money he had, and possibly make a deal of his own to free his family from under the mob's thumb. It was the least he could do after being so careless before. He nodded at Bruno and walked out of the restaurant with him.

The sunlight seemed too bright. Zeke squinted against the painful light reflecting off of the black stretch limo on the street. One of the thugs opened a door for Bruno and Zeke. Zeke slid in, sitting awkwardly on the smooth white vinyl, taking in the tricked-out interior of the vehicle. A plastic partition was in place behind him. The seat he sat in faced opposite what a normal car seat would, and he imagined it might not be easy to get used to driving backward.

Bruno pushed an intercom button on a console beside him. "Just around the block, Maddock."

The car engine started, and it pulled forward into traffic.

"I remember you, you know." Bruno eyed him with a practiced amber stare, his wolf eyes shining past his human ones and scrutinizing him.

"I didn't expect you to," Zeke replied.

"I remember all the young men who foolishly seek to date my daughter. Most of them end up dead. I assumed the same of you when you vanished. What happened?" Bruno cocked his head. It made Zeke's ears itch. Not his human ears, but the location on his head where his wolf ears would be if he shifted. He resisted the urge to change forms and scratch.

"We were stupid. Got caught running high in mixed forms. The others scrammed, I got cornered and captured."

Bruno nodded. "Did your time, I suppose. And escaped? But surely you didn't return just to endanger your family? That doesn't seem like a Costas thing to do."

Zeke shook his head. "The camp I was put in folded. I took advantage and left." His mouth felt dry. Thinking about leaving made him think about Mandi.

"You Naturalized?" Bruno asked the question abruptly, leaving no room for Zeke to answer around it.

"Yes."

"You're a liability. But I assume you know that. Any pack that takes you on will have your record to deal with. These days, that could be an advantage or disadvantage. You've done well to shake your government babysitter if you made it this far without getting taken back in. We can work with that."

Zeke waited, not sure how to respond.

Bruno shifted in his seat, crossing his legs. "I could use a wolf with sense, like you. Find a position of leadership within one of my sub-packs. And I'd allow you to quietly work off your pa's debt, if that's what you want to do. A decade of steadfast service, and he'd be free from our agreement. Might even acknowledge you as his son again, if his pride doesn't get the better of him."

"What *does* my family owe you?"

Bruno chuckled and glanced out the window, then back at Zeke. "I'm not prepared to call an ambulance if you were to go into shock. Let's just say, it's a tidy sum, and your pa won't pay it off in his lifetime unless he wins the lottery. With your help, though, he might be free before he gets to his deathbed. I made the same offer to your brothers, you know. They turned me down. I think you're smarter than that."

"It's a good offer," Zeke admitted.

Bruno leaned forward, putting both feet on the floor of the car, his hands clasped. He stared straight at Zeke, eyes pulsing with a mesmerizing sort of pull that drew Zeke in. He couldn't look away. Here was an alpha that exuded dominion.

"I can tell you feel a lot of guilt over not being here for your family these past few years. You might even think that if you hadn't been captured, they wouldn't be mixed up with me now. But I can tell you, The White City pack owns Chicago. It was only a matter of time before your old man came to me.

Your leaving just expedited the process. And now you have to decide, are you going to spend the rest of your life groveling and trying to make it up to them? Are you going to waste your alpha potential? I see it in you. You could be a dangerous wolf, a valuable asset to the right pack. But not if you go belly up to make up for a foolish, youthful mistake."

Zeke breathed heavily through his nose, feeling his nostrils flare. He didn't want to admit it, but Bruno had nailed his intentions and insecurities precisely, after knowing him for a handful of minutes. Working for Bruno, Zeke could pay back the debt he felt to his father without injuring his pride. Eventually, he could wear down his father and be welcomed back into the family pack. But would he still like who he was at the end of it?

The car slowed. Zeke glanced out the tinted windows and saw his borrowed motorcycle.

"Thanks for your time." Zeke held out his free hand.

Bruno clasped it. "Think about it. Our pack is thriving. We can support you."

Zeke's jaw clenched, more angry with himself for considering Bruno's offer than anything. He hesitated before stepping out of the car.

"One more thing. Can you tell me where my family lives now?"

Bruno ripped a piece of paper from a nearby pad and scribbled across it. "You'll see how we've taken care of them. Not just the shop. They have a nice setup, unlike that cramped apartment you were all shoved into. You'll have to tell me what you think."

Zeke took the paper without looking at it and stepped out of the car without another word. He strode over to the bike, re-attaching the package as the limo pulled away. He couldn't take Bruno up on his offer until he'd exhausted every attempt to get back into the family pack. With his father giving him the cold shoulder, there was only one option left.

The Elders.

Every pack had them. The grandsires; the retired alpha and their mate. If he succeeded in convincing the Elders, they would petition his father, the alpha, who would take their word with far more weight than anyone else. If he didn't succeed before the moon rose, he'd be forced to return to that seedy hotel to ride out the transformation.

With the sticky note in hand, Zeke sped through the streets of Chicago. The prickling of the impending transformation urged him to go slightly over the speed limit, and he pushed it, letting the thrill of speeding take the edge off of his rising pulse and adrenaline. He had hours still until the sun went down, but the pull of the moon was strong, even in the bright daytime.

When he arrived at the address on the paper, he thought he'd made a wrong turn, at first. He checked and double-checked, glancing from the numbers on the page to the manicured lawn that led up to the mansion in front of him. With a surreal sort of feeling, he parked the motorcycle on the circular driveway, walked up the long walk to the porch and pressed the doorbell.

It rang loudly through the house. No rushing footsteps followed, no shouts that someone was at the door. No stiff-faced butler answered either, which Zeke had been prepared for. Instead, the door quietly creaked open, revealing a slight young woman about Zeke's age. Zeke froze, blinking like an idiot on the porch while the woman looked on with widening eyes.

"Can I help you?" She asked, her greek accent thick. She belonged to one of the older families, or perhaps had come over from their home country. She smelled purely of wolf, not covered by any of the fake scents humans were prone to wearing.

Zeke cleared his throat. "Uh, yeah, sorry, I'm here to visit Theron and Iris?"

The young woman's brow creased. "I'm not permitted to let anyone in the house while Antonio is away."

Zeke breathed in. "I'm his son. His oldest son. Ezekiel. Perhaps you've heard of me?"

She shook her head, then tucked a strand of pretty brown hair behind her ears and folded her arms. "They do not speak of you. I have seen your face, though, I think, in an old picture." She cocked her head. "You have been gone a long time."

Zeke nodded. "Too long." He craned his head, trying to get a look inside the house. It was decorated as lavishly as the outside. "Do you take care of my grandparents?"

"Sometimes. Often the littlest ones as well." She hesitated, then opened the door wider. "You are family. You smell like family. But I hope I do not get in trouble for letting you in."

"I don't mean to cause trouble." He tried to smile without baring his teeth.

"I'm Cressida, by the way," the woman said when he'd stepped inside. "Your grandmother is usually in the front room this time of day." Cressida took off down the hall and opened the ornate bronze handle of the second door to the right of the hall. To the left, a carpeted staircase rose to another story. Zeke brought his attention to the room that opened before him.

It was dark, curtains drawn, and lit with a blueish light from a TV screen. The colors flickered across an old woman's still face, cast in enough shadow from the side of her chair that Zeke couldn't quite tell if she was asleep or not.

"Go ahead." Cressida nodded.

Zeke stepped lightly, trying to make enough noise that he wouldn't frighten the woman into a heart attack, but she didn't react to the slight creak of the floor or the scuff of his shoes on the carpet. He approached the chair, considering whether he should touch her shoulder, then thought better of it and scooted around until his body blocked the television.

"Eh? Get out of the way, Antonio. I don't have time for your antics today," his grandma croaked, waving her hand.

"Grandma, it's me, Ezekiel."

Her mouth dropped open, and her eyes grew wide as she adjusted her spectacles. "Zeky?" She flipped off the television and clapped her hands, turning on the lights automatically.

Zeke grinned and sank to his knees, opening his arms and allowing her to collapse into him. She was heavy. Not a frail, bones-and-skin woman like some grandmothers. Zeke tried not to grunt or fall backward, his enhanced strength and balance the only things keeping him upright in the awkward position.

A little sob shook through Grandma's body. Zeke patted her back, heart swelling inside him. After a moment, she sniffed and sat back up with a little push from Zeke.

"Let me take you in properly, now." She smiled through her tears and reached for Zeke's hand. He let her clasp it in her wrinkled palms. He took a deep breath in, his nose filling with the smell of her. Something floral, something spicy in the undertones, but no wolf.

Grandma was the only human in the family.

He leaned back and smiled at her. She had never wanted Pappy to change her, and it showed in her aged face and the creak in her joints. Werewolves aged much more gracefully than humans did.

"Where's Pappy?" Zeke searched her face, noting how her smile dimmed slightly.

Grandma reached into the seat of her maroon armchair. She blew her nose into a pale pink handkerchief she pulled out. "Oh honey, he passed last year."

"Passed?" A werewolf like Zeke's pappy should have lived decades longer.

"It was seeing your father get into cahoots with that Bruno fellow. He didn't agree, they got into a fight. It was nearly a full-on pack war." She shivered in her chair. "Theron wouldn't concede. It was almost as if he went mad and lost all reason."

"Dad killed him." Zeke stared blankly past his grandmother, trying to envision what would have happened had he been there. Could he have stopped it? Not likely. Two enraged alpha werewolves could rip a young werewolf apart, and would have if he'd gotten in the way. When the wolf instinct took over, even family ties were forgotten.

"Now then, where have you been all these years?" Grandma asked.

"I'd like to know the same thing," a male voice said from the doorway. Antonio stood with his arms crossed over his thick chest. He took a big sniff in, then huffed the air out with a snort. "You reek of another pack."

Zeke stood. "Dad, I—"

"Say the word and I'll chase him outta here," Robert growled from behind Antonio.

"Me too." A second head appeared behind his father, skinnier than Robert's.

"Phil?" Zeke asked hesitantly. Man, he'd gotten tall. The scrawny 12-year-old Zeke had known was practically a man, beard coming in and everything.

The smell of the three fierce males struck Zeke's nose like a wall, anger rolling off them in their scent, sending a clear warning to Zeke as if he were an intruder trying to steal their females rather than a long-lost brother.

"Look, I know this doesn't look good, but I came to make things right."

"Full moon is tonight," Robert snapped. "What made you think this was the perfect time for an emotionally charged family reunion?"

"You abandoned your pack and found another. Go back to them." Antonio gestured with his head, setting his jaw.

Zeke stepped outward, stabilizing his human form. He clenched his fists, resisting the urge to pop one in his old man's face. "Not until you hear me out."

"Pup has a death wish." Phil laughed, rolling up his sleeves.

"Not a pup anymore," Zeke claimed.

"Tony, listen to the boy. He deserves that much," Grandma chided, leaning over the arm of her chair. Her brow was creased heavily with worry. Zeke didn't want this to turn south and have her witness family infighting again. Especially not after what she'd told him about Pappy. But her being human didn't diminish her influence as an Elder in the pack, either, and Zeke could see her words working on his father.

"We'll speak in the den," Antonio barked. He turned on his heel and shoved his way past Robert and Phil, who glowered at Zeke. Little brothers, not so little any longer, their opinions poisoned by whatever his father thought of him. Deserter. Traitor to the pack. How could Zeke have thought he'd be received any differently?

"Speak to the human in him," Grandma said to Zeke's retreating back.

If only Zeke knew how.

His brothers led him to a chipped wooden door, the least kept thing about the entire house that Zeke had seen so far. It opened into a dark stairwell lit by a single bare bulb. He followed them down to a surprisingly cozy-looking space, a room filled with bean bags and a slouchy couch perfect for movies and video games and family gathering. Zeke had a hard time picturing the scowling faces in front of him smiling or laughing.

"Have a seat." Antonio gestured to an armchair at the edge of the L-shaped furniture arrangement.

Hesitantly, Zeke sat, rubbing his hands on his knees. "Thanks for seeing me. I...There's a lot to explain."

"Damn right," Rob muttered. He sat farthest from Zeke next to Phil, who nodded. They both had their arms crossed to match Antonio's stiff posture.

"I didn't run away," Zeke blurted. "I know, given how I used to be, that that comes as a surprise."

The three exchanged glances.

Rob spoke first. "We figured you ran off. Probably with some chick. Too many alphas under one roof, Dad said."

Zeke shook his head. "I snuck out that night to hang with Theresa Genovese."

"Good for nothing brat," Antonio muttered under his breath. His ignorance dug under Zeke's skin, and his blood simmered like it did when he was last under this roof.

Zeke curled his fingers into his hand, then straightened them, focusing on the movement to keep his breathing even. "I know you had issues because she wasn't a lykan, but can we let that go for now? It's not important."

"It's always important. Blood-mixing taints our lines," Antonio said.

Zeke breathed deep and managed to look at Antonio calmly. "This is my story. Do you want to hear it, or not?"

Antonio seemed to realize that something was different, now, about Zeke. He nodded curtly.

"We were hanging out, doing dumb teenager stuff. The girls dared us to shift and run across the street. It was dark, but there were people out. Most of the guys chickened out. I said I'd do it, along with this other guy. David Luciano, I think. I had all this adrenaline; I wasn't thinking about anything except impressing Theresa."

Antonio muttered something in Greek. It had been a long time, but Zeke got the gist.

"So, er, Dave and I took off down this alley, and we burst out onto the street all changed. I was halfway across when I heard the shouts. We split up. I saw the yellow lights and heard the pop of the taser before it hit me. Hurt like hell. When I came to, I was human and laying in a bed. I couldn't tell them who I really was; I didn't want them to trace my trail back to the family. That was always my first thought."

"Glad you had some sense, at least," Antonio muttered.

Zeke ignored him. "The guy left and came back with food. Said it was mine in exchange for my name. I don't know how I came up with it so fast, but I gave him one. Zeke Mandova. I told him I lived on the streets without a family. He bought the story and explained to me about the Naturalization program and asked me if I wanted to participate. He said he would give me a choice: military or the camp. I chose camp. They shipped me off that day to Camp Silver Lake in Oregon."

"They have one in Arkansas, now," Rob said.

Zeke nodded. "I heard about it. Thought about asking for a transfer, but I didn't want to give them any reason to think I had something to be out here for. Plus, by then I had my own pack to lead."

"You had your own pack?" Rob sputtered.

"No way!" Phil exclaimed.

Zeke rubbed his hand on the arm of the couch. "Come on you guys, I wasn't that irresponsible."

"Yeah, you were." Rob sat up and shifted his seat on the couch. "How the hell did they ever let you be in charge?"

"It makes sense, actually." Antonio had his hand on his face in a thinking gesture. He considers Zeke, then sighed and switched from right leg on the left knee to the opposite. "Your mother thought something was wrong with you at first. She was still pretty new to all the politics of a pack. Pappy explained it to her. 'You gave birth to an alpha,' he said. 'He'll fight until he leaves the house, and eventually, it will grow to respect.'"

Zeke shrugged. "It's not the way I would have chosen to do it."

"No, but you got it. Wish granted. You've been gone from the family so long I hardly recognize your scent anymore." Antonio stood and headed for the fridge. "Beer anyone?"

"Since when did Dad start drinking beer?" Zeke asked. No one answered.

"I'd like one," Phil replied. He glanced at Zeke. "So, why'd you come back?"

Antonio came back with the bottles, handing one out to Zeke. He took it. He hadn't had beer since before the Naturalization camp. Paranormals and drinking didn't really go together, so the camp had been dry.

"He's in trouble. Why else?" Antonio said, glaring into the mouth of his bottle.

Zeke adjusted his position on the couch, hating the tight feeling in his chest. "I knew it was time to come back. An opportunity presented itself, and I left." Zeke clasped his hands around the bottle and leaned forward, looking from his father to his brothers. "I came back because I want to help."

Rob smacked his lips after a swig. "If you wanted to help, you should have been here when all this started." He eyed Zeke. "They castrate you?"

"What?" Zeke's brow furrowed. "No. They don't do that."

"Maybe not in Oregon. But they do in Arkansas. Happened to a few friends," Rob said.

"That isn't legal." A tide of anger rose inside Zeke.

Rob shrugged. "Legal or not, it's happening."

There were channels to report abuse, but Zeke didn't have access anymore. If he could get a message to Mandi, maybe she could.

"Looks like you have other priorities. What exactly did you do for five years in a Naturalization camp? You got your card? What else?" Antonio gestured, an unreadable expression on his face.

"Got my card. Became a teacher." Zeke swallowed. "I couldn't leave the state I was Naturalized in."

"Didn't want to, is more like it," Rob said darkly.

"Yes, because I was protecting you. I couldn't tell them I had someone to go home to, could I? The entire family. Ma, the girls..." Zeke choked.

"And how do we know you won't do that now? We could be in serious danger!" Rob shouted, standing. He didn't come to full height, though, hunched over as if his spine had curved, and Zeke could see dark fur prickling through his brother's skin.

"Rob," Antonio barked. "Control yourself."

Rob growled, but the pull of the alpha's authority was strong. He fell back into the couch, the change reverting him back to full human form.

Zeke breathed out steadily. "I know about your deal with Bruno. Not the details, but enough. I'd like to help."

"What about your pack?" Antonio asked.

Zeke flexed his fists and moved his jaw back and forth to loosen the tension there. "Something bad happened at the camp. The original directors were killed, and a new witch took over."

"There's your problem right there. Witches." Antonio knocked back another swig. His bottle was half gone already.

"Anyway, she's got some agenda to lock down the camp and go full-scale rogue. The pack was discussing whether to leave or stay, and I got challenged. My co-alpha...She didn't make it. And I barely escaped with my life."

"Co-alpha? You're married?" Mother's voice came from the doorway.

Zeke jerked around, then pushed himself out of his chair. She was holding a wooden spoon, wearing the same apron he'd always known her to wear, her dark hair greying and coming out of its bun in the back.

"Ma," Zeke said. Tears burned in his eyes. He couldn't figure out how to move his legs all of a sudden. The spoon and the apron and her kind, worried eyes that somehow still held a smile in the creases brought his childhood crashing over him like a wave.

"Well, come here then." She smiled and gestured with the hand holding the spoon, and Zeke stumbled forward, falling into her embrace. He relished her warmth, the smell of olives and citrus that wafted from her skin, and very nearly broke down into a sobbing mess.

Antonio's harsh voice brought Zeke crashing back to reality. "I told you to stay in the kitchen."

"I couldn't find any of the girls to come tell you supper is ready," Ma said indignantly. Zeke straightened, sniffing and wiping at his eyes. Ma looked him up and down. "I'm glad I did come. What a secret you've been keeping from me! Our Ezekiel. I want to know where you've been. I never did believe you'd run away without telling your ma. Did you bring your little Mrs. with you?" Her eyes glittered, and Zeke shook his head.

"No, I'm not married. Sorry to disappoint."

"Then what's this talk of an alpha female and a pack you led together?" Ma raised her thick eyebrows.

"We were friends. Both of us were in love with...someone else." Zeke's mouth went dry as soon as he spoke the words. He hadn't wanted to tell them about Mandi.

Ma made an interested sound and clicked her tongue. "Tell us about her, then. So much more interesting than pack politics."

"She, uh..."

"At least she's lykan," Antonio said into his bottle. "I guess that's as good as it's going to get."

"I didn't say that." Zeke adjusted his grip on the bottle in his hand. He hadn't taken a drink since that first one. His mouth still tasted sour.

"What the hell is she if not lykan?" Antonio asked, eyes narrowed.

Zeke closed his eyes. He had forgotten about Antonio's temper, and his backward, old-fashioned ideas. Most of all, he'd forgotten just how much his dad spoke out against witches.

Antonio read Zeke's expression and his own face contorted. "This girl, not the alpha, but the one you were in love with—she's a witch, isn't she? The silence says it. You know I'd never approve."

"Antonio, why would you say such a thing?" Ma said, crossing her arms over her chest.

"It doesn't matter," Zeke said, raising his voice over his father's response. He'd rather have Antonio's anger directed at him than his mother. "She chose a different path."

Ma's expression softened. "There's a nice Greek lykan girl in the Anastas family across the street. We could invite her over for dinner if you're staying." She sounded so hopeful.

"No, I don't think—" Zeke started.

"You can stay," Antonio said abruptly. He sighed and stood, adjusting the belt on his pants. "No need to drag this out any further. Your mother has made a nice meal and it's going to burn or go cold the longer we sit here."

Zeke blinked in shock. His father had never been one to make quick decisions, and he hadn't had much hope for this one.

His father pointed a finger at him. "You may live here and work with us as long as you agree to bend to my rules. There is only one alpha here. Perhaps you could eventually earn your birthright back and one day challenge me for leadership of this pack. But you will never, under any circumstances, bring a witch into our house." Antonio pointed to the circular, sapphire *mati* hanging above the mantle. "This house is protected from that sort of evil. We don't need you and your desire for blood-mixing to ruin our lines."

Zeke laughed. It was an uncontrollable kind of laugh, born of discomfort and disbelief. "I thought somehow you might have changed. That your prejudice against every other paranormal race out there could have shifted into acceptance. You know, this is why I wanted to get away from you so bad? Not because I wanted my own pack, but because I wanted to live somewhere where they didn't discriminate based on fur-type or ear shape or magical abilities. Even the Naturalization camp respected them more than you."

"I will not be spoken to like this in my own house," Antonio said, his volume rising.

Zeke stepped forward. "And I won't stand for hearing my friends called evil."

Antonio licked his lips. "They're abominations against God, all of them."

"And we aren't?" Zeke snorted. "Nothing could be further from God's design for humankind, and yet you act as if we're somehow above the rest of them."

Antonio's expression darkened, and he cracked his knuckles. "Good thing you showed your true colors before we got used to having you back. I revoke my invitation. You'll leave, now. Tonight. And never return."

"Tony!" Ma gasped.

"Stay out of this!" Antonio burst out. He narrowed his eyes at Zeke.

Zeke's entire frame shook with the desire to unleash the wolf, but he held on for a bit longer.

"Last chance to take it back." His voice was calm, calm like the sea before a storm, calm like the center of a hurricane.

Antonio cocked up his chin. "Never."

Zeke's self-control broke into a thousand pieces. Whatever his convictions to help his family, he couldn't abide hearing Mandi spoken of that way. His muscles and bones burned, ligaments stretched and screamed. His hearing distorted as his mother screamed for Rob and Phil, her voice warbling until his ear structure perfected itself. His ears pricked back toward the lingering sound of her yell, but his head remained trained forward, watching the other wolf complete its transformation.

Zeke ripped at the material tangled around him. He was caught up a moment freeing himself, but so was the other alpha.

The ideals that had caused Zeke to transform vanished as the last of the human DNA burned from his body. The proximity to the full moon phase, only hours away from rising in the sky, obliterated his human sense, but in the final moments of transformation, a message lingered from the complex human emotions and his wolf mind translated it into a single thought: *Kill the alpha.*

CHAPTER SIXTEEN

MANDI

MANDI LAID FLAT ON her back in a comfortable bed. The hotel room was stifling in its silence. The three others she shared a room with slept, as directed by Lilith. They would go sight-seeing later, the witch had promised.

Sightseeing. Before they captured and possibly killed the president.

A chill went through Mandi, and the rose quartz in her pocket hummed in response to the rise of her adrenaline. It did little to calm her. Was the life of one human, a human who had made little progress in making the lives of paranormals better to any degree, worth the cost that a blood sacrifice would exact on Mandi's soul? A little blood magic to improve her ability to travel the astral realms was one thing. But killing a person and calling forth a demon? Mandi felt sick.

She rolled over in bed and closed her eyes, breathing in and out in a familiar rhythm that often helped her calm her mind when she was restless before bed. It was still early in the day, and she had no desire to sleep, but her appointment with the president wasn't until 4 p.m. and Lilith had insisted they all rest.

Mandi drifted in and out. When she finally heard the stirrings of the others, she sat up. Meg shared her room, along with

Hecuba and Jasper. Lilith wanted the coven to be more united, she claimed, splitting Mandi and most of her other friends up among the rooms. Mandi understood, of course, but that didn't help her uncertainty at being paired with complete strangers. She'd made her best effort to get to know them.

"Did you rest well?" she asked, not addressing anyone in particular.

"I slept so hard. I didn't realize I was that tired," Meg said, her voice stretching with a yawn.

"I meditated, mostly. Daytime naps aren't my thing," Hecuba's lower alto voice passed Mandi. It sounded as if the witch were standing in front of the window near Mandi's bed. Mandi had felt it during her exploration of the room when they'd first arrived.

A toilet flushed, and the bathroom door opened. "I sleep during the day and prefer to roam the night," Jasper said as she walked back into the room.

"Fascinating," Meg said. "I've considered a nocturnal lifestyle. It suits herbal work, I've found. Do you have much trouble with it?"

"Not these days. It's more common to keep uncommon hours now than it was a hundred and fifty years ago," Jasper said.

"Surely you aren't a day over thirty-five," Mandi said.

"As you say," Jasper replied, her tone flat in a way that made Mandi think perhaps Lilith's sisters were older than she thought. The older a witch, the more powerful, and unpredictable, she was.

Hecuba clapped her hands. Mandi turned at the sound. "I hope Lilith allows us time in the museums. I've been through the Natural History Museum dozens of times, but the number of magical artifacts contained in the exhibits always amuses me. It's fun to activate a few and confuse tourists."

"Doesn't that trigger the S.T.F. alarms?" Mandi asked.

Hecuba chuckled. "Of course. But it's simple enough to get away in all the chaos. I've never been caught."

"You have so," Jasper argued. "I got you out. And I'd rather not repeat the experience."

"Oh psh. Don't be so serious. It turned out fine."

"I've only had three hours of sleep. Don't push me," Jasper growled.

"How about food?" Meg piped up. Mandi was grateful for the distraction. She had a growing sense of unease about the two strange witches in her room adding to her conflicting thoughts about Lilith's plans with the president.

The four women left together. Mandi used her stick and Meg's offered arm for guidance down the stairs to the hotel lobby. They couldn't gather in the hotel with the others, maintaining an appearance of being separate parties to avoid any chance at suspicion or detection. Thirteen women could no longer gather together safely. Of course, a tour group wouldn't garner as much suspicion as a group that met regularly somewhere, but Lilith wanted to be careful. They would meet at the first monument on their tour list, and there Lilith would divulge the plan for the president.

The hotel had a small cafe attached, so sandwiches were purchased for lunch. It was just after 1 p.m. according to the schedule. As read by Meg, they would catch a shuttle and meet at the Washington Monument at 1:30. They had to hurry.

Mandi was crushed and squeezed and stepped on as the shuttle filled with people who didn't seem to realize that her cane meant she was blind, or rather, didn't care. Meg stood next to

Mandi, trying to make sure she didn't get separated. It smelled like peanut butter and body odor in the tight space. Mandi breathed shallowly and tried not to pass out from the warmth of the crowd. When they disembarked, she couldn't have been more relieved, stumbling out onto the pavement, last out of the shuttle to avoid the rushing crowd. She breathed in the fresh air, catching a whiff of another welcome scent: Honey's sweet herbal perfume.

"A sight for sore eyes. Glad you made it," Honey said at Mandi's side. She grabbed her in a hug, and Mandi hugged her back.

"How are your roommates?" Mandi asked.

"They're…nice." Honey's voice cracked. She paused, then continued. "Except, they don't really talk to me. I asked Serena a question earlier, and she just kept talking to Lorna."

"Maybe she didn't hear you," Meg supplied.

A fit of giggling interrupted their conversation. Mandi turned her head towards the sound, recognizing Dana's voice in their midst.

"Hello everyone!" Dana's chirpy voice said.

"You seem to be enjoying yourself," Meg said. "Like your roommates?"

"Oh yes! Isabel knows so much, and Beatrice is quiet, but so funny! I think I really like them," Dana said the last part in a whisper, as if it was a secret.

"Good for you," Mandi said. There was a sort of tension in the air, though she wasn't sure what it meant. A cool drop on her forehead distracted her from sorting it out. "Is it raining?"

"Just started spitting," Meg confirmed.

"I don't have a jacket," Honey muttered.

"I brought umbrellas!" Lilith's voice appeared as if out of nowhere. There was a rustling as the umbrellas got passed around, and several clicks and wooshes as they opened. The sheltering presence of an umbrella extended over Mandi's head.

"I'll share," Honey said to her.

"Thanks," Mandi replied.

"Okay, we're part of a rather large group, so try to stick to-gether. Especially you, Mandi. The tour guide is aware of you, but I've told her we will keep track of you ourselves and that she doesn't need to make any special accommodation. We don't want to draw undue attention to any of our party." Lilith's voice carried away on the wind, making it a bit faint.

An even fainter voice started as soon as Lilith stopped. It was the tour guide, introducing herself and the tour.

"Why the pretense?" Mandi muttered, feeling annoyed. She adjusted her grip on her cane.

"What was that?" Honey asked, her arm brushing Mandi's.

"I don't understand why we're playing tourist. It doesn't make sense."

"Fresh air makes us better thinkers, Mandi dear." Lilith said from behind her. When had she gotten there? "Truly, it is only the first monument that is critical to our cause. The tour group is a camouflage, of sorts."

That made sense. The tour guide called for them to move forward. The first stop was the Washington Monument. The shuttle had dropped them across the street from it. Mandi fol-lowed Honey's guidance and the tapping of her cane. As soon as they crossed the road and stepped onto the sidewalk, Mandi felt a rush of energy zing through her.

"Woah," Honey breathed beside her. "Did you feel that?"

"Yeah," Mandi said. "Is it...is it a pentagram?"

"A giant one," Dana said. "You can't see it, though. I think it's been drawn into the substrate somehow. The monument is at the center."

"What does it look like?" Mandi asked.

"Just a giant stone pillar with a pointed top in the middle of a field," Meg said from Mandi's left.

"It's an obelisk," Dana informed her.

"Sorry, obelisk," Meg said. "It's acting as a crystal wand, essentially, but near as I can tell, it's just made of stone."

There was a strong, thrumming energy pulsing from something large ahead, Mandi could sense it. The wind picked up, dragging her hair back and forth, flicking it into her face and then away again. It tugged at her cane. The rain increased, still just a sprinkle, but more constant. Mandi's heart rate rose. She tapped her way forward, and this time the crowd responded to her cane, letting her forward to touch the cool stone surface.

"Granite and marble," Mandi muttered, running her hand along it. "Something else...Gneiss? And Fluorite?"

"There is a fluorite core. It was installed a few months ago, just for this purpose," Lilith explained.

"Then this is where the...where it will happen?" Dana asked.

"Yes," Lilith confirmed, her voice lowered. "There are others, just like this one, at pivotal points across the U.S. When they're all activated and connected, we'll have enough power to call forth our champion."

"Power at this scope has not been required for centuries," Isabel said, admiration and longing in her voice.

"It's about time," Jasper said.

"So exciting," Selena breathed.

"It sounds dangerous," Honey said, her voice trembling. Mandi reached out and squeezed her friend's hand.

"We're going to be part of a vast change. It's unsettling, but it'll be for the best in the end," Mandi said.

"Do you really believe that?" Honey's voice dropped to a whisper, meant only for Mandi to hear.

"Gather over here, girls, and let us discuss the history of this great monument to our nation's first president." Lilith sounded like a teacher, her voice pitched higher than usual. Mandi followed Honey's lead and crowded in with the others as they separated from the tour group.

Mandi felt a familiar muffling as a spell closed around them, and Lilith's voice became clearer without the chatter of dozens of other people.

"Can you feel the energy here? It's powerful, isn't it? Imagine what it will feel like with the full moon above us, and the combined magic of thirteen covens," Lilith said.

Honey gripped Mandi's hand, and the umbrella's chill metal handle pressed into Mandi's upper arm. The tapping of raindrops increased above her head, becoming a solid downpour.

"Is it forecasted to be clear for the spell?" Hecuba asked.

"It is," Serena piped up. "I checked last night."

"Excellent. Mandi, come here," Lilith said, urgency in her voice. Mandi stepped forward, guided by numerous hands from coven sisters whose faces she could not see. She gripped her cane but held it off the ground so she didn't trip. Rain landed in Mandi's hair as she moved between umbrellas until Lilith touched her arm, stopping her forward motion. "While I speak with Mandi, the senior witches will tell the others about their plan in retrieving the vessel today. This must go off without a hitch. It will be tricky, but doable, if everyone does her part."

Conversations broke out among the others.

Mandi," Lilith urged. "I want you to go in alone. There's less of a chance that you'll be detected, and it will be far easier to get you out should any alarms be activated."

Alone? Mandi's mouth went dry. "How will that be possible? The splint doesn't allow us much distance."

Lilith's hand landed on her shoulder, and Mandi felt the coolness of Lilith's skin through her shirt. "You're the perfect one for this position. I will be nearby. When I can go no farther, I will find a place to obscure myself and enter the astral realm to aid you. So far we are able to be at least fifteen feet apart. I can perform a certain spell that may give us some more distance."

"How are we going to get an audience with the president?" Mandi whispered the words, a hushed sort of heaviness overcoming her.

"I've pulled the right strings, paid the right people. It's taken quite some time to maneuver this into place, but you do have an appointment. We just need to make you look the part."

"What part is that, exactly?" Mandi asked.

"Amanda Marckel, a representative of the Rowanite Reformists. You're a supporter of paranormal rights because your and your mother's lives were saved by a pack of werewolves when your car went off the road two years ago. Your meeting is to discuss moving forward on making some key things more accessible to paranormals."

"I have to have a conversation with her?" Mandi's voice went up in a squeak.

"Just greet her," Lilith's voice was infused with confidence. It was almost enough to calm Mandi's anxiety, but she was going to meet with—and lie to—the president! She wasn't sure anything shy of a medical tranquilizer would calm her. "Greet her, thank her for meeting with you, and offer her a gift."

"A gift?" Mandi swallowed the lump in her throat and rubbed the chilled skin on her arm. Even vigorous rubbing did little to warm her goosebump-riddled skin.

"I'll give it to you right before you walk in. It will ensure the president comes without a fight. You'll activate it with a specific phrase, and then we'll come in and deal with the rest."

"That sounds remarkably simple," Mandi said.

Lilith waived her hand carelessly. "There are some tricky parts. The government employs witches, and the others will take care of distracting them. You shouldn't run into any trouble."

"People are going to die, aren't they? Maybe not today, but as part of this plan...someone has to die?" Mandi's words hung in the air, and a chill shuddered through her. Two pistols had been found in her tea leaves. No one had died yet. She was determined no one she cared about would.

The other conversations had finished by now. Within the confines of the muffling spell, the only sound was the rain as the others, all eleven coven sisters, awaited Lilith's answer.

"It is the cost of rebellion. Recall your history lessons. Has there ever been a truly peaceful upheaval on this scale? We're talking about a radical change for this entire country, a change that could eventually move to the rest of the world. Peace comes after the conflict, sisters. We must be brave; we must hold onto our vision of a world where paranormals are no longer suffocated by oppressive laws and regulations. A few lives may be lost, but what is that cost in the face of those who have been lost already?"

Fletcher. Mandi could name a few others, friends who had completed Naturalization and moved on from the camp only to show up in obituaries later.

Her damp curls brushing her cheeks as she nodded her agreement to what Lilith had said.

"What if…what if we're not willing to pay the price?" Honey's voice floated through the air and stung Mandi's ears. She gripped her stick, twisting it anxiously in her hands. Honey couldn't be the one to leave now. Mandi needed her.

"No one is being forced to remain here. If you have doubts, then leave." Lilith's voice took on a harsh edge. "We will find another to replenish our numbers. Witches and warlocks will line up at the door to be part of this circle."

Mandi reached out for Honey, stepping forward. She knew the general direction of her friend, but she wasn't certain. To her great relief, Honey grasped her hands, guiding Mandi to her. They stood facing each other in the rain.

"Honey, I can't do this without you. I want so much for our kind to be free from oppression, to be part of all this, but I need to know you're by my side." Mandi's chest tightened as she waited for Honey's response. When it came, the words were soft, with an edge Mandi had never heard in Honey's voice.

"I'll do it," Honey whispered. "For you, I'll do it."

Mandi hugged Honey, feeling her shiver in her damp clothes. "Thank you," Mandi whispered.

Lilith raised her voice. "It is nearly time to enact the first phase of our plan. Mandi needs to get dressed. The rest of you, lunch and leisure. Be in place when the time comes. Honey, you can attend Mandi with me."

The circle dispersed. Mandi felt the space around her open up as the muffling spell lifted, and the chatter of the real tourists who had braved the rainy weather filled the air once more. The rain had lightened to a sprinkle that no longer needed an umbrella, but Honey came to stand next to Mandi still holding hers anyway.

Mandi touched her friend's arm. "I'm grateful you're coming."

Honey took a deep breath, but didn't respond.

They rode back to the hotel with Lilith. Makeup, hair, and a business suit later, Mandi felt ready for anything. She tugged at the bottom of the suit coat. Wide pant legs swished against her legs, ending just above a pair of heels.

"Lilith, what about the paranormal security measures at the Capitol building?" Honey asked as they finished up their lunch.

There was a long pause. "Oh of course. I got the idea from Mandi, actually. She's always using her stones in such unique ways."

Mandi warmed at the roundabout praise and straightened in her seat. "They really are! Most witches sort of ignore them."

"Yes, well it turns out that the detection devices being implemented by humans get rather scrambled up when crystal signatures interrupt their signals. I thought of using—"

"Black tourmaline," Mandi blurted. She could feel the energy of the stone in the room now, a low, vibrating hum. "You've got some very pure stones. I can hear them."

Lilith laughed. "Yes, I do! I charged them before we came, knowing what we might face. You'll both wear one. They coordinate with your outfits well enough. And I have another gift for you, Mandi. Something that might come in handy should something go wrong."

Lilith tucked the stone and a thin cord into Mandi's hands. Mandi rubbed the uneven surface of the rectangular stone. Black tourmaline didn't take to polishing well. Its frequencies were better amplified in its raw state. She went over the ridges with her fingertips and the stone seemed to warm in her hand, as if to assure her all would be well. She slipped the cord over her neck, remembering a time when she'd gifted Zeke a necklace very similar to this one. Did he still wear it? Her throat closed up. She forced herself to swallow and pushed thoughts of Zeke away.

"And this," Lilith pressed a velvety bag into Mandi's hands. Half a dozen crystals sang inside, telling Mandi their names, reminding her of their properties. Amplifiers and blockers, lures and penetrators. In combination, the stones could be quite powerful. Fortunately, they fit into the pockets of her loose pants.

Mandi rolled the crystals in her palm, listening to the calming sound they made when they clicked together during the shuttle ride to the Capitol. Once the vehicle stopped, Mandi tapped her cane carefully across the shuttle floor, getting to the open door and stepping down with help from Honey. The air outside was humid, but no rain fell.

"Those clouds look horrendous," Honey muttered at Mandi's side. Lilith had also exited the shuttle, although she was pretending not to be with Mandi and Honey.

"Which direction to the front door?"

Honey turned Mandi with hands on both her shoulders, until she was facing the correct way. Mandi took a deep breath and walked forward with more surety than she felt. The heels made her wobble occasionally, especially on wet cement steps with her injured ankle as she climbed.

"You'd think they'd make this a bit more accessible," Mandi huffed once she realized they'd reached the top step. She stopped to catch her breath. The click of doors opening made her straighten, and she tugged at the bottom of her suit and tried to present a confident face to whomever was walking up.

"Tourists," Honey informed her, taking her arm. They waited a moment longer. A woman with strong perfume brushed past Mandi, nearly knocking her over.

"Hey, watch it!" Honey yelled.

A box was thrust into Mandi's hands.

"I'm sorry, darling. Didn't see you there." The perfume smell disappeared. Mandi rubbed her fingers along the edges of the box. It was rectangular, and tied with a ribbon. Inside, nestled in the soft velvet, was a crystal wand. The perfumed woman had been Lilith in her disguise.

"Did she have to ram into you so hard?" Honey muttered, taking Mandi's arm again and guiding her through the front doors. Sleek black security terminals stood sentinel on either side of the doorway. The black tourmaline on the cord around Mandi's neck got warm, then hot, hot, HOT. She swore it burned into her skin, but she bit the inside of her cheek to keep from crying out and then they were through. The stone took a long time to cool. Mandi rubbed the heated spot on her chest.

"It worked!" Honey whispered gleefully. "Your stones are incredible, Mandi."

Mandi breathed in. One hurdle down. Her heels clicked on the marble floors, and she adjusted her step to keep from slipping on the slick surface. Quiet, garbled conversations bubbled around the room. Mandi focused on her breathing and walking.

Honey took her up more stairs. They were stopped at an elevator and asked their names and purpose. Their box was scanned, and they submitted to being patted down. The tourmaline on Mandi's neck heated again, but they apparently passed the test and were allowed to and the flooring changed to carpet, muffling the click of their heels. They halted.

Mandi sniffed, taking in a scent like dust and sandwiches.

"Amanda Marckel with the Rowanite Reformists. I'm her guide, Helen Ludlow." The lie flowed smoothly off Honey's tongue. Only Mandi could hear the hitch in her best friend's breath and feel the pulse quicken through her ribcage.

Mandi put on a wide smile.

The woman at the door clicked her tongue. Her pen scribbled. "Our 4 o'clock. Excellent. You're right on time, we like that. Wait just a moment."

The door opened with a slight creak and Mandi heard shuffling beyond.

"Your 4 o'clock, Madam President."

"Send them in." The president had a somewhat nasal voice that Mandi recognized from the few times she'd heard the president speak on T.V. and earlier that day at the public speech. She moved into the room, Honey at her side.

The unmistakable clicks of cameras and low murmur of many people slammed into Mandi like a wall. There weren't supposed to be so many here. The spelled object Lilith had given her, being held by Honey, would only work on a few. They had been operating under the assumption that there would be no press.

"Lilith said this might happen. What do we do?" Honey whispered, guiding Mandi by the elbow.

Mandi tried to gather her thoughts. "It's fine. It will be fine. Nothing has changed, really." There were more people who could witness their takedown of the president. But if Mandi utilized the stones in her pockets, she could amplify the effects of the crystal wand. She couldn't spread them out in her patterns like she had in her room at the camp, but she could organize them in her mind, draw upon her abilities, and hope for the best.

"Welcome to my office, Ms. Marckel. I hope you don't mind the press, with something as unprecedented as this meeting, I wanted to give the public a glimpse." A chair moved out and an expectant air hovered in the room.

Mandi squeezed the obsidian, asking it mentally to activate. It responded, becoming frigid in her hand.

Honey leaned in toward Mandi. "The president would like to shake your hand, Amanda."

"Oh, of course. I don't mind the press," Mandi lied, holding her hand out. President Evans clasped it, and Mandi forced a smile, holding the pose a bit longer than normal for the sake of the cameras. Then the president released her. Mandi's other hand roamed in her pocket for the jade. The moment it activated, the air in the room warmed. The president put a handkerchief to her head, dabbing as sweat appeared.

"Your proposal intrigued me. Do tell me more about how your group can leverage my Paranormal Work Now initiative to its full advantage."

Mandi licked her lips, then gestured to Honey that she'd like to sit down. Her hand groped for Honey's, found it, and gripped hard. This was where she was supposed to mention the gift before the conversation began. But she couldn't with all the press there. The spell would activate and the reporters and journalists would blast the evidence all over the internet. Why hadn't Lilith told Mandi this could happen? And what would Honey do about it?

"Ms. Marckel? We only have twenty minutes together. Please, don't be shy," President Evans said.

Mandi shifted in her seat and fanned her face. "Forgive me. It's so warm in here." It was warm. Uncomfortably warm. She nudged Honey.

Honey gave a nervous laugh, touching her hand lightly to her head then her chest. "I feel rather lightheaded all of a sudden. Could we open a window, perhaps?"

"No, I'm afraid that's not possible," the president's secretary said. "But perhaps a few of the press would be willing to step out?"

The room emptied. Mandi sensed a lightening of the air. "How many, Honey?" she whispered.

Honey laid three fingers on Mandi's wrist. Three press remained. They'd have to risk it. The wand should be able to handle everyone in the room.

"Thank you ever so much," Mandi gushed to the president. "I'm delighted to be here representing my organization. We have a gift. For you."

Mandi set the ribboned box on the desk and slid it across. Before it left her touch, she breathed in and urged the crystal wand hidden inside to activate, rubbing the crystal quartz hard to amplify the wand's reach.

"Oh, well, thank you. I can open it after..."

"Now, please," Honey's voice was taut. Mandi laid a hand on her arm. She was going to cause suspicion. Someone would pick up on the strangeness of the situation and stop it. After all they'd gone through to get here without detection...

"Very well," the president said, her voice tinged with surprise and resignation. "I delight in receiving...oh."

Mandi muttered a low chant, squeezing the obsidian again, and the temperature in the room dropped twenty degrees. Mandi sucked in her breath. The stone on her chest heated up like it had when she went through the sensors.

Everything went silent. Silent as a tomb.

"Come on, we've got to—" Honey's voice cut off as an alarm blared. Honey cursed, the word sounding extra harsh coming from her normally kind lips.

Mandi shrieked. "The magic—it triggered some kind of sensor!"

Honey grabbed her hand. "We're getting out of here."

"What about the president?" Mandi stood.

"I'll get her. Activate the portal." A blast opened the door with a bang, and wood cracked. Mandi froze, trying to imagine what had just come through.

Honey cursed again. She jerked Mandi around the desk and shoved her hand forward until it rested on a fabric surface. It rose and fell slowly, and Mandi realized it was the president's back.

"On three, transport," Honey said.

"Where to?" Mandi asked, gripping the fabric of the jacket tightly.

"Front steps."

"What about you?"

"One," Honey said, ignoring her concern. "Two. Three!"

Magic sizzled in the air.

Mandi's body buzzed, nearly tearing apart as she transported farther than she'd ever gone before. She burst through the fabric of space and time, stumbling and falling into a crouch on the stone ground beside the prone form of the president. A dagger-like pain stabbed through where the splint was buried in her side, and she clutched at it.

"Honey!" Mandi gasped. No response. No one came to help her, either, and she wondered where the tourists were. Mandi moaned. She was alone. Had Honey transported, or had she gotten caught?

Mandi swept the ground with her hands, looking for her cane. She'd dropped it somewhere, or it hadn't been transported with her. Her hand brushed something large and cold and hard—the pillar. She sucked in and breathed out in a great rush, then scooted to the pillar and sat back against it. Rain spattered on the pavement, a soothing sound in normal circumstances, but the rhythm of the water was maddening now. Mandi scrubbed at her eyes, cheeks sticky with tears. She was alone on the front steps of the Capitol Building.

Mandi leaned her head back against the pillar, wishing she had her shawl. Wishing she was back at the camp learning how to light candles and do stupidly simple things. Things that had driven her crazy, but at least they hadn't put her and her friends in danger. Maybe Violet had been right. Maybe she wasn't ready for this.

Mandi stripped off her high heels and hugged her knees.

Do you have the president? We're coming to get you. Be ready to go through the portal.

Portal? Mandi's head came up. She crawled to the president and hooked underneath her arms, dragging the unconscious body up with her. Perhaps Honey would be with Lilith. Perhaps she'd just transported somewhere else.

A thrum sounded to her left and Mandi turned, the warmth of the portal drawing her in the right direction. She put her hand out and it caught with a tingle in the energy waves. She drew in a shaky breath and dragged the president through.

Someone caught her on the other side. Several others removed the president from her grasp, and Mandi was led to a bed. They were back at a hotel.

"Mandi, you're all right!" Dana cried, hand tightly gripping Mandi's arm.

"Let her catch her breath. Mandi, when you're ready to answer, do you feel any pain? Any shortness of breath?" Lilith asked.

Mandi shook her head. "Honey, is she...?"

Silence met her words. Someone shuffled across the room. The lack of response put Mandi on edge.

She cleared her throat. "Captured?"

"Dead." A single word, like a knife in Mandi's chest. It didn't matter who'd spoken. She choked on her own saliva as she gasped, and what came out was a garbled sort of cry. Dana put her arms around Mandi.

"How could this happen? You had it all planned out! You made us believe as if we couldn't fail!" Mandi yelled, struggling to stand with Dana's arms still firmly around her.

"We didn't fail," Lilith said, her voice cold, emotionless. "We have the president. She lies on the bed across from the one you sit on. Our vessel is ready."

"When you said there would be a cost, that lives would be lost, I didn't think...I didn't think that it would be one of our own." Mandi stopped struggling and stood with Dana's arms clamped around her, her own arms dangling at her sides.

"Remember the tea leaves, Mandi?" Meg asked, her warm voice floating over Mandi from her other side.

Yes, the tea leaves. Two pistols. Honey had been one of them—she hadn't wanted to come, she'd been the most reluctant, Mandi knew. And now, her selfish desire to gain her sight had lost her a dear friend. She had asked Honey to stay. It was her fault. She never should have come here.

Mandi collapsed onto the bed. She put her head into her hands and sat, curled in on her dark cave, mind reeling with the realization that she was the reason that Honey was dead.

Dana and Meg and several of Lilith's sisters surrounded her, patted her and spoke with soft, comforting words, but Mandi stayed in her self-made cave until gradually, and at Lilith's urging, they drifted away to get food or sleep. They had an hour, Lilith said, until they had to move hotels.

Mandi's conscious mind processed the words, but she didn't respond. When the room was empty, except for the heavy breathing of a sleeping person—supposedly the president—Mandi lifted her head.

She had made a terrible mistake. Thinking about what she was to do that night with the coven made her stomach roil and her breath heave. She put her hand on her chest, focusing on slowing down the movement of her lungs so she didn't hyperventilate. She had to leave, had to get out of here.

Mandi stood and made her way to the door. She opened it. It swung on silent hinges.

"Mandi?" Dana's voice filled the hall. "Are you all right?"

"I-I just need some fresh air," Mandi lied.

"I'll walk you down," Dana said. Sweet Dana, ever ready to serve. No wonder she'd been friends with Honey. They were perfectly suited, completely unselfish. Unlike Mandi.

Mandi's heart broke in waves as grief washed over her. She barely managed to get the words out. "No, I just want to be alone."

A pause, and then, "Lilith says you aren't to be left alone. She says you're grieving and grief can make people do foolish things."

"Of course she did," Mandi replied bitterly, squeezing her eyes shut, tears escaping from the corners. "Please, Dana? I need to be alone, but I can't stay in that room any longer."

"Lilith cares about you. And so do I."

"Let me go, damn it!" Mandi's shout echoed down the hall. A door opened.

"All right there, Dana? Mandi?" Hecuba, one of Lilith's sisters.

"Fine," Mandi called back over Dana's stuttering attempt to reply. "It's fine." Mandi pivoted and returned to the room, shutting the door behind her. She leaned her back against it.

"Can I get you any food, Mandi?" Dana's voice filtered through the door.

Mandi shook her head, emotion overwhelming her. She put a hand to her mouth. She couldn't leave, couldn't run away from this.

And the only person in the world she wanted to talk to might as well be on another planet. Hands in front of her, she found the bed and lay down. The tiny crystal splint in her side twinged, causing Mandi to bolt upright. She *did* have a way to contact Zeke. Astral travel.

She laid down again, arranging herself so she was comfortable and could relax. She breathed in deeply and let go of her conscious mind. It was difficult to navigate past her grief and guilt for Honey, a torrent of emotion she had suppressed rather than release, but she practiced a rhythmic breathing pattern. In for the count of four, out for the count of eight...she let air flow through her body and accepted it as the only sensation, and gradually, her mind drifted to the place between sleeping and remembering, and her soul peeled away from her body.

Mandi looked down at herself. Damp, wrinkled clothes, lines of grief creasing her face, frizzed hair. She was a mess. But at least her astral self appeared more put together. Now she could go find Zeke.

Trouble was, she didn't know where to find him. How did one find someone in the astral realm?

Mandi thought about Zeke. She thought about the rumble of his laugh, the deep baritone of his singing when he thought no one was listening. He spoke Greek, something few people knew about him, and Mandi only knew because he sang in Greek. Mandi thought about the almond and honey scent of his skin, and the warmth of his lips as they pressed against her cheek when they last said goodbye.

A knot tightened in her chest, and a bright golden light flared, then shot from Mandi's astral form out to one side. She turned, facing the direction the golden line pointed. It tugged, as if urging her forward. She had heard that one had to be careful not to get lost in the astral planes. But surely the earth plane would be safe enough to travel in. As long as she remembered where her body was and didn't lose her mind, she would be safe.

Mandi flew forward, following the pull of the line. She darted high into the air until cities became splotches on the globe below her, and the stars brightened and she felt as if she were swimming among them. From Washington D.C. to Chicago, Illinois. It surprised her that Zeke would have come so far, but somehow the city suited him. Now she had to find him among the tens of thousands of sleeping individuals.

The line from her chest grew thicker. Mandi marveled at the glowing strand, wondering if it was leading her to Zeke or someone with sinister intentions, but her intuition said it was a good thing. She zipped through the air over the streets of Chicago, headed west. The moon peeked a sliver of its head over the horizon. It would be full tonight. Would she catch Zeke before the wolf transformation took him?

The thread led Mandi to a large, ornate house awash with silver light. She flew through the walls with ease, searching, heart pounding. She'd never seen Zeke. He wouldn't be able to see her, but she could finally look on his face.

Shouting in the basement, faint and garbled through the astral realm. Mandi sank through the floor and found herself in the middle of a standoff between two men. A woman sat on the sofa, fidgeting anxiously.

"Last chance to take it back, Father." The younger man stared down the older, his broad chin lifted with pride, his dreads hanging, the beads clicking. Mandi froze at the familiar sound of Zeke's voice. The line in her chest connected with Zeke's chest. It pulsed twice, then faded.

"Never," the older man spat with so much venom, it shocked Mandi. The older man was the spitting image of Zeke. Or the other way around, presumably making this man his father. They were fighting.

Mandi considered her options. She could jump into Zeke's mind and try to influence him while awake. From what she heard, it was much, much harder than when someone was sleeping.

With a roar, the two men shifted. It happened in a blink, and without thinking, Mandi leapt towards the head of the wolf that had been Zeke. She rebounded off him, a dizzying sensation, like being held upside down too long. Her astral form flickered, darkness covering her vision for a terrifying instant. *No.* Mandi held on, digging in with all the strength she could muster. Why couldn't she connect with his mind? Was it the wolf form?

If you want him to stay sane, you'll return with me. A form flickered into view. Blonde hair, white robe.

Lilith? Why are you here?

Lilith opened her arms wide, a gentle, concerned expression on her face. *To make sure you're all right, of course. I can feel a lot through our bond, Mandi. I can feel your sorrow, your regret, your guilt. You want to leave, just like Honey.*

No, I'm not going to leave, Mandi insisted. She wasn't. Not yet. She had just wanted to talk to Zeke. *I made Honey come. She never wanted to be part of this.* The wolves were circling. Mandi didn't have a body, but she could still feel the tension building, a tightness, a pulsing throb. She had to stop the fight, get Zeke's attention somehow.

Oh, he's beyond your influence now. Your Zeke. The wolf has consumed him.

Mandi gazed into the black wolf's amber eyes. They were void of all humanness, all familiarity. *He's normally so in control. Even at the full moon.*

Lilith laughed. *I knew you would come here. I wondered how long it would take you to contact him, once we'd forged the bond. You can't leave, not while we're connected. I won't let you leave.*

Can't you take this out of me? Mandi cried, gesturing to her side where the crystal splint had been inserted. *Free us both from this bond?*

Why would I do that? Lilith asked, her voice chilling Mandi to her bones. *I don't want you to leave. Why would I give you the means to do so?*

Mandi backed away from Lilith, a thick dread filling her. *I don't want this anymore, Lilith.*

Lilith's expression fell, then morphed into something like anger. *After everything I did for you? Bonding myself to you, giving you power and opportunity, you want to leave?*

My heart isn't in it anymore. I'd only be a liability, Mandi said.

The moon is at its zenith in a few hours, and we cannot risk bringing another unknown witch in at this point. We already have to replace Honey.

The casual way she spoke about Honey made anger simmer within Mandi. It felt like a brand burned within her. Her astral form lit up with a brilliant red glow.

You should get better at controlling such an obvious expression of emotion. Here, emotion can be dangerous. Lilith waved a finger in the air, like she was warning a child off some bad behavior.

The price is too high, Lilith. I didn't sign up for my friends dying.

They are going to die anyway. In the camps or in rebellion. Let them decide how their lives are best used. The real question is, what will you choose?

Do I have a choice? Mandi said bitterly.

I can make it easier to decide. Lilith flicked her wrist. The werewolf with grey streaks on its forehead lunged forward—Zeke's dad. Snarling and biting, he went straight for Zeke's throat. Mandi screamed, but no one in the room reacted. They couldn't hear her.

Stop! What are you doing to them?

Speeding things up. They were going to get to this point on their own. It was only a matter of time. And if you have nothing here to cling to, then you'll more easily make the decision to stay. The witch looked bored, examining her intangible fingernails.

You don't know that. You don't know that they would fight. They could work it out.

Zeke's mother was screaming. Mandi wished she could step between the wolves, pull them apart. Even if she had her body, it would be impossible. Two younger men ran into the room, pulling off their shirts and pants before shifting. Now it was three on one. To their credit, the new wolves seemed to be trying to break up the fight.

Admit it. You were going to ask him to take you back. Lilith's voice mocked Mandi. Mandi saw Lilith's blue eyes flash violet, like that night when she'd called the coven leaders together in the astral realm. Mandi didn't know how she hadn't felt it before, the void energy pouring off this woman and washing over Mandi like a wave. She should have, but she had been blinded by more than her physical form. The desire to regain her vision had taken common sense away from her, and she'd been in denial. Zeke had known. Honey had known.

Anger boiled, and the red glow filled Mandi's astral Sight. She advanced toward Lilith.

I'm done! Mandi yelled, swiping a hand in front of her like a sharp blade. A wicked orange slash arced toward Lilith, who flicked her hand and sent a blue slash into Mandi's, banishing it without any apparent effort. Mandi blinked and stared at her hand.

Emotions are physically manifested here, if they get strong enough, Lilith explained. She stepped toward Mandi, a grin on her face that made Mandy uneasy. *You hardly know what you're doing. Let me guide you a little longer, love.*

You don't care about me. You don't care about any of the coven. You don't deserve to lead us, Mandi said.

Zeke yelped and leapt back from his three attackers, holding one paw up in the air. One wolf approached him slowly, but Zeke snarled and snapped his jaws, leaning up against the wall. He was cornered.

All it takes to lead a coven is power. Are you going to be foolish and deny yourself the opportunity for greatness? I'm on your side, Mandi. We're going to make the world a better place for paranormals.

She sounded so reasonable until she started threatening Mandi's friends.

It's for your own good, Mandi. Lilith made a fist and punched it toward the wolves. Zeke lunged, and the three wolves buried him. They would destroy him.

Fear flooded her, and the glow of her astral form turned yellow. *Stop! Please!*

What will you offer in exchange for his life? Lilith demanded, her violet eyes flashing.

Mandi's heart tore as she watched Zeke snarling, fighting for his life. A sob shuddered through her, but she choked it back, clasping her fists to her chest. She couldn't take her eyes from Zeke, from the uncontrolled fury that consumed his normally soft eyes. He was there, underneath the rabid rage.

I'll come with you. Just stop the fight.

Very well. Lilith floated into the brawl and put her hands on two of the wolves' heads. They instantly collapsed. She touched the other two, a finger on each forehead. Their eyes rolled back and closed as they fell.

You didn't...they're not...

They sleep.

A whine came from behind Mandi. A female wolf, slightly lighter build, nosing at the wolf with the grey streaks. Zeke's mother. Mandi wished she could tell her they would be all right, but Lilith took her arm.

Come, now. It's time for us to leave.

Can I come back after the spell, when it's all over? Mandi asked, but she already knew the answer.

I think it would be best if you didn't.

Mandi's astral form couldn't cry, but she had a sensation like she was choking on her sadness. She coughed, gagging on the sensation. She massaged her throat, though the motion was pure habit and had no effect. She let Lilith pull her astral form along. When they floated up from the house, back into the moonlit night, the golden thread flickered into view again, a strand of light leading from Mandi's chest back into the house.

No wonder you're not acting with any sense. Lilith said. *That's a soulmate thread. Don't worry, we can take care of it.* She held a hand out to her side, and a blade of purple fire flashed into her hand. She raised it, and before Mandi could stop her, swung the blade downward. A freezing cold sensation seized Mandi's heart.

No! She gripped her chest, falling to her knees in the air and gasping. Her astral form didn't need to breathe, but she felt for all the world as if Lilith had just stabbed her. The thread unraveled from her chest, falling away and disappearing through the roof of the house.

There now. That pesky thing won't bother you anymore. Don't worry, the soulmate thread can be regenerated if you're ever united with your love again. Lilith banished the sword and brushed her hands together. She took Mandi by the arm again, pulling her up. *You'd do best not to enter the astral realm again without me. There's far too much for you to blunder into.*

Mandi didn't respond. Numbness spread through her body, and the grief from losing Honey and Zeke washed over her. Lilith sped them through the air, from Chicago back to Washington in the blink of an eye. She dragged Mandi to hover over her body, then pressed a thumb into her forehead.

When you wake, this will be as a dream, Lilith murmured.

Mandi struggled against the spell that washed over her mind, force-soothing the emotion that raged inside of her, plunging her under and drowning her in darkness.

CHAPTER SEVENTEEN

TYSON

"YOU WANNA NAP BEFORE I introduce you to your team?" Dak asked, thumbing the pockets of his jeans.

Tyson unfroze himself, blinking and turning back to Dak. He ran a hand through his hair. "I think I'm probably good. Got a lot of sleep at the hospital, you know?" Tyson gathered the things Becca had handed him, the herbs and oils and crystals. Everything in his hands went out of focus, then back in again. He shook his head and it throbbed. "On second thought, I'd better take that nap."

"Good man," Dak clapped him on the back. "I like it when a person knows their limits. Means I don't have to babysit you. This door here leads to some spare beds. Should be all set up." Dak gave Tyson's shoulder a pull, bringing him closer to the door. "See this com link on the wall? You need anything you can reach me on channel two." Dak explained how the com link worked. Tyson tried to absorb the information, a throbbing pain in his skull making it difficult to concentrate. He'd hit his head harder than he thought.

Dak stared at him. Tyson realized he was rubbing his head and frowning. He dropped his arm.

"You need a medic, man? We got a good one. And you *were* just in the hospital," Dak said, his eyebrows creasing together.

"No, I'm good. I'm good. A nap will do me." Tyson turned the door handle. He'd left the backpack on the couch, and after a brief pause, he went back for it, waving sheepishly at Dak, who just smiled and whistled as he walked out of the room.

The door clicked shut, and Tyson locked it, leaning against it and sighing. He couldn't collapse on the floor. Besides, the bed looked comfortable. He set the crystals and things on the bedside table. It was a tiny room, but hotel-quality, with a full-size bed with a homey-looking quilt, a modern art piece on the wall, a lamp, and the bedside table. A closet stood empty opposite the bed. Tyson stuck the backpack on the closet floor and shut the door, then opened the door again and unzipped the pack. Where was his head? He couldn't think straight. He rummaged around, finding the soft velvet of the sealskin wrapping that contained the *ulu* knife. As he pulled it out, his hand brushed the surface of the Harpy egg. An image flared in his mind.

The egg weighed heavily in his hands, quivering and vibrating. The surface heated, and a seam opened in a jagged line through the middle. The egg cracked, steam hissing from the opening. Tyson jumped and dropped it. The egg halves fell to either side, and a shadowy form stepped out, then grew to full size. Her black wings unfolded from her back, feathers damp like a newborn chick's feathers, but still a grown woman.

Harper's hand raised toward his face, but when he didn't step forward, she let it fall back to her side.

"Don't forget me," she said.

"I'll remember," Tyson promised.

"You mean like you remembered Reya?" The form of Harper smirked. She turned on her heel and walked away, ignoring Tyson yelling for her to come back, his hand stretched out towards her retreating back.

The vision vanished. Tyson's hand hovered in the air, and his throat felt hoarse. Had he been screaming out loud? The egg lay on the floor, whole and uncracked. He cleared his throat, massaging it, then stood with the help of the closet doorway. He carried the knife to the bedside table and set it down.

Had it been a vision? Or something nonsensical induced by his head injury?

Tyson blinked at the arrangement of metaphysical assistance on the table's surface. His fingers hovered over a pink stone. He touched it and it hummed. He yanked his hand back.

Stones. Crystals. That blind witch at Camp Silver Lake had loved them. She'd already been Naturalized by the time Tyson started counseling, so he'd never had a session with her, but he remembered she always had some in her pocket. She'd claimed that they cleared energy, enhanced mental function, and opened channels of communication. Tyson had never put much stock in crystals, but then, he'd been a lot thicker in the skull a couple months ago. Harper, and everything that had happened to him since, had shaken loose the close-minded beliefs and opened his eyes to how the world worked with paranormals in it. A world where they were supported, rather than suppressed. It was incredible.

Tyson touched the other three stones. A brilliant blue with gleaming green flecks. It had a pearl-like sheen, and Tyson recognized it as opal. He didn't know the names of the other two, a soft, powdery blue stone and a clear purple stone with orange streaks, but when he touched them, they matched the hum of the first pink stone. Quartz, maybe? Mandi would have known, and she was blind.

Tyson nudged the rocks around. They felt...restless. As he played with them, maneuvering them around the other things on the table, the restless feeling diminished. He put the sage bundle in the center, then at the top of a circle sort of thing that he'd created on the wood surface. The *ulu* knife rested in the center on the black surface of the seal pelt. Tyson opened one of the oils. It smelled sickly-sweet. Tyson capped it and picked up the other. He liked this one. More woody, with some sort of pine scent layered with a rich, warm scent and something else. He couldn't discern anything else familiar in the notes, but he liked the tingle that started in his fingertips. It seemed promising. The tingle moved up to his forehead, between his eyes, and the base of his neck. Tyson tipped the oil bottle and dabbed the liquid inside on the points that were buzzing.

"This is so weird," he muttered to himself, screwing the lid back on. He sat on the bed, then laid down, staring at what he'd created. He wished he could light the candle, but he didn't have fire, and that wouldn't be a good idea anyway, having a lit candle while he slept. He turned his head and closed his eyes.

He dropped into the in-between space, like he'd learned from Jaco. He intended to move through it into sleep, but maybe it was the essential oils, or the altar-thing he'd created, but it was *effortless* to separate from his body and float into the air.

Todd was nowhere to be found. It was just him, floating in the room. He could see through the walls, sort of, and beyond into the world. It was late afternoon outside. Fantasy elements from the astral realm grew along buildings. Vines and things, entire trees. Stars were visible, despite the daylight, and everything was tinged with purple light.

An orange portal glowed just beyond the walls of the building Tyson was in. He flew toward it, careful to maintain his distance. He didn't like portals when he knew where they would take him. He was extra wary of this one. He flew past it, shaking loose the perverted temptation to go through on a whim. He glanced around. It seemed quiet. A little too quiet, compared to the first time he'd come to this plane, when Todd had spoken to him and there had been people everywhere. Where was everyone now?

It didn't really matter. He was here, he needed to get a lead on Harper.

As soon as he thought of Harper, a golden line flickered from his chest, like a fishing line was stuck inside of him. It flashed just a moment, never becoming fully tangible, then disappeared. Odd.

Tyson rolled his shoulders and filed it away to ask Todd whenever he saw him next. Would the fox-man hear him if he yelled?

Todd! His voice carried through the...well, not air, exactly. The realm, he supposed. He heard the echo, felt it come back to him. He sensed that Todd hadn't heard, that he wasn't on this plane. He wasn't sure where he'd gotten that information, but he had it all the same.

He turned in the direction of Oregon, toward the west and the setting sun. Could Lilith have taken Harper back to Camp Silver Lake?

That golden fishing line flickered again, like a lightbulb about to burn out. Tyson frowned and rubbed his intangible chest. He couldn't feel anything. He tried to follow the sporadic line with his eyes, noticing it disappeared in the distance to the east. It went out again.

The light of the astral realm dimmed as a bank of fog rolled in. Near as Tyson could tell, it was a feature of the astral realm, not an actual fog from earth. For one, it glittered. And it didn't touch Tyson. A ten-foot radius around him remained clear. He walked forward, and the fog parted for him.

He would head east, just to see what he could find. Maybe there would be a clue. He walked at first, then pushed off from the ground and flew. He couldn't break through the fog—it extended for an eternity into the sky. No wind touched his face. There was no wind in the astral realm. At least, not on this plane.

A whisper tickled Tyson's ear for the first time as he passed into the Wasatch mountains of Utah. The golden line blinked and went out. Tyson saw enough to realize that it had pointed straight down.

Could it be leading him to Harper? Jaco had warned about illusions and tricks that lower vibrational beings used to lure unsuspecting astral travelers into traps. Tyson hesitated in the air, waiting for the glitchy strand of light to return. A tiny pulse, like an erratic firefly, shot from his chest to the ground. Tyson strained his eyes to follow it before it disappeared. It followed a perfectly straight path down, at a 45 degree angle. Tyson swooped down. It was oddly anti-climactic without the sensation of wind whipping past that he'd imagined flying would be accompanied by.

A tree loomed too fast for him to dodge. Tyson covered his face with his hands, bracing for impact, but it never came. He zoomed through the forest, going through the trees. Right. Intangible astral form. Laughter bubbled up in Tyson and he let it loose as he flew, intentionally aiming to go through the trees just for the thrill of coming out the other side unharmed. The golden line sent out the occasional blip from his chest, moving forward into the pitch-dark forest like a flare.

Then, it stopped.

Tyson kept flying for a while, certain he would see the blip again, but it didn't happen. He turned, looking back at the forest behind him. The golden line flashed, lighting up the trees closest to it. Tyson hesitantly backtracked, walking this time.

Voices whispered among the trees. He couldn't see anyone, but that didn't mean they weren't there. In fact, he hadn't seen anyone since he'd gotten to the realm. Did everyone else get an invitation to a party he'd missed? Har har. Tyson rolled his eyes at his own irrational thoughts. But he couldn't shake a sensation like a spider crawling on the back of his neck. He rubbed the skin there over and over, finding nothing.

Ahead, a rundown cabin stood. A flickering glow in one window suggested *someone* might be home. The flashing golden line pulsed right through the front door. Tyson's feet made no impression on the ground as he walked toward the front steps. He was halfway through the clearing when a sudden rush of alarm overwhelmed him. His entire form went rigid, seizing up with terror. He froze, mid-step, and a roar bellowed out from the trees. He tried to move and failed. Something held him in place, fear coursing through him. The pulsing line vanished. A shadow passed over the window in the cabin.

Help me! He yelled, hoping the person in the cabin would hear and come to his aid. Everything sat still.

Tyson couldn't hear his attacker approach, but the terror grew, and fog thickened around him, drawing closer until it nearly obscured the cabin from view.

Tendrils whipped out of the darkness, wrapping tightly around him. They reeled him in towards a hulking shadow hiding in the trees. Tyson struggled against them uselessly.

"Caught a sneak, caught a sneak!" A nasal voice cackled. The tentacled thing crawled forward, holding Tyson off the ground.

It entered the clearing. He couldn't quite see it, despite its proximity. It was a writhing mass of darkness. A thing born of fear.

A chittering sound sent shivers up Tyson's spine. He twisted his head around and caught sight of a second tentacle creature. It stroked a tentacle over Tyson's face. He sputtered and coughed, gasping when the tentacle lifted.

"Take it to her, yes, yes, yes."

"Take me to who?" Tyson shouted. His voice had released.

The tentacle creature cackled, and its form spilled across the ground towards the stairs to the cabin. Tyson squirmed, but the creature tightened its grip. The door opened before the creature touched it, and it molded to fit the frame, making itself fit in the tight space. Once inside, it threw him on the ground. Tyson got to his feet and darted for a window. He slammed against the window's surface and fell back, dazed. He couldn't go through it. The cabin must have been built in the astral realm.

Behind him, the shadow creatures hissed and chittered. Panic sent Tyson scrambling around the room. He went through another doorway into a kitchen-type area. He spotted a door at the back of the cabin and ran for it.

The entire room went cold and dark. The light he'd seen from outside extinguished with a quiet hiss. The chittering from the other room stopped.

Inky darkness, so black it was almost blue, spread across the back door and coated the windows. It filled the room, surrounding Tyson.

So, a lightbringer dares enter my lair. On the night of my triumph, no less.

*I didn't know—I don't know—*Tyson stammered, pivoting. The door he'd come through was no longer visible. There was no escape.

The new being laughed, a deep, throaty, distorted chuckle. *Didn't know, it says. Everyone knew. Did you not wonder why you didn't see anything else for miles in this region of the physical realm? They are far more aware than you are. They knew to avoid this place,* The voice sucked in with a sound like slurping saliva. *They knew to avoid me.* It growled the last sentence, and an icy finger trailed down Tyson's back with such a wet sensation he thought he might be bleeding, but when his hand reached back he could feel nothing. He wished he had his knife. Without the weapon, he wasn't confident he could fight the being.

Who are you? Tyson asked, trying to buy more time before the being decided to end him, or whatever happened to spirits separated from their bodies in the astral realm. He couldn't be killed here, but if he was trapped somewhere, his body would starve and die back on earth.

I am Ragranoth.

The cabin groaned at the name, as if it might collapse. Tyson's being tremored. A powerful lower vibrational being, to be sure. He stood in the center of the room, the impenetrable darkness his prison.

A pinprick of light pierced the hide of the darkness. Tyson shielded his eyes as the light grew, and a portal opened.

Todd's head stuck out. He spotted Tyson. "Hurry! I can't...hold this." He grunted and the portal opening flexed.

Tyson didn't hesitate. He grabbed a chair and shoved it against the kitchen counter, climbing up to where the portal twisted. He hooked his arms over the edge. The room behind him wobbled.

"She's going to collapse this dimension!" Todd yelled, hand reaching for Tyson's. He pulled, and Tyson pushed off from the counter, and he slid into the portal, hollering as his belly scraped the portal's edge. It vanished the moment he came through.

Todd extracted himself from Tyson and stretched his hands out, creating another portal. He grabbed Tyson's arm and shoved him through.

"Hey!" Tyson shouted. His words twisted inside the portal, and then it spit him out the other side. He stumbled into the middle of a busy city street, cars zipping through his astral form.

Todd emerged, already forming a third portal.

"Hold on a sec—" Tyson gasped.

"No time. Go." Todd kept walking, pushing Tyson before him, and they merged into the portal at the same time. This one didn't open back up. Tyson spun in dizzying wheels of motion until Todd grabbed his foot and righted him. He floated easily with crossed arms, and a cross look on his face.

"What?" Tyson asked.

"Tonight, of all nights, you had to go exploring by yourself. Do you have any idea what you were risking? That demon, for lack of a better word that you'll understand, is rising tonight. She's taken over the physical realm. Her lackeys are everywhere. It's a coup of massive proportions."

"Well now that you mention it, no, no one warned me. And you weren't there when I got here. I thought I'd just take a quick look around. If this Ragran—" Todd muffled Tyson's words with a hand clamped over his mouth.

"Don't speak her name. Unless you want to call down her lower vibrational denizens." He snarled, showing his teeth.

"Sorry. If she's rising and taking over and such, why not contact the higher vibrational beings to deal with it?" Tyson spun his arms, trying to stay upright. Or, at least the way he thought was up. It was hard to tell in the swirling blue energy that made up this limbo between portals.

"We have. They're in conference. Trying to decide if Earth is worth saving. So good luck with that," Todd said.

Tyson let the words sink in. The higher vibrational beings—whoever they were—were on the fence about saving earth?

"What happens to the astral realm if they don't save earth?" Tyson asked.

Todd shrugged. "It's connected to more than just earth. It will go on as before. The physical plane will just lose an aspect." The fox-headed man glanced down. "It's a nice aspect. I hope...Well, it doesn't matter. Hope is useless at this point."

Tyson's hand started tingling, and he held it up to his face. The fingers were turning blue and fading, almost melding with the limbo space. "Uh, Todd, is this normal?"

"Oh, yeah. We should leave now," Todd said, his tone almost bored. A portal window opened on the other side and Todd walked forward, grabbing Tyson's arm and dragging him along. They popped out into Tyson's room at T.R.S. headquarters. Tyson shook out his limbs, trying to get rid of the sensation that he was being erased.

Tyson held a hand to his chest, as if his heart was galloping. But there was no heart there to gallop, just a squeezing sensation that made him wish he'd never left his body. "Let's never do that again."

"How about you never do what you did again?" Todd crossed his arms, his accusatory gaze directed at Tyson. "And stay out of the astral realm until this blows over, all right?"

Tyson sat in silence, watching his own chest rise and fall in the body on the bed. "What if it doesn't 'blow over'?"

Todd clapped him on the shoulder. "It won't get to that point."

Tyson raised his eyebrows. "How certain are you?"

"Reasonably," Todd winked, then disappeared.

Tyson jumped into the air then dove back into his body. He woke with a gasp, and sound and sense crashed over him.

Outside the room, the halls filled with shouts and stomping feet. Tyson threw off the covers and bolted to the door, unlocking it and throwing it open. He stepped outside, dragging a hand through his hair. A woman ran into him, her brown eyes frantic.

Tyson grabbed her arms. "Hey, what's going on here? Why's everyone running?"

Her eyes widened. "Oh, you're the new guy. Come on." She pulled out of his grip and headed for the main hallway leading away from Tyson's room.

Tyson jogged after her. "Who are you? Where are we going?"

"Janae." She stuck out her hand, still walking. Tyson shook it awkwardly. "I'm the head of the T.R.S. communications department. We're headed for the briefing room."

"Why?"

"You'll find out." Janae moved from a fast walk to a jog. She turned down a different corridor and slid through a door so fast Tyson nearly missed her. He ducked in behind her. The room was packed with people. Tyson only recognized Dak, who stood at the front of the room with a grim expression. People were shouting and asking questions. Dak saw Janae and his face visibly relaxed.

"Here's the woman who can tell us what's going on. We just got a tip about something big happening in Washington. Let's quiet down and let Janae focus." Dak leaned toward Janae and whispered something. She grinned back, then placed her fingers on her temples in a focused, trance-like stance. Her eyes rolled back into her head, revealing the whites. Tyson startled, but no one else seemed to think anything was odd.

Janae whirled around, a beam of light casting onto the large television screen at the front of the room. The screen flickered to life, projecting a grainy image depicting the Washington Monument.

Surrounding the monument, as if burned into the grass and sidewalk, was the largest pentagram Tyson had ever seen. At each point around the outer perimeter stood a woman. Thirteen, to be exact. A full coven.

The image zoomed in on each of the faces for a split second, landing at last on a witch with long, blonde hair, and a smirk that Tyson would have recognized anywhere.

"Stop!" he shouted. The image flickered to the next face; a black woman with milky white eyes. Mandi. "Go back."

Every eye in the room turned to look at him. Tyson ignored their stares, watching the screen as it flicked back to the face of Lilith.

"That one. She's in charge," Tyson said.

"You know these witches?" Dak asked.

"Some of them. Not all of them, but that one," Tyson pointed at the screen to Lilith. "She possessed my friends and took them captive."

"You're on the ground with us, then," Dak said. "We've got to take this witch out. She's making some big move on the government, and it doesn't look like it's going to be pretty. It will incite a war."

"A war?"

"See the figure strapped to the base of the monument?" Dak gestured to the screen. Janae had moved her projected vision, zooming in on the center of the pentagram where a figure was tied to the obelisk. "That's the President of the United States. We're all about getting paranormals their rights back but putting the President at the center of a sacrificial circle isn't the way to do it. Based on the look of things, they're about to use a human sacrifice to summon a demon from the depths of the underworld."

"There's no underworld," another woman in the room scoffed. She nodded toward Tyson. "He knows. Don't ya? It's levels and vibrations. No demons either."

Everyone looked at Tyson. He shrugged. "She's right. I think. I'm new at this. And I was just there...Something is coming. It called itself Ragranoth."

Bethesda shrieked, covering her ears. "Are you blinkin' mad? You'll bring her down on all of us!"

Dak grimaced. "Then let's take the fight to this being first. Bethesda, open a portal. Put us down near the Lincoln Memorial. We don't want to end up in the middle of that pentagram. And stick with the newbie, would you? Maybe you can teach him something. Everyone else, get your gear. I want to be on the ground in less than five minutes. Go!"

The room erupted into a flurry of activity as people scrambled into position. After a moment, Tyson was alone in the room.

"What do they think I am? A babysitter?" Bethesda muttered, blowing a strand of greying brown hair out of her face. She tugged on her fingerless gloves and stood up from her chair.

"You're Bethesda?" Tyson asked.

"I'm not Susan," the woman retorted. If Tyson had to guess, he'd say she was in her fifties. "Look, do you know how to open a portal?"

"No." Tyson shuddered. He hated portal travel. He was even more opposed after his recent experience in the astral realm.

"Well, you're going to learn today. Get over here." Bethesda gestured, and Tyson felt a physical tug in his sternum.

"Are you…*compelling* me?" He'd read about this in college. It was highly illegal.

Bethesda rolled her eyes. "I didn't realize you were a conformist. Are you going to help me or not?"

Tyson licked his lips and wiped his hands on his jeans. He moved around the table, coming to stand near the woman. "Are you a witch?"

"No more than you are."

"I'm a dreamwalker," Tyson insisted.

"Right. Now, portals are tricky. You have to know where you're going. We want to go there," she pointed at the dark television screen.

"It's blank," Tyson said.

"If you're really that big of an imbecile, you can leave now," Bethesda snapped. She glared at Tyson, who finally shook his head. "Glad that's settled. Now then, where were we? Okay. It's like astral travel—you know what that is, right?"

Tyson nodded, trying not to bite his lip. His hands shook.

"Okay. Imagine that sensation as you fall asleep, where something catches in your chest, almost like a hook? That's what you're looking for in the air. It's a pathway. Everything is part of everything else. The earth sends messages through water, which is constantly cycling. That's how we can always find a path because water in the air remembers being part of the place you're going. We're going to hone in on the water molecules that contain the pathway and expand it until it's a stable portal." Bethesda reached for Tyson's hand, grabbing it and pulling him to stand before her. "You're going to open the portal. Don't worry, I'll help you keep it open."

The door to the room opened, and three people walked in. Janae was one of them, and two men that looked like identical twins.

Bethesda smacked the back of Tyson's head. "Concentrate. Find the pathway and tell it to expand."

Tyson closed his eyes and tried to focus. He usually had his knife for stuff like this. The only water he could sense was the sweat gathering on the surface of his palms. He wiped them on his jeans again, then sighed. "I can't do it. I need my knife."

"You don't need a knife. The knife is a crutch. The magic is inside of you, not in the knife," Bethesda snapped. "Try again."

Tyson breathed in deep and closed his eyes. He reached into the place in his chest where he often felt magic activate. It stirred. He imagined the air around him was visible, filled with tiny droplets of water. They glowed a faint blue, bobbing around in front of him. He thought of the Lincoln Memorial. He'd visited once in grade school. *I need to get there*. He thought. He wasn't certain, but he thought the droplets hummed back to him. A single droplet increased its light, glowing brighter than the others. Tyson honed in on it, focusing the energy in his chest toward the droplet. It connected and began to expand, swirling with a brilliant zinging light.

He forgot the people piling into the room. He forgot everything except what he'd just done. He stuck his arm in the portal without thinking, pulling it back through. It was damp—from the portal? Or was it raining on the other side?

Bethesda shrieked with laughter. "There you go! See, not so hard. And you didn't need your knife. You're keeping it open on your own, too."

He was. He could feel the strain in the back of his mind, like flexing a muscle while working out, but he could manage it.

"Here's your backpack," Janae dropped the worn blue bag on the table beside Tyson. "Dak told me which room was yours. I put everything I found inside."

"Thanks," Tyson said, sliding his arms through the straps.

A loud clap sounded in the room. "We all here? All ready to go?" Dak walked in, pressing through the small crowd until he stood beside Tyson and Bethesda.

"I'll go through first. We're heading straight for the witches. We've got to disrupt this circle before they kill the president. Tyson, I want you with me. If we can talk that witch in charge down and end this thing without any blood, I'll be a happy camper."

Tyson didn't think that would happen, but before he could say anything, Dak disappeared through the portal.

Bethesda nudged Tyson. "You're next, bud. Just don't close the portal on the other side until we're all through."

Tyson took a deep breath. He stepped into the portal, bracing himself for the thousand-knives sensation he'd always felt in portals before. This time, however, it didn't come. Instead, the light of the portal flowed over his skin, coating him in glittering blue light, and it warmed him, soothing all his stress and fatigue away.

He came through on the other side, immediately wishing he could go back into the portal. Rain was falling in sheets. He was drenched in a moment. He ran up the stairs of the Lincoln Memorial, getting under the pavilion's cover. Dak stood next to the seated stone giant, arms clasped behind his back. He nodded to Tyson without looking away from the Washington Monument in the distance. A giant spire that even through the rain, Tyson could see because it was lit up with a violet light.

A voice carried on the wind towards them, the words unintelligible, but their effect was visible as an opalescent purple dome surrounded the monument. A wave of dark forms emerged from the mile-long reflecting pool between the memorials. Dak cursed from Tyson's side.

"The witches have evoked their defenses." Dak looked at Tyson, as if sizing him up. "You got a less vulnerable form you can take on?"

"I can turn into a bear," Tyson said.

"Good. I think this is going to turn into a nasty fight. Arm up!" Dak shouted to the others, most of whom had made it through the portal and were gathered in the pavilion and on the steps leading up to it. "We need to get through that contingency the witches have raised and punch through the dome. If we succeed, we take the Capitol today. Who's with me?"

A roar went up from the mob of rebels. Tyson's chest clenched. He grabbed Dak's shoulder, and the man turned to face him.

"What do you mean, 'we'll take the Capitol?'" Tyson asked.

Dak clapped him on the shoulder. "If the government goes down, it's going down on our terms." He grinned and raced down the steps, leaving Tyson standing in the rain watching dark forms swarm from the pool, most of them shifting. Several figures took off into the air. Could it be...?

Swallowing hard, Tyson dropped his backpack and shifted into polar bear form. He let out a bellow to warn those below that he was coming, then leapt down the stairs, landing with a crash. The rebels nearest to him raised their weapons, one had fire consuming his fist, which he punched into the air. Energy pulsed through Tyson. He could do this. He surged forward, paws pounding on the cement.

One of the flying figures swooped down, landing in a crouch with her fist on the ground. She looked up, damp hair dangling over her face, but Tyson still recognized her.

Harper.

CHAPTER EIGHTEEN

ZEKE

THIS WAS NOT NORMAL. Some part of Zeke's mind recognized the dark influence he was under wasn't part of him, but he couldn't do anything about it pinned beneath two of his brothers. His father stood some distance off, still snarling and snapping, trying to get around Rob and Zeke's mother to get at Zeke. Zeke lashed back, yelping when Theo nipped him. Theo, of all his siblings, only sixteen but the broadest of them all, a stocky black wolf with a powerful bite that Zeke was bleeding from in a few places.

Stop fighting, Theo demanded.

You're being stupid, Phil agreed. *You moon-addled, or what?*

Moon-addled. The term weres used when someone was so taken over by the forced full-moon change that they lost their mind and essentially went rabid. That wasn't Zeke, was it?

He hasn't had the serum. Mother's voice entered Zeke's mind, cool and calm.

Dad has, though. What's his excuse? Rob growled. He barked and bit at Dad, who snarled with his ears folded back, but didn't lunge forward again.

Zeke tensed his muscles to spring, but a pulse throbbed through his skull, forceful as a strike, and yet none of the other wolves had moved. He slumped into unconsciousness.

When Zeke came to, he found that the others, also, had fallen asleep. Some mysterious influence had come over them. The silence screamed in his ears almost audibly. He twitched them, then glanced at Antonio. The large wolf stirred.

The blood-thirst woke again in Zeke, the burning urge to howl the call to challenge the alpha waited in his throat. He had to play his cards right, here. He could attack now, when everyone was groggy and vulnerable. It would be easy.

Phil and Theo got to their feet, eyeing him warily. Zeke huffed, pricking his ears forward, trying to show himself as calm. His brothers brightened visibly, their tense muscles relaxing, their tails wagging, and Zeke seized the moment they let down their guard, darting between them and snarling and snapping towards his father.

Rob slammed into his chest, flipping Zeke backward, and Theo grabbed a hind leg in his jaws, holding tight enough to break the skin, but not tight enough to break bone. Zeke kicked and struggled.

Let...me...have him. I'd make a better leader of this pack. You don't need this bigotted coward.

Zeke! Mother chided. *He is our alpha.*

He's not my alpha. Zeke glared from his place on the floor, lifting his head and curling his lip as he growled.

Rob put a paw on his head, forcing him down. *Shut it, brother. Can someone get Cressida?*

Mother huffed. *There she is.*

A dainty female trotted into the room, a pale cream coat with patches of light brown, and a dark patch over one eye.

She carried two syringes in her mouth. Her jade eyes glittered, passing over Zeke to look at his father.

Who needs it first?

Antonio already had it. Will a second dose harm him? Mother asked.

Might put him to sleep, Cressida said. *But no harm.*

Zeke first. Rob insisted, growling down at Zeke.

I'm not letting you stick me with something. Zeke said, thrashing about and nipping Rob's opposite leg. The wolf yelped, but only put more of his weight on Zeke.

The blood thrill hasn't left you yet. This will help. Cressida put one syringe down and approached Zeke, who snarled at her. She lifted her lips, snarling back, then to his shock she changed.

It should have been impossible with the full moon. No werewolf could change in the face of it. Not for 24 hours. But Cressida did, panting, and with great exertion and pain, as he could tell by the distortion of her human features as she shifted. She adjusted the band of the sports bra she wore and crouched down beside Zeke, those jade eyes holding his amber ones. Rob licked the side of her face, a blatant claiming of her, like a wolf would claim a mate. A growl rumbled low, vibrating into Zeke through Rob's throat.

Don't you dare bite me, or you'll feel my teeth. Cressida threatened. She held up the syringe. *This goes in your shoulder.*

Before Zeke could react, she plunged it down and pressed it in. It pinched, and Zeke yelped, but it was done in an instant. He sniffed the area, catching the slightest foreign scent, then licked it.

The steam in his blood diminished. He moaned as the adrenaline left him, shaking his head. The serum cooled his blood and slowed his heart. He panted. *What is this?*

"It's a serum I invented," Cressida said. "It gives the ability to calm weres during the full moon change. For some wolves, it disrupts the change entirely and they can still choose which form to take, especially if given regularly."

Cressida was hired by Bruno, Mother explained. *She oversees administration of the serum every month, as well as caring for our elders and youngers.*

And she's my mate, so don't get any ideas. Rob snarled, pushing off from Zeke and letting him up.

Zeke slowly stood, his entire body trembling. He felt sick and weak. He didn't like it. Something had diminished inside of him, some fire, some strength given to him by the moon. He whined and licked at the injection site again.

Don't be such a baby, Phil said.

It takes getting used to. Mother nosed Antonio, Zeke's father, who had just received a second dose of the serum. His eyes seemed to clear, and he recognized her, his tail thumping, and then it slowed, and his eyes drifted shut and he rested.

He'll sleep for a few hours, Cressida said from Rob's side, back in wolf form.

You should leave, Rob said, stepping forward, his hackles raising. He puffed out his chest, playing at alpha.

Zeke felt tired. The last thing he wanted to do in this state was leave a safe place, but with the eyes of the pack watching him warily, he knew it wasn't safe here anymore. Not for him.

I wanted to help.

Yeah, well, dad's alpha. And he doesn't want your help, Rob said. He glanced away, nudging Cressida as if seeking comfort. She watched Zeke steadily, panting in a casual way, but Zeke knew if he made a fuss, she'd be the first to see him out. He wished he knew her better. He wished he knew them all better. He wished…Well, it didn't matter what he wished.

Zeke bowed his head slightly. *All right. I'll…I'll see you around.* He couldn't bring himself to say goodbye. Not a permanent one, anyway. He trotted from the room. No one spoke to stop him or to bid him farewell. He should have expected this sort of homecoming.

Zeke made his way up the stairs, his claws clicking on the wood floor, paws occasionally slipping. His head and tail hung low as he made his way through the hall to the front door. He glanced at the room he'd found his grandmother in. It was dark, now, not even the light of the TV showing. He pressed the inner latch on the door that was right at his level, an installation one would only find in a house owned by shifters, an invention that allowed them to open doors in any form, at least in their own house. The door clicked, and Zeke forced his nose into the crack, pushing the door open.

Zeke. Wait a moment, my Zeke. His mother's call couldn't be ignored. Zeke turned, tail hanging between his legs. He whined, then looked her in the eyes. Her gentle, brown eyes, outlined with pale brown fur. She walked up and brushed her cheek against his, then licked at some of his wounds. They were shallow and would heal quickly. Zeke closed his eyes, accepting her administrations.

Dad might see.

Let him see, his mother said, and she continued until she was satisfied she'd found every wound. She backed up and looked into his eyes. *He's right, you know. Your father.*

Zeke flinched away. He'd never taken his mother for one to agree with such a horribly biased view.

Not about everything. His discrimination is...wrong. But about you needing to leave. You've always needed your own pack, Zeke. I knew it from the moment I first laid eyes on you that you would be different. You are an alpha, and no walls can contain two alphas.

Bruno manages, Zeke said bitterly. How the mob leader maintained control was beyond him.

Bruno requires his pseudo-alphas to give control over to him. Don't you dare think of doing the same thing. Find yourself a pack to lead, Zeke. A real pack. Forget about your father's debt. It is his to manage on his own. And he has us.

And I have no one.

Zeke, his mother chided. The brown wolf sighed, gazing into his eyes. *Were you serious about that girl? The witch?*

Yes. More serious than he'd been about anything, ever.

Then you better fetch her. And when you're settled, I'll come visit you.

Zeke forced his tail to wag. They both knew a visit would be far too dangerous, even if Antonio allowed it. The risk of his mother getting caught was too great, and Zeke would never ask her to risk herself that way.

I'll call you, he said, and he leaned forward and licked her cheek. When he pulled away, his mother had a drooping, soulful look to her eyes. If she'd been in human form, she would have been crying, and Zeke was glad she wasn't. He wasn't sure he could take it if she cried.

A howl went up, a high, clear tone pealing through the night air. It was answered in an echo from within the house, a softer sound, and then cries went up across the city.

Zeke lifted his nose and released the grief from his throat.

It ended as abruptly as it began. He glanced one more time at his mother, standing on the porch in her wolfskin, eyes gleaming brightly in the darkness.

Adio! She called. A final goodbye. More permanent somehow, spoken in the language of his heritage. He watched her go back in the house, most likely summoned by Antonio. A pull that Zeke no longer felt. Would never feel again.

He stood on the pavement of the circular driveway. His motorbike stood where he'd parked it, the package on the back undisturbed. Zeke went over, sniffing. He found his brothers' scents nearby. Of course, they would have checked it out. Apparently, they hadn't found anything amiss, because they'd left it all alone.

Zeke remembered what Cressida had said about some wolves being able to change forms. He tried, feeling for that place inside that allowed him to invoke his human form, but everything just felt numb. He wouldn't be shifting tonight, but he still had a job to do.

Using his teeth, he removed the bungee cords holding the cardboard box to his bike. He snapped them off and took the package in his mouth. It was just slim enough to fit between his jaws, though it would be tiring to hold it for any length of time. He could already feel the strain. He adjusted his grip, letting his teeth pierce the outer layer of the cardboard. Drool dripped to the cement. Great. He'd look like a sloppy, drooling fool, but at least he'd get the job done.

Fortunately, he remembered the address Jack had written on the piece of paper. The paper that was in the pocket of Zeke's now-shredded jeans, still on the basement floor inside the house. He wasn't going back for it now. He eyed the motorbike. Jack expected it back, someday. Zeke expected that his family would respect it, keep it for him. Especially if he left a message.

Zeke lifted his leg, mentally apologizing to Jack for peeing on his motorcycle. He sniffed around to make sure everything was as he'd intended, then he left the yard.

He ran down the street, keeping to the shadows. The address wasn't too far from here, he'd be there in an hour. He just had to remain unseen, or hope he got mistaken for a dog. An intelligent dog, carrying a package in his mouth.

The address took him to a run-down part of the city, where giant storage containers lined up like houses in a particularly grungy neighborhood. Street lights dotted the parking lot sparingly, their orbs of light illuminating only a small section of dark pavement, with darkness owning the gaps between. Zeke crept along, head low as he sniffed. It seemed deserted, but it was unlikely Bruno kept this bit of real estate unguarded. Which was why Zeke was there. Jack's contact, called "Blue" on the paper, should be nearby.

Zeke slunk between two of the storage containers, ears pricked. The night felt like it was brooding, a slight fog coming in and the moon above partially covered with clouds, its full surface gleaming down on Zeke like a giant eye, watching him. The fur on his scruff lifted, and a tingle traveled along his spine. Someone was watching him. He looked over his shoulder, but no figures emerged. He rounded the back of one of the units and a giant grey wolf leapt straight at his face.

Zeke was bowled over by the force of the attack. He dropped the package and rolled, then scrambled to his feet and sprang for the box, but the other wolf sniffed at it, tail wagging. Zeke froze, waiting to see what would happen. The strange wolf huffed and grunted, nosing the box, then looked up at Zeke.

Who are you? What is your business here?

I'm looking for Blue. Zeke said, taking a chance on revealing the name.

You found him. The larger wolf shifted his stance, then nosed the box again. *Who sent you?*

Jack. Met him back in Wyoming.

Blue nodded. *This for me, then?*

Yeah. Zeke was curious about what could be inside. His nose hadn't picked up anything in particular. But that wasn't part of his job. Deliver the package. Done. Now he just had to decide what to do with the rest of his life. He could return the motorcycle to Jack, possibly join the rebellion, try to make a difference. Or he could still take Bruno up on his offer to join the White City pack. Working for a mob boss didn't appeal to Zeke the same way it had when he was a teenager. But the rebellion...at least the things he did there would be for a good cause.

Blue whined. *Time to clear out. We're about to have company,* he said to Zeke.

A bark echoed through the empty lot. A second. A third. Shadowy canine figures emerged from the darkest shadows between shipping containers, entering the pools of light beneath the few dim street lamps.

From the corner of his eyes, Zeke saw Blue disappear around the corner of the shipping container. Zeke followed.

Where can I go? Zeke asked, panic rising in him. If he was caught, he'd be taken to Bruno, and he might not have a choice but to join the mob pack.

Through here. Blue sniffed at the edge of the container, then pressed his paw on a short lever near the ground. *You'll have ten seconds.* Blue said mysteriously, then he walked through the side of the shipping container as if it weren't there.

Zeke didn't hesitate. He didn't understand the magic, but somehow when he reached the corrugated metal wall, he didn't slam into it like his brain was screaming would happen. Instead, he passed through the solid metal like a ghost, and his senses exploded with sound and light and then everything fell silent. The inside of the massive container was pitch-black. He heard a sound like cardboard tearing, and then a blue glow filled the container, illuminating the grey wolf. Blue.

What is it? Zeke asked. *What was in there?*

A message. I've been waiting for this one for a while. Jack said he'd get a message to me when it was time to pull out. Looks like one of the witches on his team had a prophetic vision, and it means I have to get out of here. Now. Blue prodded the object on the floor, a sort of round disk with a flat blue light on top.

How are you going to do that? The pack is hunting us. Howls and barks surrounded the container. A thud echoed outside. *Can they get this thing open?*

They'll have caught our scent outside the wall. And yes, they can open it. Might take them a minute to undo the locks. But that's all we've got. I sent the signal. The T.R.S. should be sending a portal any minute. As Blue spoke, the air split, and a portal opened, hovering a couple feet off the ground. Zeke had seen them a few times before. That happened when you hung out with a witch. He'd never traveled through one before, however, and the swirling blue energy made him nervous. He whined and paced.

You coming? Blue asked. *I assumed, since Jack sent you.*

I'm not part of T.R.S. It was...convenient that we crossed paths so I could deliver that box. But how did they know I would get it to you in time?

Witches. Blue's tongue lolled out of his mouth. He cocked his head as the thudding outside the shipping container stopped.

That's my cue. The portal will stay open for a bit longer, but not much. Best of luck.

The grey wolf leapt through the spinning disc in the air and disappeared. Zeke stopped pacing and stared down the blue hole in the air. He couldn't see what waited on the other side. He thought of the motorcycle, still sitting in the driveway at his parents' house. He didn't have time to fetch it and return, even if he could shift right now. He'd have to return for it some day.

Metal ground on metal, screeching. Orange light from the streetlights outside spilled in through the gap, and excited barks echoed into the shipping container. He was out of time.

Zeke bunched the muscles in his hind legs and leapt. The portal flared and encased him in a billowing swath of light. Tiny pinpricks, like needle points, tingled all over his body. He shuddered and twitched, trying to get rid of the discomfort. It only lasted a second, and then Zeke landed on a paved surface, claws skidding to the edge of a long, steep set of stairs. He glanced over his shoulder, and the portal was gone. In its place sat the giant, lifeless depiction of a famous president. He was in Washington, D.C., at the monuments, and by the look of things it had all gone to hell.

Every kind of paranormal flew, roared, and fought on the ground below. Werewolves, vamps, witches, even bird shifters.

Bird shifters. Zeke recognized the two fighting a polar bear near the reflection pool. One of them was Harper, the raven shifter from Camp Silver Lake. Her eyes glowed a violet color that Zeke could see even from the distance, and he wondered whose influence the raven shifter was under. How had this happened?

He started down the steps, taking them in leaps. Behind him, a flood of wolves erupted from the portal, Blue barked from the bottom of the steps, grinning at Zeke.

Glad you made it.

What's going on here? Zeke asked.

Get to the dome. The society is trying to prevent a human sacrifice at the monument. Some witches decided they could raise a demon to take over the government. Guarantee we don't want that to happen. With that, Blue barked and the stream of wolves that had come through after Zeke threw themselves into the fray. Zeke followed, leaping to the bottom of the steps, his eyes trained on the towering obelisk.

A circle of women stood on a glowing pentagram protected by a gleaming magical dome. There were a lot of witches in the world. Was he crazy to think that one of them looked like Mandi?

A flash of gold blinked at his chest, a spinning thread of light shooting into the distance and kindling heat like a flare inside him. He yelped. Had someone cast a spell over him? He bolted, zig-zagging to get out of the line of fire, then spun and crouched, read to face his attacker. No one pursued him.

A vamp flew over him, thrown by an opponent, hissing as he struck the water in the rectangular pool. The water splashed, drenching Zeke, but he kept running. *Get to the dome.* Rain fell, making the grass slick beneath his paws. A grizzly shifter towered in front of Zeke on its hind legs and lurched for him. Zeke dodged the blow, skidding beneath the bear's underbelly. The bear bellowed, but didn't pursue. Its violet eyes flashed and it lumbered towards another opponent, already having forgotten about Zeke.

The golden glimmer appeared again, and a flood of emotion washed over Zeke. *Danger in the pack.* It yanked at him, an urge to protect so strong he couldn't ignore it. But he had no pack here. Why did he feel certain that there was another wolf here, one he needed to protect?

The sensation drew him towards the dome. He had to get to that circle of light, had to stop the sacrifice. *Protect the pack.* A werewolf ran into him, snarling and biting. Zeke scrambled away, not engaging. When he looked back, he saw the wolf's amber eyes and felt its voice in his mind.

Sorry, man!

Zeke kept running. He moved towards the line of trees that edged the walkway, keeping near the trunks. A figure stood in white robes near one of the trees, protected by the magical purple barrier. Zeke skidded to a halt, panting. He recognized the witch. The waist-length brown hair, the freckled face. It was Meg, one of Mandi's friends. His heart wrenched. He barked to get the witch's attention. She didn't turn, but her eyes darted toward him. She held a hand up, pointing towards the South. Pointing him to Mandi. Mandi was here. She was here. *Protect the pack.* Zeke barked his thanks and took off.

He ran the hardest he had ever run. As he passed the obelisk, he noticed the figure tied there. He couldn't discern who it was, but knowing they were intended for sacrifice, he ran still harder, paws pounding, lungs reaching their maximum capacity, his heart threatening to burst.

If Mandi performed sacrificial blood magic, she would never be the same. Never. He *had* to get to her first, before this magic destroyed the woman he loved.

CHAPTER NINETEEN

MANDI

MANDI TOOK HER POSITION at the edge of the pentagram. She rolled her shoulders under the robe draped over her. The fabric scratched against her arms, but at least the heavy fabric mostly protected her from the sheeting rain. The activated shield above only stopped physical beings from getting through, not water.

The rain pounded on the ground around her, the heavy droplets coating her hair, but she did her best to ignore the physical discomfort. It couldn't be worse than the empty coldness in her chest. Even back at the hotel room beneath heaps of blankets she hadn't been able to get warm. She'd had terrible dreams of wolves fighting and running away and other dark things, which she had chalked up to her nerves. But today was a good day, not a frightful day. Today things would finally change.

Lilith stood at the north point and shouted the opening lines of the incantation to raise Ragranoth. A chill zinged through Mandi, and she adjusted her grip on the ceremonial dagger she held. The slick hilt heated up against her skin. She would know the right moment to use it, Lilith had told them all, back in the hotel. When it got too hot to hold, then she would add her blood to the circle, letting it drip into the grass at her feet.

Lilith would manage the rest, drawing upon her energy and the energy of the eleven other witches who stood in the circle. Where she'd found the witch to replace Honey, Mandi couldn't tell. She hadn't bothered to get to know the woman who stood in the place of her best friend, and her heart ached when she thought of it. It was one of the few times Mandi was grateful she was blind, so she didn't have to look into the face of the woman who had taken Honey's place.

The chant echoed across the circle. Beyond it, Mandi picked up sounds of fighting. Had the humans risen up already? A chopper flew overhead, the blades a familiar thwacking in the air. Media or military? The hairs on Mandi's arms rose. She reached for her pockets, for her stones, out of habit. She found none. The ceremonial robe she wore didn't even have pockets, and she had no friendly stones with her. Hesitantly, she reached out to 'feel' the crystal core within the obelisk monument. The fluorite crystal wand sang from within its prison of granite and marble. As soon as Mandi's mind touched the stone's signature, it flooded her with strength and clarity. She breathed in the new energy.

Mandi, you've been loyal. Lilith's voice wound through her thoughts. *You've overcome so much doubt and resistance to be here. Ragranoth rewards loyal followers. She has a gift for you. A taste of what is to come.*

A breath of warm air washed over Mandi, smelling of a sweet incense, the kind she avoided burning because it filled her nostrils with a sensation like acid in her sinuses. She held her breath at the first whiff, then released and sucked it in. It burned up into her skull. Her neuropathways lit up, sparking and awakening in areas that hadn't functioned for many years. The orbs of her eyes burned as if melting into her skull.

Mandi exclaimed, reaching up to her face, as if to make sure her eyes were still there, not that it mattered...

Open your eyes, Mandi, Lilith said.

Mandi's eyelids pried upwards, blinking at the blurry blades of grass below. She gasped and looked up, her vision clearing as tears filled her dry, watering eyes. The protective shield that she heard as a throbbing hum was a brilliant, glittering violet flickering across the clouded sky. She looked down, skipping over the dark form tied to the obelisk and seeing her white-robed coven sisters. Her eyes landed on Lilith, who smiled warmly at her, and the tiny crystal wand in her side vibrated against her ribs.

Now you see what we can do together. You've made the right choice, Mandi.

Mandi straightened, and Lilith's focus returned to the center of the circle. She clapped her hands above her head, continuing the chant, then stepped forward, away from the Northpoint, heading toward the center of the circle.

Mandi's joy immediately froze, and her heart plummeted. She would see it all happen. The sacrifice, the blood, the return of the being of the lower realms with enough power to shake the earth and bring freedom to the paranormal beings that lived there. It was happening.

The ground trembled at the power of Lilith's spell. She was chanting a connection spell, connecting to the pentagrams she had initiated in other parts of the United States, where other covens would be offering their own sacrifices, creating a pentagram of a size that had rarely been seen in the history of men.

Mandi's breath caught in her throat. The grey stone rose from the ground, imposing and cold. She could feel its heart thrumming, pulsing, filling with power to be directed at the body that sat crumpled at its base.

Elnora Evans. The President of the United States and chosen vessel of the champion, Ragranoth.

The dagger in Mandi's hand heated. Around the circle she watched as one by one, the other coven members raised a hand and sliced across their palm, letting blood fall into the circle. Each new addition sent a thrill of energy zinging through the pentagram, darkening the ground at Mandi's feet until the grass had taken on a nearly black hue, almost like the night sky, and the pentagram lines showed up vividly in gold.

Mandi watched Lilith walk forward almost as if in slow motion, her dagger raised, her voice calling forth the demon.

A bark drew Mandi's attention away from the grisly scene. She looked right and saw a large black animal outside the protective shield, leaping against the surface of the spell. It made no impact, but its barking distracted her. Beyond, Mandi's eyes widened at the battle that raged. She hadn't noticed the sound, muffled by the dome as it was. An army had risen up to greet those who would disturb the magic her coven was performing.

Oddly enough, they seemed paranormal. They were either government lackeys or they didn't understand that the gathered witches intended to set them free from the tyranny that ruled them.

The knife burned white-hot in her grip. It was her time. She raised it.

The bark turned to a yelp and she looked again, this time seeing the black animal - a wolf, she realized - being torn down by two other shifters, a raven and an eagle, wings flapping, swords in hand, slicing. She felt sorrow for the wolf, remembering Zeke.

She looked away. Sight was an awful thing sometimes.

Mandi! Mandi, drop the knife! Zeke's voice, clear as day, reverberated in her head.

Mandi startled and nearly did drop the knife. The heat was growing unbearable, and Lilith glanced behind, as if noticing that the chain of blood spilling had halted. She nodded to Mandi, who stood frozen.

It was ridiculous. Why would she be hearing Zeke's voice anyway? It wasn't possible. She glanced toward the black wolf again as it broke free from the attacking bird shifters and ran at the dome, leaping up to put its paws on the surface. It barked once then howled.

It's me. Zeke. You've got to listen. If you're still you then you know this is wrong. If you're still the woman I love.

The woman he loved.

A shudder went through Mandi, a piercing of her heart and soul that shot from her chest and raced across the distance to the black wolf that snapped at the feathered wings beating at him. Seeing him fighting, fighting for her, brought back the bond that had been severed by the witch that watched her from the pentagram's center. The witch who had nearly killed Zeke, not just in a dream, Mandi realized. It had all happened.

Zeke was here. Her soulmate, Zeke. And she was holding a knife about to participate in a blood spell on a national scale, all for the chance to see.

You can't do this, Mandi. You'll lose yourself. I'll lose you.

How is this possible, that you're speaking to me? She froze, realizing he'd heard her voice just as she had heard his. *I thought only pack members could do this.*

You are my pack, Mandi. He went down under the attack of the two bird shifters, their wings covering him from her view. Mandi's heart wrenched. She looked at the knife in her hand, the ornate details on the handle and blade gleaming wickedly at her. She looked to Lilith, who waited for Mandi's blood to fall so that the spell could be completed. She looked to Elnora, who watched her with a tear-streaked and filthy face and pleading in her eyes. All things she never would have been able to see without Lilith, without the power they were raising, and yet, she couldn't bring herself to make the cut.

"I won't do it," she said aloud, dropping the knife to the ground.

Lilith whirled on her. "Pick up the knife, Mandi. It's too late now. Can't you feel the power? It has to go somewhere."

"Send it back, then. There has to be another way." The earth rumbled again, this time feeling angry beneath Mandi's feet. The power in the giant wand screamed for release.

Lilith shrieked and transported. In an instant, she bore down on Mandi, looming at seven feet tall, hair dark and flying, eyes flashing violet, skin draining to grey. Mandi didn't know what Lilith was, but she wasn't a witch. Not anymore.

Mandi ducked, covering her head as Lilith swiped towards her with claws growing from the ends of her fingers. The claws raked her back through her robes, and Mandi screamed.

"Finish the spell!" Lilith roared, her voice a voice of thousands. A demon's voice. Ragranoth somehow spoke through her.

Mandi glanced around, terrified, overwhelmed by her new sense. The ceremonial dagger lay a mere foot away, shining against the darkness of the pentagram. Mandi reached out and grabbed it, standing and swinging the blade to fight back the being that attacked her. She hardly aimed, just swung, praying she'd make contact.

The blade leapt with her hand and sank into flesh. Mandi tugged.

Lilith's voice gurgled, and blood dripped down from her throat, soaking the robe and the ground below.

"What have you done?" the otherworldly voice bellowed. Lilith's head lolled and her form crumpled. Mandi fell back, throwing the knife away from her, sobbing at the body by her feet.

The obelisk cracked, the outer stone falling away, crumbling and revealing the inner core. It gleamed blue and purple and green, the natural colors of the fluorite crystal. The protective dome vanished with a sucking sound and a crackle of violet lightning, and as it fell a cosmic boom shuddered through the atmosphere and struck the pentagram, shattering it and everything nearby.

CHAPTER TWENTY

TYSON

SHE HAD A SWORD. A glowing sword. It zinged through the air in Harper's hands. Tyson dodged, his polar bear bulk barely getting out of the way in time. An acrid, burning smell coated the air, and Tyson glanced at his side at the smoking patch of fur. Time for a change of attack. He breathed in and shifted from bear to bird. Now a raven, he took off into the air.

Possessed-Harper's violet eyes followed his flight. She put away the sword and took off after him, swooping over the reflecting pool. How could he get her close enough to touch without being killed himself? If he could touch her, he could possibly see how to disrupt Lilith's hold on her.

Tyson glanced into the water, the normally smooth surface shattered into a hundred thousand bits by the rain and the battle raging around it.

"Paranormals are advised to stop fighting and turn themselves over to the Supernatural Task Force officers waiting beyond the memorial grounds. Stop fighting and turn yourselves in," the megaphone message echoed from speakers on a helicopter flying above the mele. Tyson stayed well below the vehicle, diving towards the line of trees on the ground. He wove in and out of the trunks, fully aware that Harper followed closely. Her hand reached out and brushed his tail feathers, and Tyson squawked.

She had been flying a lot longer than he had, and she had the advantage of human limbs, but he had the advantage of size. He banked sharply away from a tree trunk and winced as Harper ran into it with a thud. She dropped to the ground, landing on her feet, and launched back into the sky, seeming no worse for the wear than a few rumpled feathers. But then, would her possession allow her to rest if she was truly injured? He had to end this, and fast. The only way to do that was to get to Lilith, who was currently under the protection of the massive magical dome.

Tyson flapped his wings and reached his beak towards the clouds. He focused on the reservoir inside where he sensed his magic. It was mostly full. He hung in the air, flapping hard to stay suspended, and concentrated on forming a pointed casing around himself, a protective shield that might also be able to punch through the magic covering the pentagram.

Below, the ground turned black with clear, gold lines tracing the pentagram. The earth rumbled, throwing fighters off balance on the ground. Lilith, her platinum blonde hair flowing, strode toward the obelisk and the person tied there, as if the movement of the earth had no effect on her.

Tyson gave one last glance around and didn't see Harper anywhere. Had she stopped her pursuit? Had striking the tree caused an injury that prevented her from flying? Tyson put it out of his mind. He had one shot, and it very well could injure or kill him, but if it stopped Lilith and freed Harper, it would be worth it. He shot down toward the dome, the magic he had formed sparking with brilliant oranges and reds. He closed his eyes, bracing for impact.

A massive force struck his side, throwing him into the air and breaking the magical battering ram he'd created. He spun end over end, feathers flapping uselessly as he tried to right himself.

A pair of arms grabbed him, stopping his chaotic tumbling, but crushing his feathers. The raven shrieked in Harper's hold.

She would rip off his wings. She would snap his neck. He had to *do* something, but he didn't want to kill her.

An idea blossomed in his head, and Tyson didn't stop to consider the implications. He shifted back into human form. The sudden change in weight caused Harper's wings to buckle mid-flap, and she plummeted, releasing Tyson. She caught herself after a split second, but Tyson still fell, the ground coming in swiftly.

And that's when the dome exploded. The magic filled the air like a million tiny shards, glittering in the air around Tyson. Tyson tried to shift back into a raven, to save himself, but the charge of the magic in the air directly contradicted his efforts, and he couldn't muster the amount of concentration he needed to make the change.

He squeezed his eyes shut, then opened them, looking straight up at the night sky. This was how it ended for him. Splatted on the pavement like rotten fruit.

CHAPTER TWENTY-ONE

ZEKE

ZEKE DROPPED HIS HEAD, nuzzling Mandi's face. The rain had stopped, but everything was muddy and damp. He stepped over her and pushed with his snout, rolling her onto her back. There was mud and blood, but everything he sniffed had Lilith's scent more than Mandi's. There seemed to be no reason for her to be dead, but a powerful spell had been interrupted, and none of the other witches were moving either. Were they all dead?

A crowd gathered at the broken base of the Washington Monument. Stones were tossed aside, and a cheer went up when they reached the center.

Zeke closed his eyes and laid himself down beside Mandi's body, closing his eyes.

A hand stroked his head. Normally, he would have snapped in warning. He wasn't a dog to pet. But he only cracked an eye and slightly lifted his head, until he could see that the hand stroking him belonged to Mandi.

Mandi.

Her eyes fluttered open, and she smiled at him. Zeke leapt to his feet and licked her face, making her sputter.

"All right, all right. That's enough of *that*," she chided. And then she froze. She blinked, putting her hand out in front of her face. She closed her eyes, squeezing them, then opened them again.

"Zeke," she whispered. "I can *see*."

Zeke barked. He couldn't help it. Some sort of miracle had happened. His tail wagged full force, moving his entire body with it. He wished he could be human, to hold her, but with the moon's hold still strong as it gleamed above, it was unlikely he could manage the change. But he could try. Zeke sat, stilling his body so he could concentrate. He breathed into the tightly locked space inside that held the key to his shifting ability. The place where the wolf and the human melded together and became one.

Something felt…different there. Maybe it was because of the serum he'd received in Chicago, or maybe miracles were being passed out in droves that day, but he felt the subtle click and grind as his bones started to move and a gentle, liquid fire moved through his veins like lava flow.

When he opened his eyes, he sat on the wet ground in nothing but black biker shorts, and next to him, seeming frail but certainly alive, was Mandi.

And she was *looking* at him. Straight at him, and as the helicopter flashed its probe light over them, Zeke saw they were a brilliant copper color. The pupils seemed too large, and somewhat splotchy with the light shining in them, but perhaps that was some lingering effect of the magic or a trick of the search beam.

Zeke scooted closer and took Mandi in his arms, pulling her into his lap. His hand stroked her face, trying to ignore the mud and blood mixing on her cheek.

"Did you mean what you said?" she asked, eyes searching his. "About me being your pack?"

Zeke cleared his throat. "I did. I mean, if you want to be."

Mandi nodded vigorously. "I do." She flung her arms around his neck and pressed her face in tighter, her entire body trembling.

He could have sat like that for ages longer, but a mob had gathered on the lawn surrounding the once-proud obelisk. Now, it lay broken, revealing a cracked crystal that had been obscured in the center. It still sparked with some kind of magical lightning every few seconds, erratic and dangerous. Zeke loosened his grip on Mandi as she turned her head to look.

"That spell...I shouldn't have survived when it failed, Zeke," she murmured. "Did...did any of my sisters survive?"

Zeke glanced again at the prone bodies strewn about the circle. None of them had moved. He swallowed. "I don't think so, Mandi."

Mandi closed her eyes tight. "Two pistols," she whispered. "I should have known better."

Zeke opened his mouth to say something that might comfort her, to reassure her that it wasn't her fault, but the angry shouts from the gathering crowd had grown louder.

The possessed paranormals seemed back to normal, the violet glow of Lilith's influence gone from their eyes. They were shaking heads and hands, explaining to others what had happened and that they weren't really the enemy. The fighting had stopped completely. Some wandered away from the crowd, clearly bewildered as to how they'd come to be there.

Zeke followed one young woman as she headed for the trees, only to see her freeze, holding up her hands, as a soldier approached in full riot gear, holding up an impressive-looking gun.

The National Guard had arrived, and with them, the Super-natural Task Force. Zeke could see their neon green vests flashing in the brilliant light of the spotlight from the helicopter as it passed over. A second helicopter had joined, this one bearing media insignia.

The sound of the crowd became an angry buzzing as they noticed the military forces pressing in on all sides. Shifters who had returned to human form, those not affected by the moon, were shifting back, pawing at the ground, preparing for a fight.

The grizzly shifter from before bellowed from the middle of the crowd, and a rapid string of shots answered, cracking in the cool night air.

The bear went down. Screams erupted, and the mob turned to panic, growls and snarls and shrieks ready to answer for the bear shifter's death.

Another shot fired into the air, and everyone fell mostly silent. Zeke watched as a line of soldiers stepped through the trees, each armed and ready to fire, and at their head a man clearly distinguished as their leader. One of the helicopters highlighted him with its spotlight, the whirring blades almost drowning out the tense muttering of the crowd.

The commander held up a megaphone. "I am General Howel. This is your final warning. Surrender to S.T.F. forces and no one else gets hurt."

Zeke put an arm protectively around Mandi, glancing around for the quickest way through the crowd should all hell break loose. It was only a matter of time before one side attacked the other, and then a real battle would begin.

"I know an easy way to settle this." A man's voice carried through the air, projecting loud and clear. Paranormals shuffled aside to make way for a small group holding a stretcher.

The man gestured to the woman on the stretcher, who cradled a broken arm and had bandages wrapped around her head, but otherwise seemed coherent.

The man held the end of a gun against her temple.

"As you can see," the man continued. "We have the president."

CHAPTER TWENTY-TWO

HARPER

THE EXPLOSION OF MAGIC shocked Harper's brain. Sparks like lightning danced along her neural pathways, reawakening forgotten functions and connections.

Her eyes flew open, and her wings flared out to catch herself. She stared down at the body swiftly falling, getting smaller, staring up at her with a plea written clearly on his face.

Tyson.

It didn't matter how she'd gotten there, or why Tyson was falling. Harper's wings snapped against her back, and she tilted into a steep dive. Wind beat at her face, and a second wave of magical influence buffeted Harper, pushing her slightly off course. She leaned, adjusting her flight path, urging her body to fall faster, to be heavier, begging gravity to come through for her for once.

She didn't want to see his body mangled on the ground before her eyes. She didn't want to lose him before she'd even gotten him back again.

Harper surged forward and swooped beneath Tyson, snapping her wings out and stopping for an instant mid-air. She reached out, and Tyson slammed into her. They tumbled together with the force of his momentum until she righted herself, flapping to slow them down. Her shoulder blades ached as if her wings had been wrenched nearly from their sockets.

Tyson glanced down. They were only twenty feet from the ground, now. He sagged against her and met her gaze, his blue eyes searching hers as if looking for something.

"Do you think it's safe to land?" she asked, her voice husky with unuse. She coughed.

He looked surprised that she'd spoken to him. "Yeah, I think it's fine."

"Good." She breathed out with a huff and dropped the rest of the way, stumbling as she landed. "Because you're heavy."

"Hey, now." He grinned. "Are you going to put me down?"

"When I'm good and ready," Harper said stubbornly. She hesitated a moment, then set him on his feet as if it had been her idea, but not because she couldn't handle his weight. Her biceps ached.

Tyson didn't give her a moment before he pulled her into an embrace. He buried his face in her neck, hands clasping her back. Hesitantly, Harper's hands found his waist, and her stiffness slowly melted. She breathed in, noticing he smelled like soap, and something spicy that tickled her nose.

He dropped his arms, and Harper reluctantly stepped back, but he didn't let her go far, putting his hands on her elbows and keeping her within his reach. His eyes seemed to drink her in, and she wondered what could have happened to make him look at her like that. Like he had never expected to see her alive or in control of her person again.

Her head swam, memories tangled up in each other, blurred and distorted. She remembered meeting Chief Aguta, her grandfather, at the Tulukaruq village. She remembered Lilith's arrival and her mark activating, and then…nothing.

"How long have I been…gone?" Harper asked.

Tyson licked his lips, and a sigh shuddered through him. "A little more than a month. I didn't know where you'd gone, and when I found you in the astral realm, I couldn't reach you." His words tumbled over themselves as he raced toward an apology.

Her lips quirked upward in a small smile. "Not everything is your fault, you know. It was my own stupid mistake that got this mark on me."

She held up the hand that Lilith had marked what seemed like an eternity ago at Camp Silver Lake. The skin was smooth and bare, without even an impression of the spell that had enabled Lilith to control her. She rubbed at it, frowning.

In the field surrounding the shattered Washington monument—why didn't she remember coming here?—a dozen or so figures lay prone and unmoving, their white robes flashing in the helicopter beam.

Tyson tapped her shoulder and pointed to one with pale hair. "That's Lilith. I saw her fall."

"Are you certain?" Her heart rate increased.

Someone should check, make certain the witch was dead, but it was as if her feet were rooted in cement. She couldn't move. Her gaze drifted, landing on a half-naked man cradling a woman in white robes. The man's thick dreads triggered a memory.

"Tyson, that's Zeke."

"And Mandi. I know. What are they doing here?" Tyson asked.

Harper didn't know. She wasn't sure of anything.

Helicopters whirled above, their silver lights probing the crowd. People swarmed on the ground, gathering in a crowd and facing the oncoming row of military enforcement. Someone jostled against Harper's wings. The crowd loomed like a tidal wave behind her, hungry for justice, for action. She knew what that felt like.

A stretcher parted the crowd. Harper recognized the president. She didn't know the people who held the stretcher, or the man who held a gun to the president's head.

"As you can see, we have the president," the man said. He exuded the confidence of an experienced leader.

"That's Dak," Tyson leaned in. "T.R.S."

"So, he's on our side?" Harper asked.

Tyson grimaced, but nodded.

"Deliver the President to us and we will be lenient," the commander at the front of the approaching military contingent shouted through his megaphone.

"That isn't how this works, General," the man said. "We'll put the President somewhere safe. Nice and comfortable, too, and then you and I will both dismiss our people and have a talk about what things are going to look like from now on."

A werewolf growled from Harper's side, pawing the ground.

Harper eyed the line of military. They'd crept further through the line of trees, and beyond them, she could see a large gun being set up on a frame. That didn't look promising.

She focused on the General. He appeared to be having a discussion with a second at his side. A messenger? She noticed the S.T.F badge on their arm. All she could see were soldiers in front of them, except for this one lone Stiff.

As the Stiff ran off, she followed him, losing sight as he went behind the trees, then spotting him again as he crossed the lawn some distance away and met a line of Stiffs lurking on the opposite side of the monument. She looked over the crowd. It was larger than she expected, but still small and penned in by opposing forces now.

The General cleared his throat into the megaphone. There was a scuffle in the crowd, and a squad of Supernatural Task Force agents attacked the men holding the stretcher. They'd made their move.

A gun went off. Someone screamed. The man—Dak—held up a silver disk on a cord around his neck and grabbed the president, and then the two vanished.

Harper saw the General's hand form a clear sign at his side.

"Run!" she screamed, leaping into the air and flapping her wings to gain altitude.

The big gun opened fire, the soldiers in front of it hitting the ground and covering their heads.

To Harper's amazement, a turquoise shield blossomed from Tyson's outstretched hands and surrounded the crowd of paranormals in a protective bubble, including Harper. It lit up the darkness, illuminating the terrified faces. A few people had been hit, she could hear crying, someone asking for an ambulance. An ambulance would never get through this mess.

"Harper," Quinn called out, joining her in the air. "We have to do something."

"Singing," Harper said, remembering the gift of her people. They didn't know all of the songs yet, though.

"I think I remember the tune Tarkik whistled to get that van to leave," he shouted over the agitated noise of the crowd below.

"You think that will work on that many people?" Harper nodded toward the soldiers, who had picked up their guns and sprinted across the grass shooting at Tyson's shield.

From the inside, a bear shifter pounded on the surface, raking with his claws and bellowing to be unleashed on the enemy. If

Tyson released that shield, they'd be dead meat. The soldiers were loading up their machine gun again. With the onslaught happening from both sides of the shield, Harper didn't know how long Tyson could hold it up. In the gleam of the shield's light, sweat trailed down the side of his face.

"Do you have a better idea?" Quinn asked.

Harper squeezed her hands into fists and shook her head. "You start. I'll pick it up." She flapped her wings again, swooping in the tight circle Tyson had created.

Quinn did the same, flying in the opposite direction. They passed each other.

It started with a whistle. The pure tone arched through the air and landed among the soldiers, clearly directed away from the paranormals below, but some of the yelling and struggling stopped.

Harper matched the tone. Her hand drifted up to finger the amulet totems around her neck that had been gifted from her grandfather. The notes of the song flowed out instinctively, weaving around Quinn's. She put all the force she could muster into the notes, to calm and to distract the soldiers. Some of them fumbled on the trigger, missing the brilliant glowing dome. Others straight up turned around, shouting back at unit leaders with confusion.

A discordant whistle caught Harper's attention and she looked to where the S.T.F squad had been. They were closer now, only ten, fifteen feet away. The whistle came from an orb that spun through the air and landed on the outside of the dome, sticking there. The magic flickered.

Tyson cried out and crumpled. The shield fell, and chaos broke loose.

Weres roared, sprinting towards the soldiers, many of whom were retreating.

Harper increased the volume of her whistle, trying to direct it at the attacking rebels as well as the human soldiers, but her voice cracked. She just couldn't reach them all on her own, she wasn't powerful enough. Her head grew dizzy, and black spots danced in her eyes. She lost sight of Tyson and hoped someone was helping him, she couldn't stop the Singing, it was still having some effect on the soldiers, but it wasn't enough.

A light streamed from above, the blueish silver of a portal being opened. She glanced up, keeping the song going, and watched in awe as a stream of flying shifters soared out of the portal. Their feathers flashed all different colors - browns and whites, even the red of a cardinal, but only one had the same pitch-dark wings as Harper and her brother. A woman.

Help had arrived. The woman with the dark wings opened her own mouth and Sang, and it was unlike anything Harper had heard before. The other bird shifters joined in, each with their own tone, their own whistle. While they sang, they dove towards the soldiers, dropping nets and shooting with slingshots, of all things, knocking them out without harming them. A net fell on the bear shifter, a group of werewolves. A final note rang out, high and haunting, and everyone on the ground froze.

The contingency of bird shifters landed, gathering on the ground, the helicopter's strobing light giving their wings a sterile silver sheen. Harper landed, and Quinn with her, and hesitantly they approached the contingency together.

"That was good work you two. Thanks for holding the front line," the female with the dark wings said. Her face was shadowed from the angle of the light, making it difficult to make out her features, but something about her voice...Harper craned her neck, but someone turned around, standing in her line of sight, disrupting Harper's focus.

"Shoot. Tyson. Quinn, can you see him?" she asked her brother, spinning back towards the place she'd last seen him.

Quinn didn't answer. Harper nudged him. "Hey, I need to know if you saw Tyson?"

"He went down over there." Quinn gestured vaguely. He was staring at the woman with the dark wings, his eyes wide.

The woman barked directions, and bird shifters split off in twos and threes as she sent them away. "Let's unfreeze this lot. I want to talk to Dak and secure the president. Has anyone seen Jack? Did he make it yet?" the woman asked.

Harper searched among the frozen bodies for Tyson. It was creepy the way the bodies lay prostrate, arms flung over each other, some in their shifter forms.

A Song broke out among some of the bird shifters, and the cluster of bodies moved, people stretching and standing up, bewildered expressions on their faces.

Tyson sat up not too far from where Harper searched, shaking his head. Harper held out a hand to him, and he took it.

"What happened?" he asked.

"We got backup." Harper gestured towards the woman with the dark wings, who was crouched by the stretcher, talking to the men who had stood by the president when she vanished.

Tyson's eyebrows shot up. He looked from Harper to the other raven shifter, and back to Harper.

"What?" Harper asked.

"What? You don't see it? The resemblance?"

"Don't be ridiculous." Harper waved away his words, but glanced at Quinn, who stood staring at the woman with an expression just like Tyson's.

"Mom?" Quinn asked, his voice quivering and small. The group around the stretcher stopped talking and everyone looked at them.

Harper pushed through the crowd. She needed to be with Quinn. She needed to guide him away and talk him out of this confusion he was clearly caught up in.

She put her hand on his arm. "No, Quinn, it's not her. Come on."

The woman spread her wings, and the light reflected off them. Her face caught the full beam of the helicopter circling above and in an instant, Harper saw it. The same round face, though scarred. The same short-cropped dark brown hair, though edged with grey. The same brown eyes, though framed with wrinkles. It was like looking in a mirror.

"Quincey!" The woman spread her arms, and Quinn ran, stumbling over the torn ground, collapsing into her and sobbing.

Harper stared, unblinking.

After all that had happened, after every effort to search for her parents had seemed to take her farther and farther away, her mother stood before her.

Tyson touched her elbow. "You okay, Harper?"

Harper's bottom lip trembled. She covered it with her hand, but she couldn't look away from the joyful scene, mother embracing son. Embracing her brother.

"I don't recognize her," Harper whispered, voice breaking.

"I think she recognizes you," Tyson said, and as he did, the woman looked up over Quinn's shoulder and her smile broadened. She gestured with her hand, motioning for Harper to join them.

Tyson's hand pushed her shoulder gently, and Harper walked forward in a daze, letting the woman pull her in and whisper in her ear.

"We're a family again."

Harper's heart clenched until she thought it would burst.

The full moon shone in the sky and the helicopter whirred, making silver circles on the grass. All Harper could see was the Beryllium Orb with her hands fixed on its surface, and she wondered what price she would pay for her happiness this time.

Don't miss the final installment of the Wings of Rebellion series, Rebel Sworn!

SPECIAL THANKS

Writing a book is no easy task, and I could never do it alone. Thanks to my writing group for trying to keep up with my lightning-fast pace, for cheering me on when things get hard, and for being there for everything else. Here's to another eight years writing together!

Special thanks to Beth, Rachel W., and Amanda for being alpha readers and making it through my roughest drafts. This book would suck without you.

Local coffee shops make everything possible. Thanks to the Lost Canvas and Swede n Co. for refreshing drinks and tempting treats.

I want to thank my faithful readers, especially those who have stuck with me since "Woven" was first published. You've kept me going with your fantastic reviews. If you like this book, please take a split second and give it a star rating on Amazon or Goodreads. It makes my day every time.

I owe so much to my husband, who keeps the house functioning and manages children when I need to escape and write. Consider it an investment: someday I'll retire you with my books.

Bree Moore lives in Iowa with her husband, seven children, and two cats. When she's not busy homeschooling or folding laundry, she sneaks off to write more fantasy.

Bree writes urban and epic fantasy to explore different worlds with amazing creatures and magic systems. She enjoys giving her readers a story that is both entertaining and emotional, with a healthy dose of romance. When she's not writing, Bree can be found foraging for edible plants, watching fantasy shows and movies, or hanging out with her husband and kids.

Published works include: *The Shadowed Minds* series, the *Lost Souls* series, and *Shadows of Camelot* series. She's currently working on *The Plague King Chronicles*.

Visit www.authorbreemoore.com for a FREE fantasy book!

tiktok.com/@breenovels

instagram.com/breenovels

Shadows of Camelot
The Lady's Last Song
The Queen's Quiet End

Shadowed Minds Series
Prequel: Thief of Lies
Thief of Magic
Thief of Aether
Thief of Bones

Wings of Rebellion Series
Prequel: Raven Blood
Raven Born
Serpent Cursed
Coven Bound
Serpent Turned
Siren Called
Rebel Sworn

The Plague King Chronicles
The Keeper of the Well
The Quill and the Vial
The Arrow and the Ivy

Of Dusk and Dawn Collection
Sacrifice for the Standing Stones
Vows Beneath the Frozen Stars